Ascension

Ascension

Sabrina Strong Book 1

Lorelei Bell

In Memory of Barbara A. Bell,
My Mentor, Friend,
And Mother All In One.

Chapter 1

The full moon poured silvery light down around me as I arrived about eight minutes late for my job interview with a vampire. Mr. Paduraru had kindly agreed to meet me in my little town of Moonlight, instead of giving me confusing directions to some place in the city, that I'd never before driven to by myself. I chose a bar that was easy to direct him to from the tollway. The Saloon resided on the corner of Sunbank and Route 30.

Normally, it would only take me ten minutes to drive from my house to this bar, except that a huge John Deere tractor, hauling just-picked corn, took up the whole damn road, and I had to follow it the one mile from my house to turn onto Sunbank.

This was not your ordinary nine-to-five office job for which I was applying. The ad had read, "Clairvoyant needed. Only serious applicants need apply." Disbelief had filled me as I read the ad, and I read it five or six times before I dialed the number. It was long distance—a Chicago area code—and I made mistakes before I'd gotten it right.

Yes, I was nervous about the interview. I didn't know he was a vampire until I spoke to him over the phone, of course. How I knew this was second nature. Sometimes all I had to do was walk up to a house I'd never been inside before, and I *knew* the layout of the place; or, the emotions of the people inside a room would sometimes flood me, and every once in a while, merely by speaking to someone on the phone I would get a "read".

This was how I *knew* that Mr. Paduraru was equipped with fangs, and drank blood.

Mostly, though, I only needed to touch something to get a read, sometimes they came as visions. I didn't do that often. Not at all, if I could help it. Being a clairvoyant sometimes sucked, especially on a social level. Early on, I'd had to learn to shield my mind against this ability, or hide in a closet—literally—or go insane. The gloves I always wore were my only other protection. I'm a Touch Clairvoyant, which is very rare.

Climbing down out of my Jeep, I took in the other vehicles in the lot. There were seven cars—well, three were cars; the rest were pickups. Not many people here, but it was Monday.

Black and sharp, my shadow advanced ahead of me on the gravel lot as I walked toward The Saloon. I'd turned twenty-one four weeks ago, and had only been here once. I spotted a sleek, black Jaguar parked near the building. This could not belong to any of the regulars inside. It had to have been Mr. Paduraru's.

Curious, I angled for it and stopped next to it, pulled in a little breath to steady myself, and closed my eyes. Suddenly, my mind sent me a flash of an image: *Twin white spires cutting skyward over a Chicago skyline.*

Whoa. I had a little bit of a head-spin as I opened my eyes.

As the spinning stopped, a wave of energy hit me, totally and inconceivably savage, and possibly carnivorous. A tangled emotion that, as a human, I couldn't fully appreciate. In fact, I didn't know where it came from.

That's when I saw a low shadow ease from a dense copse of trees, around the far side of the building. When it emerged from shadow into the light recognition threw me; I could hardly believe what I was looking at. Large and gray with four legs, and big yellow eyes staring right at me, the creature growled low and menacing.

Keys still in my hand, I froze and surveyed my surroundings. I was alone. The wolf stood between the tavern and me. Behind me, and about fifty yards beyond my Jeep, the two roads that converged at the corner didn't have a lot of traffic. The closest house was simply too far away.

Without warning, the wolf lunged at me.

I screamed. For one frozen moment, I thought I was dead. All of my twenty-one years flashed before my eyes.

Big, sharp teeth grasped my free arm—the one I held up to protect myself. I batted at the animal with my purse, smacking it pretty hard, and it let go of me. I kicked him, connecting a blow to the rib cage, but this did little to deter him. By the loping, little jump he made to stay clear of my swipe, I sensed this was play to him.

The wolf snatched my purse and ripped it out of my hands, then shook it as though it were a living thing. Tossing it aside, he snarled and lunged at me again, snapping at my left hand— the one that still gripped the keys. Automatically I had made sure that I had a few keys sticking up between my fingers, like a weapon, when his mouth clamped shut around my hand, sharp teeth scraping my fingers and knuckles through my gloves.

My first reaction had been to run like hell, but then, I'd decided to fight for all I was worth.

My hand was now trapped inside the animal's mouth, but he didn't crunch down, but held it there firmly while making a terrible growling deep in his throat, and then *pulled*, as though he was going to take me somewhere. I planted my feet, and skidded about five feet as he pulled. Fear seized me temporarily, leaving me unable to comprehend why this animal had attacked me, or what it wanted.

Although perhaps a minute had elapsed while dealing with this beast, I wondered if anyone had heard my screams inside. Well, no. For one thing, they were all into the football game on the big screen TV—I could hear their boisterous cheers from inside all the way out here.

The keys rattled around in the huge wolf's mouth as he renewed his grip. Then the creature made a sudden whine, as though he might have bit down on one of the keys wrong, and they had stabbed him, and he let go. My hand came away from the grip the animal had on me, and with the momentum, I fell on my butt. Sharp gravel bit and scraped my backside and legs through my nylons and cotton skirt. Rolling over to my knees, I scrambled to gain my feet, but he knocked me down from behind. In the next moment, the horrible beast was on top of me, big paws on my back, pushing me back down to my knees, sharp gravel knifing into me, making me screech again. He had hold of my dress and I heard it rip.

Why couldn't anyone in the bar hear me screaming?

Something dark lurched from the edge of my periphery, pulling my gaze about ten feet away. Renewed fear reverberated through me.

Another damned wolf.

Screaming, my heart reeled as though it would jump out of my chest. Utter terror gave me strength to push nearly to my feet, but it was no use. The second wolf leaped and tackled the other one with a vicious growl. A yelp of pain resounded through me as my knees and hands took the brunt of the combined weight of two huge beasts. They tumbled off me in a flurry of fur, teeth and claws. A sharp yip from the first wolf told me that its attacker had hurt him. One fled, the other chased; I could hear the garbling growl of the pursuer. Then, there was no more sound.

The hole in my nylons spread up my thigh, and that was so out of context it wasn't funny.

Panting, and simply too relieved to worry about what happened to either wolf (or my nylons), I tossed my long, dark brown hair out of my face and tried to brush myself off.

Searching for my keys, I shuffled toward my Jeep. A sound made my head turn toward the building. A handsome guy with black hair, wearing an un-tucked, button-down green shirt and jeans, dashed down the steps toward me. Here I was tousled, my clothes ripped, wearing holey nylons, and one of the cutest guys I'd seen in a long while was rushing toward me, a sort of pity glowing in his eyes. I was hoping he was an off-duty paramedic. He'd tend to me, surely.

"Nicolas!" he called out loudly, as he darted toward me where I struggled to stand upright. My feet felt as though I had roller blades strapped to them, my legs had turned to rubber hoses and I sagged against the Jag.

"Ms. Strong, are you hurt?" the handsome guy asked as he darted swiftly to me—I thought I'd blacked out for a few seconds. Suddenly one hand was clutching my arm, and the other one went around me, holding me up.

"Who are you? How do you know who I am?" I said numbly, trying not to lean against him too much. He was only a few inches taller than my five foot four stature that was, at this moment, compromised by my slumping. His black hair and dark eyes contrasted harshly against a complexion that looked like pewter in the moonlight.

Oh, damn. Vampire!

"Ms. Strong, are you—" He stopped, and eyed my arm. He looked worriedly up at me. "You're bleeding." His face went through an alarming metamorphosis of emotions. Concern had vanished, now something like a wicked smile drew his lips back off his teeth, and his fangs slid out. I could see this situation was above and beyond his ability to handle, what with me bleeding and him being a vampire and all.

The glove of my left hand was ripped. My eyes zeroed in on the sticky wetness. Blood. *My* blood. It glistened darkly in the overhead lights of the lot. Raising my gaze, my heart wrenched as I saw a wolf pad toward us from the shadows. "Look out!" I cried, and braced myself against the younger vampire, who had hold of me and wouldn't let me go even if I could get my legs to move right.

This wolf stopped and made an odd whine as it looked curiously up at us. A wisp of smoke obliterated the wolf, and in a moment, a man emerged from the smoke. He looked to be about thirty, in human years. Wearing a dark brown suit expertly matched with a lighter brown silk shirt and gold-green silk tie, he surged toward us, looking as though he had merely been out for a stroll. He straightened his tie, and then ran his fingers through his slightly tousled, iron black hair, smoothing it away from his heart-shaped face. I questioned my own sanity at that point. Clearly, if I told a policeman that a wolf had just attacked me, and then I saw another wolf change into a man, at that point, he'd take my keys away from me and call a paramedic. Probably this would have been the best scenario, but no policeman was available. Unfortunately.

"Ms. Strong?" This new man's voice charged the air around us—a magnificently smooth-as-whipped-chocolate voice, and I wanted to hear it again.

"Mr. Paduraru?" *I presume.* Still shaken I had to pull in a breath and simply stare. He had deep-set eyes—the kind that held mystery behind them. Dark brows arched distinctively from a narrow, slightly hooked nose. His unblinking stare was a little haunting. Hypnotic. His pale skin was almost opaque, but I noticed his cheeks had a little blush to them.

He inclined his head. "At your service. What a horrible ordeal! I beg you forgive us for not having come to your rescue much sooner!" he said in an apologetic tone as he neared me. His glittering gaze engaged the other vampire beside me. As though something telepathic happened between them, the younger vampire stepped away from me, lowering his head, as though giving way to a monarch. "Seeing that you were late, we worried. We came out, heard you screaming, and saw that you were in trouble. Do forgive us."

"And so you turned into a wolf to chase it off?" I wanted to make sure he could easily explain the inexplicable.

"I did." He smiled knowingly. "You seem to be taking the shock of all this quite well. I mean, you understand what we are—Steve and I?"

I nodded. "Vampires," I said simply. Yes, I certainly did know that vampires existed. My mother was one, after all.

"We have not come out into the open, and have retained our anonymity down through the centuries for our own security," he explained. "But we employ many humans to do many tasks. The job I was to interview you for pays handsomely, by the way."

I nodded, barely able to yank my mind out of the terror-induced few moments of before to the idea of taking a job for vampires in the city.

He moved closer in a liquid way that seemed to defy gravity, and the use of his feet. I think he merely floated over to me. I felt the power from his eyes—a sort of hypnotic bondage. A weakness, or a deep lassitude overwhelmed me, and I sagged. As though anticipating this, he caught me by the arms, his minion caught me from behind, and they held me upright between them.

"One important thing, Ms. Strong. Did the wolf bite you?"

Making a befuddled effort to remain on my feet, I groaned weakly, "yes," and shakily held up my injured arm. My black glove was tattered and pulled halfway off my hand, and dark blood covered it.

"Hold her still," Paduraru said, and I heard the scuff of shoes in gravel as Steve pulled me up against himself, his arms around me from behind. If anyone had come along at this point, they would have thought two men were accosting me.

The efforts of the two vampires, however, went on without interruption. Only an occasional shushing of a vehicle going by on Route 30, or stopping at the stop sign at the juncture of the two main roads, let me know that I was still conscious. Barely.

Very gently, and with care, Paduraru peeled off my glove, one finger at a time. "Steve is here merely to assist me tonight." Well, I had news for Mr. Paduraru. From such close contact with his younger assistant, I was getting that what he really wanted to do was yank me into the bushes and ravage me. The only force that kept him from doing so was Mr. Paduraru's power over him. I was still of the old school of belief that as soon as a vampire comes into physical contact with a human, they became irreversibly locked into the hunter-prey relationship. Had Mr. Paduraru's thrall not paralyzed me, I'd be screaming at the top of my lungs again, trying to escape this mayhem.

Unveiling my hand, my fingers looked as though dipped in blood. A wound at my wrist was bleeding freely. Suddenly Steve snatched my hand and began licking my fingers as though they were the best buffalo wings he'd ever had.

His fangs out, he said, "Oh, fuck, she's delicious!"

I gasped, startled by his fangs, and words. A terrifying sinking feeling came over me. It looked as though I was about to become his snack. Right when I wondered how I would get out of this, Paduraru's voice shocked my senses.

"Stop tasting her!" Paduraru hissed vehemently.

Abruptly, Steve let go of my hand, then let go of me, bowed, and backed off. I could tell that Mr. Paduraru had a definite power over Steve.

"Sorry. She's your human," Steve muttered apologetically, his tone a tad jealous. Tongue slipping out, licking his own hands of my blood, his teeth and lips had become blood stained. "You have to do something, or she'll become one of *them* at the next full moon!" he all but begged him.

I didn't know what Steve meant, or what Paduraru was going to do until he swiftly brought my arm up and covered the bleeding wound with his mouth. Alarm went through me like a bolt of lightning when he sucked—not a little bit, but he attached himself to my arm like a Hoover on a throw rug. The feel of it—of him—sucking my blood from the wound, made my head spin suddenly. A cold sweat washed over me. Little sparks lit across my eyes, and everything went black.

At some point, I woke up. Understanding emerged slow as molasses that I was on my back, my head was in someone's lap. Lights flashed by the windows of the car.

This had been my vision, I realized as I groggily came to with my head in the lap of the driver, his one hand on the wheel, the other soothingly touching me on the temple. I gazed up to see Paduraru's face looking down at me.

With a quickness that shocked me, I righted myself and sat in the front seat of his Jag. We now eyed one another warily in the semi-darkness of the interior of his car, and headlights of nearby traffic—we were on a four lane.

"How do you feel, Ms. Strong?" Paduraru's voice was gentle. Only now did I realize he had a slight, eastern European accent. Possibly, it had been all the excitement of those moments back there that this one detail had escaped me.

"Alright—" A movement from behind and to my left made me shriek, and I jumped, flopping against the car's door, hitting my head as the flight mode took over. Fists at the ready, back to the door, I saw Steve leaning between the front seats, a black bottle in his hand, eyes gleaming at me, a sneer on his lips.

I let out a relieved gasp, although I really didn't know why I felt relief. It seemed two vampires had abducted me. It would be a while before I'd quit being so jumpy. Steve took a pull on the bottle, brought it away and smiled at me. Dipped in red, his fangs were out. I had to look away quickly.

"Steve, see if there's a juice box in my cooler, will you, please?" Paduraru requested.

Steve disappeared from his spot between our seats, but quickly reappeared with a juice box. He handed it to me.

"Drink it," Paduraru said to me. "It will help you recover."

Finding his concern with my physical state a great relief, I took it, found the little straw and struggled to tear it away. I finally had the straw jammed into the little hole and sucked on somewhat cool grape juice. My left arm ached all the way to my fingernails. Although I couldn't really examine my hand or arm, since it was mostly dark inside the car, I did notice its neatly wrapped bandage.

Sucking the drink gratefully down, I looked out the windows trying to get my bearings. "Where are we?"

"Aurora, I think." Paduraru squinted, eyes darting to look into his rear view mirror.

"Yes. We just went through the Aurora Toll Plaza," Steve supplied, between sips from that black bottle. I eyed it. Red lettering across it identified it as *Real Red*. That was all. It didn't take my clairvoyant abilities to tell me that the content was blood. No wonder he looked like a contented puppy at his mother's teat.

"Aurora?" I said, feeling anxiety hit me.

"Tell me, Ms. Strong, how is it that you knew that vampires existed?" Paduraru asked quickly before I could make a comment about the direction we were going.

I hadn't talked about this in a long while, and I had to go slowly. "I happen to know that my mother is a vampire."

He squinted questioningly at me. "How is it that you know that your mother is a vampire?" he asked gently. "Tell me what makes you think this."

I made a deep sigh, and plunged into the story. "I was ten when my mother disappeared. It was summer. Everyone looked for her, thinking she'd gone into the field behind our house, looking for me, or maybe our dog, and had got lost—you can really get lost in a tall cornfield. Anyway, they never found her, dead or alive, but one night, maybe the third or fourth night she had been gone, I woke up, thinking about her. I got out of my bed, looked out the window, and I saw her down in the backyard.

She wasn't a ghost, either. She was solid. I waved to her. She waved back. Because it was summer, and we had the windows open, I heard her say she loved me. And then she was gone." My hand went up and wiped the tears from my eyes automatically.

"I see. I'm very sorry," he said quietly. "How long ago did you say this was?"

"Eleven years ago."

"What was her name?"

"Julia."

"You say she disappeared?"

"Yes."

"And, you are certain that when you last saw her it was night, and she spoke to you?"

"Yes. It wasn't a dream or anything like that. She was there. She was real and solid. Not a ghost." In my mind, I could see her standing out in the yard, under the light. This memory sparked another, more sinister memory. Squeezing my eyes shut, I chased it away before it took anchor in my mind, too frightened to let it take purchase.

"She wasn't one of our turns," Paduraru said, abruptly interrupting my thoughts. I nearly said "thank you" out loud to him for bursting in like that.

"Beg your pardon?" I finally blurted, a little disoriented.

"What I mean to say is The North American Vampire Association did not create any new vampires in that year, and I know for certain none have come across my desk from this quadrant of my ward. I will take this information back with me; see if I can't bring her up on our computer system. If she's in there, we will find her."

"She might be listed under the European Vampire Association?" Steve suggested.

"Yes, thank you. She might be," Paduraru said distractedly.

I sat there trying to make sense of what the both of them had said. I was a little confused. "North American Vampire Association? European Vampire Association?"

"Yes—uh—we have an extensive listing of all vampires in the world in our data bases. We have listings of every vampire, whether they are rogue or not," he assured.

"Okay," I said slowly. This really sounded complicated. "Well, thanks." I tingled slightly with the thought that my mother might finally be located, and my one sighting of her verified. I'd told only a few about seeing my mother. My brother had told me I was sleepwalking—I never sleep walk. The only other person I had ever told about this was my best friend, Jeanie Woodbine. If my mother was a vampire (I was certain she was), who but vampires would know her whereabouts? "T-that sounds really wonderful. I-I mean if you can do that." I stuttered, then paused and took in a shaky breath, pressed my fingers against my eyes and let it out. I needed to push all this talk of my mother out. I had to somehow make him take me home. "Now if you'll just turn your car around somewhere and take me back to my Jeep, where I'd left it, I'd really appreciate it."

Paduraru's head turned to me and he said, "No, Ms. Strong. I don't believe that is possible." Before I could protest he said, "Go to sleep, now, Sabrina."

My lids drooped. I fought against his thrall, but he was too strong. The last thing I heard was Steve saying, "Her blood is sweet."

"I noticed that," Nicolas said, his voice echoing in my head somehow.

"You're not strong enough to keep her safe. She needs a—"

"—Master. Yes."

Chapter 2

As I came to, I heard voices. One of the voices I knew who it belonged to.

"She is resting, now. She will be ready to travel when she wakes," that deep, smooth-as-velvet voice spoke in a calm, reassuring tone. I remembered, now. His name was Nicolas Padauru. Somehow, the whole situation felt like déjà vu. Like some half-forgotten dream, or a vision.

"You have arranged for someone to take her home?" the other male voice asked. A deeper voice than Nicolas', more authoritative, resonated pleasantly. Soothing, but at the same time commanding. Formidable. I liked its sound.

Pulling myself from the groggy spell I'd been under, I found myself prone, looking up into a mulberry-colored ceiling. I knew this was not my ceiling, of course, but at the same time, I found it visually relaxing.

Taking stock, I knew I was in a bedroom—Nicolas Paduraru's bedroom. My left arm felt tingly-numb, almost like someone had injected it with Novocain. At least it didn't hurt like hell anymore. Then I remembered a wolf had bitten me, and Nicolas had sucked on my arm—sucked my blood.

He took my arm into his large mouth and bit ... warm blood ... the two funny red marks, later.

I was sedate and calm and that struck me as odd. I should have wanted to jump up and dash out of there. I reasoned I was experiencing the vampire thrall, still.

Gradually, I took in my surroundings. The walls, were cranberry, and tastefully contrasted with dark furniture and the mulberry ceiling. There were no windows.

Mr. Paduraru, or Nicolas—I figured since I was in his bedroom, I had a right to first name basis now—was standing in front of a bureau mirror, only it wasn't a mirror. I didn't see his reflection, but there was someone in it, talking. I concluded it was one of those flat-screened TVs. But the oddest thing struck me; Nicolas was speaking *to* the person there, and that person was answering back. Was I hallucinating everything?

Draped in a luxurious dark blue, velvet robe Nicolas looked like he was ready for bed, or had risen for the night. A part of me wondered what time it was, and that I needed to get the hell out of here. Suddenly I remembered I hadn't driven. Nicolas had driven me. *Great. Now what?*

I took stock. I was on top of the made bed. My clothes were still on me, my dress was smoothed down over my thighs in as modest a way as possible—but that meant nothing. As far as I could tell, my underwear and pantyhose (shot through with holes), were still in place. Reassuring, but still, I was in his bedroom. Lots of room to go to the gutter on this (my mind was already there).

My arm began to ache. It ached at the bite site, or maybe somewhere above that. I was too out of it to really tell.

Dazed, as though someone had hit me with a hundred pound pillow, I moved to sit up. Unable to hold my head up, I fell back. Nicolas glanced over his shoulder at me, but quickly turned back around.

"She is awake," Nicolas announced to the image in the screen.

"Give me an up-date on her recovery. I regret I could not meet her today. Tomorrow night would be better," the man on the screen said. I noticed he had long, blond hair and dark eyebrows over incredible blue eyes. I thought he looked like a rock star, or maybe a god.

"Yes, my Lord," Nicolas said with a bow. He held a TV remote in his hand and pointed it at the screen. The man's image on the TV suddenly vanished, and in its place, there appeared a mirror. The mirror now reflected Nicolas' image. I made note of this. Why did everyone think vampires didn't have a reflection? That was stupid. They were solid, weren't they?

Smiling, Nicolas turned around to take me in. He'd taken a shower. His hair was still damp and slicked back. I could smell the soap's perfume, warm and spicy; a somewhat rich scent that I found intoxicating.

He stepped toward the bed. "How are you?" His voice was soft, bedroom soft.

"Fine. I should go home." I wanted him to understand that I didn't want to be here any longer than necessary, but I also needed to take care of a whole lot of personal things immediately as well.

Once more, I tried to get up, but a dizzy spell returned me flat on my back.

"Rest a moment, Miss Strong; you have lost a generous amount of blood."

Tell me about it.

I noticed he still had a nice rosy glow, thanks to the blood I'd supplied him. My deepest fear was that the want ad I'd answered had been a hoax, and I was to be his blood host from now on, too buzzed on his vampire thrall to care one way or the other.

"Let me see the arm," he said, reaching out to me. Reluctantly, I let him take my hand and arm in cool fingers and he removed the bandaging carefully. We both examined the bite, now. It looked red and ugly, but the skin was no longer torn. It almost looked somewhat healed. I found where the wolf's teeth had done their damage on my forearm, but it didn't look as bad as I'd expected.

In fact, it looked as though two days had passed since the bite, mostly scabbed over, only a few spots still healing with a bit of scar tissue. I couldn't have been out that long, could I?

"How long have I been here?" I asked suspiciously. My stomach roiled at the thought I had become his victim, kept here for whenever he needed to satiate his blood lust.

"Several hours," he said.

"It looks—" he cut me off.

"It will take time to heal, Sabrina. If you wish, I would happily supply you with a little of my own blood, and it will heal completely, in a matter of moments," he offered. The offer threw me off-stride.

"Thanks. Think I'll pass," I said. "Am I going home at some point? Or not?"

"Yes, of course. You've been through quite an ordeal tonight," he said. "You understand that I couldn't allow you to go home in your condition. I had to make sure the wound would heal with my ministrations." Still holding my arm, and sounding like a doctor who was about to give me his devastating prognosis, he went on. "You need to know—that is, I'm afraid that you have been bitten by a werewolf."

"A what?"

"A werewolf. I sucked out as much of the venom as I could," he went on clinically, "I took the venom for you."

I frowned. "Venom?"

"Yes. It will not affect me, as my blood will counteract it. But had I not, it would have definitely turned you into a were-person at the next full moon."

"Were-person?" We were being politically correct, I guessed. "But, because you took the venom, I won't turn?"

"I am not at all positive what will happen during the next full moon. Perhaps you will only feel slightly different; possibly you will have better hearing, your senses heightened."

"And if you didn't act quickly enough?" I swallowed dryly. The whole idea of my turning into a were-person didn't settle well. I'd gotten through some rough times already, damn it, what with my father dying and all. I deserved to have a smooth road for a while. I wanted to date. How can I date if I have to worry about turning into an uncontrollable beast every month? Along with the other monthly visitor, I'd become a were-bitch.

"As I have said, I do not know if I have gotten it all. The only way to banish it totally would be for you to drink some of my blood." *Yish.*

"Didn't you just offer your blood to me a moment ago?"

"Yes."

"And I refused it, right?"

"Yes."

"So, I don't think I'll go that route," I said, as he released my hand.

"Very well," he gasped lightly, relenting. "I merely wanted to offer you everything that I could."

"Well, you have, so—"

"I need to ask you something else," he said, brows still knitted as he stared intently at me.

"What?"

"Where did you get that other mark on the inside of your arm?" He pointed at my inner elbow of the same arm.

I knew what he meant, and didn't have to look. I gnawed on my lower lip. There were segments of my life that were a big question mark. For example, the scar on my inner elbow was one of them. I didn't really know for sure what it was from. I had concluded a long time ago it had to be a dream—or a nightmare. It was too far-fetched, and scary to accept as real. I remember finding the two marks—about the size of pencil erasers—there, only sometime after my mother had disappeared.

"I-I really don't know," I answered slowly. "I think I was ten when I first noticed it."

"May I?"

"What?"

"Try something. I won't hurt you."

Where had I heard that before? "Okay," I relented.

Holding my arm with one cold hand, he touched my funny scar with cool fingers of the other hand. I watched, wondering what he was up to.

"Did you feel anything?"

"Not really. Just your touch."

"Let me try something else." He bent down to my arm, his face going down toward it, eyes watching me. I tensed up. "Don't be frightened, Sabrina. I'm not going to bite you."

"I can't help it. I'm—"

"Don't be frightened." His voice was intoxicating, and I couldn't help but relax.

His breath brushing against my arm felt warm. Suddenly a hard twinge exactly there at the scar site caught me by surprise.

Startled, I yelped and jumped, yanking my arm away from him.

"Did that hurt?"

"Yes!" I scowled at him, holding my hand protectively over the old scar.

He drew back and eyed me with some measure of suspicion. "You are certain you do not know how you got that scar?"

"Yes! I'm certain!" This was a lie, at least in part. I had struggled with admitting it to myself, like I was keeping some dirty secret.

"Think, Sabrina. There must be something, something a long time ago. Even if you think it is nothing, or that it was merely a dream. Did someone ever come to you at night while you were asleep?"

I gaped at him, chills going up, and then down my spine. The memory flooded me. "I do remember something exactly like that."

"And what was the nature of his calling upon you?"

"I don't know!" Irritated by his question as though he was accusing me of something dirty, or evil, my voice became louder. To think that someone could actually steal into my bedroom at night while either one or both of my parents were home was outrageous.

"Do you remember him biting your arm, there?"

Unable to speak, I nodded. Tears burst to my eyes. How did he know this? Was it him? Had he been in my room that night? But I knew it hadn't been him, unless his hair had been much longer, and I also remembered the accent. It had been French. *Why am I remembering this now?* While Nicolas' accent was eastern European.

"Sabrina," he said softly, almost sagely. "You have been marked by a master vampire."

Horrified, I covered my face, but couldn't hold back the gasp of despair.

Nicolas nodded. "Only another master can cancel it out by biting you."

I gaped up at him. "You have to be kidding me, right?"

"I do not joke." His deep-set eyes never leaving mine, the vampire thrall was working on me. I actually had to force my eyelids to fall into a blink in order to break it. "That is one of the sweet spots. That is no ordinary bite," he went on. "You had pain when my breath touched it, signifying that no other vampire can claim you, except another master. I am not a master. Tremayne, however, is."

"Tremayne?"

"Yes. You will meet him soon. Tomorrow night, possibly."

"Was that who you were talking to, in that mirror thing-y?" I asked, thrusting a hand toward his mirror on the bureau.

He smiled tightly. "Yes. It was. That is our communications system. Ingenious, don't you think?"

"Yeah, whatever. Tremayne's a vampire too?" He was handsome whatever he was.

"Yes. You are still willing to take the job?"

"The clairvoyant job? I'll need to think on it," I said. I really did need to think this through. "Right now, though, I need to use the—you know?" I announced, moving to sit up and found that if I moved slowly, I could overcome the vertigo.

"Of course." Leaning toward me, he took my hand. Slowly, I swung my legs over the side of his bed, and planted my stocking feet on the deep plush of his carpet. I took in his bedroom, and found it ensconced in warm, dark colors; the carpet was a beautiful wine color, furnishings were walnut. The comforter was a tasteful mix of these colors in diagonal patterns and splashes to match the room's decor. Sure, I should have been able to get all that through my clairvoyant powers, but as I worked on why nothing was coming to me—his mind melding with mine kept me sedate and my inner eye wouldn't work through all that.

"This way," he said, handing me my shoes and purse. "You have had a long night."

That was putting it mildly. I edged out into the dimly lit hall, but I could find my way well enough.

"Down the hall to your left," he pointed. "Take your time."

I padded swiftly to the door on the left. His bathroom was large, done in black and white tile, with a Jacuzzi up on its own level, and a large shower on the other side of the room. Gratefully, I used the facilities, and discarded the ruined nylons into a stainless steel wastebasket with a lid and a foot lever to open it. Running the hot water, I gazed at my reflection and nearly went into shock. My dark hair was a snarly mess.

While I washed up, and combed out my hair, I thought on what Nicolas had revealed to me about my childhood boogie man. Why, after all these years, didn't I realize it? I had to acknowledge that he had been real, and whoever *he* was—and the feeling was vague—he'd had everything to do with my mother's disappearance. I wanted to find him. Ask questions.

And then I'd kill him.

There was nothing more I could do about my state of dress, so I emerged from the bathroom, shoes on, face washed, ready to face whoever else was in the apartment with him—there was another person there with us, I knew that without trying very hard.

Human, not vampire. Thank God.

Nicolas appeared at the end of the hallway.

"The papers you need to fill out are in the living room."

"Papers?"

"Everything for the job, all the information on Tremayne Towers is in there as well."

"Oh. The job. Thanks," I said, clutching my purse in front of myself.

"I am certain you would like something to eat before you go home?" he offered.

"Oh, don't go to any bother," I said. I wanted to go home, and I knew he must need to go into his vampire sleeping state.

"It is nearly dawn," he said, as though reading my thoughts. "I must regenerate," he added, as if to make sure I understood. I nodded. "But Toby will take care of you."

"Toby?"

"My human servant."

"Oh," I said. Toby, his scion—someone who did his bidding during the daytime hours while he slept, someone who would guard over him.

"Come," he said, guiding me up the hallway. "Toby?" Nicolas called as he continued up the passageway; his robe was long enough to brush the wine-colored rug under his feet.

We emerged into an open space. Ahead of me, heavy black, floor-to-ceiling drapes hung across an expanse of ten feet, interrupted by one large pillar. The rest of the apartment opened out into a living area done in warm tones with a fireplace tucked into one corner. Huddled before it were a couch and two chairs made of deep chocolate suede. Bisecting this living area, and the kitchen, ran a breakfast bar positioned at an angle to the rest of the apartment with tall black stools on this side of the room.

In the center of the kitchen area, stood a scarecrow-thin young man in a mauve button down shirt and black Dockers. By my estimation, he was at least six foot tall, possibly eighteen or nineteen, but looked older. Turning toward us, he shook his shoulder-length blond hair out of large blue eyes. I thought they gave him an androgynous cast. Honestly, if I saw him on the street, I'd have to really look to make sure if he was a man or a woman.

"Yes, Nicolas?" the young man said in a nice, medium range voice. A lithe finger brushed longish bangs out of his eyes off to the side. I noticed that his hair wasn't naturally blonde; he needed his roots done.

"Sabrina, this is Toby Hunt. Toby this is Sabrina Strong," he introduced, hands stuffed inside the deep pockets of his robe.

Flitting glances at one another, we exchanged hi's. Then, uncomfortable at eying one another, we settled our gazes back on Nicolas. "Toby will take care of your needs, today," Nicolas said.

"Thank you," I said, trying to hide my slight discomfort of being cast into yet another stranger's care. Toby was younger than me by a year or two.

"Well, I'm off to bed."

"Alright," Toby said. "Sleep well."

"And a good day to you." Nicolas then turned to me. "I hope to see you tonight, Sabrina?"

"Tonight?" I don't know why that shocked me.

"Yes. After you have filled out the papers, we will need to get you into the system," he explained. "I will come 'round to pick you up. I will call to let you know when. Oh, get her number, Toby."

"Of course, Nicolas," Toby said.

I hadn't signed anything, so I could still decline. I was still in two minds on this.

"Tremayne is excited about your joining us, Sabrina. He's willing to give you a generous sign-on bonus of one thousand dollars," Nicolas informed.

My mouth fell open then. I deducted several bills hanging up on a billboard right then that I could suddenly pay.

"Well, good day." Nicolas turned and disappeared down the hallway.

After thirty seconds of quiet, I said, "Nice place."

"Thanks," Toby said as he poured something into a glass. "May I offer you breakfast, Ms. Strong?" he asked, bringing over a tall glass of orange juice on a little tray. "Would you like cereal? I could whip up some oatmeal. Or some eggs?" He set the glass down before me.

Setting my purse on the nearby chair, I searched for my gloves. "Oh, don't go to any trouble," I said slightly distracted. "And call me Sabrina."

Smiling, he said, "No trouble at all, Sabrina. You can call me Toby."

"Okay, eggs sounds fine," I relented. I was hungry, and seeing that I had about an hour's travel back home, I knew I couldn't stave off my hunger much longer. Obviously, Toby was comfortable in the kitchen.

"You're to drink that, by the way." He pointed at the glass of juice.

I complied. Tasty, cold, and no pulp, I drank it down.

"So, you work for Nicolas?" I asked while he cooked the eggs.

Spatula in hand, Toby half-turned to glance at me through a curtain of spun gold and caramel, and sent me a look that made my face flush slightly. Especially with his next words spoken in a way that left it up to me to decipher.

"Whatever he needs me to do, I do it." That could include a whole lot of things. I was getting a slight read from him, too. Since Nicolas' thrall had left me, I was beginning to pick things up. Realization made me snap to, and I had to begin blocking him, best I could, while Toby trekked between the stove and fridge.

Protectively, I brought my hands up to my chin one clutched in the other, and took in the rest of the condo. Behind the black curtains there would be windows because of the various lush plants growing in pots stationed along the expanse. The fig tree, trailing vines, and ferns looked healthy. I wondered what floor we were on, and what the view would be like. Would I see the Chicago skyline, or Lake Michigan?

After a few moments, Toby brought two matching black, square plates to the breakfast bar. One held my eggs with a sprig of parsley off to the side, and the other with orange slices—fanned out, no less. He'd placed a maraschino cherry in the center. Nice presentation. It looked as though he'd made this all up ahead of time; slicing and arranging an orange this way took some time as there were no membranes on the orange sections. This guy was a chef.

"You must be taking culinary courses?" I said, picking up the fork with my bare hand. Silverware what went through the dishwasher didn't give me much of a read. I had a fleeting image of him in a cooking class.

"As a matter of fact, I am. University of Chicago," he informed me happily.

"Coffee's done. You want some?"

"I'd die for some." I squeezed my eyes shut. "Sorry, that sort of slipped."

Smirk in place, Toby poured coffee into a square black cup. "Don't worry. No one's ever *died* from my coffee." I chuckled nervously as he set the cup of coffee with a matching sugar and cream on a little black serving tray before me.

"No. I'm sure," I said, feeling like he was jerking me around. I looked for my gloves again. I was beginning to pick up things from the objects he was handling.

"You're a super-sensitive," he said, switching subjects. I looked up at him from spooning in two spoons of sugar into the coffee.

"Yes. And you're Nick's-uh-I'm sorry, should I use the word scion?"

"Maybe I should explain our relationship to you." Heat blossom into my cheeks once more. "Oh, a woman that still blushes! I like that." He'd gotten the reaction he was striving for. Yeah, I still blushed. I was not a worldly woman in any sense of the word. I'd lived in the country all my life, and preferred it over any city and the jaded people who lived there. Vampires and scions included.

"It's really none of my business," I said, pouring a little cream into the coffee, watching it swirl and come to the top. I had made this easy for him—his being able to tease me. I had to quit letting myself get backed into corners like this. *Damn it all!*

"No, actually, I don't mind telling you. I'd rather you understand our relationship, rather than assume it. I'm Nick's human slave. Or, if you prefer, the word is *scion.*" I couldn't quite decide if he was proud of this fact or slightly disgusted with himself.

Nodding, I dabbed my lips with a cloth napkin. The orange slices were juicy. "Right," I said. "I mean, well, it's what I'd thought." Did I sound as stupid as I felt?

"Did you?" he said, looking smug, large hands splaying onto the counter top.

"Look," I began somewhat exasperated. "Last night I was bitten by a wolf—ah-a werewolf. That's the only reason I'm here this morning. I had no desire to be here in the first place, and would just like to go home. Okay?" Why did I have to qualify myself to this scion? I wasn't Nicolas' lover or *anything.*

"I know, and totally understand." Leaning forward, he brought his forearms down on the counter and laced his fingers. I noticed his manicured fingernails. "I was here when he brought you in." His glance slid to my arm. "How's it feel?"

I held up my injured arm to show him. "Not perfect." I checked the wound. It covered a large section of my wrist, and was easy to identify as bites from a large dog-or in my case, a werewolf. "But, I'll live." I wasn't about to discuss my other scar—ever again—with anyone, if I could help it.

"Nick gave you a gift," he said, glancing away from me, and across the room toward the hallway to where Nicolas' room was. "He took the werewolf venom." His eyes flicked back on me. "Vampire blood cancels were-venom, did you know? In fact," — he straightened, hands resting on the counter again— "vampire blood heals nearly everything from wounds to disease."

"He offered his blood to me, but I turned him down," I stated flatly.

"Oh." Quickly, he pointed toward the plate. "Done?"

I nodded, clutching the cup of coffee with both hands.

He swept up my breakfast dishes and sauntered to the dishwasher where he quickly stashed them. Before I could move from the breakfast bar, I had a vision of a different and much younger Toby. It all slammed into me in quick flashes: A teenager abused by adults; using crack, jamming a needle into his arm; someone brutalizing him from behind, his screaming. I realized too late that these visions were coming off the cup I held, and siphoning right into me.

I slammed the cup down, letting it go, castrating all those frightening visions. *Crap! Where are my gloves?*

Startled by the noise of the cup, Toby jerked up from the dishwasher to stare at me.

"Sorry," I said. I'd dumped coffee all over my hand and a brown puddle was oozing its way across the counter. I only now felt it burn, the visions had so completely grabbed my focus a second ago.

"You okay?" He brought over two black towels—too nice to ruin with coffee. Oh well, what did I care? He gave me one and wiped the counter with the other. "Did you get burned?" he asked, sounding concerned. He looked at my hand. He found it red, and gave a grunt of surprise. I'd done things like this before—much worse things, in fact.

"I'm alright," I mumbled, embarrassed. I moved my hands away, avoiding skin-to-skin contact with him when he tried to reach out to me. I didn't want another, stronger vision of anything else about him. That was plenty. I couldn't dare let him know I suddenly knew his past. That really made people frightened of me. I didn't know what Nicolas had told him. For that matter, Nicolas didn't know what kind of a clairvoyant I was, either.

Toby shrugged and snapped up the towels, then tossed them into the sink.

Damn it, where were my gloves? I looked around. "Toby, Nicolas said my things were out here, somewhere?" I asked as politely as I could, trying to sound nonchalant to cover up my nerves. In reality, I was panicking; my heart raced, my head throbbed. The gloves wouldn't banish the visions I'd had, but they would prevent more. I really wished he wasn't the one to drive me home, but if I had my gloves on, and set up my shields against his emotions, I'd be okay. It wouldn't be a comfortable ride home is all.

"Over on the couch," he said, scraping the pan off into the garbage disposal, and then loaded it into the dishwasher as well.

While Toby banged around in the kitchen, I found my jacket draped over the couch—I missed seeing it when I'd entered the room earlier. Inside the pocket, I found my gloves with the right-hand glove badly ripped. I realized someone had washed them. I slid them on thankfully. The cloth would help shield any residual emotions coming off any surface I touched.

Long legs took him out of the kitchen. Picking up a remote, he aimed it at the drapes. Like magic, the drapes slowly slid opened. Brilliant light washed into the room like a huge spotlight. With hands at hips, he stood squinting out for a moment. "Looks like a lovely day."

"I know this is going to sound stupid, but where are we, exactly?" I asked.

"Where?" Turning, he dipped toward a glass-topped table, picked up a large, red watering can and began to water his plants.

"I know I'm in Chicago, but where is this?"

"Tremayne Towers, of course."

"I've heard of it." I nodded.

Toby made his way around the plants, watering them as he went. "This is vampire central, in case he didn't tell you." He threw me a quick glance as he watered a jade plant that was the size of a bush. "We work and live here, on the north side."

"North side of Chicago?"

"No, North Tower. There's two, North and South Towers. The South Tower is the human side."

"So, Tremayne Towers is where vampires live and work. Got it." I nodded. "What sort of work do they do?"

"Oh, lots of things. We have the hotel, suites, and condos for both humans and vampires. There's Tremayne Air, his clothing line, as well as anything else that he manufactures, like Real Red."

"Real Red?"

He stopped what he was doing to look up at me. "Bottled blood, of course."

"Human?"

Moving around the plants, Toby tested the soil of the Boston ferns that grew so lushly before administering the water. He was tall enough not have to use a step stool to reach them. He paused to eye me. "What?"

"The Real Red. Is it human blood?"

"It's one hundred percent human. Given by donors, of course."

I grimaced and stood up on tiptoes to catch a glimpse out the window taking in the top portions of dark gray skyscrapers, against azure blue background of sky. I edged closer to the window.

"I've never been up this high in a building before."

"Really? Well, here," he said, and undid the latch and slid open the glass door. "Have a look, and don't fall."

Sensing that he was goading me to see if I was afraid of heights—I wasn't—I eased out onto the balcony. Skyscrapers filled my vision, below us ran a river. Large boats were slipping across its surface.

"Is that the Chicago River?" I asked.

"Yes."

"The one they dye green for Saint Patrick's Day?"

"Yes. We're only a block from the Magnificent Mile. The Wrigley Building and Tribune Tower sort of flank us." I nodded, feeling like a tourist as he pointed out various points of interest.

I was about to ask what floor we were on when my foot hit something unexpected. I looked down. Rope. Lots of it wound up in a tight coil—the kind I supposed rock climbers used. I noticed the clips they might use to hook to when they climbed. But why it was here, I hadn't a clue.

"What's this rope for?" I asked, pointing.

"Oh!" he said, sounding slightly alarmed. He recovered from whatever my observation had caused him. "They're still working on the windows, or something. Anyway, the workers left it." He shrugged.

I'd had enough vertigo to last me, so I backpedaled into the relative safety of the room. I slipped on my coat, trying to give him the hint I wanted to leave. My coat had been ripped by vicious wolf teeth, saving my dress from being torn completely. My dress, on the other hand, had minimal damage (using the bathroom mirror, I'd learned this). I had envisioned that the whole back side had been ripped up. But that wasn't the case.

"Are you ready?" he asked, striding toward a closet. He donned a black beret, and a tan corduroy jacket. He looked a little on the beatnik side, but it suited him.

"Yeah," I said, moving for the door.

Keys jangled as we exited. Toby locked the deadbolt, turned and looked up at something. He did an air kiss and then a finger wave.

I looked up to see a camera stationed across the hall, directed at the door.

"We're being watched?" I asked, incredulous.

"Yes, there are over a thousand cameras in Tremayne Towers." He giggled and strode away. Following, I realized he was having a bit of fun at the expense of whoever had the tedious job of watching hallways all day long.

While we got on the elevator, Toby asked me to recite my telephone number and I considered lying. Mentally I kicked myself. Six months ago, after my dad had died, my brother and I were left with a sizable inheritance—I got the house, so his cash portion was larger. My portion was dwindling. I'd had to pay taxes on the property, after all. I would have to buy propane for the winter—and that wasn't cheap by any means. If I didn't get a good paying job soon, I'd have to consider selling the old farm house. I didn't want to do that. I gave Toby my number and he entered it into his Blackberry. All the papers dealing with the job were in a large envelope I held, and I'd look it all over when I got home.

"How tall is Tremayne Towers?" I asked as we rode down.

"Ninety-seven floors. The top one is s condo for Mr. and Mrs. Tremayne. Of course…" he paused, and did something incredibly sexy with is mouth as he considered his next words. "Mrs. Tremayne is no longer with us."

"Oh. I'm sorry."

"She was murdered," he supplied in a low tone that sounded slightly gossipy. "I hear she was shot with a bolt to the heart."

I sucked in air. "No kidding! How awful!"

"Letitia was a vampire, by the way. Just like Mr. Tremayne."

Meeting no one the whole way, the doors hissed open and we stepped out into a huge garage. I found it dank, despite the overhead lighting. He beeped open a red Scion with a black rag top. Classy, with tan interior. As soon as we were in motion, he pressed his CD player and something with guitar and jumping beat came on.

He drove out of the garage smoothly, and stopped at a small building, barely large enough for a person to stand or sit inside. This was obviously a check point. There was a twelve-foot iron gate closing off our exit, with a four-foot barricade running between the exit and entrance. Toby's window slid down, and he greeted the guy in the little gatehouse. While the gate electronically opened, they exchanged niceties, and then we pulled into sudden traffic and noise.

An unbroken line of tall buildings towered over us, and traffic snarled before us. Rush hour. All I saw were cars all around us, and traffic lights up ahead of us as far as my eyes could see. *How do people deal with this day in and day out?*

As he made a left turn onto Michigan Avenue, turned onto the Stevenson Expressway and drove through a tangled area of bridges and exits, then over the bridge that crossed the river. I turned to look past him out the driver's window. Spectacular white twin peaks rose into an azure sky above, my gaze kept sliding up and up to find incredibly sharp tops among the other sky scrapers.

"Do you live with someone?" he asked, either trying to make conversation, or digging.

"No. I live in my dad's house, but I'm alone, now. My father just died, and my mother has been, well—missing—since I was ten." Again, a pang flared up in my gut when I told him this. It wasn't easy for me to talk about my father's death, because it was still so recent. I had to hold myself in tight check to keep from bursting into tears. Being parent-less was hard at such a young age. I would've expected my dad to pass away when I was, say, in my sixties. Not in my twenties.

I saw Toby jerk slightly, as if the news had hit him as a surprise. "Oh, I'm sorry," he said, gaze back on me. "Then we have something in common."

"We do?" I said, surprised.

"Yeah. I'm an orphan too. Been one nearly all my life."

"I'm sorry," I said.

"I was born to a crack addict. They put me in foster care when she died. I went from one home to another. At eight, ten, and twelve, I ran away. I kept running away until they quit looking for me."

"Wow." Elbow against the window ledge, I leaned my chin on my fist. "That's really sad, and terrible." I repressed images leaking from him. I really didn't want to know more.

He shrugged. "I wound up on the streets, pretty much like my mom had. Once you've had it in your system, you can't get rid of it.

"And then Nicolas found me," he went on, his tone of voice changing slightly. "He took me in, cleaned me up. Vampire blood. The ultimate high." His smile broadened.

That stopped me. "You mean you've had his blood?"

"Yeah. That's the only way he could clean me of the drugs. It was a drastic cleansing," he explained. "He would take my blood, not a lot, but enough to put me on the brink, and then I was given his, to replace in me what was taken."

I wanted to gag thinking about drinking blood. "I thought blood was an emetic, that if you have too much it's rejected, and makes you vomit."

"Not vampire blood," he said, smiling. "It's decadently sweet."

I strove for the rest of the ride home to block his emotions, and all else emanating from him. Easy, like holding my breath under water.

Chapter 3

I lounged back in my tub of bubbles and hot water. I couldn't help the flitting images of my night—what I remembered of it. I let my mind go with it, knowing good and well I'd only be haunted later tonight if I didn't allow them in the forefront now.

Nicolas would call me tonight. He expected me to sign up with Tremayne Towers. I had to find out more about this job before I dismissed it—he had said it paid "handsomely". Admittedly, I was curious.

On one hand, I feared I would be making a mistake. On the other hand, my savings account had dwindled from the fifty-five hundred left to me from my father to about two thousand. The never-ending bills ate away at it. Of course, my not working was not helping things. This job was an opportunity that had practically fallen into my lap.

But work for vampires? In Chicago?

My mind conjured up the handsome man's image in the mirror that served as a monitor in Nicolas' bedroom. Was that Tremayne? I was certain of it. My heart thundered at the mere thought of that handsome vampire with the bluest eyes—they'd had a depth to them, like an ocean.

Emerging from the warm, lavender scented water, I grabbed my towel. That was when I thought of the darker thing. My *other* bite mark. The one I directly associated with my memory of the dark-haired stranger at my bedside when I was ten. I shivered all over suddenly. Nicolas had told me I'd been bitten by a master vampire. I didn't want to believe him. But what other explanation was there? The man who had come to me one night, long ago had been a vampire. He'd marked me for his own. Why?

I now examined both bites on my arm. Oddly enough, my older scar looked red, swollen—almost as if I'd been recently bitten. Shocked, I wondered what Nicolas had done to my old scar to make it look like that.

While dressing, I thought of the more pressing matters I needed to address. Like food. My refrigerator was so empty, it tempted me to clean it. My logic was that if I kept food in it, I wouldn't notice the grime. So, grocery shopping was high on my list, and either call or see my best friend, Jeanie Woodbine. The things I had to speak to her about were not something we could talk about openly. We could do lunch and I could fill her in. I had to get this off my chest and Jeanie was the only other human I could share this with.

I thought of Constance, my brother's wife, and my immediate need for money. I didn't want to take anything out of my savings, or the checking, which was low. Constance owned an antique and gift store, downtown Moonlight. My job was to help with the cash register, put out new items, clean, or whatever she needed, and she would pay me for my hours—minimum wage, of course. I was happy for the money, but it was part-time and it wasn't enough to pay all the bills. This was my normal day to come into the shop, so she would be looking for me. I could go to the grocery store after work with the cash she'd give me.

But I really needed to talk to Jeanie first. Jeanie worked at the only other bank in town—the one I didn't have an account in.

The crystal blue day was typical of mid-October northern Illinois weather. Leaves on trees ablaze in orange, gold, and crimson caught my eyes along my route, while golden corn fields blanketed my surroundings as far as my eye could see. Halloween was around the corner, announced by decorations in windows and carved pumpkins on doorsteps as I drove into town. My mood had become cheerful. That emotion had really been lacking in me for the past several months, since the funeral. I had to examine why I'd come away with this feeling after what had happened to me last night. I couldn't understand it—unless possibly, it was the job offer. The only good one I'd had—ever. A job that might end my worries about my future. *I really shouldn't turn it down.* I had been in turmoil, earlier, but now I was more inclined to take this job, no matter that it involved working for vampires.

Ten minutes later, while reliving last night in my mind, again—between my thoughts of bills, and money worries—I pulled up to the only stop light in Moonlight. It stopped traffic on Route 30 and Main. The First National Bank was a towering (for a rural town this size), four-story sandy-colored brick building—the only four-story building in all of Moonlight—on the same corner as the stop light. As the light changed, sure enough, someone vacated a diagonal parking spot right next to the bank, and I smoothly pulled into it. Since Constance's shop was across the street, I could leave my Jeep here all day. We didn't have meters here in Moonlight.

The time on the bank read 9:14, and the temperature was a nice, crisp 62°. A chilly wind made me pull up the hood on my sweatshirt. Once out of my Jeep, in a few strides I surged through the door of the bank and was blasted with the smell of money. Jeanie was a teller. She enjoyed dressing up nicely. The job suited her. Her cupid-bow lips stretched into a big smile when she spotted me. Jeanie had a sparkling personality to go with her bright, blue eyes, and short, naturally blond hair. She was pretty, compared to my cute. She winked at me over the head of some little, white-haired woman she was waiting on. I stood at the high counter, pretending to fill out a deposited slip so I could stand in line. I kept on thinking as much as I came in here to see Jeanie, I should change my account over here.

I got in line behind a tall, broad-shouldered blond man wearing jeans, a flannel shirt, sleeves rolled up to the bulging forearms, work boots that had seen better days, and the standard wallet-chain. His wavy blond hair was pulled back into a long tail. He was a good six two, and there would be no mistaking him for a woman. Tattoos covered muscular arms. Being so close to him, I got a read that he worked for some construction company. I had a brief flash of him laying bricks. As I closed in, I detected a heavy musk about him. Oddly enough I thought that I knew him from somewhere. But his face wasn't familiar.

"Hi, Frank. What can I do for you today?" Jeanie perkily asked.

The man she called Frank shuffled forward.

"Hi, Jeanie, I just need to get some money out of my account. Going on a little trip." He smiled wide at her. His teeth were large, thick and surprisingly white. Leaning an elbow against the counter, he half turned his body, and cocked one leg over the other as though he were ordering a beer at his favorite well. "I'll take it in fifties and twenties, if that's no problem."

"No problem at all," Jeanie said. "I'll have that right up for you." While Jeanie's fingers pounded out keys, they exchanged some pleasantries. In a moment, she was counting out the money. It all had come to two thousand and sixty-nine dollars, no change. A big sum. I couldn't figure out what a guy needed with such a big sum for traveling. Maybe he didn't believe in credit cards.

Jeanie told him that it closed out the account. He nodded. "Yep," he said, unconcerned.

Then she asked him where he was going. He said he was going east. I tried to block him, because he was such an easy read. I knew he had a Harley for a ride, and he was going west, not east. I saw, with my inner eye, the California coast, which looked different from the east coast—I knew it from trips I'd taken with my dad.

Big Sur. His saying he was going east was a big lie. I wondered why lie to Jeanie, who he seemed to know.

"Thanks. Talk to you later," Frank said, stuffing the money into that huge billfold with a chain leash. He swung around with his head down. Taking a step closer to me, he looked up and our eyes met. There was some initial shock of recognition between us. My pulse increased, and I grabbed onto the counter for support. I knew the vision was coming.

It was dark, quiet, when the woman came into view in the parking lot. He approached her quietly, at first. Sensing her fear, he loped toward her. Aroused by her scent he couldn't help himself, and bit her...

I staved off the rest of the vision; the moments of last night coming at me from a different angle—the wolf's memory—and the emotions were hard to read from a human level, but the base need to mate mingled throughout all of it.

Wary sapphire-blue eyes flicked down and then up my form quickly, taking me in. A smile curved large lips. "Excuse me, little lady," he said in a polite tone, and strode passed me. That heavy musk rolled off him, and it wasn't aftershave.

Moving toward Jeanie, I turned my head to watch his progress. His big head swiveled back to take me in. He smiled again. *Great. Now he thinks I'm interested.*

A chill slid down my back. In the same moment, I realized he was the werewolf who had attacked me last night—there was no question about it. I turned around and grasped on to the counter in front of Jeanie's window before I fell over.

"Brie, you alright?" Jeanie asked, concern in her voice. That pulled me from the horrible looping images of the wolf attack that had lodged in my head. I shook it off and looked up at her through the opening in the teller counter. She wore a light blue pantsuit that seemed tailored for her heavy bosom. It not only brought out the color of her brilliant blue eyes, but showed some cleavage, in a tasteful-for-her way.

"I'm fine. Now." I leaned as far into her window as I possibly could without drawing suspicious stares that I was robbing the place. "You know that guy?" I jabbed a thumb over my shoulder toward the entrance.

"'Course! I see him at The Saloon, and Trails End a lot," she informed, bright smile in place. "What's wrong?" Perfectly plucked eyebrows collided with concern. "You see something?"

"Oh, you'll never believe me."

She made an unladylike like sound with her lips. "Brie, it's me," she said low. "You've never kept secrets from me."

"True. Just don't go out with him tonight, whatever you do."

"I wasn't intending to, but why?"

"Not here," I whispered hoping I hadn't drawn attention to my klutz act. "Anyway, I have real good news. I may have that clairvoyant job!" I announced.

"Wow, really?" Leaning her arms on the counter she beamed brightly.

"I'm going to work for Tremayne Towers, in Chicago. If I want the job, it's mine."

"Get. Out!" she said, her already large eyes widened. She looked around quickly. Her boss, Bob Haticker, was nowhere in sight. One teller several feet away handled the drive-up window. Another woman down at another window was waiting on the only other customer in the bank.

"I answered that ad for the clairvoyant," I explained.

"No way! Really?"

I nodded; yesterday I had told her briefly about the ad. "He offered me a thousand dollar sign-up bonus."

"Oh, we have to talk. Lunch? Eleven-thirty?"

"Of course." I began to step away.

"Subway?"

"Where else?"

After saying our good-byes, I stepped out onto the sidewalk, glanced across the street and spied my sister-in-law's shop's sign, *Moonlight's Antiques and Collectibles*, catty-corner to the bank. Crossing the street with the light, I jogged to Constance's store entrance. I looked past the various antiques, birdhouses and crafts she'd placed outside on the walk, through the large window. The building, like most in downtown Moonlight, was built back in the mid-to late 1800's. It had once been the original mercantile, and then had been the local grocery store, complete with a meat locker in the back. They had moved the meat locker up front to use for displays.

Constance had gone from one small space to another, before she'd finally moved into this long vacated, much larger spot. She was doing a booming business, now that she was smack dab on a busy route, plus she advertised heavily. The old mercantile was big enough to allow her to bring in larger antiques than before. The eighteen-foot ceiling had given her room enough for my brother and some of his friends to build sturdy shelving all the way around the shop to display certain large antiques that didn't sell all that quickly. They'd used barn wood for the walls from three different barns—perfect for displaying antiques, and crafts.

I stepped through the door, making the cow bell ring. Constance stood at her horseshoe counter (it had once been part of an old tavern), with a customer. The warm scents of candles and potpourri washed over me as I sailed in and waived my greetings.

"Hey, kid-o!" Constance hailed as she rang up the sale. "The new Boyds are in!" she called over her shoulder.

"Oh, good!" I slapped my gloved hands together and rubbed them to show my enthusiasm. I was wearing my white cotton gloves for the job. I had extra pairs of gloves here, in case I got them dirty. Plus some disposable gloves for handling the cash register. You would think I wouldn't need to use gloves unpacking new items like teddy bears or candles. But you wouldn't believe the aggravated thoughts I would pick up—minutely—from such items. Once I had touched an innocent-looking antique bear with my bare hands and learned that the child that had last touched it had actually ripped the poor thing's head off. It had been sewn up by the mother, of course, but the image had stuck with me all day. I didn't like coming across those images or any residue emotions from the things I touched in her store. Antiques really packed a lot of memories, and residual emotions in them.

I stepped past the Boyd's Bears display, and couldn't wait to add the new arrivals to it. Constance had a large back room for storage, now. Her last place had always been so cramped; we barely had room to move around.

I found the boxes of the new arrivals and opened them up. Constance liked how I used various small toys and some of the other accent pieces she had in the store to help the display. Since Halloween was around the corner, I was using a lot of black and orange, pumpkins, and witch hats, and skeletons for decor. She had let me go at it, using my imagination, adding only a few small suggestions here and there. She was wonderful, really, and had a certain decorative flair that I could only marvel at.

"So?" Constance said from the doorway, bringing my head up from my joyful moment of unpacking. She was holding a brown Hull mug of coffee. The aroma of hazelnut floated over to me, and I suddenly wanted some too.

"So, what?" I asked, trying to keep a poker face as I stepped toward the counter where the coffee maker and mug tree was. I poured coffee into my own mug and dumped cream and sugar in-making it "undrinkable", as my brother would accuse.

"You have your job interview last night? How'd it go?"

"I've got a job!" I wanted to trickle the information in bit by bit.

"Yeah? Doing what? Who with, and how much does it pay?" she prodded in her sexy, slightly husky voice. Constance was a little taller than me. Thick, wavy honey-blond hair was streaked in a way that made it look like sunshine was hitting it under the fluorescents. Today she had it up in a crazy sort of bun. It looked sort of sexy, and I wondered if she would show me how to do that to my own hair—as if I could achieve it with my straight, angel-thin hair that refused to take a curl no matter how much mousse I put on it. I figured she had one hell of a hair dresser— a pricey salon where they pour wine, and exotic music played softly in the background—that she went to every six weeks without exception. I'd learned to like her at some point after she took my brother away six years ago. But truthfully, she was the best thing for him, and I loved her.

"I'm going to work in Chicago."

She made the give-me-more gesture with her hand.

"I don't have all the particulars, yet. I'm going in tonight, get more information, have a tour, you know."

"Oh, honey, that's great!" She put down her mug of coffee and gave me a hug. I hugged with a big squeeze back. She'd felt pity for me since the funeral, I knew this without her telling me. She'd given me more hours in her shop after that, knowing I didn't have a job. "What sort of job is it?" she asked as she turned to retrieve her coffee mug.

This was the tricky part. I didn't exactly know the details about the job, and I couldn't tell her that I'd be working for vampires in the city. No matter how long I'd known Constance, there was only so much she could handle. I had to do some creative lying.

"We're going to hammer out the details tonight, actually. Last night I was—ah—interviewing for a job with Tremayne Towers."

Her cornflower blue eyes went wide as saucers and she pulled the cup away from her lips. "Tremayne Towers? Really?"

"Yep," I said, trying to hide my conflicted thoughts, and took a sip of coffee.

"Well, come on. You have to know more." Her voice was breathy and excited as she poured more coffee into her mug.

"Well, I'm going to use my clairvoyant abilities, but that's all I really know," I explained.

"But doing what exactly?"

The bell over the door rang. That saved me from over embellishing. I could really get myself painted into a corner if I was allowed to continue.

"Con? Con, you in here somewhere?" My brother, Randy's voice came closer as he made his way to the back room. "There you are. Hey, Brie," he greeted, appearing from around a large quilt hung over the door of the office/storage room.

"Hey," I said.

"What are you doing here? I thought you were out playing garbage man," Constance said on a chuckle. My brother worked for the county on road maintenance. Mostly he mowed ditches during the summer, plowed snow in the winter, filled potholes in between. Constance turned toward him. I leaned against the counter, sipping my coffee. I *knew* he was going to say something significant. I felt his emotions, and they were going off the scales.

His tortured gaze flitted between me and Constance, hesitating. Hands on hips, he looked like a guy who had come across something bad or disturbing.

"Spill it," Constance said, cocking her hip. One arm had gone across her middle; her free hand cradled the elbow of the other while she sipped her coffee. She had no idea what he was about to say. Although I couldn't read his mind, I could feel his emotions, and they were almost tangible.

"Okay, I may as well tell you both. Before you start hearing it all over town. There's been a body found over on Howard Road."

Constance pulled in a sharp gasp. I did too, but it wasn't as loud. We both gaped at him.

Hands out, doing his usual don't-get-excited gesture, he said, "Hasn't been identified yet. All we do know for certain is, it's a woman. They got the county coroner out there, and half the damned county's sheriff's police searching every blade of grass. Anyone wants to rob the bank, they'd get clean away." He chuckled grimly at his own joke. Sometimes my brother really got animated, and sometimes he went with embellishing things. Today, he was doing both.

"Bob dropped me off to talk to you, and he went to see his wife over at the hair salon to do the same. We wanted to make sure you guys were safe, and to warn you not to go anywhere, or do anything alone. Especially at night." He eyed me on that last part. Guilty as charged. If only he knew what had happened to me last night. It had me thinking about werewolves and the guy in the bank who left on a trip with two thousand dollars in his wallet.

"What do you mean?" Constance said, verbalizing my own question.

"I mean, don't go anywhere after work. It gets dark out early now, and you know there's been cattle mutilations out by us… I want you to be safe."

"But, I need to shop. We're out of food!"

"Close up early," he suggested.

"Close up! I'd have to close at four!"

"That's right. I don't want something to happen to either of you." His eyes slid to me. "Brie, you really ought to think about staying with us. Until they get this solved. Some are saying it's a person trying to make it look like animals attacking cattle. No telling what kind of nut we got out this way." He paused, and looked around—as if there were a crowd in the back room with us—and lowered his voice, although there wasn't anyone in the shop at the moment. "Hell, he might even be a local guy."

"Local?" Constance said. "Why do you think that?"

"I'm just saying you never really know someone, do you?"

Yeah, you just never know.

"Where exactly was the body?" I asked.

He glanced at me. "In the ditch. Partly covered up with a blue tarp—kinda looked like they'd moved it in the tarp. I didn't want to mow over it. Got off the mower, and tried to move it, and—holy shit! I got an eye full!" Looking green-tinged, he did some swallowing before he went on. "I lost my breakfast, I'll tell you that much. Called 911 right after." He began to pace the little area that was clear and ran his hand through his thick brown hair. I'd never seen him this way, except after we were told my father had had a heart attack while flying his Cessna 172 Skyhawk, and had crashed in a field up in Wisconsin.

Constance made a half-whimper, half-disgusted sound as she went to sooth him, patting him on the back. They gave each other looks of concern.

All his years of working for the county, my brother would tell about all the dead animals he would come across only to gross us out. This was simply too much for him—something no one wants to come across is a dead *human* body.

"Well, I gotta go. Bob is waiting. I only came in to tell you this."

Constance kissed Randy on the cheek. I slipped out of the office and into the shop to let them have a little private moment. A minute or two later he said 'bye to me and stalked out the door. Something told me he would have a beer with lunch today. And maybe something stronger tonight, when he got home.

I didn't like the things that were popping into my head. My job (the one I was offered), would most likely have me leaving the house at night. Although it took me away from town, I didn't feel safe, not in the city with the shootings, and crime, not to mention driving through the insane traffic. Oh, hell I was going to work for vampires, as if *that* was safe. My brother's news sort of blew a hole through my joyous moments of before.

Coffee cup in hand, Constance said, "I know we don't have a lot of room," she began, "but you're welcome to stay over tonight."

"Thanks, but I'm probably going to have some really weird hours. Like I said, I'm supposed to go in tonight, get some things taken care of. They might have me start."

"Are you sure?" she said, brows knitting. "The girls would love it if you came to stay overnight."

"Yeah, I'd love it too. But I'll be alright. Besides, I'm getting a ride in tonight." My stomach tipped at the thought of being with Nicolas in his car again—and this time I'd be alone with him.

"Okay, but you know you always have a place with us," she assured. "We worry about you being out in that house all by yourself."

I thanked her again. This was the same offer they had given me back when my dad had died. Randy had said if I'd want to, I could stay with them. They had suggested I sell the house, and stay until I got my own place. I didn't want to sell the house. Besides, the house market was really bad right now.

I spent the rest of the morning pricing the Boyds bears, and arranging them in whimsical poses. This task took my mind off of all this business of cattle mutilations, and people getting killed after dark and working with vampires. I couldn't wait to run all this by Jeanie.

At eleven twenty-five I walked downtown, along the busy main route of Moonlight, went past the only other bar in town, Trails End, and the only dentist and chiropractic clinic in town stood on the last portion of the block where I had to cross after the small parking lot. Excitement bursting in me, I trotted toward Subway the last half a block.

Jeanie was already getting her sub built when I joined her in line. There were only two other people in the sandwich shop—exactly why we liked to get here early.

In five minutes we both had our lunches, and slid into a booth.

"So," Jeanie prompted as she unfurled her sub from the wrapping paper, "tell me about the job interview. How'd it go?" The light blue pantsuit made her bright blue eyes bluer. She looked especially nice today, I thought.

"God, I've been holding it in all morning. I've got to tell you before I absolutely explode!" I gasped, pulling in the aroma of red onions and tuna fish on whole wheat. "I'm going to work for Tremayne Towers, in Chicago. If I want the job, it's mine."

"That's great!" she said, her large eyes popping.

"The guy hiring me," I leaned forward and whispered, "was a vampire."

"WHAT?" she gasped loudly. We both glanced around. No one looked our way, so I went on.

"His name's Nicolas Paduraru. He works for Tremayne Towers, in Chicago. His boss is a—" I mouthed the word *vampire* to her. Her eyes went large again. Jeanie was the only person I had ever told that my mom was a vampire—and she'd believed me. Incredible, but she also believed me when I told her there was a ghost in her parent's barn (I learned he had been a caretaker from the nineteenth century who'd hung himself.) She believed me because she was aware of the story about it, and she'd never told me the story until I told her I saw his ghost. I had really spooked her when I'd told her. So, she knew I wasn't making the vampire thing up.

"Get out! Did you meet Tremayne?"

"No, he wasn't there," I said quickly, making a gesture to keep her voice down. "But, I saw him in a two way communications monitor. Believe me, he is hot!"

Jeanie took a sip of pop, swallowed, then said, "So, you're taking it. Right? The job?"

"I'd be stupid not to. But I'm not sure what they want me to do. I mean—*vampires?*"

"You're a clairvoyant. Why not make money working for someone?" She had a point.

"There's something else that happened, last night, I've got to tell you about."

"Okay," she said, wiping sauce off her cupid bow lips, along with her pink lipstick.

I looked around the place, found that no one was close by, and went into the story about the wolf attack. I told her how Nicolas had sucked the venom out, and ended with, "I woke up in Nicolas' bed."

"No shit?" She made a suggestive sound.

"Hey, he didn't do anything to me."

"Don't count on it." She made a provocative sound and wiggled her eyebrows.

I rolled my eyes exasperatedly. "Still had clothes on."

"That's never stopped a guy. Is he cute?"

"Handsome. Probably about thirty, in human age." I gave her a few little tidbits about Nicolas and his scion, Toby.

After several moments of gobbling down some food, I told her about my brother finding a body in a ditch.

"No!" she nearly sputtered on her drink. "Really?"

"Yeah." I paused as we stared at one another knowingly.

"Think it's that Cole woman?"

"Anyone else we know who's missing?" I asked.

"I heard she was having an affair."

I gaped at her. "How do you know?"

Before she could answer, the door swung open. Three guys strode in. All of them said hi to us, and we said hi back. One was Jeanie's brother, Mark. One of five brothers, and nearly two years older than us he stood six foot two, with golden blond hair that he had finally allowed to grow, and was still single. Ensconced in tight fitting jeans, dirty from working in the nearby stair building factory, his tanned arms and face gave the impression he worked outside for a living. He was an avid sun worshiper, spending weekends at his parent's pool. The other two guys were work mates. I'd had a crush on him since fifth grade. I'd played with the thought of calling him for a date, now that Jack and I were through. But I didn't have a big enough ego to go through with it. He barely looked at me now.

"How do you know Dee Dee was cheating on her husband?" I whispered across the table.

Taking a sip of her drink, she shook her head—"Can't say"—and snagged a chip from her pile of cheddar chips. Popping one into her mouth, she nosily crunched away as if I hadn't asked her a question at all.

"Would her husband have killed her?" I prodded, seeing that she wasn't forthcoming with any answers.

She lifted her sandwich with both hands. "I really don't want to discuss this, now. Let's talk about what happened after you met Nicolas. Are you sure he didn't—" she made a biting motion with her mouth, and I totally got what she meant as she bit into the meatball sandwich. We both were avid fans of vampire fiction, movies, and anything about vampires. We got into the sexual connotations of having a vampire bite you from the movies and books, wondering if it were true you could have an orgasm.

"No. He didn't." Now it was my turn to look covertly around. Her brother was still getting his sandwich built, and no one had sat near us. "Just the werewolf."

"Werewolf?"

"Yes, and I think I know who it was. I met him in human form in your bank this morning."

She looked clueless.

"Hint: He took two thousand dollars out of his account."

Jeanie's mouth fell open, which was really gross, and she immediately covered it with a napkin. She swiped her mouth, then swallowed. "Frank?" she garbled.

I nodded.

"You mean Frank Lundeen?"

"Yeah."

"Oh, come on!"

"I'm telling you. It was him. I'm sure of it!"

"It's not to say Frank isn't a wolf in person, but a *werewolf?* How do you know?"

"This morning, in the bank; I got a vision from the wolf's angle—from him."

"What?" She gasped.

"Shhh!"

"Well, I can explain that," she said simply. "Frank has a wolf as a pet."

I paused and said, "That's illegal as hell! And, no, it was *him*!"

She shrugged.

"How long have you known him?" I asked.

"About a year," she said. "He's a regular at The Saloon. And damn it! We were talking about you, not me!" she complained bitterly, and then took a big bite out of her sandwich. Sauce oozed out, and one meatball plopped onto the paper in front of her. I don't know how she managed to not get sauce all over herself, but she never did. Not one speck. Must have been her Italian side.

"How did you get away from the—you know—werewolf?" Jeanie asked low.

"Nicolas turned into a wolf just in time to chase him off," I said, pausing to give her a significant look. "My nylons were ruined."

Jeanie burst with laughter, but covered her mouth with a napkin. She slid a look at her brother and his friends. They were slinging their legs over their usual seats near the door, laughing at some joke one of them made.

"Does it still hurt? Can I see it?"

"Here." I pulled up my sleeve, and edged my glove down, and showed her the bite. It had healed remarkably since this morning. They were now angry red welts. It actually looked as though I'd been bitten a week ago.

"Looks healed," she noted. "Does this mean you'll turn into a werewolf at the full moon?" She was smiling. I didn't see why she thought this was funny.

"I don't know." I said, my voice going serious.

"What's going on with that?" she asked, pointing at my old scar above it. I looked down, startled to find that the *other* bite mark—the one I now knew was a vampire's bite—was red, and a little puffy. Plus, it itched some.

"Wow, I don't know. I—"

Jeanie bent her wrist to gaze at her watch. "Oh, shit. Look what time it is!"

"You've got ten minutes," I said. It didn't matter when I got back. But she had to get back to her job.

We snarfed down our sandwiches. In eight minutes we were done, and heading out of the shop. I wanted to know more about Lundeen, and waited until we strode out of the shop before I asked, "Okay, so, how did you meet this Frank Lundeen?"

"I actually met him at The Saloon. He offered me a ride on his Harley," she admitted. I knew her penchant for guys with Harleys. No other bike would do. Her brother, Chad, had one. This was her addiction, I surmised. I recalled watching her hop on the back of Chad's bike and zoomed down the road, the distinctive loud muffler noise could be heard for at least a mile around. She didn't come back for hours. I had gone home a little bleak and jealous.

A trucker honked his air horn, interrupting us. Jeanie of course knew him and waved. The driver was her youngest brother, Brian, who worked for his father hauling grain to the elevators.

"When do you start?" she wondered.

"Well, it's not official, yet. I have to fill out some papers. I'm meeting Nicolas again tonight."

We stopped at the corner where the lights had stopped traffic so she could cross the busy intersection to go back to the bank. This was where we parted company.

"You have an assignment," she said, sunglasses glinting in the autumn sunlight.

"What's that?"

"I want a full report in the morning." As I stood and watched her sashay across the street, a noisy delivery truck rumbled by and in a moment she disappeared inside the bank. I suddenly had the overwhelming feeling that this was the last time I would see Jeanie.

Later that afternoon, back at home, the phone rang. I lunged for it, hoping it was Jeanie, but it didn't feel like a Jeanie ring—I usually *knew*. This time I knew the voice on the other end would be Nicolas.

"Hello?"

"Sabrina?" Nicolas' mocha-smooth voice traveled through the phone lines, directly entered my brain and nearly melted me like ice cream in the sun. I slumped into the handiest chair.

"Yes?" My arm, the one with the vampire bite, itched, and I had to switch hands and itch it.

"I'm happy to have caught you home. May we talk?" he asked.

"Sure," I said, noting the fact it was still daylight out.

"I'm coming to your house, in a little while, if you would tell me how to get there?"

Panic rose in me. I switched hands and ears with the phone.

"Sabrina?" he said, sounding a little concerned.

"Yeah, I'm still here," I said, itching my scar. Realizing that I was scratching it again, I stopped and pulled down my sleeve.

"I sincerely hope all is well?" he asked in his distinct accent and some earlier-century lingo. "I do hope you haven't changed your mind about working for us? May I offer you my most abject apology for any unbecoming conduct of myself, or if my scion has wronged you in any way?"

"Oh, no. Really," I interrupted him. "You need to explain the job to me."

"Of course. That is why I am coming to pick you up, if that is agreeable?"

"What time will you be here?" I think I went into hyperventilation mode at that point; I was nowhere near getting ready to go anywhere.

"The sun has not set, yet," he said. "But, I am about an hour's drive away. I believe in two hours? That should give you plenty of time to get ready."

"Well—" I hedged. "I have to eat dinner, first."

"I will treat you to dinner, if that is suitable?"

I blew a puff of air from my lips, making me sound a little like a horse. Embarrassed, I stopped the noise. "Dinner?" I said, trying to not sound too hopeful about getting a meal out of him. This was business, after all. I wasn't expecting him to treat me to a meal. But if he was offering, why not?

"Yes, unless you are busy, of course."

Who would be busy on a week night? Especially since I had dumped a boyfriend not so long ago.

"Not at all." I gave him directions to my house from the toll way.

I decided on my gray slacks, a simple white sweater, and since my black jacket was ruined, I had another jacket, that was brown. I wouldn't wear it unless I had to. October nights could get chilly. I would wear black gloves (I did have several pair).

I looked at the clock on the wall. Nearly four-thirty. I surveyed my house. If Martha Stewart came in right about then, she'd probably throw up and scramble the hell out of there. You'd think with no one to pick up after, I'd have an easy time of it. Not true. While my mother was said to have been able to keep the bathroom and kitchen floors clean enough to eat off (in all my recollections no one had ever set the floor with our best china), I was a total slob. I ran around the house picking things up, did some light dusting, and straightening. I folded the square brown and white afghan I had made myself when I was thirteen. It looked good on the tan couch.

By the time I heard car tires crunch on the gravel in front of the house, I was dressed and the place looked presentable. I didn't over do the make-up, or my hair. I wanted to project a business-like persona. I checked myself in the large mirror in the dining room over the old buffet.

That's when my old scar itched again. *Why is it doing this?*

Chapter 4

I waited for the knock and made my way to the front door. I pulled in a breath and opened it to the five foot ten, dark figure of Nicolas Paduraru standing there. I pulled in his scent. I had to steady myself against the memory of last night flashing through me, as well as his thrall. At the moment, it didn't feel as strong as last night.

"Hello, Mr. Paduraru. Or may I call you Nicolas?"

"I like your calling me Nicolas," he said, smiling. "You look very nice, by the way." His eyes swept over me in a hungry way.

"Come in, Nicolas." I backed away from the door, hoping that was enough of an invitation to a vampire to enter my home.

He took a tentative step forward. "Is it only you at home?" He was wearing a dark blue suit of the same cut and ilk as the one he'd worn last night.

"Yes. I'm alone. My father was killed in an airplane crash about six months ago. I'm not married, nor do I have any children running around, as you can see."

He stepped further in, looking everywhere. It made me think of my cat I'd let inside once. She had looked all over, taking a few steps at a time, stopping to sniff everything. Nicolas wasn't sniffing things, but I could tell he was out of his element. Maybe he was taking in little sniffs; he wasn't being obvious about it.

"And we know about your mother, of course," he said as he stopped in the middle of dining room, near the buffet, still looking around. "How long ago did you say she disappeared?"

"Eleven years ago."

"What was her name?"

"Julia."

"I assure you, Sabrina, I will see if I can't bring her up on our computer system. If she's in there, we will find her."

"That's really nice of you."

"My pleasure. You know," he began tentatively; "it is in all likelihood that your vampire was the one who took her."

I glanced away. "I know. It's crossed my mind."

Turning away, his gaze swept the room. The pictures on the buffet caught his attention and he strode forward, and picked one up. It showed my father, the last one ever taken of him (we didn't know it would be), at a picnic in the backyard. He was wearing aviator-style sunglasses, and a Cubs hat.

"My dad," I said.

He replaced it with a nod. "He was a handsome man."

"Thanks," I said, and watched him choose another portrait. One of my mother.

"This is your mother?" he asked, gently running a finger down the side of the frame almost reverently. "The baby, is you?" A smile quirked his lips.

"Yep. That's me," I confirmed. Mom was holding me. I was one. She wore a blue bandanna around her head, denim shorts and a red and white top. "That's my favorite picture of her—of us together," I said, smiling, feeling a bit sentimental.

"I see a certain resemblance." He smiled up at me. For the first time since I'd met him, I took him in. He had a solid stature, his carriage, and demeanor were nothing but robust. He had a presence about him. If he were not vampire I was sure I would feel it.

"Would it be alright if I took this picture?" he asked. "It would greatly help in locating your mother, if she is a vampire. Many times, when a new vampire ascends, they take another name. With a picture, it would be easier to match."

"Oh. Sure. As long as I get it back."

"I assure you, you will get the picture back as soon as I am done with it," he said, then stuck the picture of my mother into his inner coat pocket.

"Now, do you have the papers I've given you signed, and filled out?"

"Oh, Yes." I'd actually had some time to fill them out, while waiting. I picked up the envelope and handed it to him.

Opening up the envelope, he examined the contents. "Good. Good." He nodded.

He moved away from the bureau. Nicolas' skin looked paler than it did under the dim lighting of his apartment. His eyes were the color of bitter chocolate, and against that paper-white skin, he looked scary. Vampire scary.

Nicolas turned to face me once again. "We will finish our business at dinner," he announced.

I pointed toward the mirror. "You have a reflection."

Turning, he gazed into the mirror. "Ah. Yes." He straightened his tie; the image straightened his tie too. "A myth. One of many," he said by way of explanation. "Another myth is that we sleep in coffins—in fact some of us never sleep at all. Our hair and fingernails *do* grow." He raked his fingers through his hair, examining it as though to see if he needed a trim.

"So why do you need me? I mean you have all this supernatural power. What do you need me for?"

He chuckled lightly. "You over estimate us, and underestimate your own worth."

"But, I don't know if this will work out for either of us." I'd argued with myself all day long about this. I knew I had to at least give it a trial run. I would give it a week. If I was still alive at the end of it, I'd keep the job—my joke of the day.

"I'm sure you will work out well," he said, and glanced at his watch. "I have reservations. Why don't we continue this conversation in the car?"

We strode toward the door.

"Did I mention I have been given permission to offer you a thousand dollar signing fee?" he said. I plucked my purse and coat off the back of a chair and strode to the door with him.

"Yes, you did," I said, shoving the key into the lock on the door. He was standing next to me. I couldn't help but pull in his individual scent. No, not cologne, but him. Spicy vampire scent. It was all I could do not to fall into his arms.

"Plus the usual perks," he went on, as if unaware what he was doing to me.

"Perks?" There were perks? "Like what?" I asked, trying to hide my inability to carry on a conversation.

He held the door open for me. "I believe there will be a car for your use, and your own parking space, and a few other things."

"Wow. Cool." I locked my front door and stepped down to join him at his Jag. He opened the car door as I caught up with him. It glistened like show-room new under the incandescent of the yard light, and the full moon coming up over my barn. He held the passenger door for me. I folded myself into that buttery-soft leather seat, and took in the wonderful smell. *Oh, I could so get used to this.*

He slid into the driver's side and closed the door. Starting the Jag, he put it into gear and smoothly drove the loop back onto the gravel road. The smell of burning leaves caught in the vents. I figured that old Mrs. Bench, who lived right across the road from me, had been out raking her leaves this afternoon. She always did this in the fall, and then set fire to them. I found it somewhat soothing. One of those recycled memories that helped anchor me to this place.

I was silent for a while, trying to focus on the now, taking in the new car and leather smells, feeling myself surrounded by luxury, next to him. I decided his smell was somewhat clove-y.

"So, where exactly are we going for dinner?" I asked, my voice a little thin. He had said he had reservations—I presumed for a normal restaurant. One that served regular human food, not a smörgåsbord of blood types.

"It is five-star," he said, as soft music came on. I didn't see him reach for any button, but I had seen his thumb press something on the steering wheel. The elegant sound of violins and cellos—a quartet—filled the car. Possibly a Bach composition. I let my eyes return to the gravel road ahead, my stomach making terrible butterflying tumbles. In a few minutes we were on the tollway. He didn't stop because he had I-Pass. I hoped that would probably be one of my perks he'd mentioned—that I wouldn't have to pay toll.

"Would it be too personal to ask how old you are, I mean in vampire years?"

"I do not mind telling you my age. I have been a vampire for six hundred and forty-eight years."

Wow, I mouthed. "And how long have you lived here?"

"I have lived in America for about two hundred years, now."

"Where are you from originally?" I asked.

"I was born in Petrovgrad, Yugoslavia," he said.

"I thought I detected an accent."

"Yes. My mother was Romanian, my father Hungarian." He was quiet and then asked, "I understand that your father was in an airplane that crashed?" he asked it with a genuine empathy, I thought. I didn't think vampires could care one way or another about us humans.

"No, he was *flying* an airplane—and he'd had a heart attack, and it went right down. It went into a field—" I cut myself off.

"I am very sorry," he said. "Your father flew a plane for business?"

"Yes. He flew everything from passengers to medical equipment, and once he flew a heart from a hospital in Chicago all the way down to New Orleans for someone—free of charge."

He was nodding. "That was good, what he did."

"Yes. On this last flight he was about to pick up some passengers in Milwaukee, so no one was on board when it went down."

"That would have been more tragic," he said. I nodded. "You must have been very proud of him?"

"Yes." I barely got the word out. It felt like a lump stuck in my throat with the pain of loss still raw in me. That surprised me. I thought I had been doing fine, getting back into the normal routine, and not stopping to cry in the middle of something. But, it had gotten a little better every day.

"And you miss him terribly," he said, glancing my way. "I can tell."

"Both of them."

I sat back, listening to the music he'd put on.

During our ride we made vague attempts at small talk, and before I knew it we passed the interchanges for Aurora. After that, the lights and city sprawl crowded my vision. I rarely came to the city. I had no reason to. Back in high school I had gone to some lame play, and the art museum, and couldn't wait to get back home and wash the city grime off of myself. All concrete, pollution, and tall buildings, looking formidable, and cluttering the horizon. The people where rude and had hard looking expressions and never met my eyes. I had no reason to return to such a place at all. Give me the uncluttered sky, green grass, fields of corn and beans, and a few houses with trees clustered around them any day. Boring, for sure, but uncomplicated.

Of course that was before I knew vampires existed in this city. All my life I had known I was different. Now, I knew that my life would forever be changed from this night forward.

I stared at the panorama that played out before me. Lights blanketed the horizon as we closed in. Billboards cluttered the sides of the road advertising everything from booze to insurance to housing and everything in between. The traffic slowed us down, and I began feeling a little claustrophobic.

"Are you all right, Sabrina? You look nervous," Nicolas' voice came out of the void at me. And I was boomeranged back to my present situation.

"Can you blame me? I'm going to be surrounded by vampires."

He chuckled. I decided I liked his laugh.

"Sabrina, I want to assure you. You will be safe. We no longer hunt humans."

"No?"

"No. There are laws in place."

"Laws? Whose laws?"

"Vampire law." He shook his head. "These are things I wished to speak to you about, tonight. Perhaps, if you can indulge me for a little while, until we are at dinner?"

"Sure."

"Perhaps I can ease your tension a bit with some history? In the old days, hunting our food was a daunting task—not to mention avoiding getting caught. So many of us didn't survive. Many humans believed to be vampires were sacrificed unnecessarily," he explained. "We now have our own human donors. We make certain they rotate week to week, so that we do not take too much blood from any of them. They are paid well, have benefits too. We have learned how to manage our hunger, so that our donors keep coming back to us."

"Hmm. Happy donors," I muttered, but I don't think he heard me. Or else he ignored me.

"And we have our own blood drinks, as well," he went on. "Some are human and others are a blend of human and animal. It staves off our needs. But we still crave the real thing. It helps ease the need in us, until we can properly feed."

"That sounds… convenient," I said, nervously pulling on the fingers of my gloves. "Like what Steve had last night?" He thought on that a few seconds.

"Yes. We manufacture it."

"You mean you can have it brought to you, like at a restaurant and no one knows what you're really drinking—except the server."

"Yes."

"Where you're taking me tonight, they have this, uh, blood-in-a-bottle?"

He chuckled richly at that. "Oh, yes. There are several kinds, in fact. There is Real Red—that's what I prefer, and other names such as Old Coffin, Organic Red, and Crawl."

I made a face at that. "Crawl. Yeah, that really wets the appetite, I'm sure."

We both chuckled.

"I believe it was named that for the joke factor."

Our conversation was light after that. Once Nicolas exited the tollway, we were traveling in two-way traffic, hitting stop-lights about every block, and yet Nicolas drove as though it didn't bother him, even when cut off by a taxi. Skyscrapers rose above us; their towering masses looming into a night sky, each window became small beacons of light against their dark, massive forms. The city looked different at night, I realized. Actually, I found it looked pretty, all the lights shimmering everywhere.

As we crossed the Chicago River, I looked out my window to see Tremayne Towers reflected on the water, growing up out of the ground to narrow points like giant white fangs.

Oh my God, I get it.

Before I realized it, Nicolas turned into a parking garage, powered down his window, and showed the watchman some sort of I.D. The little gate went up and he drove down an incline, and continued into the garage. We passed many expensive cars before he slotted his into a space with his name on it.

Briefcase in hand, he opened the door for me. I slid out, and he escorted me to an elevator. He pulled out a card key and inserted it into a special slot. The elevator doors opened up. We got on and rode it up to Main. The doors opened up to an atrium. Before us stood a twelve foot black wall of marble, water slipping down its side. In stark contrast to the black marble, the words TREMAYNE TOWERS were in white, arranged so that the two red T's were close in juxtaposition to one another, slightly curved, and pointed at the ends. And then I realized they were red fangs. Okay, clever.

"This way." Nicolas gestured, leading me around the waterfall, and we walked right into Earthly Pleasures. Lit up with tiny white Christmas lights draped through trees—I couldn't tell if they were real trees, or plastic ones—and another smaller waterfall cascading off to one side through various lush plants gave the place a somewhat paradise quality.

"Mr. Paduraru," the hostess purred demurely. Her svelte form ensconced in a black dress that had a scooped neck, the hem hung in a jagged line around her calves; she looked like she was going for the Goth look. Especially with the red and purple-dipped hair, cut longer in the front than the back. "Would your guest like a regular menu?" she asked him and gazed down, and then up my form snottily, as though I weren't good enough to lick her shoes.

"Yes." Nicolas apparently found nothing wrong in her attitude. Maybe she was paid to act this way toward humans.

With long, slim, legs, the hostess skittered out from behind her station and led us further inside the establishment. We followed her through a low-lit lounge, then through ornate French doors that stood open, down two steps and into another low lit, and richly decorated dining area. The tablecloths were crimson, with contrasting black linen napkins and brass napkin rings. The floor was rich in color as well, but I found it as dark as a theater in here. I hadn't expected bright lighting, but I hadn't expected the lack of it either.

Nicolas had no trouble negotiating the darkness, and I let him guide me with his hand barely touching my arm or my back. That whispering touch gave me a little thrill. At first I wondered what was wrong with me. Of course, I hadn't been with anyone in a few months, but I wasn't *that* hard up. I'd left my first and only serious boyfriend because of his philandering ways. However, as we sat down, it hit me. Nicolas' vampire pheromones were rolling off of him, filling me with a sedate, yet lustful feeling. How unfair was this?

We were seated at our table. A candle burned warmly in a gold-colored glass globe, in the center. It gave off enough illumination for me to see the table, and for us to see each other, and that was about it. The hostess placed the menu in front of me, and began to place one before Nicolas. He held up his hand. "I do not need one. I know what I'm having," he said, but didn't look up at her. Instead he looked directly at me.

"Very well. Your waitress will be with you momentarily."

The moment she swished away, another woman in a short, red dress swooped in, placing water glasses on the table. "Hi, I'll be your waitress tonight. My name is Pam—Oh! Hi, Nicolas."

"Good evening, Pam," Nicolas said.

She placed a wine and drink menu in front of me. "Would you like anything to drink while you're deciding?" her high, slightly too-sweet voice pierced all the other restaurant sounds around us. I glanced up at her and realized she had asked this to me. Her dress allowed for cleavage viewing, while a short white apron girdled her slim waist, making her look less like a waitress and more like a lap-dancer. My gaze went to Nicolas. He glanced up at her only once, and met my gaze again.

"Give us a few moments for the young lady to decide."

"Very well. I'll be back in a shade," she said in that syrupy voice.

As I picked up my menu, Jeanie came to mind, and I blanked out. I knew I was on the verge of having a vision. These visions usually lasted only a few seconds. But for the person who witnessed me go into one, they knew something weird was happening to me. Jeanie had once told me, "It's kinda like watching someone having a spell, like a mild epileptic episode." I would get a blank look, and I wasn't there. I was somewhere else. Yeah, that about sums it up—I'm somewhere else.

I was trying to pull in on Jeanie's face when I felt something invade me—inside my brain.

Suddenly, like a bubble bursting, the vision was gone.

"Sabrina?" Nicolas said. "Sabrina? Are you alright?" His voice went in and out weirdly and his hand came over mine. The chill from his hand hit me as if an ice cube tray had been placed there. At the same moment a little shift, or a ripple of time made me feel light headed as I tried to pull in my surroundings.

I blinked, and found myself back in the dark restaurant. I noticed that people had shifted around; they weren't where they had been when I'd last seen my actual surroundings. In my vision I'd seen Jeanie in a parking lot. She had turned to a noise behind her, cell phone in hand. I recognized the place—Moonlight's Market, our local grocery store.

"Sabrina?"

"What?" I answered, irritated.

"Are you alright?" Stygian eyes returned my stare. His face was without any emotion at all. Then, his blank expression re-arranged itself. Giving me a raised-eyebrow look, all the harsh lines, etched there in the amber candlelight, disappeared almost at once.

"I'm fine." Embarrassed, I turned my attention to the menu that had a lot of choices. A regular restaurant—an expensive one at that—with a separate wine list. Twelve dollars for a single glass, plus a corking fee. *Yikes!* Five-star, he said. These were five-star prices for sure.

"Have anything you want," he said. "I've unlimited credit here."

"Really?" I said, peering at him over the menu.

"Yes."

"You must be paid really well then," I observed.

"It is more than adequate," he said almost smugly.

"You haven't told me how much this job will pay," I said with a casual air while I studied the menu.

He reached into an inside coat pocket and pulled out a pen and a checkbook. "I'd nearly forgotten the sign-on bonus," he said with a tight smile as he wrote out a check. He handed it over to me and I took it with a shaking hand.

"Wow," I breathed looking at the zeros. A whole thousand dollars. This would come in handy. I was hired. There was no point of my saying no to the job now.

He was pulling something out of his briefcase. It looked like a small silver notebook. He opened it up. "Perhaps this will help you understand who we are, at Tremayne Towers. This is used, more than anything, to advertise the hotel and suites." He pushed a button and turned it toward me. A video began on the little screen and music began to play. It showed the skyline of Chicago with the Sears-now-Willis Tower, and all the other tall buildings against a blue Lake Michigan. The sun glittered against the water. Sail boats, and other marine vessels bobbed on the dark blue water. The sky was azure blue, with a few puffy clouds. A typical of a summer day in Chicago.

Nicolas stood. "While you watch the short video, I need to leave you for a few moments." He bowed, and walked away. I didn't know where he was going, but the voice from the video pulled my attention back to the screen.

"The Chicago skyline has just become more dramatic," a woman's silvery voice sounded over the music. The camera panned down and across, until it filled with two sharply pointed pristine white spires. "Tremayne Towers, situated on the Chicago River and in the heart of the Chicago Loop. Easily accessed from O'Hare Airport, more than qualifies this as the most sought after luxury rooms and suites throughout the world. It has won many prestigious awards for design, as well as the use of solar energy, and recycled materials.

"Bjorn Tremayne, owner and CEO, of Tremayne Towers, has made this an ultimate destination for those who take to the night and shun the sun," the woman boasted in her energetic voice.

I gaped at the screen as it phased out from the view of the towers, and then phased back to a really tall man with long, wavy golden hair, and dark blue eyes. Dressed in light blue denim pants, and western shirt with the sleeves rolled up. Large forearms roped with muscles as he crossed them in front of himself. A necklace of turquoise ringed his neck. His skin was chalky to opaque, and yet he looked amazing to me. Broad shoulders, narrow waist; he looked like a Hollywood celebrity. I couldn't take my eyes off him.

"Welcome to Tremayne Towers," his deep, liquid voice resonated through me. "Come and enjoy the most secure place to stay in all of North America. Relax with no worries, no hassles. Donors available upon request. Be my guest. Welcome to Tremayne Towers!"

When the video cut away from him I wanted to press a rewind button. His voice had intoxicated me, as had his looks. Like he'd looked right into my eyes from the video and hypnotized me.

"...Tremayne Towers is well known for its top-notch security in both the north and the south towers," the woman's voice broke into my little fantasy. "Over a thousand cameras are monitored twenty-four hours a day, seven days a week by a staff and crew currently numbering in the hundreds..."

Before I knew it, the video was over. Nicolas returned to our table. His vulpine face in half-shadow as he shut down the video on the notebook, and placed it into his briefcase, shutting it with a snap.

"What did you think?" he asked.

"It was… interesting," I said with all honesty. "That was Mr. Tremayne in the video?"

"Yes."

Before I could say something inarticulate, the waitress was back to take our order, and to give me one of her best acid looks, as though she hated my guts. I really didn't know why. Did she think I was his date?

Dismissing this little distraction, I went with the lobster, ordered the salad with French dressing, and rice, not potatoes. The waitress made a wine suggestion. Something from Napa Valley, and something I couldn't pronounce—even after she'd said it. Because she was being so snotty, I went with the opposite. I chose a slightly sweet champagne, (it had said "slightly sweet" on the wine menu). I'd learned from Jeanie, when you're with someone who tells you the sky's the limit, you go for the most expensive food and drink, and eat like you'll never eat again. I couldn't wait to see what Nicolas would order—or rather how.

The waitress turned to Nicolas. "And you, Nicolas?"

"I'll have the Real Red," he said smoothly, as though he were ordering the best wine in the house.

I watched the waitress's expression. Smiling tightly, red lips curved up at the ends, she said, "Of course, whatever you wish, Nicolas." She paused. Nicolas looked up at her.

"What is it?"

She cast me a strangely nervous look, and then flicked her gaze back on him. "Later tonight? Your place?"

"Eh…" Nicolas cut his eyes to me. "Not tonight. I'm… working."

In a huff, she snapped up my menu and darted away. So quickly, in fact, I think she merely vanished.

"Is she your girlfriend, or something?"

"No." He said forcefully.

"Really? I mean she really looked angry at you, and jealous of me."

Nicolas' eyes had a strange cast to them. His gaze broke away from me for a second looking away from me, then slid back onto my face.

"Other than my needs, she holds no interest for me." His fingers drummed absently on the table.

"I'm sorry. I didn't mean to pry," I said, fingering the cutlery, and pulling it out of the napkin ring.

"She is a human donor. On occasion," he added, looking distractedly at his cell phone readout.

"Yours, though?" I don't know why I cared.

"Eh... yes. One of my regular donors." He breathed wearily. "She, like all of them, becomes slightly jealous of one another, or any other human who happens to be within my reach. It's so ridiculous, these human emotions."

"But I'm not a donor. Right?" I paused long enough to straighten the flat wear on my black linen napkin. "I don't want to donate my blood to you, or any of the others."

"Never fear, Sabrina. You are a super-sensitive. You are not on the same level as a donor, or any of the other humans who work for us. You are more special."

"Special. Because I'm a super-sensitive?"

"That, yes. But also because, you are my ward."

"Ward?" I repeated. "What does that mean?"

"You are my responsibility while you are here, in Tremayne Towers. You live under my jurisdiction," he explained patiently. "I oversee a one hundred mile radius. You are inside that area. Therefore you are my ward." He paused. "It is difficult for you to understand as you do not know our world, our codes, and laws— yet. You do not know our ways. Because of that I must advise you in everything you do while you are with me, or among others like myself. You must do as I say, or—"

"Or?" I became wary now. I wasn't especially crazy about what he'd told me, as if I now belonged to him, or something so eighteenth-century. My great-great grandmother had been an indentured servant. That's about what this felt like. I worked for them, therefore they *owned* me.

"You are my responsibility, Sabrina. Whenever you are at Tremayne Towers, or on an assignment, you will have to remember our rules do apply to you as well, and your being here requires the utmost caution. Do I make myself clear?"

"Yes. Crystal." I was *so* not liking this situation. "Am I in danger, I mean, if I wander off without you? Not that I would, but in case there's a fire or something, I have to be prepared."

"There are certain things that will help keep you from becoming an unwilling victim."

"Okay," I said hesitantly, leaning forward to listen on his every word.

"Never walk in front of a vampire."

"Why?" I had walked in front of him when we came inside this restaurant tonight.

"The vampire will automatically become the pursuer. The fact that you walk in front of us can trigger the hunger centers. You must think of yourself as prey, and we the carnivore, if that helps."

My skin suddenly crawled. I had figured there would be some perils in working for vampires. But this was very scary.

"What you're saying is the vampire behind me will want my blood?"

"That, yes, or—" he paused, eyes slipping shut briefly, then he blinked those obsidian pools open. His voice going lower in a seductive whisper, he said, "Our sexual cravings are equal. In fact they are dual needs for us. Any vampire who believes you may welcome his advances will pursue you. We are ruled by powerful primeval forces that cannot be ignored, or denied. Once we are locked into this roll of pursuer, we cannot easily be stopped."

"You mean that I could be raped, or my blood taken against my will?"

"Believe me, Sabrina," he purred low, his voice intoxicating, "it would take so little effort to make you *think* you wished to be bitten. Once bitten, your pleasure centers couldn't refuse more. Our pheromones are designed to set your human desires on fire and, and depending upon the vampire, on how well he can control it, he can make you become fatigued, listless, so he can advance on you at his leisure. Or for some vampires, simply a look can make you feel as though he had just made love to you without ever having touched you at all."

I had lost the grip on my serrated knife and it clunked to the table making the exclamation point of my evening. I stared at him. His explanation gripped me like a cold hand around the neck.

"Another thing you must remember—and this is very important—do not look directly into our eyes. Eye contact makes you extremely vulnerable. It also is an invitation by you to be enthralled."

Realizing I was staring right into his eyes, I dropped my gaze. This wasn't going to be easy. "Okay. No eye contact and I'll follow *you* from now on." I flicked my eyes up. I realized his gaze had a rapacity of its own.

"You will be introduced to the others, in good time. My—eh—scent will be on you, and the others will know you are my human."

"Hang on," I said. "What makes you think I'll take this job? Walking into this building sounds dangerous."

"It pays fifty thousand a year. Plus bonuses. Much like the one I've given you?" he reminded.

I nearly choked. "That's an offer I can hardly refuse," I muttered. I spied the bonus check still on the table. I stuffed it into my purse.

"Exactly." He smiled.

The waitress slithered back, ladened down with our food—well, mine, anyway. She delicately placed Nicolas' goblet down on a round, lacy paper doily. The goblet was dark glass—better not to see what was in it. "Your Real Red, Nicholas," she said sweetly, almost as if she'd opened her own vein to fill it. She came around to me and served up my salad and lobster and all the trimmings, along with the champagne, and left us alone. Yes, a good thing I wasn't in charge of tipping her.

Starved, I began eating, while Nicolas sampled his drink, and set it down, his hand draped over the rim while it resided on the table. This would take a little getting used to, knowing I was having dinner with a vampire. Out of all my daydreams about someday meeting a vampire, I had never once envisioned this.

We were quiet, enjoying our separate meals. I decided to ask some more questions.

"Since you oversee my district," I began, "what about that werewolf last night? What do you think that was all about?"

"That is very unsettling," he said, eyes holding an utterly perplexed expression in them. "Werewolves don't normally act that way. They do not bite humans, not to make more of their kind. What concerns me the most is the one who bit you last night might have been a rogue—a lone wolf, as they call themselves."

"A lone wolf?" I now recalled the look on Lundeen's face as recognition hit the both of us. Was he a lone wolf? I backed out of telling him I thought I knew who it was. What could he do? Damage was already done, wasn't it?

"Yes. All Weres belong to a pack. If they do not, they have probably been ousted for some very serious crime. Werewolves do not attack humans unless provoked. As far as I know you didn't provoke him, did you?"

"No, I—" My eyes went out of focus. I felt an unbidden vision coming on.

Pain... darkness... blood... where is he taking her?

Someone grasped my hand firmly. My eyes flashed open.

"Sabrina!" I felt his mind-melding with mine. He was in there with me—a cold viperous undulation that neither felt pleasant, nor unpleasant.

We now stared at one another.

"Are you having a vision?"

"I *was*," I corrected, angrily. "Until you climbed in there with me."

"I'm sorry, Sabrina. Are you willing to share it with me?"

"I think I saw Jeanie," I said, closing my eyes briefly, but I had lost contact with her. I shook my head. "It's gone."

"Jeanie?" he asked.

"My best friend, Jeanie Woodbine," I explained.

"I see. What was your vision?" he asked, his voice sounding slightly intrigued.

"I saw brief snitches," I said, clenching my fists with my frustration. "It was confusing."

"Take your time," he coached.

Breathing through my mouth, I closed my eyes. "I really can't make it out. Only that she was in a parking lot, at our local store." I opened my eyes. "I can't get it back. It comes when I least expect it. Then—poof—vanishes. I have little control over the visions."

Nicolas studied me a moment. "Believe it or not, I understand how friendships are so important to humans. She has been your friend a long while?"

"Yes. Nearly all my life. We're very close."

"Does she have a cell phone?" He pulled out his own cell phone.

"Yes!" I was thrilled he'd thought of it.

"I will dial it," he offered.

He punched the numbers as I rattled them off, and handed me the phone.

While I waited for the number to connect, he sipped his drink.

The line was busy, and I got her voice mail. I didn't want to leave a message. I hung up, and handed the phone back. "I guess she must be alright."

"Then, it was possibly a false alarm?"

I made a noise of doubt, but shrugged it off.

"Perhaps we can get down to business?" he suggested, stuffing the phone back into his coat pocket.

"Certainly." I nodded, lifting my glass of wine to my lips.

"One of our own was murdered recently," he said. "We are almost certain it was an inside job."

"I'm sorry." His rapacious eyes were hypnotic, and I knew if I stared too long into them I would be vulnerable to his thrall, and it both frightened and exited me. I had to avert my eyes somewhere to my plate of food. I really would have to remember to not look directly into his eyes.

"What were you saying?" I'd lost my train of thought.

"Someone has been killing our kind."

"Oh. I'm sorry." I didn't know if vampires could grieve, or love, or feel the more tender emotions. But I thought it was only right to say what I would expect said to me under such circumstances.

"She is—or was—Tremayne's life-time mate. Her name was Letitia. It was a terrible blow to Tremayne." A somber look washed over his face. He glanced away, watching our waitress— the one who he took blood from on occasion—travel across the room to a distant table.

"Toby sort of mentioned it," I said, jabbing into my lobster, then dipping a chunk into a little dish of warmed butter sauce. This was too good to go to waste, and it was better warm.

A look of concern crossed his face. "Really?"

"Yes, only this morning," I said, spearing another piece of lobster. Maybe I should have put the silverware aside to listen, but I was famished. I felt as though I hadn't eaten in two days. I hadn't had lobster in years. I slid the fork into my mouth, held the buttery lobster on my tongue, closed my eyes and smiled. Beyond delicious. I thought this was as close to heaven as I would ever get. I wondered fitfully if they had a decent chocolate mousse.

"Tremayne needs you, Sabrina," Nicolas said, his voice becoming deeper, prompting me to meet his dark gaze. A stern look replaced the sad one of a few moments ago.

"He does?" I said, continuing to enjoy my meal.

"Yes. You will become part of his inner circle, which includes me and a few others who are extremely loyal to Tremayne. You might say we are not unlike investigators, as we look into certain problems dealing with the supernatural races. This is our first murder—of this century," he explained with a quirk of a smile.

"Okay." I figured it would take cunning and swiftness to actually kill a vampire. My thought was only another vampire could do it.

"Yes. We are stumped," he went on quickly. "We need you to help us find the murderer. What we will do is have you visit certain sites where, shall we say, these unfortunate altercations took place? Read a room for us, or in some cases, touch an item that may have been left, like the murder weapon for instance, or something found on the body, to get a read," he explained at length.

I nodded as a shiver went through me—like an acute sense of excitement, but also one of dread. "It may only take me a few minutes to read a room, or a whole house. Or pick up emotions. I might get a visual of the person who actually held the murder weapon—that's what I assume you want?"

"Precisely."

But did I really want to do this? There was a good reason I wore gloves. I had avoided touching other people's things all my life. To suddenly go out and purposely touch objects other people have touched was not in my best interest. Especially if they had committed murder.

"I see this bothers you," he said. "I assure you, you are not required to do more than that, in this aspect of your job."

"It does bother me, but not in the way you're thinking. I have never purposely touched anything I thought might give me a synaptic over-load since I realized what it would do to me. It could put me in the hospital."

"I understand," he said, lifting his elixir to his lips. "I assure you we are able to get around this." He took a sip. I watched as he put a napkin to his mouth; his fangs had slid out. My nerves butterflied in the pit of my stomach. I was reminded of last night, how he had taken my blood without biting me. A part of me wanted to experience that—his biting me. I knew vaguely how it would make me feel. It wasn't like thinking about letting a man kiss me. This was beyond kissing, or petting. I knew the sensations from a vampire's bite would take me higher than mere sex had ever taken me. I found it all so darkly alluring and quite terrifying in a literal sense. I had had dreams of someone doing this very thing to me. But the face in my dreams wasn't Nicolas'. It was someone else's face—an exotically handsome vampire, with large eyes and full lips. I wondered—now that I was in vampire central—would I eventually meet him?

"Sabrina?" His voice yanked me back to the present.

"How do you get around this?" I had to divert my gaze back to my plate quickly. My thoughts going into hyper-drive about allowing a vampire to bite me a little disconcerting, maybe a tad aberrant. Okay, maybe a lot aberrant. I cleared my throat, trying to shove my crazy thoughts into that dark little hole where I kept them.

"A little memory tampering. Melding a vampire mind with yours. It is simple, painless, and you will be fine afterward, I assure you." He set his glass down.

I stared at him. "Isn't that what you just did to me?"

"Yes, as an illustration." He smiled. "However, some of us are able to tamper with your memory as well. Some of us can read your memories, as easily as if your brain is nothing more than a video."

"Really?"

"Yes. Each one of us has our own special abilities. Some are better at one thing or another. I happen to be very good at mind altering to the point that I can not only erase a memory, but invent a new one."

The hairs on my neck spiked. I realized how dangerous he was. With this ability, he could do a lot of mind altering and who would be the wiser?

"What's involved? I mean do you have to touch a person?"

"Oh, yes. I would also have to have bitten them, if I want to really reinvent things in their head."

"You must be a real hit at parties," I blurted without thinking.

He actually chuckled, and gave me a slightly sheepish look. "There have been times where I've done some mind altering on people—shall we say—in upstanding or important government positions."

"The tabloids know about you?"

He chuckled sinisterly. "Enough about me." He brought his hands together and rubbed them as if to generate warmth. "We have what may be the murder weapon."

"The murder weapon?" I knew it wouldn't be a gun, of course. "What is it? A wooden stake?"

"A bolt, actually," he said, sliding his fingers down the stem of his glass negligently. "No one has touched it. I have requested that our operatives not touch a thing until we get there."

Licking my lips, I had to cut my eyes back to my plate.

"You mean something happened? Today?"

"Yes. It happened nearby, but not to one of our own. Possibly a rogue vampire who still roams the graveyards at night. He would have found protection with us, had he looked for our site on the Internet."

"You have a site on the Internet?" I said in a disbelieving tone.

"Yes."

"It must be well hidden, then," I said. "I've never found it."

"It is a link from Tremayne Towers, actually," he informed.

"How do you know the vampire is a man, the one who was shot tonight?" I asked. "Don't you all become dust when you die?"

"No," he said. "That is another lie." Okay, I was re-learning everything tonight. "We have spread those lies, actually, to help protect us." He paused, then added, "Only the sun can destroy the body, almost immediately—except in some of the very old vampires—and if the body is beheaded."

"So, you have a murdered vampire, and you want me to use my abilities on the—what was it?"

"A bolt from a crossbow."

"And we're going there tonight?"

"Tremayne has given me permission to take you to this one site tonight, the most recent one. If that is alright with you?"

"Do I have coverage? I mean if I go into the hospital?"

His brows rose. "You do not trust that I can keep you safe?"

"Wel-l-l," I sang.

"During your employ with us, you are covered one hundred percent, from tonight on. We merely have to get you into the system."

"System?"

"Computer system. Everyone is in it. All humans, and all vampires, whether they live or work here, or are under the sovereign, are in the system. Makes tracking individuals so much easier."

"I see." *Big Vampire Brother?*

"Also, Ms. Strong, I must advise that you are to tell no one of your business with us, or that you work for vampires." He went on swiftly. "Your friend must not be told exactly what you do or who you work for. Understood?" *Oops.*

"Yes, of course," I said with a curt nod. It would be hard not to tell people what I do to make enough money to stay in my father's house. "What do I write down on my tax form?"

"Consultant."

We finished our meal, Nicolas tucked a credit card into the little black folder our waitress settled on the edge of the table. She whisked away with it, and came back pretty quickly with his card. He replaced it inside his coat, and we exited the establishment.

Crossing the open atrium, we headed to a bank of three elevators. I saw him take out the same card as before and shove it into a slot next to the middle doors. It was the only way to summon this elevator. The others had call buttons, but not this one. Obviously not everyone could gain access to this elevator. The doors opened. We got on and again took our places opposite each other.

"Where to now?" I watched him choose a button on the panel marked Level C.

"Down to Data and Personnel. You'll need to get your identification badge made," he said as the elevator descended.

Chapter 5

My knees buckled when we came to a stop. The doors opened on Level C. I discovered it was located *below* the garage. I didn't understand this, but all things in their good time. We turned down a hallway that eventually opened out into an area with a glassed-in room in a central area with hundreds of computers. An army of people gazed into these computers, or moved about the room with files looking stressed-out.

"This is the monitor room," Nicolas thrust his hand toward the glass-encased room. Like one giant fishbowl, people were seated watching the monitors. They mostly looked bored, staring like zombies. Then I noted their skin tones. Some were vampires, others were humans. They worked together pretty well, side by side, I thought.

"This is where they watch what's on all those cameras?" I asked.

"Yes," he said. "This way." He directed me along the wide hall that separated the monitor room from regular offices. Some offices had wooden doors, while some had large windows and glass doors.

A middle-aged woman with glasses perched on the end of her small nose sat behind the counter in Data and Personnel. The glasses had a decorative chain that looped around her neck.

"Oh. Hi, Nicolas," she said brightly, throwing him only the briefest glance, and then looked at me. "Someone new?"

"Yes, Sally, this is Sabrina Strong, and these are her papers, everything you need is here," Nicolas said, plopping down some of the forms I'd filled out.

"Sally will put you into the system, make you the ID, and dispense the keys you'll need to come and go around here." Nicolas' words were directed at me and I turned to him, realizing he was leaving me alone. "I will take the rest to those who need them to save some time."

I thanked him and smiled back at the woman—who I was happy to see was human.

Sally, it turned out, was an efficient woman. Large eyes and full crimson lips took up nearly all of her face. Her jet black hair—I knew it had to be dyed because she had to be closing in on sixty—was styled nicely into soft curls around her face. Her fingers flew over the keys of her computer, clicking her mouse and moving it around. She had all my information in the computer within moments of my arrival.

When she was done, she took a photo of me, like they do in the driver's bureau (only it actually turned out half-way decent because she asked me to smile). Once the card came out of the laminating machine, she looped it on a long, red nylon ribbon I was to wear around my neck, and she placed two keys on the counter. Pointing to each one she explained the green plastic one (like the one Nicolas had used), was for the elevator, and access to other places in the towers. The regular door key was for the bathroom.

"Bathroom?" I asked. "Why do I need a bathroom key?"

Sally gave me the drollest look over the rims of her glasses and said, "You'll be using the human bathrooms and if we don't lock them, the vampires use them."

"What for?" I asked.

"Honey, you really don't want to know."

My eyes went wide. "Okay. I guess I don't."

"Vampires have their own bathrooms," she explained gently as she gathered up the papers, stacked them and punched them with her stapler.

"I didn't know they needed one," I said, and immediately felt stupid about saying it until Sally smiled back.

"You'd be surprised, my dear. I keep on saying I should find another job, but the money and benefits are too good. Plus, three weeks' vacation, my own free parking—in this town, who can beat that?"

I smiled. "Yeah." I didn't know how much Sally got for doing her job, but mine probably paid a little better, plus it had perks. I didn't hear about any vacation. Maybe I should have asked. I remembered that check in my purse and made a mental note to go to the bank tomorrow.

I took my new I.D. and looped it over my head, making sure it hung right. I took up the two keys and held up the gold one and said, "Bathroom." I held up the green plastic one. "Elevator."

Sally winked. "You got it, sweetie. Good luck."

"Thanks Sally. Hope to run into you again some time."

"Oh, you will. In two weeks you'll be getting your check from me. I hand them out to everyone here. You didn't have it down as automatic deposit, right?"

"Right. I'll see you in a few weeks, I guess." We said goodbye. I had made one good human friend here tonight.

Hearing two male voices—one that I was attuned to—I turned, to see Nicolas with a blond man chatting and laughing. They both stopped a few feet from me.

"And here she is. Sabrina Strong, this is Andrew Morkel, head of the Donor Pool Department, and also heads the Sanguine Team," Nicolas introduced.

Morkel returned a bright cornflower-blue gaze. "Nice to meet you, Sabrina," he said pleasantly enough. I extended a gloved hand, and didn't apologize. I never did. People were curious, naturally, but explaining my condition produced more problems. I went with their assuming I was crazy about wearing fancy gloves. He didn't seem to make any notice of the gloves—or pretended not to—and took my hand in a gentlemanly way and didn't squeeze too hard. I knew before he shook my hand he wasn't a vampire. His skin was a nicely tanned tone a Caucasian would have to get at a tanning place at this time of year. I had to wonder if he didn't do this to make himself stand out against a nest of vampires. His hair was sandy brown with some gray at the temples, I now noticed, making it look blond. A little crow's feet running from the corners of his eyes, I figured he might be in his late thirties to early forties. He was good-looking in a general way; nothing really stood out, except that his ears were pointed. Okay. Not a vampire and definitely not a human. This had my mind swimming with the possibilities.

"Sabrina has signed on as a consultant," Nicolas said, sounding somewhat proud.

"Wonderful, wonderful," he said, and the conversation went flat suddenly.

"Level eight," Nicolas added.

"I see." Morkel smiled back at me, eyes glittering. I wasn't sure why Nicolas had added that last part as if my "level" was somehow important to him, but probably was.

"Well, I hope what I gave you helps," Morkel said. "Have a good evening, and nice meeting you, Ms. Strong."

"You too," I said. Morkel walked away and stepped through another door, at the end of the hall.

I turned to stare at Nicolas. "Okay. What was he?" I asked.

"A member of the fae. An elf," he added the last because of the confused look I fed him. I guess he wanted to see my reaction. Smiling wide enough to show uneven, but white teeth while rubbing his hands together, he explained, "We have a team of elves who run the Donor Pool, the hospital, as well as the Sanguine Team."

"What's the Sanguine Team?"

"They—eh—specialize in the blood aspect of our lives. We are allergic to their blood, so they make good nurses and doctors."

"Good to know you hire minorities here."

Ignoring my droll comeback, he strode across the hall with me in his wake. We passed a few office doors and stopped at the middle one. Entering an open area I found myself in a maze of drab brown cubicles. I could hear male voices, somewhere in one of the cubicles.

"Good. Sounds like my partners are in," Nicolas said, moving into a larger cubicle, and set his briefcase down on the desk. His office was clean, functional with two black leather chairs placed at an angle facing his desk. Behind the desk was one black, five-drawer file cabinet, a large wall map of Chicago, and a narrow bookcase filled with books stood in the corner.

"Heath? Leif?" Nicolas spoke in no louder a voice than if he were addressing me.

The voices in a nearby cubicle stopped.

"What?" said a man from somewhere to my right.

"I've brought Ms. Strong in for you both to meet," Nicolas said.

"Right then. Be right there." I caught the British accent.

Motion from behind made me turn toward the newcomers. I hadn't heard them, as much as sensed that they were suddenly there, behind me, and I turned swiftly, remembering what Nicolas had said about vampires lurking behind me becoming the hunters.

"Leif, Heath, this is Sabrina Strong," Nicolas introduced, really rolling the r's this time. "Sabrina, this is Leif and Heath Sufferden."

I found myself seeing double. Twins. I guessed they were in their early-twenties when turned. One was dressed all in black, the only color—a gold tie—pulled my eyes to him. A pair of blue-tinted glasses sat half-way down his nose. He gazed over the rims at me.

The other twin wore expensive-looking faded jeans, and a black turtleneck under a burnt umber sports coat. His wavy, dark blond hair was a little longer than his brother's, and parted down the middle, touching his shoulders. Their whiskey-brown eyes and saucy lips were their most dangerous features; they could have been on the covers of romance books, they were that gorgeous.

I put out my hand. The two gaped at me, smiling.

I pulled back my hand. "So, vampires don't shake hands?" I asked.

"It is an act of intimacy," Nicolas explained quickly. "A vampire's touch acts on the pleasure centers of a human brain. Our touch would trigger your pleasure receptors easily."

"I had no idea," I said, drawing back. "Thanks for the warning." I turned to Nicolas. "Although I'm wearing gloves?" I held up my hand to him.

"Even without touch a vampire can bring on an erotic rush, luv," the one wearing the glasses said. He took me all in and I felt like I'd been eye-fucked. "Of course it takes an older-than-dirt vampire to do it with a thought." *Yeah, thank God!*

"Yeah, like Tremayne," said the other, and they both chuckled darkly. "Tremayne will like her," Heath added.

"He likes them young." Leif eyed me again. I wanted to kick him, then run like a big chicken. I stood there chewing on my inner lip and took the abuse.

"Who doesn't?" his brother agreed, also eyeing me.

"Could we get back to business, now?" Nicolas asked, sounding slightly annoyed.

"Of course, Nicolas. Whatever you want. We're just admiring your choice in birds."

Birds? I didn't understand his British slang at all.

Leif smiled wide at me, showing a little fang. My heart lurched suddenly.

Reaching for something on his desk, Nicolas brushed against me. I got a sudden flash. I staggered back. I didn't know who had caught me.

A sea of headstones filled my vision as the moon's silvery light illuminated the largest graveyard I'd ever seen. The moon's light glowed on the hundreds of grave markers, crosses and tombstones that went on and on, beyond the grim distance.

"What is it?" the voice entered my head, and like someone turning out the light in a room, the vision was gone. A mini-vision.

I returned to the present, and my head felt oddly hollow, until I caught up with things. The room swam for a few more seconds and then adjusted itself.

Holding my forehead I said, "I don't know. A vision—of tombstones."

"What?" Nicolas was in front of me, head bent to look into my face.

Dizziness gone, I blinked up at him. "Someplace—it looked like a cemetery." I shrugged.

"Graceland Cemetery. Of course." Nicolas turned to the twins. "I think you'd better be going, before we get an angry call from V.I.U. They don't like it when we stall."

"Right," said Leif, on the move.

"Great. A cemetery," muttered Heath as he followed him out of Nicolas' cubicle. "Nothing like larking about the tombstones again, eh brother?"

"Speak for yourself," Leif said as they strolled down the hall and disappeared from view. "I'll drive."

"Oi, you always drive," Heath complained.

"Fine, if you want to drive, please do. I've a belly of your complaints tonight."

Twenty minutes later, Nicolas negotiated the narrow lane of Graceland Cemetery. Blue lights eerily flashed in the distance. These were not the red, blue and white lights, of police cars. From further away they were hardly noticeable. We neared the parked cars—a dark sedan gleamed in the moonlight, a red sporty car, and what looked to me like a hearse, also was parked along the narrow lane.

"Is that the police?" I asked as Nicolas drove sedately toward the parked cars.

"No," he said. "No. It is the V.I.U."

"The who?"

"Vampires' Investigation Unit," he said.

"You guys have your own investigation division?" I said, incredulous.

"It is not run by us, but demons. We couldn't expect the human police to take care of this," he said.

Demons investigating a vampire's death. Naturally. What was I thinking?

"And there's a body of a vampire somewhere here?" I asked, trying to understand this.

"There is." He glanced my way.

"And he was killed by a—what?" I was slightly confused.

"A bolt."

"What's a bolt, exactly?"

Coming to a smooth stop, he put the Jag in park. "You will see one soon. But it is a small arrow shot from a crossbow."

Someone was stepping toward us in the cone of our headlights. A cloud of vapor enveloped him as he lumbered toward us. I at first thought that maybe he was smoking a pipe, but nothing like that appeared to be in his mouth or in his hand. It swirled around not only his head, but around his whole body. Strange.

"I see they have already bagged the body." Nicolas powered down the window as the man who was somehow producing smoke—or maybe a mist—approached. The cool night air stole the heat inside the car. I was glad I'd brought my coat, now, and pulled the collar up. Then I realized that the demon wasn't producing smoke, but his body was probably so hot, and the cooler air around him produced the steam. Interesting. *Remind me not to touch him.*

"Paduraru," the man said in a deep gravelly voice.

"Crimmins," Nicolas replied stoically. "I see you've got everything under control here."

"As always," said Crimmins as he bent a little further, ducked his head into the window and peered in at me. He graced me with an unfriendly smile. All blocky teeth, it looked more like a grimace, and it didn't reach his eyes. I didn't much like him. "A Neophyte?"

"No. Human. This is Sabrina Strong, our new super-sensitive," Nicolas introduced me.

"Pleased to meetcha," he said in a heavy Chicago accent. "Wang's just released the body," Crimmins said to Nicolas, pulling back out of the window and nodding in the direction of the hearse. I looked to see a heavy-set oriental woman signing something on a clipboard. Her thick upper body strobed continuously in blue.

"Good." Nicolas opened his door to exit the car. "Looks like you can go home, Crimmins, since it was a vampire, and not a human death." He took delight in saying this to him, almost like he wanted to get rid of him.

Crimmins made some unintelligible sound and stalked away, limping noticeably, in the opposite direction of the crime scene and toward the dark sedan, mist billowing all around his body against the blue flashing lights.

I heard two more car doors shut behind us. I looked back to see two men striding toward us. I recognized them from their hair cut and similar build; Leif and Heath were joining us. Nicolas said something to them, but it became lost in the slamming of the car door. I remained inside the car, waiting until I was needed. Their voices were too low for me to hear what was said as they spoke amongst themselves. Then, Nicolas motioned to me. I angled out, and strode toward them.

As I joined them, I watched the hearse speed off. The oriental woman ambled up to us. She stood much shorter than the rest of us—probably at five foot.

"The driver will take him to the Towers?" Nicolas asked her.

"Is that where you want him to go?" she asked, sounding exasperated in her slight accent. "I thought you said he was a rogue." She handed him a thick type of clipboard and a pen. He took it from her, signed it and handed it back to her.

"He is, but Tremayne will take care of his remains," Nicolas said tersely.

"Well, alright." Wang had her cell phone out, and pressed a number and spoke, "They say to take him to Tremayne's place... yeah. Right, right, right." She snapped the phone shut. "That's it for me, I'm done here, unless you want autopsy."

"No. You said he died from the bolt, and we'll go with that," Nicolas said.

"Fine." She thrust a small hand up. "My work here is done." She turned and trundled on short legs for her own car further up the line.

In a moment, Wang's car followed the other two—Crimmins' and the hearse—down the lane. Now there were the four of us standing in the cemetery. Despite my coat, I was freezing. The vampires acted like it was a summer evening.

"You have the weapon?" Nicolas asked the two.

"Of course, Nicolas," Leif said with a smirk. "Would you think we'd leave it in plain view?" A large envelope appeared in his hands. I saw the word EVIDENCE in large letters across it. Leif held something out to me. Partially wrapped up in a handkerchief, I saw the narrow piece of bolt. "Here you go, beautiful. Do your thing." I eyed it as he carefully uncovered it, trying not to touch it himself.

"This is the bolt?" I gave him a doubtful look, not really sure I wanted to do this.

"Yes," Nicolas said.

I hesitated, staring at the sharpened length of wood that looked like a very short arrow.

Nicolas placed a comforting hand on my shoulder. "You will be fine. I will not let anything happen to you."

I looked into his eyes; they held a preternatural light in them. It freaked me out to see that. A slight panic washed through me, at first. Then a soothing calm replaced it. I knew then that he was reaching into my mind and controlling me. It felt like a seductive invasion that I couldn't control, and God help me, I didn't want to.

Without trepidation, I turned to Leif, and pulled off a glove. Then, I reached for the bolt. Often, whenever I touched something that had been used by another person, there was always this hesitation, a vacuum of time where I simply waited for it to come. Like when you step into an elevator and the door closes, and you anticipate the surge of movement before it happens. This was similar. Anticipation overwhelmed me for a few seconds. Then, I knew as I held the weapon something was going to hit me, and it was going to hit me hard.

I gave a groan—"Uh!" All at once, I felt hot and then cold. I didn't know if I was still standing, or flat on the ground; leaned on someone, or had passed out completely. All I saw was the vision. My whole being was the vision. The only thing I did know, I had to purge it as it came rapid-fire, and my lips and tongue moved as rapidly as I could make them, my voice went hoarse, my breath slipped from me. I couldn't purge it fast enough.

"Oh, God... a cat... a... black cat..."

Black cat... womancrossbowboltblood... NO! Bolt... it's coming, it's coming at me... Blood! Omygodblood... redonblue, redonblue... Too much blood! Too much... blackcatwomanblood...

Chapter 6

"You haven't bitten her, so you can't claim her."

Two male voices floated in and out of range, like someone messing with the volume on a TV, or a radio. I strained to listen in; I wanted to tell someone to turn up the volume.

"May I remind you she is my ward," the voice furthest from me said sternly.

"You think she's the sibyl?" the other asked, his voice had gone down a notch. I sensed that the subject seemed almost taboo, the way he'd nearly whispered the question.

"I have no idea." I knew this voice belonged to Nicolas.

"She's a very good clairvoyant." This voice was inside my head, and also above it—somehow—at the same time.

"Unquestionably," came the response.

There was a length of silence, and then the one above me spoke again.

"Your scent isn't strong enough on her at the moment to thwart another vampire, mate. Bloody hell! I'm having a time not wanting to jump her right now!"

This jolted me fully awake, but I kept my eyes closed. Icy fingers touched my temples, I realized then. They felt like large eraser heads. Cold ones. At the same time I understood this voice belonged to Leif, and it still came from right above me—and inside my head. I pictured my head in his lap.

"She's awake," Leif announced. His icy touch withdrew, and that slight pressure, which I hadn't been aware of until now, left me.

My eyes snapped opened and I stared up at his face hovering over mine. My head *was* in his lap. Crap.

"Hello, luv," Leif said, breaking into an impish grin. Hands cradling my head, he gazed down at me over the rims of his hippie glasses as we sped along some dark span of roadway.

I was in the back seat of a car. With Leif. And I could tell he was *so* liking where I was in relation to him. His domination over me was too apparent, and I was now breaking at least two rules of touching—or being touched—by a vampire, and looking into his eyes. In the diminished light of the roadway I picked up that black eclipsed the blue irises.

He leaned in and whispered, "It's been a long time since I've had a bird in such a compromising position." Although his voice was saturated with amusement while his smile broadened, I caught a flash of fang in the red backwash of a semi's taillights as it thundered by.

Goaded beyond endurance I snapped, my hand whipped up toward his face. But, before it could make contact or get close, his hand snatched my wrist in a vice-like grip.

We stared at each other.

"Na-ah-ah," he simpered playfully. "Play nice or not at all, luv."

"Go to hell!" I snarled, and struggled to sit up.

The one hand clutching my shoulder, held me down easily. Annoyingly superior grin in place, his glittering eyes looked down at me like deadly torches over the rims of his glasses. This was one vampire I did not want to be alone with—I could read the lust in his eyes. Those rules Nicolas had warned me about came blazing into my mind again. My heart thundered in my chest and my stomach lurched.

"Let me up," I said between gritted teeth.

He snickered, and wouldn't let me go.

"That's enough, Leif," Nicolas warned.

"Not unless you say 'pretty please', luv," Leif teased, a slight chuckle escaped him.

"Let me up! Please!" I was still gritting my teeth, but was closer to tears with my anger. Which is stupid. I hated that my emotions—anger and fear—were so tightly bound to one another.

"Very well, luv." He released me, still snickering.

I rose, and scooted as far away from him as possible into the corner of the back seat. We were, of course, in in the back seat of Nicolas' Jag. Nicolas was driving. His silhouette black against the red tail lights of the semi in front of us, and the soft blue of his dash lit up his face.

Red. *Blood.*

My brain seized on this for some reason, red flashing in my mind, like it would flood it forever. I shook my head to clear it. Slumping forward, I clutched my head. I had a hellacious headache all of a sudden. I knew now that Leif had been there to keep me from falling into a deeper trance-like state. But the price of melding his mind to mine was something on the order of a hangover after a night of binge drinking—not that I had ever experienced such a thing (and at the moment wouldn't want to for the feeling of my head). This was the worst I think I'd ever felt in my life after a vision.

"How do you feel, luv?" Leif asked, as if he didn't know. He wanted to rub it in. I decided that he was a sadist asshole.

"Like crap. Thanks for your concern," I muttered acidly.

"Anytime." He snickered quietly at me. "I know what would cure it."

"Leif," that same warning tone came from the front seat. "Behave yourself."

"I'm trying to, but this has me worked up. I need to go and get me some, or I can't promise I'll have control over me acts back here." I believed him. I didn't want to be there beside him another moment. I knew what he was capable of, without reading it from him.

"Very well, go then." Nicolas said, and relief poured through me.

The rear window next to Leif powered down all the way. The rush of cold wind as we traveled at seventy miles an hour tousled my hair.

"Alright, if you insist," Leif said over the road noise. "See you later, luv." He leaned slightly toward me and wiggled his brows in a lecherous way. Then, as if he were made of paper, he whipped out the window and was gone.

I gave a start, looking at the spot he had occupied, now vacant, and the open window as though it was a giant vacuum hose that had sucked him out.

The window powered back up. My hair settled all over my head and I frantically brushed it out of my face.

"What the hell happened?" I asked, really perplexed.

"Leif had to leave, thank goodness," Nicolas said, exasperated.

"Out the window? He went out the—"

"Window. Yes. I know. He's very good at doing that. He likes going out the moon roof too, but this car isn't equipped with one."

I think I stared at the window for about ten seconds, before looking back at Nicolas while he drove on.

"Would you be more comfortable up front?" he asked.

"Yeah, I think I would." With some effort, and as little grunting as I could manage, I climbed over the console between the front seats. I settled myself in, and strapped the seatbelt around myself.

"My apologies, but Leif is good at mind melding, I had no choice but to use him when it appeared that we were about to lose you."

I mulled that over a bit. "Did I say anything helpful?"

"You don't recall?"

"No. Not too much of it. But... I sort of remember something about a lot of blood."

"Yes. Something about a lot of blood," he repeated.

"Was that all?"

"No. You saw many things. The things you saw you couldn't translate fast enough into words. It would have been impossible to interpret what you were seeing, because your mind works much faster. Unfortunately we weren't prepared to siphon the images from you. Possibly, this would be how we will have to proceed with you, when you are to have a vision, or a read."

"Do what?"

He drew in a breath and let it out before answering. "The next time we have you read anything, no matter what it is; one of us will have to meld our mind with yours."

"Oh, my head," I moaned, holding my pounding head. "It hurts like someone hit me with a sledge hammer."

He chuckled lightly. *Not funny.* "It will subside. And it is far better than allowing you to fall into a deep trance where no one can reach you for hours, or longer."

"Yeah. That's no fun for me either," I groaned.

"We would rather keep you around awhile. There are stories of very adept clairvoyants, not unlike yourself, going mad for the things they see."

"Yes. I know," I said. "Why do you think I wear gloves?" I held up a gloved hand, then realized I didn't have my other glove on. Before I could start ranting about missing it, Nicolas held it out, producing it from somewhere.

Feeling my emotions surge toward relief, I grabbed it and slid it over my hand. "I have to tell you, I'm still not sure about this job. I'm afraid that I'll wind up in a lunatic asylum after this."

Nicolas chuckled.

"Not funny."

"No. It isn't. But, I assure you, that will not happen, not as long as one of us is there with you."

Sighing, I sat back and watched the dark contours and lights in the distance as the miles went by. I was reminded there were other things I wanted to ask him. Things that were brought up tonight by Leif, but I had been wondering a few myself, long before this.

"Nicolas?"

"Hmm?" He glanced over at me.

"What is the sibyl? I heard Leif ask you if I was the sibyl."

"It is a very old Greek legend."

"Well, what's the legend?" He breathed out a slightly annoyed breath, but I knew he would indulge me.

"The sibyl was a powerful seer who was the offspring of a nymph and a shepherd. Her powers were derived from Apollo."

"And?" I was certain there was an 'and' in there.

He sighed as if the whole subject bored him somehow. "She will wear the mystic ring which holds powers that allows her to walk among vampires and not be enthralled by them."

I frowned. "Can't be me," I said. "I don't wear any rings." It wouldn't make any sense for me to wear a ring. No one would see it.

"I know you are not. You would not be affected by our thrall."

"Not at all?"

"No. Besides, you are past your prime."

"You make me sound old," I grumbled.

"You must understand, this legend came about when girls married as soon as their menses started. About eleven or twelve."

"Okay," I said, slowly. "Why? I mean what's the point of finding her?"

His mouth bent into an evil smile. "The chosen master would mate with her."

"Oh-h-h." My face flushed. "Oh," I repeated, and chewed on the inside of my lower lip in thought. "You're saying vampires can mate with human women?"

"No. Only masters are able, or viable." He shrugged. I saw the slip of fangs and had to shift my glance away.

"I see." Relief flooded me. Possibly it was all his talk about a vampire's dual needs, and the whole idea that a vampire *could* mate with a human woman was simply all too much for me to accept.

"I do not hold much faith in the old Greek legend," he said on a gasp.

"Does Tremayne?"

"I'm not sure," he said hesitantly. "Although he has been acquiring a number of seers in the past two hundred years." His brows furrowed with this thought.

Ready to move on, I said, "I overheard something else you were saying, before I sat up—you and Leif?"

"What was that?" he asked.

"Leif was saying that your scent on me wasn't strong enough to thwart other vampires—him especially."

"It is true, I'm afraid. That is why we must be careful, when you are not with me, as another vampire could try and claim you."

"But you told me how to avoid being hunted," I argued.

His hand tightened on the wheel. "True. However, there are those of us who adhere to the rules, and those of us who do not. Make no mistake, Sabrina, you must be very careful when you are in the company of other vampires, besides myself. Never look directly into their eyes, and never let them follow you."

"I know, I know. But you said it's against your laws—"

"Those who do not consistently obey our laws are considered rogues."

"So, what is Leif? He wanted to bite me—and other things—I could feel it."

"He wouldn't."

"Right."

"Not while I am around."

I grunted at that. I figured it was like people speeding, or going through stop lights. As long as they didn't get caught, what difference did it make?

I saw signs telling us we were getting close to my exit. I still had questions—millions of them.

"Explain the donor pool. Why would someone do that? I mean let a vampire bite them?"

"They are paid well, have a great benefits package. Plus, the added attraction is that they have an orgasm."

"Wow. Benefits package," I said, nodding, holding back my snort. Nicolas glanced at me. A smile crimped his lips when he saw I was joking with him. "How does it work? I mean what does a vampire have to do to get a meal?" Or laid?

"A vampire who doesn't have his or her own personal donors can call the donor pool, and a donor will come to them. It is all done in a private room, sometimes in our suites. Never out in the open. The donor pool also assures that the donor does not become the property of that vampire, unless there is mutual agreement. However, some of us prefer our own private donors, and share them with no one else," he explained.

"Wow," I breathed out. "Sort of like pizza delivery."

He chuckled. I liked his rich chuckle; somewhat devious and evil-sounding.

"Something like that, yes."

"Sounds like you vampires have worked this donor thing out in great detail."

"Yes. We have."

"Then, would you have sex with a donor, too?"

"Only if it is agreed upon up front by both parties."

"Would you have bitten me last night?" I asked, wanting to know because it had been bothering me all day. "I mean if the opportunity presented itself."

He shifted slightly. "Against your will? No. I would not have bitten you. It would be considered hunting. Which is against Vampire Law."

Thank goodness for Vampire Law.

"What about... the other thing?" I asked timidly. I wanted to know what his plans for me were. I couldn't go on wondering if he was going to try and put me into a compromising situation in his office, or a couch—or the back seat of his Jag—at some point.

"The other thing? You mean sex?"

"Yes." *What else was there?*

Staring straight ahead he said, "Yes. I want you, Sabrina. I want both things from you."

That hit me to the core. His answer, spoken in that deep ethereal voice of his threw a jolt of desire through me. A twinge below which wasn't there before caught me by surprise. He'd set off vampire pheromones into the air and I was sucking them in like I was starved for oxygen.

"Before I can do so, I must ask permission."

"Permission? From who?"

"From Tremayne. He is my sire, and sovereign. I can take no donor, nor have sex with any one, unless they are a registered donor, *and* he gives me permission. Of course, if he does, you would have to change your donor card."

"How... structured," I said, trying to sound as though the whole subject didn't make me uncomfortable as hell. "And do I have any say in this?" Was it getting warm in the car? Or had he triggered my hormones into a higher gear?

"Yes. Of course. Unless I have your complete consent, I would not force you."

"You wouldn't have to," I said. "You've got that vampire thrall thing going for you."

"Again, we are not permitted to press our advantage."

Right. Whatever.

"So, let me get this straight, whenever you want to bite some-one, or have sex with them, you have to ask Tremayne?"

"Only if they are not in the donor pool, or one of my regular donors."

"Right. Are you going to ask him?"

The light changed, and he made his turn. We crossed the over-pass and were on two lanes, heading for the back country roads to my house. We'd be there in ten minutes or less.

Nicolas made a heavy sigh. "I was not going to have this con-versation with you tonight." He sounded terse. I got a rise out of a vampire. Hooray for me.

"When were you going to have it?" I asked heatedly. This re-ally perturbed me. I was no longer just an employee; I was the object of his twin desires. Great. I would probably have wel-comed his advances, if it had happened over the course of a couple of weeks, say. But now that I knew I was on his list of de-sirable female donors, it made me a little uncomfortable, being that he was my boss.

"I wanted to make sure you felt more comfortable with me," he said, finally.

"Okay. Change of subjects," I said abruptly. "When will I meet Tremayne? Or, will I ever? Is he like the Wizard of frigging Oz?"

"You will meet Tremayne, soon. He has been grieving, the last few days, but he will ask me to bring you before him soon."

"Grieving?" I prompted.

"Yes. His life-time mate was murdered in her apartment, the other night. He has been grieving."

"Oh, right. I guess you did tell me that."

"He wants answers, and that's where you come in."

"Me?"

He turned down Ram Road, the one that would take us to Sonata Road, where I lived. "He will want you to take a read of the apartment, and maybe the bolt that killed her."

"You mean, he'll take me himself?"

"Yes." He sounded slightly agitated by this.

"And that's bad because?"

"I don't know if he will allow me to escort you."

Chapter 7

An amber moon hung in the night sky as though by some ethereal force, as Nicolas turned into my drive. The embers from the pile of leaves that Mrs. Bench had burned earlier glowed eerily. I wondered if she was still out there watching it.

I thought I saw someone's shadow, but it seemed too large to be her. And too quick. I knew only that her husband had died when I was young, but I didn't know more than that about her. She had come to my father's funeral. I could still remember her cold, ganglion and blue-veined hands taking mine (I had worn gloves, of course), in hers, and telling me I had to come and see her *soon*. Making it sound important I did. At that moment I knew something about her too.

She was a card-carrying, potion-making witch.

"Who was that?"

I jumped from Nicolas' voice, jarred back to the here and now.

"Oh, uh, I don't know," I said, turning in my seat. "Someone must be visiting Mrs. Bench tonight." I hadn't thought that with Nicolas' vampire vision he could probably see clearly enough to identify the person in Mrs. Bench's yard. I was simply too tired to get a read. I didn't feel there was any threat, so I let it go and turned back around.

When we pulled up to my house, I found that I was absolutely drained from my night. I was amazed that it hadn't turned out worse than it had, all things considered.

Unfolding myself from the Jag, I spotted the full moon, and the werewolf's image swept through my mind. I was wondering if he was on the loose tonight, and possibly hadn't had a good enough werewolf time last night.

Of course, I was still worried about Jeanie, and the visions I'd had earlier about her.

"Sleep will do you good," Nicolas suggested as he walked me up to my porch.

"Yeah," I sighed. My porch light helped me take the steps without tripping. Keys jangled as I extracted them from my purse, then dropped them.

"Sorry," I apologized as Nicolas dipped to pick them up.

He moved smoothly to unlock my door. Sticking the key into the lock, he stopped and backed off, palm up. "I believe I will let you open the latch." He eyed my keys. "The silver on your key chain," he said. "It burns a little."

"Really?" I examined them, then saw the silver heart that dangled from my key chain. Made of real silver. A birthday present from Jeanie, she'd had the words, *Friends Forever* engraved on it. It had probably saved me from the werewolf last night when he'd had them in his mouth. I remembered how he had whined and let go of me then. Nicolas couldn't touch it either. One thing about vampires stood true enough. Silver was something they couldn't touch. That was why I'd seen so much gold jewelry tonight.

"Here," he said, and I turned. He handed me something small enough to fit in his hand. "Yours. You are on our 'family' plan." He was holding out a cell phone. "If you ever need to call me, I'm on speed dial."

"My own cell phone? Gosh, thanks," I said, feeling the rush of excitement. "Is this one of the perks?"

"Yes, it is."

"Thank you," I said.

"Get some sleep, Sabrina. Good night." He backed away, as though knowing if he gained entry, he would not be able to control his actions. I couldn't be expected to, either.

His shoes tapped down the stairs as he left me. Leaning against the door jamb I watched him angle into his Jag and start it up. He eased out my driveway, the red tail lights blinked on as he turned onto the gravel road. He tapped the horn, and I waved. I hoped his toot hadn't woken Mrs. Bench. But, she was awake. I was certain whoever was in the yard as we came home was visiting her. I was also nearly certain it was a man. Odd how my Knowing wouldn't reveal it to me. I merely saw his silhouette against the yard light.

I closed my door, clicked the dead bolt home, turned off the downstairs lights, and headed up to bed. My head was churning with all the events of the day. I found that I simply couldn't think about it any longer.

I washed my face, smeared on wrinkle cream, got undressed, and slipped into my peach long-sleeved nighty. It would be warm on such a chilly night. I was already half asleep when I slipped between the sheets. It didn't take me long to drift off.

Something woke me. My eyes popped open, and my adrenaline was charged. I heard a soft thump close by. My eyes flashed to my window.

Someone was out there. A dark silhouette at my window in the shape of a man sent alarm through me. With a start, I sat bolt upright, blankets pulled tight against myself, I thought I heard wings flapping—large wings.

What the hell?

When I blinked, I saw nothing blocking out the rectangle of light from the pole light. Had I only imagined it? Had I been dreaming? Again? What did this make? Maybe the fourth time in a row I'd woken up this week thinking I heard someone on the small porch roof over which my window looked.

Stock still, I listened. Waiting. Nothing stirred.

With a prick of dread, I was now certain I'd seen—and heard—someone outside my window. Was it the vampire who had marked me years ago, come to claim me?

I was all the way upstairs, without a phone. The house phone was downstairs. But who would I call? Police could do nothing if it was a vampire.

I had no one. Except the vampire, Nicolas, who swore he would be my protector.

Oh, stupid! I remembered I now had a cell phone. I had to call Nicolas, remembering he was on speed dial on my new cell phone.

The cell phone. Where had I put it? I went into panic mode, nearly hyperventilating. Quickly I squashed these invasive, unhelpful emotions in order to think.

I retraced my movements and remembered I'd set the phone down on the counter in the bathroom while I'd washed my face. Stupid place for it, but I had been so sleepy, I hadn't thought about taking it into the bedroom with me. Fortunately the bathroom was right across the hall from my bedroom. Without turning on a light, I slipped out of bed, shoved my chilled feet into my warm slippers, and padded as quietly as I could to retrieve the phone from the bathroom.

I hadn't heard any more sounds in those few moments it had taken me to creep across the dark hall and retrieve the phone, and scurried back to my bedroom.

My fingers were shaking as I went to menu and pressed the fast dial for Nicolas. I hoped that the battery was still charged—I would need to ask him for a charger tomorrow. Relief spilled through me when I heard it ring, and then his voice.

"Yes?"

"Nicolas!" I hissed. "It's me. Sabrina."

"Yes, I know. What is wrong?" he asked at once.

"I think someone is outside my house. Can you come?" I looked toward the red numbers on my alarm clock. It read 4:08 AM. Would he be able to come to my house, investigate, chase whoever off, and then go back to the city in time before the sun came up? I quickly calculated that the sun came up between six-thirty and seven o'clock.

"Where are you now?"

"Upstairs, in my room."

"Is there a lock on your door?"

"Yes."

"Lock it. I will be there shortly."

"I did that. Wait—" his line went dead. How would I know when he got here? Would he come in his car, or would he fly? I remembered how Leif had zoomed out of the car window, and was gone in a flash.

Shivering, legs curled up to my chest, I was scared out of my mind. I found it hard to think straight under these circumstances, and I rocked a little bit, and took a bunch of deep breaths until I calmed down.

A dark memory made an unbidden return. I hadn't thought about it since I was very young. Grimacing, I clenched my fists and squeezed my eyes shut, wrestling with the fear that this memory had instilled in me from when I was a child.

I was an adult now, not a child. But I was alone in this house. The sound outside, if I'd actually heard it, was probably the usual night noise. Being alone made any small sound seem like something was trying to get inside. But still, I couldn't lay here being frightened, not knowing for sure.

A vampire couldn't enter a house unless invited, I reminded myself. But he *had* been invited eleven years ago. Did the invitation still stand?

I'd heard nothing further since the original sound that had woke me. My bedroom had two windows. One was on the south-facing side, the other faced east. I had seen the shadow in the east window, where the pole light illuminated anything that moved.

I edged closer to the window, fearfully watching, hoping whatever had been standing there was really and truly gone. My dad had had these newer windows put in five years ago, and they slid effortlessly open without a sound. Looking around, I found nothing on the porch roof. I opened the storm window, and listened for noise. Gaining control over my fear, I then pushed the screen up as far as it would go, then surveyed the yard as best I could. The windowsill was practically flush with the roof. The cold caught me by surprise and I clutched my nightgown to myself as I looked as far as I could toward the tall, big-leaved catalpa trees in the backyard, and then the other way across the street, to Mrs. Bench's house. Her house was dark. The leaves on her big soft maples had turned golden-yellow and were fluttering in a gentle breeze. I could still smell the vague odor of her burnt leaf pile. All other night sounds, like crickets and owls where oddly silent.

Something whooshed in front of the open window, startling me. Screaming, I skittered back.

Someone caught me by the arms. "Don't be frightened," the familiar voice said. "I am here."

I looked up into Nicolas' face, he was holding me close.

When I recovered, I asked, "How did you get here? I didn't hear your car."

"I do not need a car, if I wish to get somewhere very fast."

"You flew, like Leif?" I managed to utter, feeling as though my knees would go at any moment.

"Yes," he said. "Where is your intruder?"

"I don't know. I haven't heard anything in a while."

"Did he try your door?"

"No. He was here, though. I know I saw his shadow in my window." I pointed to the window where he had come through. Simply saying it now renewed my fears.

"Are you sure?" Nicolas clutched my hands in his. They were oddly warmer than mine. He kissed my fingertips. I gazed at him, feeling decidedly less frightened. Of course. His thrall held me together.

"Yes." I nodded, tears slithering down my cheeks.

"Fear not, my child, I am here," Nicolas soothed, pulling me into a warm, reassuring hug. "I will look around outside," he said, drawing away from the intimate hug. "You will be safe in here." Noticing my state of dress, he pulled off his coat, and snugged it around my shoulders. He made me sit down in my reading chair, beside my bed.

I murmured my thanks, and watched as he whooshed out of my window. Pulling my feet up, I hugged my knees to myself, trying to keep warm with his jacket, but I shivered anyway. I should retrieve my robe, it would cover me better, I reasoned. But I sniffed at his incredible scent from his coat, and couldn't part with it as I pulled it into my lungs. Was it odd that it actually calmed me?

In a few moments, Nicolas was back, smelling of fresh outdoors. "I saw nothing out of the ordinary. But someone has been here," he said. "I caught his scent."

"Vampire?"

"Yes."

"He didn't break in?"

"No. And if he has been invited, he would not need to break in, as you put it." His smile was humorless. "Now, you are alone. I have made sure."

Alone. With him. In my room, and me having only a nighty on. Good grief, could this get any more melodramatic?

Without preamble, he picked me up and effortlessly carried me to my bed. Nicolas wasn't the vampire guy of my dreams; I'd known this since the first night we'd met. I had hoped that he *would* be the one. He was dashing, in a John Stamos sort of way.

As Nicolas settled me on my rumpled sheets and covers, his coat slipped off my shoulders. He took it and placed it neatly on my chair. Now he was wearing the light blue shirt, and only now did I notice his tie was missing. The top two buttons of his shirt were undone, as though when I'd called him he had been relaxing. But I now noticed something dark was smeared on his collar; I caught sight of it in the light beaming in through my window from the pole light outside. Blood?

My savior was a blood-drinking vampire, and that's what he'd probably been busy with when I'd called. I stifled my desire to bring this to his attention. Usually blood on the collar of a man might mean that he'd cut himself shaving. A vampire, on the other hand, blood on the collar would carry a whole different meaning altogether.

"I'm sorry to be such a pest," I apologized, sliding my chilled feet beneath the covers and pulled my knees up to my chest, hugging them to myself.

"You are not a pest," he said around a small chuckle. He settled on the edge of the bed beside me. Grasping the covers, he pulled them up to my neck. I shivered as I gazed at him, letting out little nervous gasps. The erotic overtones of having him in my room were not lost on me. I wondered what might happen, since I had invited him in—and he wasn't leaving.

"You are cold," he said, his face partially in shadow, the other half glowing in the light slanting in through my window. His pale skin was stark against his black hair, eyes, and brows.

I reached to turn on the light. He stopped me with his voice. "No. Leave it off… for now."

I retracted my hand, settled it on top of the covers and stared up at him.

"You are a temptation to me, Sabrina." His voice was low, vibrating in my ears in a way that perhaps a cello might. Calm, sedate, and yet with the promise of something wonderfully exciting, and something wicked hidden beneath the beauty of this other worldly creature here in my room. I could hardly believe this was happening to me. But it was. Either I was extremely lucky, or extremely stupid. One way or another I would have an experience I wouldn't soon forget.

His chilly fingers feathered over my brow, moving strands of my hair away from my cheeks. Those same fingers slid down my cheek to the side of my neck, and paused at the pulse there at the jugular. My eyes slipped shut. Was he using his vampire charms to seduce me?

He released a breath.

Opening my eyes, I found he studied me in the dark, his hands slipping across the edge of my nightgown at the ties of the neck. He loosened it, and spread the material open, availing my neck and the upper portion of my chest to him. My breath caught in me.

"Are you going to kiss me?"

"Yes." He leaned in. "Do not move," he whispered. His breath slipped over my skin as his head dipped down and I somehow not only held still but held my breath.

The face hovered over me... long, wavy black hair cascading down... I saw his face, stark against the black of his hair as he bit me on the arm... I thought he was the most elegant-looking man I had ever seen.

I gasped as my memories played back things I hadn't remembered while Nicolas' lips feathered kisses along my chest, angling up one side of my neck. My pulse quickened. A small whimper escaped my lips. I suddenly craved his ruby lips on mine. I wanted to feel them. I wanted to feel his teeth pierce my skin. I knew what it would do to me. I knew, because it had happened before. A long, long time ago. But I was too young to know why I had felt the way I had, and could do nothing about it—then.

He was close. I knew all it would take was his bite and I would be sailing on a forbidden ecstasy I could never reach with a human man. I wanted it. It was *so* close, and yet so elusive, like trying to touch a butterfly's wing, only to disintegrate before I could snatch it.

Desire dangling until I couldn't stand it, I slipped one hand out from beneath the covers, and grasped him by his shirt and *pulled* him in. My invitation was the response he was waiting for. His lips covered mine in a demanding way, pressing me back into my pillows. He shuddered over me as his lips clamped themselves over mine hungrily. His fangs grew against my lips, cold and hard. A stab of desire skittered through me.

I moaned into his vampire mouth before his tongue filled mine, and dove in and out quickly, the rhythm obviously conveying to me what might happen, if we continued this. I ran my fingers along his cool-as-marble, collarbone, then slid around to the back of his neck, feeling the feathering of hair at his collar. I was going to explode if something didn't happen soon. As though reading my thoughts, his hand slid beneath the covers, slipping along my thigh, fingernails scraping my skin, giving me chills. Then his hand slid between my legs, and brushed over my mound, then pressed me there, sending a shudder through me.

I arched into his touch wantonly. Knowing fingers slid between my panties and skin and touched and stroked me in places I'd barely been touched before. He lowered himself onto the bed beside me, drawing my legs down until he had one of his legs between mine, controlling me, his lips still claiming mine. A sense of hungry urgency thrilled me as his lips went to my throat, the long, sharp fangs grazing my skin. His lips, then his tongue hotly trailing down and then up my neck. His finger slipped inside me, and I shuddered uncontrollably.

I moaned with the exquisite feel of his fingers stroking me inside and out.

With a sudden growl, he was no longer kissing, or touching me, or leaning over me. One moment he was with me, the next he was across the room. His sudden absence threw panic in me.

"Nicolas?"

"No!"

Shaken abruptly and rudely from the euphoria that nearly was mine, I pushed myself up onto my elbows to gape at him. What had happened? Why had he stopped?

"I beg your forgiveness, Sabrina," he said, his voice had lost some of the softness of earlier. More edgy. Harsh. I could tell he was terribly upset.

"For what?" I said. "We were enjoying—"

"NO!" he roared, cutting me off. I jumped. His eyes blazed red, and then the next few seconds they segued to their normal blackness.

"No," his voice becoming softer as he brought himself under control. "No. I have not asked permission to make you mine." He muttered a string of words I knew were in his own tongue as he gazed up at the ceiling. He flicked his obsidian gaze back to me. "I crave you, *dulceață*. But I, myself, cannot ignore our laws."

I bit my lower lip, gazing at him, watching him pull himself together. He'd nearly bitten me. I had wanted it too, and now I fought off the last of his thrall. This was confusing. Was it all him? Hadn't I wanted it too? I suddenly became aware of my inner arm burning. Swiftly I pulled my arm up to examine it, but I couldn't see in the dark. I covered it with my other hand. It felt hot to the touch. Burning in fact.

"He is near," Nicolas whispered harshly. His lips were crimson against the white fangs as they slowly receded. "His mark upon you, he will find a way to call you to him, soon."

"But, he was here," I said, fear lacing my words.

Desire smoldering behind his eyes, he said, "I am loathe to be the one to inform you, but Tremayne has caught your scent on me and he is more than terribly interested in meeting you. Thus you have more to be concerned about than the one who was at your window tonight."

Frozen with dread by what he had revealed, I leaned back against my pillows, shivering.

"I must go. Now that I am certain you are safe," he scoffed, then snagged his jacket from the chair and slipped it on.

"Thanks for coming to my rescue." I didn't want him to leave, but I could think of no way to keep him here. I knew what it would lead to. *Am I insane?*

"May I offer you my most abject apology for my unbecoming conduct," he said on a gush. Buttoning his suit coat, he nodded toward me. "Adieu, Sabrina. Close and lock your window, lest you wish to attract *your* master."

Frozen with dread and wonder, I leaned back against my pillows, shivering. Not from the cold, though, but from what I knew had almost happened and where it would have lead.

Chapter 8

Everything that had happened to me in the past 48 hours, and every worry that had plagued me, crashed in on me when I opened my eyes the next morning. I trudged into the bathroom and took care of my immediate needs. I tied a soft flannel robe around myself, and bumbled down the stairs, wondering irritably why I didn't move my bedroom downstairs so that I didn't need to climb these stairs every night, and then nearly fall down them in the morning.

I could move all my bedroom furniture into my dad's old office; it was large enough. I didn't need an office, after all. This had been a thought in the back of my mind for a while; about a month after my father's passing. Now it had becoming a nagging thought. There was a full bath downstairs, since it had been the original bathroom when we had moved in. The one upstairs had been added. I figured if I offered a nice dinner to Randy, and maybe a few of his buddies (maybe Jeanie's brother, Mark, might come too if I offered his favorite beer), I could probably get them to move all the furniture from my bedroom downstairs in one day, and get things the way I wanted without too much trouble. Maybe with my bonus check I could get a nice new rug, paint the walls, and hang new drapes in there. Really make it mine.

Shuffling into the kitchen, I went straight for the coffee maker. While my coffee brewed I stuck my head into the refrigerator and grimaced. Toast was my only choice for breakfast.

While nibbling on a piece of butter-and-cinnamon toast, I glanced out the window at the bright new day, and what looked like a black beret on someone's blond head as they sat on the porch swing.

Shocked, I nearly choked on the bite of toast in my mouth. Looking further into the driveway, I saw a cherry-red car. A Scion. Toby's car. And if I wasn't mistaken, that was the back of Toby's head I was seeing. I heard his voice speaking softly as if to a child, or—more likely—to one of the barn cats.

With the aroma of coffee perking me up, I went to my door, unlocked it, and swung it open. Arms wound tightly about myself to keep in the warmth, I stepped outside. The sun felt toasty on my slippered toes as I edged onto the porch.

Toby looked up from his perch in the swing. Sure enough he held two cats in his lap. One was the calico mother cat; the other was one of her kittens, a black one with orange markings all over, a white bib and two white paws. I had named him Halloween for obvious reasons.

"Toby? I didn't know you were here," I said.

"Hi," he said. "Nicolas told me to bring this to you." He handed me a plastic bag.

I took it from him and looked inside. I found the charger for my phone, still in the box.

"Oh! Thanks." I reached down to pet the mother cat in his lap. "I just got up," I said around a yawn. "You want to come in and have some coffee?"

"Sounds good." He picked up the mother cat, who had curled up in his lap, and set her gently down. Halloween jumped down from the bench and went into his cat-stretch.

"How long have you been here?" I wondered as he rose to his full height.

"I don't know. Maybe six-thirty when I pulled in," he said, following me inside. I shut the door.

"God, you must be hungry."

"Not really. I had something on the way. I'm good." He stood inside my kitchen and sniffed. "Coffee smells good, though."

"Hazelnut. My favorite," I said, and took two cups off a mug tree. "I've got cream and sugar, if you want."

"Just sugar," he said, eyes going over my form briefly.

"Okay," I said, looking down at myself. "I wasn't expecting company."

"If it bothers you, I can go outside and wait until you're presentable?"

"Only if you're bothered," I told him. I didn't know how to tell him I felt more like a sister to him.

"Not in the least," he said. He looked straight in my eyes, not over my form. I was guessing I was not his type.

"Well, I guess we're good, then." I turned and eyed the coffee. The brew still dripped into the carafe, and so I turned back around, leaned against the counter and folded my arms across myself. Well, okay, self-consciously. He was still a man, after all. I worked on shielding Toby, remembering all his emotions that had hit me yesterday morning. I didn't have my gloves on as yet—wouldn't need them in my own house. But now I considered it.

"Nicolas tell you what happened last night?" I asked, noticing the coffee was done.

"No. He told me I was to bring that charger to you."

"Well, Nicolas brought me home last night." I turned and poured the coffee. We took turns spooning sugar into our cups.

"He left, and I went to bed. Later, a noise woke me up. Someone was outside." I added creamer to my coffee with a shaking hand, stirring it in. I stepped toward the table and deposited myself into a chair not able to believe that really happen last night.

"Really?" Leaning against the counter, his gaze roamed the kitchen. I noticed he hadn't shaved, but his stubble gave him an epicene look. He seemed slightly taller than yesterday, but maybe that was just me. He also had dark circles under his eyes, against a white-as-milk face. I hadn't noticed that yesterday either.

"I speed dialed him on my new cell phone, and he was here within five minutes," I went on, but from the distracted expression on Toby's face, I was wondering why I was relating this to him at all, as though he was my buddy. It struck me that he wasn't really my friend and maybe everything I'd said to him was making him privately hate me because Nicolas had come to me last night; I'd caught him in the middle of a feed. I remembered the blood on Nicolas' collar. Who had he bitten before he'd come to me? Toby? Those dark circles indicated that he'd lost some blood.

I now questioned why Nicolas had sent Toby with the charger, when someone else could have brought it to me later on. My suspicions went on the alert. I'd handled the bag with the charger box actually, having felt *something* coming off Toby. A slight *something.* But it was important. Red flags went up.

"Yeah. He can travel pretty fast when he wants to." He took another sip of coffee. "This is pretty good coffee."

"Thank you," I said, crossing my legs. A chill came over me. He was here on his own agenda, I *knew* this. What did he want?

Maybe he wanted to know how good a Touch Clairvoyant I was. I became suddenly on edge. Weird that someone was interested in my abilities, instead of freaked out by them.

I sipped my coffee contemplatively for a moment, considering where Toby's visit would lead. I wanted badly to know what was up. Why he came here. I could simply wait until he leaves and touch his cup to get a vision. It might, or might not tell me what he was up to. But I had to keep him talking. See if he'd slip up some.

I glanced at the clock and remembered Jeanie. Jeanie would be at work by now. "Excuse me, I need to call someone."

"No problem," he said. I padded out of the room.

The phone in the office took messages. The light wasn't flashing. This really disappointed me. Jeannie would have had time to call me by now.

This was going to bother me until I spoke with her. I dialed her work phone number, hoping I'd at least find out she was fine. A woman with a slightly hoarse voice answered, I didn't recognize the voice, or the name when she'd said it.

"Hi, this is Sabrina Strong; could I speak to Jeanie, please?"

"I'm afraid she's not in." My stomach dropped to the floor. "What do you mean she's not there? Who is this?"

"This is Laura Hill," she said, and I got a visual of a middle-aged woman with gray hair and glasses. "You're her friend, aren't you?"

"Yeah. What's going on? Why isn't she there?" I asked, holding my hand over my stomach because it ached in a worried-sick way. My mind replayed some of those visions from last night. I'd seen Jeanie in the grocery store parking lot. Something had made her turn, and she'd dropped her phone—that part I was certain of. The rest was fuzzy.

"We don't really know. We called her cell phone and left a message. She hasn't gotten back to us," she said in a vague tone.

A sick feeling plummeted deep inside. Visions from last night returned clearer than ever. My knees went, and I nearly missed my dad's large oak office chair. The chair creaked loudly as I dropped onto it.

"We called her folk's house, just to make sure nothing happened, you know—like an accident? Her mother said she hadn't come home," the woman said.

"Oh," I said, gripping the receiver as though it were a live thing trying to wriggle out of my grip, I was shaking. "I see," I managed to croak.

"Like I've said, we haven't heard anything since we called."

"Okay," I said with a little catch in my voice. "Thanks—uh—Laura."

"You're welcome, sweetie."

I cradled the receiver and hung my head. My emotions came to the surface and I had a hard time cutting them off.

"What's the matter?" Toby asked quietly. Surprised, I looked up and found him slumped in the wide doorway of the living room, one leg hooked over the other, sipping his coffee. He looked slightly concerned, but not overly.

"My friend hasn't been to work today, she never got home." His eyes squinted, and a corner of his mouth quirked, teeth flashed, and then was gone. I didn't understand that.

"You mean—like—she's missing?" His voice didn't reflect any genuine concern. It was one of those things. Maybe like other people he assumed Jeanie had gone out with someone and had spent the night. Jeanie wasn't seeing anyone, and she didn't sleep around. She wasn't like that. Last night was something else. Someone had come up to her in that parking lot. I was sure of it, now.

"I don't know exactly." I wasn't going to rehash my visions from last night, not to him and not to myself. They had pummeled me as I spoke to Laura, a moment ago. I didn't like how clear they now came to me after-the-fact. It didn't set well with me.

A sudden thought hit me. Of course. Vampire thrall had held my visions back, last night. Plus, every time I'd gotten one, Nicolas interrupted them. I made a small gasp, and somehow swallowed the bubble of horror that knifed through me. *I could have saved her.*

"I'm sorry," Toby said in that gentle voice. I didn't trust it. His synthetic attempt to sound concerned went flat. He was not my friend. Warning bells were going off. I had learned not to trust people, unfortunately, throughout my life.

"I don't know what to—" my voice faded. The vision took precedence, and as always, it consumed me. Eyes unfocused, I bent forward. *The car. Of course. It would still be there.*

"Sabrina? Are you alright?" Toby's voice came from an area closer to me—right in front of me, in fact. My vision cleared and I stared into Toby's face; he was kneeling down in front of me. He had cornflower-blue eyes, but looked a tad bloodshot. I also noticed that he'd had his roots done. He must have had it done yesterday. I'd lost time—a minute, maybe two. How easily he had approached me while I was somewhat out of it. He could have done anything while I had my mini-vision. He could have riffled through my personals—anything like that.

"What?" I said. My brain and vision still scrambled.

"Jeanie. You could try and find her through your clairvoyant abilities, couldn't you?"

I stopped and held my breath. A wave of something dark emanated from him and I had to shield him big time. He was way too close to me. The dark circles under his eyes made him look slightly psychotic.

Abruptly I stood, steadying myself on the chair and desk. He rose, too, staring at me. "Uh, thanks for bringing the cell phone charger to me, Toby. That was really nice of you." I stepped stiffly into the dining room, working to look casual as I put the table between myself and him, getting as much distance between us as possible. "I've got something to take care of, if you don't mind, and really need to get dressed."

"You sure you don't want me to hang around a bit?"

"No. I've got a bunch of things to take care of today, so..."

Twenty minutes later, I was driving south on Sunbank Road toward Moonlight. Toby had left my house—I could tell reluctantly—and I'd locked the door before I went and got dressed. I didn't know what Toby was up to, but it was something significant. Like some plan he had hatched, or was part of, and I was somehow the one thing in the way of it all working for him.

I feared that if I went into a full-blown vision in front of him I'd be out of commission and that would make me too vulnerable. Already those few moments that I was gone, he'd seen whatever he'd wanted to see—and in a way, so had I.

After he'd left I tried to locate his coffee cup. It didn't surprise me that I never found it. He was wise to fear my abilities. I wished he hadn't been so careful, but his taking the cup told me to be careful as hell around him.

Passing The Saloon, I came to the stop sign at the junction of Route 30. Judging by the cars parked in Moonlight's Market parking lot, there was the normal amount of business. My heart beat wildly inside my chest as I turned into the store's parking lot, and tried to locate Jeanie's silver Malibu.

When I spotted a silver car parked about halfway back, all by itself, my heart began a deep beat of dread. I swung to the back of the lot. I was certain this was her car; her license plates were personalized with CUTE 1 on them.

My indecision vexed me as I pulled up next to Jeanie's car. I wanted to feel relieved in finding it, but couldn't. I'd had several visions last night. I remembered blood in some of them. I didn't know whose blood. Mine, I'd thought, at the time. But now, I wasn't so sure as I pulled around, and glanced at the trunk. Something dark was swiped onto it. It looked like the letter V. I didn't know what to make of it.

The vision I'd had during the evening while at Tremayne Towers, repeated itself now in stark contrast to the air of normalcy all around me.

Cell phone falling from her hand as Jeanie turned around, startled...

I had to lean my head against the head rest, because seeing this had thrown me. Sickened with the knowledge that I *had* seen this in my visions last night, and basically ignored it.

No. I hadn't ignored it. I had done the only thing I could do, I'd called her. I'd gotten a busy signal, meaning that she was on her phone and everything was okay. Later on, of course, I'd gotten through to her voice mail and had left a message. Somewhere in between those calls something had happened to Jeanie. Was I seeing something in the future? Or, had it happened already?

Something vibrated against my hip. Startled, I looked down—my new cell phone was vibrating. I pulled it out and saw the number—Jeanie's mother's number. That startled me until I remembered that I had tried Mrs. Woodbine a couple of times during the drive out here and the line had been busy. She must have seen my number on her missed calls read-out. I knew right away she hoped that Jeanie was okay and with me. I wished like hell that was the case.

"Hello, Mrs. Woodbine?" I said shakily.

"Sabrina? You get a new cell phone or something? Is Jeanie there with you?" the woman jabbered in my ear breathlessly.

"No, Mrs. Woodbine." I had to swallow a lump in my throat. I now knew what it was like to be the person who delivered bad news. Although I really didn't know what had happened to Jeanie, I knew it wasn't good. "I've been trying to locate her as well. But I do know where her car is."

"You do? Where?"

"Over here at the supermarket lot."

"Stay there. I'll be right out," she said, and she was gone.

I stepped out of my Jeep, went over and looked inside the Malibu. I saw Jeanie's purse and cell phone on the front seat. That was curious. I stepped back to my Jeep and sat with the door open, waiting. About ten minutes later a red and gold Explorer wheeled around the corner, and flew into the parking lot. Dust from the gravel roads she had to have traveled on billowed up, creating a gray-yellow cloud. I don't think she had the vehicle in park quite yet when she threw open her door. I waited for the dust to dissipate before getting out to meet her.

Wearing faded jeans that formed to her slim legs, and a southwest designed coat, the svelte woman launched herself from her vehicle. I hadn't seen Mrs. Woodbine since my father's funeral. Then, she had been teary-eyed. Today she wasn't much different. Distraught more than teary-eyed, as she jogged past me and stopped before Jeanie's car. She stared at it like she expected it to do something like spew her daughter out of some mysterious place, like some hackneyed magic act.

"How did you know it was here?" she asked me, finally turning to acknowledge me. Turquoise and silver earrings caught the sunlight, as did her matching watch.

I pressed my lips together. If Mrs. Woodbine didn't know what I was capable of after all these years, I sure as hell wasn't going to help her out on this one.

"Oh," she said softly, her realization registering in her face. "Right. You just get here?"

"A while ago. Before you called," I said.

"I called the police," she informed, looking around as if she were expecting them to speed down the road at that moment. "They said she can't be considered a missing person for twenty-four hours!" Frustration wedged in her voice while her arms went up and fell with a sharp slap to her sides. "Can you *believe* that?" She made a short sniveling sound, shook her head as though trying to not go there, and then let go an exasperated gush. "I've heard that a body was found in a ditch near the Fairfield Farm." Her mouth quivered and unshed tears pooled in her eyes. *Shit.* I glanced away. I couldn't go all to pieces now.

"It's not Jeanie," I said as calmly as I could. That body had been found yesterday, after all.

"What?"

"It isn't Jeanie, Mrs. Woodbine. Believe me." I was certain that Jeanie was still alive, but I didn't know where she was, and that really frustrated the hell out of me.

"Oh, I know that. Did you try the doors?" she asked, her voice back to normal.

"No. I didn't think—" She stepped over and opened the front door of the Malibu.

"It's not locked? And her purse is in here!" Sounding scandalized, she turned to send me a look of complete astonishment; dark eyes wide, mouth unhinged.

"I'm going to try and get a read," I told her, walking toward the car. "Don't touch the purse."

Watching me, she looked half-terrified, and half-astonished.

Pausing, I wondered if this was the right thing to do. What if I merely saw a vision of Jeanie getting out of her car? I convinced myself I'd see something. If not, I'd try her phone.

"I might faint," I informed. "Could you be ready to catch me?"

"Oh... sure." Mrs. Woodbine slipped her cell phone into a pocket. "Where do you want me?"

"Stand behind me, get ready to catch me," I told her.

"Okay. This is like that trust thing. You fall back and I catch you." She got into position. I realized that she wasn't really expecting me to *see* anything. I was sort of happy about that, because whatever I did see I knew I wouldn't be able to tell her about it, merely because the people involved weren't humans. This much I was positive about.

Pulling off a glove, I paused, then reached for the handle of the blue purse. I hoped to only get a read from Jeanie—what she last saw or experienced.

Closing my eyes, I slipped my fingers beneath the handle and felt its weight in my hand—heavy, like any woman's purse. Everything was intact. Nothing stolen. That was easy. The vision I waited for took maybe a few seconds. It came like a title wave.

Darkness girdled the pool of lights of the parking lot, overhead. Moonlight's Market's sign glowed red letters against brick. The store was still open, but not real busy.

"Night," I said, still standing, but feeling myself tremor.

The scrape of shoes came from behind, made Jeanie wheel about. "Who's there? Oh shit!" In an instant everything happened; there was a scuffle...

"Someone is here," I said. "In the parking lot with her. Jeanie turned to him."

Someone was there, but wasn't the one who grabbed Jeanie. Someone stood in front of her. His face glowed ghostly white—

"I can't see his features!" I said, frustrated. "It's all blurred. Black hair..." *coiled around the blank, white face, falling in waves down the shoulders. It looked like someone had placed a wig on a mannequin with no features.*

Gasping, I held on, trying to get the read in before everything went black.

His mouth rimmed with terrible fangs came closer, closer. A knifing pain at my neck came sharp and unexpected, and I couldn't stop it from coming through me. No, not bitten by the vampire in the front, I realized, but from the one behind.

The vampire's mouth released Jeanie. The one in front of her dipped two tapered fingers into the blood on her throat. He—or she—turned and made the mark on the trunk of her car.

The sharp scent of ammonia brought me to. I don't know how long I was out, but I found myself laying back, looking up into the azure sky, until Mrs. Woodbine's face swam into view.

"You okay?" Mrs. Woodbine's voice pulled me from the darkness.

"Wow," I said, my head swirling. She gave me another dose of the smelling salts and I swatted at her hand. "Where did you get that nasty stuff?"

"We have it at the hospital. I always carry some." She put it to her own nose. She merely blinked, her eyes watered a little. "Works like a charm."

"Did I say anything?"

"You said a few things, but screamed, mostly."

"Really?" I still felt cob-webby as I sat up.

"What did you see?" she asked anxiously.

Knowing full well I couldn't tell Mrs. Woodbine the truth, but could think of nothing better to tell her, so I lied and said, "I couldn't get a clear read."

Chapter 9

I'd been home an hour, thinking about everything that had happened this morning, when my cell phone rang, and I had to dig it out.

"Hello?"

"Sabrina," Nicolas said, rolling the r. He didn't say it as a question, as he knew it could only be me answering this phone.

"Nicolas?" Relief came over me at hearing his voice. It was middle of the afternoon. He was up?

"Are you alright? I've only just risen, and only now learned of your friend Jeanie's disappearance. Toby has told me."

"I'm—" I had to let out an exasperated breath first and think of how I did feel. Of course I was devastated, sick to my stomach. "I'm doing a little less than okay," I said, finally. I'd wanted to call him earlier, but I didn't want to disturb his sleep. I found relief talking to him, but I wasn't sure what to tell him.

"Toby said you had a vision while he was there. Was it about Jeanie?"

"Yes. I saw the person who abducted Jeanie." Since this morning, I'd had time to put things together. It was the rogue vampire. *My* vampire. The one who had bit me eleven years ago, I figured out. The hair. That's all I could go on.

"You did?" he asked, sounding uncertain, suddenly.

I was pacing around the dining room table as I spoke. "You know any vampire whose name begins with the letter V?"

There was the longest pause.

"Nicolas? Are you there?"

"Sabrina, we need to talk. I'm sending one of the twins to come for you in a little while."

* * *

I was dressed in charcoal gray slacks and a matching knit top, taking a long look in the mirror over the bureau when a car pulled into the drive—I heard the distinctive crunch of gravel, and engine noise. Headlights flashed across the windows, into the dining room. All I had left to do was apply my lipstick—a light plum. It made me look a little older.

The loud banging on the screen door startled me and I nearly shoved the lipstick up my nose. I capped the lipstick, and spun on my heel. Grabbing the black jacket, I stepped toward the door. I yanked the door open with my free hand while slipping an arm through an armhole.

I'd turned on the porch lights, showing I was expecting company, and now took the young handsome vampire in. Dressed in a gray suit coat, a black T-shirt, a gold chain hung from his neck, becoming a single strand, ending in a heart. He looked a little like a rock star, I thought. He wasn't wearing glasses. But I was still uncertain.

"Heath, or Leif?" I asked, squinting.

"Heath. Are you ready, then?" he asked. I loved his accent.

"Yeah," I said, pulling my arm through the other sleeve of the coat.

He stepped back, holding the screen door open as I yanked the door closed. I locked it and we both thundered down the wooden steps.

He had a super nice car, of course. A maroon Eclipse. What my brother would call a 'babe car'. I was beginning to see a pattern. These vampires all had new cars. Must be a perk with the job.

"Nice car," I said. I ventured a glance to his face (avoiding the eyes). I found it reassuring that Heath looked normal in a human way, save for the parsnip-white complexion, of course.

"Thanks," he said. "Comes with the job."

"So I figured," I said. "You and your brother are from England, right?"

He glanced my way. "It was me accent that tipped you off, then?"

I chuckled. "Yes. It's an interesting accent. What part of England are you from?"

"Proudly from Liverpool."

"Really?" I said. "Same as the Beatles?"

He threw me a surprised look as he drove out of my drive. "You know about the Chaps from Liverpool, then?"

"Sure. My dad had a lot of their records, then he went with CD's. So, you're from the same town?"

"Same town, same era. In fact we were roaring Beatles fans, back then."

"Oh, wow! Did you actually go and see them?"

"Of course!" He hit a button and sound blasted from his speakers. The Beatles' "Ticket to Ride" came on.

"We went to the clubs where they drew huge crowds," he spoke over the music. "The Cavern, those sort of places. It was great to see them larking about on stage, making jokes. Before they became respectable blokes, you know." He laughed, and I chuckled.

"Sounds cool that you can say that you saw them back then. It must have been wild."

"Wild. Crazy. The girls all went nuts over them, fainting, throwing notes—and unmentionables—at them. We guys grew our hair and sang 'yeah, yeah, yeah', hoping to attract the birds, you know?"

"Okay, that's slang for what?"

"What? Oh, you mean birds? Yeah. Means girls."

I chuckled again. My mood had definitely made a U-turn.

We talked about the Beatles for a while, enjoying the music. He reminisced about those times, running around with his brother. I was simply amazed by it and wanted to hear more.

"You became a vampire about that time?" I asked.

"Right about then. Yeah."

"Can you remember it?" I asked carefully.

"We went with these two birds, see—" he paused, frowning. "I don't remember their names, but we wound up at this house in the country, and it was a wild weekend of drinking, drugs, rock and roll, and sex."

"Oh. Like an orgy type thing?"

He chuckled as he turned onto the toll ramp. "Exactly like that, yeah!"

"So, it happened then? You were turned?"

"I guess it must've, yeah. I haven't any memory of who bit me or what. Sort of happens, I guess when you do things like we did. Trying to be cool and all. We paid for it, I guess." He sounded down suddenly.

"Hey, I'm sorry. I didn't mean to depress you."

"Oh, nah. Look at me. I'm twenty-one forever. How could it get any better?"

"How true."

"I wish I could remember those two bird's names. Now it's gonna bug me."

Enjoying the music, I looked out my window at the indigo-night sky, and noticed the silver disk riding the sky about halfway up.

"Nicolas told me about your friend," he said, and sped up to pass a semi.

"Jeanie?"

"Yeah. Bummer," he said. This reminded me of something I wanted to ask.

"Heath, do you know of any vampire whose name begins with the letter V?"

"You don't mean Vasyl, do you?" he asked, sounding slightly alarmed.

"Well, I don't know. Why?"

"He's a free radical that one is!"

"A what?"

"He's a freaking loony. Mad, I'm saying." A hiss escaped him as he shook his head some.

"A vampire who's crazy?"

"I said he was, didn't I?"

"Wonderful. A lunatic vampire has abducted my friend."

Our eyes met. His were like cat's eyes when the lights from the other cars shown in them. It reminded me quickly what he was. I found it had been easy to forget he was a vampire during our chat. I turned my head away quickly, remembering rule number one.

"Nicolas will know what to do," he assured. He didn't like the song that came on, "Yesterday", and he hit a button and, "All My Loving" came on.

"I'm just worried," I finally managed to puff out.

"About meeting Tremayne?" He reached over and turned down the music.

"Tremayne?" I said, astonished. Great. Now my mind played back what Nicolas had told me last night (after he'd nearly bitten me), that Tremayne *so* wanted to meet me. I found myself suddenly trapped inside some surreal soap opera, where vampire men wanted to bed the new clairvoyant girl in the office.

"Yeah. I'm taking you to the meeting," Heath said, smiling.

My stomach tightened at the thought of meeting the hot-looking, tall blond master vampire that I'd seen in that video.

"Yeah. You've become a part of our little circle," he said fondly. "Tremayne wants to welcome you to his fold." Heath sounded like part of the clergy, like I was going to join his church, instead of going to a strange job where vampires were my bosses.

"I'm a clairvoyant," I said. "I mean, I can't fight Weres like you guys do."

"True," he said, smiling. "But you have powers we don't. You're very important to us, and believe me, Tremayne will take care of you. He won't let anything happen to you. If there is an outlaw Were or rogue vampire in your area, Tremayne will put someone out there to watch over you during the day *and* night."

"Really?"

"Yeah, really."

We were sailing on the toll road, I didn't want to know how fast we were going, but it was *very* fast. His reflexes were so much faster, and more acute than a human's that we were switching lanes, zooming around cars, at an alarming speed. I had to close my eyes at one point when he maneuvered the car, and placed us right in front of a semi—who blasted his air horn. Nicolas had not driven this way last night. I didn't think I was going to survive the ride. But before long, we were downtown Chicago—and going at a sedate speed, comparatively.

Crossing the bridge of the Chicago River, I checked the reflection of the lights from tall buildings glistened across its black surface. Twin peaks of the Towers, scythed into the night sky. In two minutes, he turned and stopped at the gatehouse. Heath greeted the guy inside, showed him his ID badge and when he peeked in at me, I showed him mine. The gate lifted.

He drove down into the parking garage. Lit only sparingly by overheads that gave me a sudden foreboding. I couldn't see much beyond the cones of headlights. It spooked me. Something wasn't right. Although we had gone through security, I had a terrible feeling. My stomach clenched—like something was about to happen. It took me by surprise.

Heath fell silent, as though feeling it too. Maybe that preternatural knowing had come over him. He looked at me.

"What's the matter?" he asked.

"I-I don't know. I just—" I shook my head to clear it. A whole bunch of things slammed into me all at once, and I had to expel a breath with the review of my vision from last night: Blood, a black cat prowling around—in exactly this location—and maybe a woman too. I didn't understand it.

"You okay?" his voice pulled me out of my intense reverie.

"No. Not really," I said finally.

"Nervous about meeting Tremayne?"

"Yeah. I guess," I said, chuckling, trying to dispel his concern.

"That I can understand. Believe me." He leaned toward me and spoke low. "Sometimes he scares me, too." I knew he was trying to make me feel better. We both exited his car at about the same time.

Tense, thinking about meeting Tremayne, I was unprepared for what happened next.

As I bent down to grab my purse from inside the car, I heard a *thhhunk*. Heath gasped sharply. I straightened quick enough to see him jerk back, and then go down.

Blood. Spurting. Turning the blue shirt purple in a star pattern.

I dashed to the other side of the car where he was slumped. A dark splotch blossomed on his chest over the black shirt, a bolt sticking out of it. I had been wrong. He hadn't worn a blue shirt, but a black one. But there was blood.

"Oh God!" I shrieked.

"Oh, shit! Bloody hell! Oh shit!" Heath spat, legs jerking, in obvious pain—and yet he had taken the bolt more like a vampire, not at all like a human since he was still conscious and talking—and kept on swearing. I stood there stupidly, unable to move or do anything useful (like dial 911, because I wasn't used to having a frigging cell phone on me).

"Get down!" he growled.

I dropped. While crouched at the front end of his car, I looked out fearfully into the mostly dim garage, saw the dull gleam of other cars across from us. A noise shifted my attention. I'd heard someone's shoe scuff along the cement floor somewhere nearby. Then a different noise, like a little beep pulled my attention toward Heath who was leaning against his car. Cell phone in hand, he talked quickly into it, "Get someone down to the garage, I've been hit... yes... oh, shit, I'm hurt bad!" He groaned, panted, then hissed another string of expletives.

Adrenaline making me shiver, I wrapped my arms around myself, tried to get the image of Heath's bloody shirt out of my head, and failed. It reminded me too much of my own wolf bite, the blood on my black glove gleaming dark and thick. I crumpled to a seated position, feet out in front of me. My back against the bumper, little white dots swam across my vision. I opted to lie down on the cold cement before I fainted. I breathed in and out, concentrating on that, and not the blood. I kept on swallowing, trying to keep from throwing up, aware of the cold concrete floor beneath me. I spied a black beetle scurrying across the cement floor along the wall, escaping into a dark shadow. I wanted to be him—escaping.

Within moments, a flurry of steps tapping along the concrete reached my ears.

Voices shouting, "Where are you?"

"C-Two!" Heath said, coughing thickly.

I heard more scuffing and tapping along the cement. Then something like a high pitched expulsion of air, and a clattering noise of some object dropping, echoing briefly. A woman shouted an expletive. There were more shouts pell-melling around us. I remained motionless, as another sharp shriek reached my ears. It sounded more like an alley cat, and she was full of fight. I heard flesh smacking flesh. More shrieks. Then nothing.

Footfalls came closer.

"Sabrina! Heath!" Nicolas called. Relief washed over me at the sound of his voice.

"Over here!" I shouted, but it came out more like a sob. I thought that maybe Heath lost consciousness because he wasn't moving or saying anything.

"Bloody hell, over here!" Heath cried.

I made to rise off the cold cement, and looked over the hood of the car, through the windows. Nicolas and Leif were running toward us. I got to my feet and threw my weepy self into Nicolas' protective arms. I buried my face into his chest. His pheromones calmed me almost at once.

"Brother? You trying to stop a bolt with your body, then? That's been tried. It doesn't work out well, I'm afraid," Leif said.

"I'm dying and you're larking about!" Heath grumbled.

"Don't be daft!" Leif admonished. "If it had hit your heart, you'd be dead already. Now, hold still, I'm going to pull it out."

"It'll hurt!" Heath bellowed.

"Probably hurt like hell, but it has to come out, unless you want to walk about like this."

"Go ahead then and be quick about it."

I heard Heath grunt as I imagined Leif grasping the bolt in his hand and with vampire strength pulling it out. Heath gave a groan of relief. A lot of panting followed. Then he swore some more.

"Yes?" Nicolas said. I looked up, and found him speaking into a Bluetooth. His voice vibrated in my ears. "We're in the garage," Nicolas said calmly. "Yes. A bolt."

"Do you have it out?" Nicolas called to Leif.

"Yes. It's out," Leif said, and Nicolas repeated the same into the cell phone.

"Leif, what was the name of those two birds who took us to that house?" Heath asked.

"What house? What birds?"

"You know, when we were turned. What were their names?"

"Oh, them. Astrid and Jane. Why?"

"Been bothering me I couldn't remember their names. That's all."

"You daft son of a bitch," Leif said. "Here, drink. It will keep you until the Team gets here." I didn't know what Leif was offering his brother to drink, and I really didn't want to know. My nose picked up the heavy metallic scent of blood, making me nauseous. I turned my nose into Nicolas' coat and breathed in his scent. *Ahh, better.*

Garbled voices and faint shouts made me turn. I saw a woman with a choke-hold on a dark-skinned woman. Both women were sleek, and muscular. Long waves of black hair were drawn back into a thick tail on the African American woman. I couldn't really see the other woman's face, but she was blond, and most likely a vampire since she'd picked the other off the ground. Three men in white shirts with security badges converged on both of them. But they held back. They spoke into walkie-talkies.

"The crossbow is back there," the blonde said, with a jerk of her head in the general direction. The men with walkie-talkies ran in the direction she'd indicated. "She was trying to re-load."

Blondie shunted her prisoner toward us. "I've caught our murderess!" she said between gritted teeth, looking positively proud of herself. That's when I saw the fangs.

"Easy, Darla," Nicolas soothed. And when I looked again, the vampire—the one Nicolas had called Darla—had moved her face up against the woman's neck, nostrils quavering as though sniffing her. "She must be taken alive, to be questioned," Nicolas said in an authoritative voice. "Keep her under your thrall, until we get her detained."

Darla sneered, a grimace so horrifying I had to look away. "Don't worry, my pretty," Darla snarled again. "You'll live to see the morning. Tomorrow night is another thing altogether." The prisoner's eyes were glazed over. She didn't struggle at all. She must have been under Darla's thrall.

"Yes?" Nicolas spoke again, but not to any of us. He was on his phone again.

"What's the situation?" a deep voice asked over the phone. I knew his voice well, now. I would meet him soon and my stomach quivered suddenly with anticipation.

"Heath was hit with a bolt," Nicolas answered.

"What is his condition?" the question was asked in calm, calculating way, and answered in the same way.

"He lives. He needs blood, though."

"Do you have the perpetrator?"

"Yes. We have her. She is under our control, and will be taken to an interrogation room shortly," Nicolas assured.

"Very good. Where is Ms. Strong?" When he said my name, his voice vibrated through me, as though he had reached all the way across the phone connection to me.

"With me," Nicolas answered. "She is fine. Unharmed."

"Excellent! When you get your prisoner secured, come down. Bring Ms. Strong."

"Of course."

When the phone conversation ended, two women raced through the garage, both wearing olive green smocks and matching pants, and white shoes with thick soles. One carried a black bag. Her long black hair was pulled into a flowing tail. The other was a redhead, and they both had pointed ears. Elves. This shouldn't have surprised me, but it did.

"Where's the entry site?" the one with black hair asked anxiously.

"Right of center," Leif said. "I've given him some of my blood—"

"He needs human to replace what he's lost," she said briskly, and pulled out a bag of blood, like the ones you see in hospitals. She swore lightly as she stuffed it into Heath's mouth. "He's really hurting, and I only have two." She turned to her redheaded partner. "Janet—"

"On it—" the redhead said, and then spoke quickly into a little mike on her collar. "We need two donors from the pool. Stat! Send them to the garage, C-two."

"I need to get you out of here," Nicolas said, and shunted me forward, away from the scene. I went willingly.

Ahead of us, the two security men who I had seen earlier now had control of the would-be vampire slayer. Her hands were bound behind her back, but she didn't struggle at all. The one named Darla was walking along behind the group, looking pissed.

I turned to Nicolas. "What's going to happen to her?"

"She is being taken for questioning," he said calmly.

They guided the would-be slayer into the elevator. The doors slid shut.

"And then what?" I asked.

"We will determine if she is a real threat; if she has been the one killing our kind."

We reached the elevators and had to wait for its return.

"What if she is?"

Nicolas regarded me sharply. His pause made me anxious.

"She will be reconditioned," he said finally.

"Reconditioned? What's that mean?"

He didn't answer me right away. His gaze went back toward where they were still working on Heath.

"Her memory will be altered."

Chapter 10

We stepped out of the elevator, onto lush, deep crimson carpet with gold designs twisting, and intertwining vine-like along the edges. The walls had been covered in similar patterns and colors half-way up. The rest was red all the way to the black ceiling. Indirect theater-lighting ran along either side of the wide hallway, and gave off the needed light for my human eyes.

"You were going to talk to me about this vampire, Vasyl?" I tried to be assertive, but I sucked at it. Especially when Nicolas' eyes went fiery when they flicked back on me.

"Where did you learn of his name?"

"Heath. I asked if he knew a vampire whose name started with the letter V."

"Later. I'll talk to you later," he said hastily, as though the subject was too sensitive—or irritating.

The elevator pinged again. The doors slid almost soundlessly open, and out strolled Leif and Darla looking like they were on a catwalk. Now that I had an unrestricted view of Darla—without a woman in her grasp—I noticed she wore her streaked, short blond hair in wild spikes. Not a lot of women could pull off this look. Darla's features were hauntingly beautiful. Dangerously so, since she was a vampire. I imagined a man would most likely not care that she bit him—anywhere. Wearing a shell pink camisole beneath a black leather jacket, allowing uninhibited view of cleavage, and a matching micro mini skirt, with fishnet stockings, and black leather boots with spiky heals, she looked like she'd stepped off the cover of *Glamor Magazine*. She obviously had no problem flaunting it.

"Darla, this is Sabrina," Nicolas introduced. I remembered not to offer my hand. This time, it was more a matter of self-preservation than anything relating to vampire-human etiquette.

Darla slinked down the stairs as though she had no actual bones in her body. I couldn't move like that if you sent me to modeling school, *and* paid me a million bucks. Although I wasn't a guy, I found her beauty intoxicating, and I noticed her eyes were absolutely green, like a cat's. I simply couldn't look away. She was putting a whammy on me as she looked straight into my eyes.

Shit. I'm so-o-o stupid. Looking into a vampire's eyes was fatal mistake number one, and if I didn't get that down, I was going to be dinner some night. Donor card or not.

"Sabrina," she breathed huskily. Her gaze flicked off me and onto Nicolas, and the thrall, like a cold blanket, lifted from me. I didn't think Nicolas had realized she'd glamored me. I glanced back at Nicolas. Nope. He wasn't any the wiser. "Pleased to meet you. Are you here for the meeting?" Her gaze cut back to me. I quickly flicked mine to her outfit, avoiding her gaze at all cost.

"Yeah, and nice meeting you, too," I said. "Love your outfit. You buy on line? I love the color…" I realized I was rambling and shut my mouth as I caught the looks from Nicolas and Leif.

"Uh, yes. She is here to meet Tremayne," Nicolas answered for me.

"How delightful," she purred. Smiling, she revealed a hint of sharp fangs along the cage of her red mouth. It was a feral, cunning smile. "Tremayne will find her yummy, I think." The tone in her voice was somewhere between cunningly sweet, and lecherous, grinning deliciously as she gazed up at Leif, and they exchanged longing looks.

In return, Leif's hand slid to her back, then he leaned in and kissed her neck. She responded as though he'd sent an electric current down her spine straight to her libido. I saw his lips move, but couldn't hear what he said—but she sure did. Darla twisted into his embrace, eyes half-closed, bringing one leg up higher than his hip, crotch to crotch, as he kissed her on the mouth.

Okay, someone tell me when the porno show is over.

"Be good, luv," Leif admonished, loud enough to allow me to hear it, his gaze directly engaging mine.

The two sauntered over to us and pulled up alongside Nicolas. "I've heard you're going to bring the neophyte, Steve, into the fold tonight?" Leif asked.

Steve? The same Steve from the first night? I wanted to ask, but didn't get a chance.

"You've heard correctly. He will become my minion with Tremayne's blessings." Nicolas' smile went tight. I saw the jaw work a little.

"Lucky you," Darla smirked.

"Sweet," Leif said. "Where did you find him?"

"I found the cowardly wretch in an alley, feeding on a homeless person, near Grant Park." I became suddenly uncomfortable, like I had been listening in on a conversation that wasn't meant for my ears. How would I ever get it into my head these were vampires, and they spoke of horrifying things right in front of me, no matter if I were brand new to this world of theirs or not. I looked away, wanted to simply walk down the hall and never come back. I saw no exit sign.

Nicolas motioned with his hand, "Shall we?" His eyes caught mine, and saw my wavering decision to actually continue this one way walk toward what might be my own doom.

Somehow, his waiting posture and the other expectant gazes, made me move forward. The unwilling novice human. *How quaint, and delicious,* I imagined they thought of me.

We stepped some twenty or so paces, following the curve of the hallway. A panel of floor-to-ceiling windows looked down two stair-stepping floors. In the space directly below, people were seated at round tables, cafeteria-style, enjoying their meals.

Another level below that was what looked like a billiards room, with the usual video games stationed along the walls. A huge plasma TV hung from the ceiling and pool tables stood unused at the moment.

We continued away from the wall of windows, the hallway curving to the right, a fork to the left. We continued right, entering a long hallway with marble columns on either side. Other vampires were going about their business. I could tell they were vampires because of the skin tone: cottage cheesy to ashen. I noticed women wore nice pant suits or dresses designed for the office. Men wore expensive-looking suits. Although I had worn the best outfit I owned, I felt under-dressed. I wondered where they were going, and what they did here. They all seemed preoccupied, and didn't notice me, since I was the only human there.

Before us rose black marble stairs ending at white double doors that stood open. The place looked less like an office— or whatever this was supposed to be—and more like an Italian palace. I had expected bland gray office cubicles with ugly gray desks with tense-looking people hunched over computers, typing away, cradling phones on their shoulders, with faxes and printers going non-stop.

Pleasantly surprised, I wondered what the rest of this underground palace looked like. Would I walk into a room filled with Victorian style furnishings? Would there be vampires draped across them, feeding on their randy hosts? A scene from one of Goya's paintings, perhaps? I knew if only by the fact that I couldn't get a read that Nicolas had his thrall all over me, and I wondered why. Or was it simply that vampires couldn't help but press their advantage whenever a human was within range?

Pulse quickening, and my stomach doing lazy flip-flops, I strode unsteadily forward. Our steps tapped along the marble floor until we came to two white doors in an arched frame, barricading some inner sanctum. Off to the side was a curved, white desk with a flat-screened computer. There was no receptionist. The white doors were interrupted by two large crooked red T's—longer than my forearm. I remembered I had seen this yesterday and had interpreted them to be fangs. They were arranged so that each T was on either side of the separation. Nicolas took out a key card, passed it through a locking mechanism. It buzzed and the doors snicked open for us, like an elevator. Impressed so far, I was about to get bombarded by something more intriguing and bizarre than my over-fertile imagination could ever dream.

Red met my eyes first. It took a while before they could adjust to it all. Like looking down a tube after being subjected to squares. Smooth surfaces and absolutely no right angles at all greeted us as we wound through a large, smooth tube. Our walking surface was the only thing that was flat. Crimson lighting was indirect, and cast seductively against curved walls and what served as the ceiling. I compared it to walking into a piece of modern art, or one of those odd rooms in a fun house—but really not that much fun since it made me somewhat dizzy. It took me a few moments to realize that the surfaces were actually white, and the lighting tinted it.

We soon emerged into an elliptical room with a type of sunken seating area. The vampires took the few steps down to a main level. Beyond this level was the sunken area. The seating in this pit was a continuous couch curving around the wall. Crimson cushions and red carpet allowed the only disruption to the white color scheme of the room—enhanced by more red lighting.

Beyond this seating area, on the main level, curved a white counter or workstation. There were several flat-screened computers lined up along the horseshoe-shaped desk. At the farthest point hung a huge, flat-screen TV screen—one of those plasma monsters—and I saw people, bigger than life, scurrying around on the screen in a dark hallway. I unraveled the mystery of the scene, and soon realized it wasn't some reality TV show. It showed the madness we'd left moments ago, down in the garage. I now saw myself, scrambling into Nicolas' arms. Taped and now replaying for our viewing pleasure.

My vampire comrades had all stopped at the top of the stairs, waiting. I stood taking in the place, but mostly watching what was on the screen. The scene switched. Presently two men in white shirts placed the African American woman into a room. It had to be the woman who had shot Heath. Someone stood outside the door to guard it.

Suddenly, the screen went blank. *The end.*

Stationed behind the desk was a white, tall-backed leather chair, turned away from the room. I had to presume the person seated could only be the mysterious Mr. Tremayne himself.

Nicolas, Darla, Leif, and I stood in front of the sunken sitting area. No one coughed, or said a word. We simply waited.

The leather chair turned, slowly revealing the master vampire. He had thick, wavy blond, hair parted in the middle; it fell loose well beyond his shoulders. I inspected him in more detail, and without realizing it, I found myself staring into startling blue-green eyes. He took me in too. There was no question about it; he was terribly interested in me, as his unblinking gaze roved me up and down. From a distance I thought he might be thirty-something. He had the most striking eyes I'd ever seen, and the large, hawk-like nose on his large face looked noble. He smiled pleasantly, affluently, when he leaned forward in his chair, hands clasped on the smooth counter.

My mind dredged up what little I knew of the man from before I'd answered the ad. Tremayne had remained a focus of interest while this singularly unusual building was in the works. Controversy concerning Tremayne was that no one knew where he had come from; neither how, nor where he'd gotten his money, but that he was worth billions. And as everyone knows, money talked in the workings of city government, and he'd finally gotten his way. Construction on Tremayne Towers began two years ago. Finishing touches were still on-going, as far as I had heard. No news cameras were allowed inside the building beyond the hotel lobby after it had been opened. The media harped on the fact that the building had the fewest windows of any sky scraper, bar none, and were curious about the design. Obviously, they knew nothing about the vampires who now lived and worked here.

The other curiosity about Mr. Tremayne was that he was rarely seen, and—as Jeanie had pointed out—no one had a photo of him. Obviously, Mr. Tremayne was either camera shy, or being a vampire, his image was unable to show up on film—unless he wanted it to.

An odd twang of energy flowed around me. I went into full alert.

"*Carpe noctem,*" the large vampire greeted. His voice was deep, resonating, and pleasant. It offset his somewhat brutish hulk. Were he human, he could have easily been either a full back in the NFL, or an All Star Wrestler. Although seated, I had to guess the vampire was well over six foot-six, and possibly weighed in at two hundred-eighty to three hundred well-muscled pounds. It wasn't that he seemed muscle-bound, but he had broad shoulders and a heavy-looking chest. He filled out the deep maroon, button-down shirt. The black silk tie may have been a last moment addition. I could see it had been hastily tied, it hung slightly crooked. I smiled to myself.

"*Carpe noctem,*" came the chorus from the others. The vampires next to me went into a genuflect—I heard them, before I saw the motion from the corner of my eye—like a precise military guard snapping to a soundless command. I was struck by this, but at the same time confused as to what to do. I went on one knee and bowed my head. When in Rome...

"Nicolas, Leif, Darla. Well done." The r's were soft, like a British accent that had me at first think he was British. But his inflection and where he put the stress on words was all different. Though his voice was deep, he spoke in an innocuous, pleasant tone. The others rose from their obeisance, and so did I. His blue-green stare took everyone in.

Then those flecks of ocean fell on me. His smile grew broader as he rose—and kept rising. I suddenly had to revise my first assumption—he was impossibly tall, possibly seven foot tall, with a powerful chest, as though he had swung a broadsword at some point in his distant past, or, as a hunter, carried a huge carcass home on his shoulders when he was a living man. As an undead, he was possibly the largest vampire I'd ever seen. Even without his superhuman powers, he could throw any one of us across the room.

"Nicolas, make the introductions, please?" Tremayne said.

"Certainly." Nicolas turned to me. "Bjorn Tremayne, may I present Ms. Strong."

"How do you do." Tremayne stepped from around the desk in a gliding, easy manner. Graceful, liquid, and yet strange. I would not have expected such grace from a man of his size and bulk. But I quickly reminded myself vampires did not always move as we did. Legs ensconced nicely in a pair of black slacks, he strode around, and slouched back against his ultra-modern desk.

"Hello," I replied, feeling as if I were the most interesting person in the room.

"Please, come closer." His words flowed toward me like a slow-motion rope, surrounding me like a lasso, and tugged me forward. I wasn't aware that my feet had moved, but suddenly I was about three feet away from him, craning my head back to take him in. He stood almost three feet taller than me.

But that wasn't the half of it. An odd sensation twinged my vampire bite, then it turned to something else altogether. My libido had a rude awakening. It was sudden, unexpected, and mostly unwelcomed, since this was neither the place nor the time—plus, he was a total stranger.

I was aware that I was unable to move, unable to do much of anything but stare into those deep teal-blue eyes of his. Unlike the way Nicolas had used his vampire charms on me, this was different. I could feel this vampire's mind touching mine. Lightly. Almost a brush, as if he'd feathered his fingers across my cheek in an admiring way. It wasn't exactly unpleasant, but not the most comfortable thing I'd ever been part of either. Thrilling, but at the same time a chill of danger stabbed me: If he could do this, without touching me, or having had my blood, what else was he capable of?

"Welcome to my abode, as it were," Tremayne said, thrusting his hand out to indicate his strange office. "May I present Dante Badheart, my magus?" He directed my glance toward someone standing across from us on the main level, in partial shadow.

I looked across and saw a man dressed entirely in black. He stepped forward, allowing the light to fall on him. His black suede leather coat was fringed along the arms, and over the chest. His T-shirt had some sort of large emblem on it—two interlocking swirls, silver on black. Black jeans were tucked inside black suede moccasin-styled boots. A proud nose and high cheek bones were arranged on an angular face that looked to have seen age thirty, at least. His eyes were the most unusual color of what I could only describe as smoky-gray.

He was handsome, I thought, and the only other human in the room, and this made me feel slightly more at ease.

"Dante, this is Ms. Strong," Tremayne introduced.

Dante slid his smoky eyes to me. They had a feral cast to them. He didn't move toward me with an out-stretched hand, but made with a simple nod. Straight, raven-black hair, lustrous with firelight, fell over his waist to his hips. He wore it parted down the middle.

We exchanged hi's. Since he didn't extend his hand, I didn't either.

He had a smooth, resonating voice. His mouth was wide and framed by a Fu Manchu mustache. Cinnamon-colored skin made his heritage Native American. But the name Dante threw me. I wondered how he had wound up with a 13th century Italian poet's name.

"A magus?" I said. "Like a magician?"

"I prefer the word shaman," he said, a slightly crooked smile bent his lips.

"Perfect!" Tremayne's voice boomed. "My alliance is now complete. I have my magus as well as my seer."

I looked up at him questioningly.

Tremayne's gaze shifted toward me. A cunning smile made deep creases in his otherwise flawless face. "A master vampire's rule is determined by those he surrounds himself with, Ms. Strong," he explained patiently. "You are my latest addition, and as we seem to be the target of a vampire murderer, I am certain you will help us in discovering that individual." Tremayne laced large fingers across his middle, and I saw an intricately woven gold ring on his middle finger.

"Okay. But no pressure. Right?" My joke went over all their heads. Except for Dante, whose snort I caught as he hid his face in the draping of his long hair.

"But we caught her!" Darla protested.

Ignoring her, Tremayne went on, "I'm having Nathan, Devin, and Bryan check the entrances, including any sewer lines. See how she got in."

"She must have found some other way in besides the entrance," Nicolas argued. "They would have seen her. Surely."

"Cat," I blurted, remembering the vision I'd had the night before.

Everyone's attention slid to me.

"I saw it," I said almost too briskly. "Last night, when I touched the bolt, I saw a cat turn into a woman. I didn't understand it then."

"No. You made no sense at all," Leif agreed, eyes glittering from me, to Tremayne. "She did call it though. Amazing."

"The woman is able to change into a cat," I explained. "She was able to come inside, getting past the guards as a cat, and changed herself back into a woman."

"Shiftchanger," Dante supplied in a neutral voice.

"Of course," Tremayne said, looking pensive. "But how did she get her clothing and the weapon inside?"

No one spoke. We all looked at one another.

"Nicolas, I want you to question her, or meld your mind to hers if she refuses to answer. Find out who put her up to it. Obviously, somehow the crossbow and her clothes were placed inside for her to use."

"You don't believe she is the one who has been killing our brethren?" He sounded somewhat crestfallen.

"No. The MO is all wrong," Tremayne said. "If she had been, she wouldn't have missed. I saw the replay of the tape," he went on. "She missed his heart by inches. Every vampire that has been killed so far was shot at close range. Within a few feet. Not several yards. This was messy."

"Yes, of course, sire." Nicolas bowed. When he straightened, his eyes didn't engage Tremayne's, but found me, instead. Some dark emotion crossed his face, and in a flash was gone.

"Besides, when they were attacked, the victims were always alone. There were no witnesses," Tremayne went on. "No, I think she's a plant. The real killer is trying to draw us off his trail."

All of us exchanged pensive glances. All, except for Nicolas, whose eyes went vacant for a moment, not really looking at anything.

"Darla and Leif will accompany you to question our little would-be assailant. I'd also like Dante to join you as well," Tremayne said. "And, once done, alter her memory, as usual. Then have her followed."

"Who?" Nicolas asked.

"I want Darla to follow her. Maybe Leif should go with, just in case. Use any method to follow her, as long as she doesn't see you." Tremayne shifted away from the desk and stood. "I want to know where she goes, what she does, and who she sees along the way."

"I will go," Dante offered, taking a step forward. "If she shift-changes again, I am more than qualified to follow her."

"Excellent idea," Tremayne said. "However, I have other plans for you."

I glanced over at Nicolas. Gaze cold, he turned away from me. It was as though I had done something wrong. But what? I had merely told them the woman was a shiftchanger. Wasn't that what I'd been paid to do?

There was a slight pause in action and words. Then Tremayne said, "I think we can begin the blood rite, now. I know the neophyte has been waiting a while." *Blood rite? Ew.*

Turning his attention back on to me, he said, "Sabrina, I think you should stand next to Dante, if you would, please?" He thrust his hand toward Dante.

I complied and angled toward him. Relieved, I stood next to Dante, watching the autocrat vampire. I realized he'd released me of his powers. His focus was totally on something else. He turned slightly and bent toward the counter behind himself.

"Send in the initiate," he spoke into an intercom.

"Yes, sir," came the muffled response.

I noticed that Leif and Darla had moved further around on the same level as Dante and I. Arms wrapped about one another, they gave each other affectionate nips. They seemed somewhat excited about whatever was about to happen. We formed a staggered half-circle around the main floor, looking down into the seating area.

Nicolas stepped down into the sunken sitting area. Removing his coat, he folded it neatly, methodically, and placed it on the couch that wrapped around the pit. It made my mind jump to last night, when he was with me. A rush of guilt hit me and I arranged my face so it wouldn't show that I was having lustful thoughts about Nicolas.

At the same moment, a different set of doors—I hadn't noticed them—off to one side, slid open with that characteristic swoosh. My guess was correct. Steve from that first night—the one who had such a hard time holding back his lust for my blood—stood there dressed in black slacks and a white shirt with large, roomy sleeves, unbuttoned down mid-chest and belted around the waist. At the moment, I was slightly confused as to why he was dressed as though he was about to attend a Renaissance Fair. I tried to make sense of it with what I'd overheard, and, of course with vampires I was unable to get a read from their emotions—other than they were all extremely excited about this. Darla especially, by the way she kept on nipping at Leif, and Leif had to hold her wiggly body still a few times.

Steve stepped up to the edge of the stairs and went into the full bow, both knees on the floor, head all but touching the floor, showing the master vampire obedience. I remembered them saying he was a neophyte. I remembered Crimmins had called me that and Nicolas had corrected him.

The room went dead still. I could sense that something significant and possibly terrible was going to happen to Steve. I was startled that my clairvoyant abilities were able to work at the moment, but I realized none of the vampires' attention was on me.

"I bid you welcome to my realm. Please, step down." Tremayne invited.

Steve stepped down into the pit, and went into the bow once again. "My lord," Steve said. "I request you give me safe passage and that my eternal days be free of guilt, pain and fear, and that I live out my life obeying you and only you."

My eyes slid to take in the smirk on Tremayne's face. I imagined that the words may have been said a hundred times, maybe a thousand times—possibly a million times—to Tremayne, but obviously they gave him great satisfaction in hearing them.

"Who is your sire?" Tremayne questioned.

"My lord, I do not know. He did not come for me, and I awoke in an abandoned apartment in the basement one night, hungry and alone. Give me sanctuary my lord." He spoke the last in a harsh whisper. I noticed he trembled slightly, the lengths of his dark bangs quavering against the white of his shirt.

Tremayne had assumed a relaxed stance, crossing his arms and one leg over the other as he leaned against his desk. I noticed Tremayne's shoes. They were cowboy boots made of snake skin, dyed gray.

"Who found you?" Tremayne asked. I understood these questions were all part of the rite. Obviously Steve had to become part of this den, or nest of vampires, and it required his going through these motions and words.

"Nicolas."

"If that is so, Nicolas, say aye. If not, say nay," Tremayne said, nearly sounding bored.

"Aye. I was the one who found him preying on a woman in a back alley like a starving animal. I brought him into my confidence. I am, to this point, his sponsor."

"Do you consent to be his sire?" Tremayne asked.

"I do," Nicolas responded as he rolled up his shirt sleeves. Then he loosened his tie, and undid the top button. These curious undressing actions had me worried and a little confused.

"Initiate, will you honor and obey the rules and do the bidding of myself, or Nicolas?"

"I will," Steve said, not budging an inch from that bowed position.

"Very well. As Nicolas has advised you completely in the rules and laws of my state, I hereby welcome you into the fold." He paused. "Nicolas?" Tremayne gestured toward Steve. "You may take him as your minion."

"Stand," Nicolas commanded. Steve stood, head still bowed slightly.

Nicolas moved to stand behind Steve and gently, almost reverently pulled his collar away from his neck. I didn't know what to expect, and yet I knew it would not be good. When it happened my stomach lurched as I saw Nicolas' head snap back, jaws opened, and out popped the fangs. Dante's hand gripped mine firmly as I glanced away, and covered my eyes with my other hand. Before I could block it out completely, I saw Nicolas' fangs dart toward Steve's neck from behind. I couldn't drown out the sound of Steve's horrific groan of pain, twined by some terrible growl coming from Nicolas.

I muffled a scream, and looked away. Dante drew my head against his shoulder in a protective way, shielding me from the view, like a parent might protect a child from seeing some horrific scene in a movie. I couldn't express to him how grateful I was of his standing there with me. Obviously, he had seen this same rite before—possibly many times—and it didn't bother him.

When Dante's hand released mine and he removed his other hand from my head, I stole a look. Nicolas was stepping casually away from Steve, daubing his lips with a black handkerchief. Steve was sprawled upon the floor. He looked as though he was dead. A sort of panic went through me. Then I saw the fingers of his outstretched hand twitch, and he moaned.

"Nicolas, do you consent to exchange blood with Steve?"

"No," Nicolas said in a manner that seemed as though it were repugnant.

Tremayne's movement toward the intercom was slow. Leaning down, he said, "Send the Sanguine Team in."

The same doors snicked open and out rushed several people. Three, wearing the same olive green uniforms as those who had come to Heath's aide, converged on the area beside the vampire on the floor. I noticed a red swirl on the sleeves of this medical team. It was some sort of emblem, I decided. Two others, a man and a woman, were casually dressed, in their mid-twenties and stood by as the three attendees bent to the vampire on the floor.

"He took a generous amount from this one," the woman with red hair snarled. I realized she had been one of those who had been with Heath only moments ago. I remembered her elfin face.

"Nicolas?" The fair haired man looked up at him. I recognized him from last night. Andrew Morkel, head of the Donor Pool. He wasn't in a suit tonight. He wore the same olive green uniform as the other two. Andrew exchanged glances with Nicolas.

"Hurry, we need one of you, now!"

Morkel's edict put one of the two humans into motion. The man already had a sleeve rolled up. Kneeling, he pressed his wrist to Steve's mouth. The elf nurse slapped a pressure cuff on the donor, and placed a stethoscope over it. The male nurse held Steve's head up. Steve clamped down on the wrist like a rabid dog. I had to look away again, remembering the way Steve had greedily licked blood from my fingers that first night.

"Nicolas, you amaze me, as always. You knew when to stop, just in time. Two donors may not revive him, I fear," Tremayne said casually, leaning against his desk, arms crossed over his chest.

"I was excited by the blood… earlier," Nicolas said by way of explanation.

Tremayne's voice pulled my attention away from what was happening down in the pit. The Sanguine Team had gathered Steve up, who was able to walk unsteadily with the help of Andrew Morkel.

"This will all be cleaned up," Tremayne said almost as a way of pulling everyone's attention away from Steve and the Team. "Meanwhile, I will take our clairvoyant up to Letitia's apartment. I'd like to see if she can get a read." Shaking his buttery mane out of his eyes, he paused, and took them all in. When none of them moved, he said, "Well, you have your orders. Go."

Dante left my side as the others turned away. Nicolas threw me one last glance, his face unreadable as he turned to join the others. They all streamed out of the room, leaving me all alone with the powerful vampire magnate.

Chapter 11

"Are you ready, Ms. Strong?"

I looked over at him. Tremayne had stepped away from his desk. He rolled down the sleeves of his shirt, and fastened the buttons at the wrists.

"Where are we going?" I asked, heart pounding. I felt like a trapped rabbit.

"I'm taking you up to Letitia's apartment."

Confusion must have riddled my features because he added, "Letitia Westgate was my life-time mate. She was shot, the other night with a wooden bolt."

"Oh. Right. I'm very sorry," I added, watching him climb the steps toward me with long, strong-looking legs. He stopped four feet or five in front of me, and my head went back, and back. God, he was tall. A girl could get whip-lash trying to kiss him.

"Thank you." Tremayne's face was unreadable. I couldn't tell if he was mad, glad, or merely annoyed.

"You want me to read her apartment now?"

"Yes. We would have had you do this last night, but I was... indisposed. I had Letitia's body cremated only yesterday. I had to witness the cremation, to make sure that it was done correctly. That's why I wasn't able to meet you."

"I see. Of course." I averted my gaze, both trying hard not to crinkle my nose at the thought of what he'd said, and not look directly into his eyes. "How long were you—um—together?" I asked, because that seemed the polite thing to do.

"Eight hundred and eighty-one years, and two months." He wiggled his broad hand. "Somewhere around that."

"That's a long time."

"Yes. It came as a crushing blow. I discovered her body," he went on, his gaze going to the far end of the room. "It will take me time to recover from the loss." I didn't hear him say he loved her in so many words. But perhaps for vampires, it was a little different.

"We will take my private elevators." He motioned toward elevator doors recessed slightly in the wall doused in red light.

He strolled in that lithe gate, and was already across the room before I could turn to join him. I think my hesitation drew more from the fact that I really didn't want to be trapped with this powerful vampire on an elevator, after having no problem glamoring me at a distance of twenty or so feet. A five-by-five cubicle was the *very* last place I wanted to be cooped up with him. As a human, he would intimidate me. His being a vampire was a thousand times worse.

"How's the arm?" he asked, as he swiped a card key through a swipe pad on the wall.

I blinked and probably looked clueless.

"I heard that you were bitten by a Were?"

"Oh, um, yeah. It's fine, thanks," I said, lifting my arm slightly. I blew out a frustrated breath, hoping he didn't hear it. Why was I acting like this was my first day at junior high? *God, Sabrina. Get hold of yourself.*

I pulled in a breath and let it out, steeling myself against my nerves, or panic—whatever this was—and we stepped into the elevator. No red lights in here. The elevator doors snicked shut.

Swallowing, I tried not to think so much about being trapped with such a large and incredible hunk of a vampire. Reaching past me, he pressed one of the many buttons on the panel.

I pressed myself against the wall, holding onto the heavy chrome bar for support—and out of sheer unadulterated fear. Meanwhile, the powerful and attractive vampire leaned against the opposite wall, trying to look harmless as he folded his arms and cocked one leg across the other, hiking his pant leg up revealing those gray snake-skin boots.

For some reason my fear subsided. Coincidence? I hardly think so. The vampire pheromones had to be really heavy in such a close room.

Aside from his commanding aura, his scent filled the small space. Warm. Woodsy, with a hint of deep musk. It invoked thoughts of walking in the woods. I had a sudden vision of Tremayne holding hands with a faceless woman, sunshine casting deep shadows along a forest floor filled with yellow jonquils. They were laughing, and then he grabbed, and twirled her in his arms and they fell as lovers, into the yellow ocean of flowers, still laughing.

I decided he'd telegraphed this pleasant image to me to banish my terrified ideas of him.

I shook my head to clear my thoughts. He was trying to calm me. But enough was enough. I had to find some way to keep him out of my head. He was simply too strong for me. Maybe I should go hunting for a silver cross to wear.

Casting my gaze upward, I noticed an arrangement of repeated symbols, or runes, all along the top edge of the wall of the elevator in a continuous panel. I didn't know what they were, or what they meant, but I recognized two of them. I hadn't thought that these symbols might actually mean something. It was the first time my attention was drawn to them, without other things going on around me.

"What are those symbols?" I asked, pointing up.

Tremayne looked up.

"Ah, yes. Those are ancient vampire runes," he said.

"I didn't know that vampires had an ancient language."

He made a scoffing noise. "Some vampires don't know of it. Anyway, they were rediscovered recently," he explained, and then pointed to one. "This one represents blood." He pointed to the odd swirl that ended in what looked like a red drip.

"Like on the shirt sleeves of the elves who came to Heath's aide," I said.

"Yes. That's the Sanguine Team," he said. "And this one represents the beast." He pointed to the two interlocking swirls. The symbol that Dante had on his T-shirt.

"Beast?"

"Yeah, shiftchangers, and Weres are into this symbol heavy."

"Dante's a shiftchanger?"

"Yes, among other things."

"And I'm your seer?"

"Yes."

"What will I be doing, I mean, after we solve the mystery of who has been killing vampires?"

"Don't tell me you're worried you'll be unemployed, Ms. Strong." His serious mien melted into a smile as he slouched back against the wall of the elevator.

"Well, I don't know what to think, to tell the truth," I said.

He shook the hair out of his eyes. "You only need to know that you are on an elite force—"

"Of vampires, wizards, and shiftchangers?"

"Something like that," he smiled, staring at me with those incredible eyes. I noticed they were the color of the ocean, definitely a beautiful blue-green. Why the hell did he have to be so damned handsome? His weathered face and the deep crow's feet around his eyes—now more evident in the overhead lighting of the elevator—did not make him less attractive to me. He didn't come off as an older man to me. If anything, mature was the word I was scrounging around for. I realized he had been someone who'd been exposed to sunshine and maybe the sea, when he was alive. *Viking?* His exact age in human years was difficult to ascertain, but he looked around the forty mark. Some people who spend a lot of time in the sun, and elements look much older than they are in actual years. I put him at thirty-eight, maybe. His blond hair—now under pure white light—was butter-yellow, and abundantly thick, with a little receding along the temples. I noticed he had longer-than-was-in-style sideburns, and, like his dark eyebrows, was darker-almost brown, in fact.

He caught my gaze on him and I had to shift mine to the floor.

"Nicolas informs me that your friend disappeared?"

"Yes."

"And tell me if I am mistaken, but I believe you had a curious vision?"

"Yes," I whispered, near tears.

"When you had this vision, it was of your friend *and* this vampire?" he carefully worded his question.

"Yes. Only—"

"Only what?"

"I couldn't bring his face in. That was weird." We both became silent for a moment, contemplating this.

Tremayne interrupted the silence with a new question. "Nicolas informs me you were bitten by Vasyl when you were young?"

"Yes."

His eyes focused somewhere above my head in thought. "Interesting." His gaze flicked down to me. "I wonder if he..." his voice trailed off.

"What?"

"No." He shook his head. "Never mind."

"Why did he choose me? I was only ten. What does he want of me?" My voice had become a little louder. My hands were shaking and I slid them behind my back.

"That is for Vasyl to explain, should he ever get the chance to. He marked you. That's *so* old."

"Who is he?" I asked.

"A rogue master. He won't conform to our new vampire laws." He pulled in a breath and let it out, almost creating a whirlwind as he did. "He moves around quite a bit." His eyes slitted at me. "You will call either myself or Nicolas at once if he comes to you. Do you understand?"

"Sure. But, he took Jeanie," I said a little heatedly. "You must know where he might have taken her."

"No, I don't. I'm sorry." He re-crossed his arms.

Hopelessness filling me, I dropped my gaze. Jeanie was in trouble, and it was all because of me. I had to find a way to learn where she was. If Vasyl was hunting me, why did he go after Jeanie? And then he'd left that clue with the blood on her trunk—the letter V. Maybe he was crazy as hell and wanted to play some terrible game with me.

I couldn't hate him more at this point. First my mother and now my best friend.

The elevator came to a slow and easy stop on the ninety-seventh floor. The doors slid open to a dim and short hall. No soft pinging noise to announce us. That was odd.

"Here we are. This is mine and Letitia's penthouses," he explained.

Penthouses. Plural. So, they'd had separate dwellings. We stepped into the short hall. Two doors faced one another. They were like any door you might see, with brass handles instead of round door knobs. A small panel next to each door had a tiny red light next to a slot. He turned to the right side of the hallway and faced the door. I stood behind him. This was the first time I'd seen his entire backside—or noticed it. He had a nice butt. The pants he wore fit him snugly, and they weren't Dockers or anything I recognized. The logo on the back pocket's flap were two red crooked T's—Tremayne's logo. Tremayne had his own line of clothes. Toby had said that Tremayne had a number of businesses. He was quite the entrepreneur.

I jerked my eyes away, ashamed I had been admiring the vampire's derrière.

Reaching into his back pocket, he took out a plastic card and inserted it into the slot next to the door. A click and a little buzz, and he opened the door. Pleasant perfume wafted out to me. He pushed the door wide, allowing me to enter. I quickly strode through, and turned so he wasn't directly behind me—in the hunting pose. He turned to a panel and pressed several numbers in a sequence. I presumed he had disarmed the alarm.

Show time.

I have walked into places I've never been before and had a wave of Knowing come over me, unbidden. I can't explain it other than I simply *knew* the layout of the whole apartment at once, although I had never been inside. It came as second nature. At an early age, I thought everyone could do this. But obviously not.

"My hope is that you will be able to get a reading from her things, without having to resort to you touching the actual bolt that we found in her," Tremayne explained.

I barely heard what he had said while getting my bearings. I closed my eyes. I knew the way to the balcony—the one where he'd told me Letitia had perished—through her bedroom. At the moment we stood in a large room done up in beiges and browns with cream-colored, wall-to-wall carpet as thick as sheepskin. There were mirrors all over the walls—another vampire inside joke. In a far corner stood a grand piano. White with gold accents.

"Ms. Strong?"

With a stalling hand, I stopped him from speaking further. He understood what was going on and remained quiet. Good.

I opened my eyes. "The kitchen is to the right," I said, pointing. "Letitia had wonderful taste, by the way. She also has a large collection of ceramic dogs kept in several glassed curios, in a room off the kitchen."

A smile leaped to Tremayne's lips. "A silly collection," he said, shoulder lifting. "But I indulged her."

I smiled knowingly. "She liked the bull dog, said it reminded her of you."

He gave a sharp laugh. I'd thrown him with that one.

I stepped further into the room. A throng of personalities poured over me much as if I had been drenched in a tidal wave of voices, music, faces, and conversations all at once, from a recent moment. *The opening of Tremayne Towers—ahh, yes.* I saw people in evening attire, drinking, talking, and laughing. Their images superimposed in a watery way over the existing surroundings. I recognized a number of famous people. I closed my eyes and pulled in tighter on certain individual faces.

"Elton John played that piano," I said, pointing toward the grand piano. "Oh," I said, as more faces came into view. "Looks like a lot of politicians, actors, and entertainers came here."

"Our launch party for the Towers." He nodded, eyes darting around as though he too could see what I was seeing.

Face becoming warm, I saw Letitia—I simply knew it was her—slipping a hand on a well-known actor's butt. The man smiled, kissed her on the cheek (I remembered that he and his wife had gotten divorced recently, and it was in all the tabloids).

"Actors, entertainers, a lot of famous people were here for it," I said.

"Yes," he said, looking impressed. "You are taking a very good read of this room. Letitia loved to entertain. She loved the actors, and I liked to bump heads with the politicians." He made a sound in his throat. "Don't get me started on politicians. They're all pompous know-it-alls. None of them suspected Letitia and I are vampires." He made the sound again, a sort of half-laugh, half-snort. "If we announced ourselves to the world tomorrow, I know there would be mayhem."

I couldn't concentrate on what he was saying. I was doing what I'd come here for. I opened my eyes and looked around at the tastefully decorated room.

"The balcony is through that hallway," I said, and strode toward it, but then stopped and cocked my head. Some other vision had caught me off guard. I had a vivid vision—on a different night—of several young men, each of them with a drink, talking casually amongst themselves.

"I see a little party. This is the most recent event from everything I've seen so far." I was surprised that I could single this one vision out of all the others, but probably because it was so recent it had more power behind it.

"Yes?" Tremayne said eagerly. "Tell me. Tell me everything."

"I see about a dozen men. All of them good looking, young—in their mid-twenties—talking, drinking. The room is dim, lit only by candlelight and a few low-lit lamps in corners," I said, my eyes slipped shut to get the full vision.

"Who—?"

I stalled his question once again with hand up, motioning him for silence. He didn't speak, as I frowned into my vision. "Yes. All men. They're chatting amongst themselves."

Then, a face loomed out at me. Toby? What was he doing here?

Tremayne made a sigh of impatience, but he didn't interfere.

Toby was among the young men here, in this room, on some evening, not very long ago. I didn't say anything because I wanted to see what was going to happen.

"What do you see?" Tremayne asked, startling me, and I lost Toby when he ducked out onto the balcony through a sliding glass door.

"Ah, well, Letitia's pretty, with long, wavy, copper-colored hair." I paused to listen and observe. "She knows every one of them. Greets them all by name—Blane, Roan, Reggie, and others. She touches them, asking how they all are."

I followed Letitia, mentally, of course, as she drew one of the men to the bedroom, in a seductive way, holding his hand. The man was large, curly black hair, his skin tone like chocolate milk. I thought his name might have been Wayne, or Dwayne. He looked as though he didn't know what to expect, but was eager to get things rolling, I could tell.

They didn't make it to the bed, and he was kissing her on the mouth, his hands all over her in a rush to have sex. The flash of her biting the large man on the neck, caught me (and Dwayne) by surprise, and he came into his pants right away with a groan.

"Oh, crap!" My eyes snapped open.

"What is it?" Tremayne was insistent now.

"She's taking blood from one of them."

"Her donors. Of course," he said, unconcerned. He shrugged. "Is that it?"

Nettled, I frowned at him. "I think so."

"She liked to throw parties—"

I stalled him again with my hand as another little image popped into my head. First, I saw Toby stepping back into the room from the balcony—no one else in the room, or the apartment with them. He'd waited until everyone was gone. He wanted to chat with her. Well, it was more than a friendly chat. He was arguing with her. I heard the conversation in my head.

"Why not?" I said this, but it was me speaking as Toby spoke. These types of visions were always awkward when they happened, because I sometimes couldn't help that I sometimes played the part of some of the people there in the vision.

"Why not what?" Tremayne's voice infiltrated the world I was in at the moment.

"Because, you are Nicolas'," said Letitia's voice through me. "And I'm not authorized."

The image and voices vanished, and I opened my eyes to see Tremayne waiting for my explanation.

"She refused to turn one of them. He became angry and stormed out." I now wondered if this had been the secret Toby was holding inside, and didn't want me to know about. Somehow it didn't seem like that big of a deal. I wished I could have followed Toby from there on, and see what he did afterwards, but the vision died.

"Of course," Tremayne said. "We aren't allowed more than one turn in a hundred years. That's been in place for about sixty years, now. Only if we have lost a life-time mate are we allowed, and also in extreme circumstances," he explained.

An annoying ache in the back of my head began to throb. I'd had too many strong visions lately. I stepped gingerly toward the hallway. I never knew when another image would hit me.

Tremayne followed me on silent feet, so I turned around to face him.

He made an annoyed sound with his tongue. "I'm not hunting you."

"Right," I said. "You go on ahead. I'll follow."

With a sigh, he relented and strode forward.

Three doors opened up along the short hallway, and I knew that the one I wanted was second from the end. I paused in front of the door, not sure I really wanted to do this.

Tremayne reached past me and opened the door for me. I paused to gather myself. Only once before had I gone into a room where someone had died—not murdered, but died—and it seemed so sad to me; it had depressed me for weeks. It had been the only other time when I had fainted dead away, and had been in bed for three days. How would I confront a murder scene?

Tremayne stood beside me, waiting patiently. I glanced up at him, but looked away quickly.

"I know," he began gently, "that it is difficult for you to continue. I have had various clairvoyants in the past that would go into deep trances. This is going to be difficult for you, I understand that. Take your time. But perhaps I can persuade you to continue? I will pay you a thousand dollars for your read, tonight, on top of the wages promised to you."

I blinked, astonished.

"I'll write you a check," he added. "Free and clear. No matter what the outcome. Even if you get zip."

I knew this was important to him. And another thousand dollars would definitely help pad my savings and checking account.

I took a deep breath, gave my head a little shake, and took a step forward. As I did, the lights flicked on inside the room—motion sensitive lights, I presumed. The bed was large, done in a soft peach, some ribbons of beige and cream with a leaf motif woven throughout. The headboard was huge, in dark cherry and simple design. The room was conservatively modern. There were no windows, obviously, because she was a vampire. But there was a balcony, with a sliding glass doorway, like in the main living room. The glass was darkened, for obvious reasons, with creamy sheers, pulled back, revealing the night sky and lights of tall buildings nearby.

I walked toward the bed and looked around. This was a woman's room. I could smell her scent—the perfume she used; fragrant without being overwhelming. Gentle, almost like an ocean breeze. Ah, of course, Tremayne's favorite.

I slowly pulled off my gloves, feeling a little bit of pressure in my chest when I did. I didn't understand that. I had to take a few more deep breaths. I sensed Tremayne behind me, watching me, but trying not to interfere with what I was doing. In fact, he was trying to stay out of my way so as not to interfere with my read. He understood this part of it, and I was glad of it.

I watched Letitia saunter around in her apartment. She had stepped out of the shower, her hair was still wet, and the wavy dark lengths spilled down her back. She slipped into a light peach robe. A glass of her favorite wine—yes, wine—stationed on the bedside table awaiting her, the glass sweating slightly.

The evening was soft, and she wanted to step out onto the balcony. I moved, almost mirroring her motions.

"She stepped out onto the balcony, after her shower," I said over my shoulder. I wanted Tremayne to know what I was seeing. "She wore a peach robe and night gown..." I continued toward the sliding glass doors. For some reason I was unaffected by my fears of only moments ago, and stepped out into the night air, felt the chill hit my face, a stiff breeze brush my hair back. We were ninety-seven floors up—the top floor—and the many tall buildings of the Chicago skyline surrounded me, and Letitia. I stopped and breathed in the chilly night air. A crisp, clear autumn night, with a moon sliding overhead like a pale lover's face. I was still with Letitia, with her ghostly presence. She was happy, enjoying the moment. She had fed on the blood of one of her male donors while having sex with him—oh! There had been three of them—and she was feeling quite marvelous. I could almost feed off her elation and relaxation from wonderful, repeated sex.

"She was here," I said, and reached out to the balcony railing. When I touched it, everything slammed into me all at once. Something hit me like a stabbing jolt in the chest. I screamed. It hurt like living hell.

Chapter 12

The sensation of cool fingers against my temple gave me a start, and I jumped. Tremayne jerked back, his physical contact with me broken. I now stared back at him. This was exactly what Leif had done last night; fingers to my temple, manipulating my brain functions, somehow short circuiting the overload of information to it. The vampire-mind-manipulating thing, again. I knew that this was all that kept me from going right into La-La-Land. I appreciated it, really I did. But somehow the idea of a vampire touching my mind like that, so intimately, gave me big-time willies. What else could he be doing in there? Giving me subliminal messages?

I moved to sit up.

"Slow, slowly," he cautioned, helping me. He propped plump pillows behind my back. "How do you feel?"

"I'm—" I looked around. This wasn't Letitia's penthouse. I was in some other place entirely. Not a bedroom, surely. The place was dark, with dark furnishings, dark wood, dark green carpet. Cave-like. I had envisioned Tremayne's place looking exactly like this. Heads of animals—trophies—hung on the wall; gazelles, lions, zebras, and other things I didn't know the names of.

"Is this your place?"

He sat back on the ottoman. "Yes."

Someone behind him handed him a glass of water. His face was a network of wrinkles, head balding. He had kind, gray eyes that looked sincerely worried about me.

"Master, is the young lady going to be alright?" he asked.

"Yes, James," Tremayne said as he held the glass of water to my lips. "Drink."

I did. The water was cold, and I could tell it came from a bottle, not the tap.

I was still unused to vampires ministering to me or mind-melding whenever I fainted from a read.

I handed the empty glass to Tremayne, he handed it back to James.

"Thank you, James. Leave us."

At Tremayne's words, the human servant, James, bowed slightly, and left.

Tremayne looked back at me anxiously. I had it all still in my head, and I wanted badly to purge it.

"She turned toward a sound, I think," I began. "She was startled, I could feel her tension, and then there was someone there. Someone all in black. A man, swooping down—somehow?" I said this as a question, because I wasn't sure, and my over-worked brain was trying to tell me I'd missed something. But what? "I saw the crossbow in his hands." I paused. "She was shot, in the heart."

"He came down from above, then," he said in a harsh hiss. "You saw nothing else? Not his face?"

"No," I said, closing my eyes momentarily. "He was covered totally, head to foot in black. I see him kneeling over her—oh!"

"What?" he hissed. "What else do you see?"

"I think he may have drunk her blood." I frowned deeply. I had to shake my head; that was totally disgusting.

"What was that?" Tremayne asked, noticing my expression.

"He drank from the wound in her chest." I suddenly shivered from the thought.

Tremayne straightened to his full height. Eyes blazing, he bellowed a word I'd never heard before. I only knew it wasn't English. Anger was too soft a word to describe the emotion going through him at this point. He looked like he could kill something with his bare hands right then. I didn't like that I was the only person—a human—in the room with him. I wanted to melt back into the sofa and become a small speck of lint.

"I'm sorry," I all but whispered, as though I were the cause of everything.

Great hands balled into fists, looking like sledge hammers hung at his sides. He took a few deep breaths, letting each one out shakily. His shoulders moved up and down, his back expanding and contracting as he did. The shoulders relaxed, head came up—his golden hair falling like a waterfall in the sun, rippling down his back. He let out a breath and on it a single word, in that other language.

Slowly, his gaze fell on me and it took my breath away. "No need to apologize, Ms. Strong," he said, finding a gentle voice. "You have accurately described Letitia's condition when I found her. Her heart *had* been drained of blood. I have told no one about this. No one," he repeated. "Not even Nicolas."

I passed the Litmus test. Big gold star for me.

"Wouldn't that be a lot of blood to drink?" I asked, a little amazed, remembering from biology that a human body held five quarts of blood (it was on a biology test and this bit of information I'd retained for some odd reason). I wondered if a vampire held that much too.

"Not really," he said, glancing at me. "A vampire holds much less blood than you might think. On a daily basis we can get by with anywhere from one pint, to four." I blinked at his explanation. "It depends upon our activities, during our waking hours. And it is flushed through the system on a daily basis."

"I see." And now I knew why vampires had their own toilets. I guess it all had to go somewhere.

"There are reservoirs in the heart, stomach, brain and sex organs," he went on. "The heart being the largest. The stomach sends it to various places as needed, but the heart would be the place to bleed a vampire first."

I was having trouble not grimacing with his clinical and detailed explanation. I had one more question, however, and thought I'd better ask before I got side-tracked. "Would a vampire drink the blood of another vampire?"

"No. Not to feed upon, anyway." Turning, he stepped away from me. "We do so only when we want to control a weaker vampire, or when one of us is mortally wounded—both things that you have witnessed tonight, Ms. Strong." His movement was inhuman. Liquid. One moment he was beside me; the next, he was a few feet away from me. "No," he said this word more softly. "A vampire would have nothing to gain from drinking large quantities of blood from another vampire."

"How about a human?" I remembered what Toby had said to me that first morning that vampire blood could make a person high.

"Possibly," he said, swiveling his head around to regard me. "We do hear about vampire blood being sold on the street from time to time. Humans get a high from vampire blood. It's short-lived, but it's a high. However, drinking too much vampire blood can turn a person."

"Really? How much is too much?"

"It's more a matter of ingestion on consecutive nights, as well as the amount." He paused, and then asked, "Is it possible he took some into a syringe? Or somehow siphoned some into a container?"

"I'm sorry; I didn't see anything like that. The vision simply ended." I sat up, and swung my legs over the edge of the sofa and sat there momentarily waiting for the head spins to quit. "I wish I could have seen more."

"You have done well, Sabrina." His voice had a little catch in it, then. He cleared it. "Our murderer is more cunning than I had anticipated." He turned back around to face me. He brought the tips of his fingers together and moved them toward his lips, as if in prayer. He was deep in thought for a moment. I didn't interrupt him. "I have the bolt," he said. "I will have you touch it. See if it helps you identify him."

"It won't," I said, feeling really nervous again. I found my gloves next to me on the coffee table and I pulled them on, clenching and unclenching my hands, feeling the material become taught around my fingers and knuckles. Their protection in place, relief washed over me.

"Why?" He gave me a harsh, critical look then.

"It will only give me the most immediate information—of it going into the person's body."

"Very well, then." He stepped toward me, then held his large hand out to me. I took it, glad that I'd re-placed my gloves on my hands, and he helped me to my feet.

He was holding an envelope before me.

"The money I promised you," he said.

Flicking my gaze from it back up at him, I took the envelope, resisting the urge to open it right away. My mind had it all spent in a matter of a millisecond before my plans were disrupted by Tremayne's deep velvet voice.

"Sabrina, I will pay you one hundred thousand dollars more if you reveal the murderer to me."

I think my jaw dropped to the floor at that. All my money problems would be solved in one felled swoop—for years to come. Possibly a life time if I didn't spend it on anything crazy.

"I can't promise you," I said finally. "I never know if what I'm going to get are emotions, or a face, or like what I saw back in there." I motioned with my hand, meaning back in Letitia's penthouse. "Also, I don't know if it's the past, present, or the future, either."

He returned his blue-green gaze. "Nevertheless, do we have a deal? My promise to you is solid. You reveal his identity to me, I will pay you. But I want you to promise me one thing in return."

I paused. Thoughts of sudden wealth fading. I knew there had to be a catch. "What?"

"Stay on—with me—in my alliance. I will allow you to come and go as you wish."

My mouth went dry. What was he saying? Come and go as I wish? Didn't I already? And what did he mean about staying on with him in his alliance? Did he mean in his firm? I already worked for him.

I worried that he had other plans for me that had nothing whatsoever to do with my clairvoyant talents.

"I don't think I understand what you mean," I pressed.

Brushing a hand through his thick mane to pull lengths of it out of his face, he straightened. His eyes pulled me in. I suddenly forgot what the conversation was about. It's an odd feeling to have a vampire blank your mind, and although I knew he had, I had no will to protest.

"I'm hungry. Are you hungry?" he asked.

"I am. A little." I said, unsure.

"What are you up for?" he asked, gliding through the penthouse on silent feet. A man his size should make the whole floor shake with every step. Not him. "Lobster? Or, perhaps a nice porterhouse steak?"

Suddenly, I was keenly aware that I was hungry. The peanut butter sandwich I'd had earlier was gone. His mention of food really sabotaged my desire to get the hell out of there. Damn him. Could he have put that into my mind as well? Probably.

We headed out of his penthouse, and went straight for the elevator. Getting on, we took our respective positions across from one another once again.

We began our journey downward when I had a blank moment. I knew I must have had some residual vision because I was now up against him, almost like we were dancing, but we were still in the elevator.

"Are you all right?" his deep voice vibrated in my ears, and against my palms.

I snapped to. Blinking up at him, realizing my hands were on his chest. I yanked my hands off him, and tried to back away, but he still had me in his grasp. Our eyes locked for a few more seconds. My fingers memorized those muscular contours.

"What?" I was terribly confused.

"You said something about a black bag."

"I did? Just now?" I tried to pull away, but he held me close.

"Yes."

"Where?"

"I don't know," he said sounding frustrated.

"The garage," I said, squinting, my surroundings fading in and out. "That's where Solange got her clothes and the crossbow. Look in the garage, by a pylon, near where she was found."

"Solange?"

"The cat-woman. That's her name. Look down there and you'll find the black bag."

Chapter 13

The sign for Earthly Pleasures filled my vision and I hesitated. I was going to dinner with a vampire. Again. I'd sit and eat, while Tremayne would drink from a wine glass of some sort, and I would know all along it was blood. Damn it all. I wanted to go home. But, I needed a ride back. Would he allow me to bow out like this, now?

Tremayne turned and gave me a look.

"What is it?" he asked, frown creasing the area between his brows.

"I'm not exactly hungry."

"I think you are," he said, looking at his watch. "You must be! It's nearly ten o'clock. I'm sure it's been hours since you've eaten."

I hesitated.

"What is it?"

I couldn't voice my thoughts.

"Sabrina, like it or not, you are now part of my realm. What I ask of you, from this moment on, you will do without question."

I frowned. "What am I now, your property because you paid me?"

People around us were gaping at us, hearing our argument. I didn't know if they were humans or vampires and I really didn't care at this point.

"No," he said, a stern coldness in his eyes, which had suddenly turned more gray than blue. Lowering his voice he dipped his head toward me. "You are a powerful clairvoyant. Hell, do you think I'm the only vampire in the state—in the whole country, hell, maybe the whole fucking world—who was looking for you? And there you were, right in my realm. Nicolas seized upon the moment to hire you because if he didn't someone else would have."

I was startled by his words. "What do you mean? I answered an ad in the paper!"

"Right," he said. "Whatever you want to believe. Another vampire enclave would have pounced on you, and believe me, out of all the other power-hungry vampires you could have wound up with, I'm not the worst of them. I at least offered you salary, up front"—he counted off his fingers—"gave you freedom to come and go as you wish, benefits, even offered you the usual perks only my entourage gets."

"Oh, yes, how I love the perks," I said, folding my arms. "I can't leave when I want to. Some perk."

"Leave?"

"Go home," I clarified.

"Home?" he repeated. "I need to get a few things straight with you before you go home tonight, sweetheart."

"Like what?" We were having a heated debate in the middle of a mall. People were walking by with shopping bags in their hands, gaping at us. I could only guess what they thought. Four, or five young women slipped past us giggling, heading into the restaurant. I couldn't help but notice they were looking at Tremayne wantonly. They were dressed to the nines, and every one of them was pretty. Tremayne made no eye contact with them whatsoever. He was intent on me.

"Vasyl has bit you and now is calling to you, and that concerns me a great deal more than anything else, right now," he said with a gush of impatience. "Let's go inside. I have my own private room. We need to talk about this."

I would have gone numb at his mentioning Vasyl, except for his last words to me. In all my haste to get away I'd forgotten that I needed him to help me find Vasyl—or at least try and get Jeanie back somehow. How was I going to face a dangerous, "crazy" vampire and demand he release my friend without other vampires to back me up? God I was lame sometimes.

A sound bite of music interrupted us. Tremayne's cell phone was in his hand and he answered it swiftly and trekked through the entrance of Earthly Pleasures. I surged to catch up. Tremayne's cell phone to his ear, he was barking orders for someone to get down to the garage and look for a black bag.

The same hostess as last night spotted Tremayne and picked up one menu—the human one.

"Mr. Tremayne, very delighted you could join us, this evening," the hostess said, trying it in a husky voice as she sailed out from around her little booth but it ended in a hurried, breathless one as she had to trot to keep up with us. "Your guest is human tonight?" she asked unnecessarily, giving me a quick little smirk as she dashed ahead of me like a sprinter.

"Yes," he said, slipping his phone back into its holder on his belt, long strides taking him well ahead of us.

"Your usual room is ready," she almost shouted, as she led me through the dining area, Tremayne was nearly through to the end of the room, ignoring her. His gate easy and smooth. Predatory. Every eye in the place followed us—well, him, anyway. I was the dressing. Probably they all thought I was his newest donor. They could think whatever they liked. Of course, Tremayne being who he was, and as tall as he was would stand out in any crowd if not merely for his sheer size.

A mixed crowd, tonight. Some tables held only vampires, and some held only humans. But there were places where humans and vampires shared a table. I had to presume some were donor-dates, or something along that line. I had a lot to learn and understand about modern vampires. I was getting a real education tonight.

We stepped by one table ringed by five young women—the same ones who had passed us out in the hall. Their eyes followed Tremayne's progress. Each of them was dressed in revealing dresses with spaghetti strings, or something that scooped dramatically to reveal their neck and cleavage. Their giggles sounding like tinkling wind chimes, as we walked by.

To me, all of them looked like call girls waiting to score. But the dark circles under their eyes, and clear bite marks on their necks told me differently. *Donors.*

I glanced back at them, and one stared right into my eyes. Embarrassed, I dropped my gaze and walked along a little more swiftly.

By this time the hostess had caught up to Tremayne and held open the curtain to a private room, and allowed and me to step in and then Tremayne ducked through. The table was much like the other tables in the restaurant, except larger, and his chair was more like a throne of carved wood; heavier than other chairs, with arms, and a high back and generously padded with red velvet. *Only the best for the master vampire of his empire.* But once he sat in it I realized no ordinary chair would hold his massive body. He would look ridiculous in a regular-sized chair. He was very much like a modern-day athlete who was too tall, or too large for ordinary furnishings—or clothes.

The oddest thing about the room, however, was a padded bench that encircled three walls. Red velvet cushions, lots of gold, black, and crimson pillows in every shape, size and design resided along this continuous couch. It appeared decorative in an innocuously pleasant way.

But, as with every new room I entered, my brain was feeding me visions of what transpired in this one with great regularity. I saw women lounging upon these pillows, smiles upon their lips, with expressions of sheer bliss on their faces. The vision vanished almost as soon as it came to me. I had to shake my head to clear it of the sudden dizziness.

"Your server will be with you in a moment," the hostess purred as she set the menu before me. She turned to Tremayne and bowed. "When you are ready, the offerings await you," she said low to Tremayne. Then, with a graceful turn, she exited.

Tremayne leaned over the table and said, "Have whatever you want. I want you to enjoy yourself."

Yeah, in present company—not gonna happen.

I opened the menu.

In a few moments a young man with black hair glided up to our table. I was startled when I looked up to see Steve. "Hello. My name is Steve, and I'll be your server tonight, Mr. Tremayne, and Ms. Strong. May I take your orders, please?" he said while into a bow, showing Tremayne the greatest reverence.

"Take the lady's order first," Tremayne said to him, thrusting his large hand out toward me. "I will take my repast in a little while."

"Very well, my lord," Steve said.

"Hi, Steve," I said. Steve gave me a side glance. His movements to fill the water glasses well-choreographed, yet, I noticed his hands shook a bit. Nervous?

"Good evening, Ms. Strong, may I suggest the prime rib? It's the house special tonight. The other humans tell me it is quite delicious," Steve said.

"Prime Rib?" I said, and wrinkled my nose at the thought of a rare piece of meat floating in red juices. Then I caught Tremayne's arched brow.

"Okay, but well done," I said, folding the menu closed. I gave him the rest of my order—salad with raspberry dressing, rice, not potato, and hell with it, I went with a burgundy.

Steve turned to Tremayne for his order. "Real Red for you tonight, my lord?"

"Not now," he said, lifting his fingers from the chair's armrest to dismiss him, his other hand pressed into his cheek, elbow resting on the other armrest, smoldering eyes resting on me.

I should have been relieved he wasn't ordering, but somehow I wasn't. It had everything to do with the vision I'd had when we'd stepped inside this private dining area. I had a funny feeling in the pit of my stomach I was going to actually get to witness it—whatever actually happened in this room.

Steve took my menu and was gone. But as he left, he dropped and closed the drapes of the room.

"You know Steve?" he said, eyes looking slightly suspicious.

"Uh, yeah. He was with Nicolas the first night I met him."

His eyes went off me in thought. "I see. He must have wanted to keep him nearby," he said distractedly. "He's a newbie." He waved a dismissive hand.

Soft piped-in music interrupted by the distant clinking of silverware and china, the give and take of conversation somewhere outside our little world, the only other sounds. That, and possibly my knees knocking and my heartbeat thrumming, and no doubt Tremayne could hear that, too.

"I spoke to Nicolas a moment ago," Tremayne informed, coming out of his distracted expression.

"Yes?" I reached for the water glass. I took a couple of gulps from it, wishing it was a glass of wine.

"They finished questioning the woman. Her name is Solange—as you'd said. She's from L.A., and as you so brilliantly detected with your powers—is a shiftchanger. She'd changed into a cat to gain entrance into the garage."

I nodded. Swallowing, I replaced my glass. "What about the bag?"

"Leif and Darla have gone down to find it." He went on swiftly, "She wasn't aiming for Heath, by the way. She was aiming for you."

Shocked, I stared at him open mouthed. "What? Me?"

Tremayne drummed the fingers of his free hand on the arm-rest. "Yes. My educated guess is that our killer knows about you, and wants you out of the way. You are the only one who can identify him with your clairvoyant powers." He shifted in his chair, staring intently at me. "Anyway, I've been informed Solange was bitten. My guess is a rogue vampire is behind this." His gaze went off me, looking pensive.

"But I thought we agreed that the killer was a human."

"The one who shot Letitia, yes. But the master-mind behind this must be a vampire. A human can't be hypnotized to the point of killing another person, unless they were already a murderer. No. She was enthralled by a vampire. At any rate, we've identified our little shiftchanger as Solange LaPrima. She's from L.A. and that's all we got from her. Her mind's been blanked of anything else."

"And you're saying a vampire bit her and sent her here?"

"Yes, sent her here to shoot you." He squeezed his eyes. "I don't like that they knew where to wait for you. Or what you looked like." He made a weary sigh. "I hate turf wars. But I have no idea who is behind this. That's why I've hired you, Sabrina."

Wonderful. I had no idea vampires had wars. *Where was that damned wine?* Picking up the glass with a shaky hand, I sipped more water instead.

Tremayne leaned forward. "I would suggest you staying here, but since our killer knows the ins and outs of this building as well as I myself, it would be a bad idea."

"I agree." My heart was thumping madly. I glanced at the closed drapes. *Where is Steve with my wine?*

"Therefore, I will put a bodyguard on you. Someone who can be with you day and night."

"Who?" I didn't relish the thought of someone shadowing my every move. "Not Nicolas?"

"No. Not Nicolas." He placed one huge hand on the table. My eyes were drawn to it, as though it were some exotic part of his body. Perfect, it appeared to be chiseled out of marble by the most adept sculptor. I looked up to engage his wary eyes.

"Sabrina. Understand, you aren't a donor," he said in a quieter voice. "You're a super-sensitive. If you weren't so special, I wouldn't keep Nicolas from taking you as his own. You understand that for a vampire the needs for blood and sex are equal?"

"Yes." My whole body quaked.

"Some of us can't separate the two. But know this, Sabrina; I never confuse a meal with a lay. If I want to feed, I feed. If I want to fuck, I fuck." He was tapping his finger on the table to make his point. It sounded like he was hammering a nail.

Stunned, heat rushed into my face at his bluntness. His eyes were keen, like cold twin oceans wanting to wash over me. I forced my gaze downward.

"Sabrina. Look at me."

I made a little helpless gasp as I fought against him, but ultimately he won and I couldn't help but bring my eyes back up; tears pooling. I wanted out. But I couldn't move. I really, *really* was unable to move any group of leg muscles in order to get up from the chair. It was as though he'd tied me to it.

"I am the master over every vampire here in my realm. This includes all of eastern United States. I get first choice. And I want *you*," he said calmly, almost dispassionately. "Not for blood. Though I'd like to sample it, of course."

My throat constricted. I grabbed the water glass again and sipped cool relief. But it only alleviated the dry throat, not my discomfort concerning the vampire before me. My legs were still non-respondent.

"Don't be so surprised, Sabrina." He smiled, made a half-scathing, half-chuckle sound.

I wanted to jump up and dash out of there. I should have screamed at him, or thrown a drink in his face. Something. But I couldn't. I found myself helpless in the lap of his glamor. It was like he had found a tuning fork inside me and he'd hit it *just* right, and I was really humming. A warm surge of pleasure shuddered through me, making me tingle, turning into a delicious throb began between my legs, shocking me.

What the hell?

I stared at him, helpless and breathless, trying to mount a comeback or an insult, but nothing came.

He sat back slightly, and I saw something leave his face, all the determination, or *something* simply left it. Also, his eyes looked different. And then his thrall lifted as though it had never been. Yep. He was a dangerously powerful vampire if all he had to do was look at me and, *boom*, I wanted to be his whore. I should have given the check back to him but I needed the money.

Finally the words came. So did the anger. I trembled as I sat there working my mouth. "I won't work for someone who wants to control me. Especially like that."

"That's good to know, Sabrina," he said, his tone had taken on a lighter quality, but I read the look of resigned tolerance, and sarcasm in the grin. "Since you've been bitten by Vasyl, and he's been calling to you, you need to know exactly what you're up against. I had to show you what *I* can do. Like me, Vasyl is a master, and is just as strong. And he's not going to let you go if you go to him."

"But he has Jeanie!"

"I know!" he all but growled. "He took her because you ignored his call. That bite must really burn like a bitch." He nodded at my arm. "I'm surprised he didn't crash into your bedroom to fuck and bite you. The invitation must have worn off, or changed because you didn't originally invite him inside."

I gasped at his blunt words. Frustrated, I blurted, "Who the hell is he?"

"He's not like any vampire I know."

"Why?"

"He's—" he broke off to gasp at what he was about to say. "He's *religious*." He said it as though the very thought was detestable.

"A religious vampire?" I said, my voice flat, disbelieving.

"Yes, he is. I've heard that he wears crucifixes. At any rate, he doesn't conform to our rules; he more or less defies them—as far as he can go, in fact."

"Crucifixes? A vampire?"

"Yes. Or so I've been told."

"Wow." I glanced down at the table, trying to get my mind around that.

"Most likely he's looking for the sibyl—" his words were interrupted as Steve swooped through the drapes at that precise moment with my meal, and—*thank you!*—my glass of wine. What timing. I nearly wanted to kiss him—*not*.

I stared at the plate of food, as he slid it before me. It looked less appealing than the thought of it was before when I'd ordered. I eyed the basket of steaming bread and slab of butter and pounced on it at once.

"Anything for you, Master?" Steve bowed to him.

"Yes," Tremayne said, an odd curl to his lip. "Bring in my disciples. Send them all."

"Of course, master." Steve threw me an uncomfortable look, bowed and left the room.

I dug into my meal, not exactly knowing what was about to happen, and, not wanting to go hungry the rest of the night, I gobbled some of everything down, and took sips of wine in between. I was surprised I liked the not-so rare prime rib. I'd never tried it before. *Maybe I'll have this more often!*

I gazed over at Tremayne as I took a big quaff of wine. He was undoing his tie, then removed it completely. Folding it neatly, he set it on the table before himself, reminding me of the undressing ritual Nicolas had gone through tonight before he bit Steve in that blood ritual. I halted a choice piece of prime rib to my mouth when he unbuttoned three or four buttons. This revealed plenty of chest hairs that disappeared seductively behind the rest of his shirt. I could almost envision him as a Viking warrior, swinging a club or a broad sword. Dashing, like a damned pirate who was all about himself and what he wanted—treasure, and women.

"What are you doing? A striptease?" I'd said it before I realized it came out of my mouth. He chuckled darkly, like he knew what he was about to do would send my senses reeling again.

"I think you'd enjoy that," he said, smirk in place. He stood, and moved his chair back a little ways, as though he needed the room. "What you're about to witness is a special treat, Sabrina. I don't allow humans to watch this. Only those who are chosen share this with me."

Forewarned, I grabbed the glass of wine and took another healthy swallow, ate another piece of bread—after swabbing it through my plate of meat juices. Whatever was to come next, I could only guess, having seen the vision of women lying back, looking as though they were in the throes of some sort of ecstasy brought on by Tremayne's bite.

The curtain parted with a hand, and five women sauntered in, making a slight bow to him. Each one was greeted by Tremayne as they marched in, one by one. "Celeste, Jessica, Jasmine, Ashley, Chastity. Good evening."

As they stepped past him, they took me in with glares like I was competition. One woman's eyes locked on mine. This time I didn't look away. I could feel the heat of her gaze, like she wanted to hurt me somehow. I breathed in and then let it out steadily. I could play this staring game too. Finally, she flinched and her gaze went to my hands. The gloves. Her eyes flicked back to my face, and she looked away. Maybe she suddenly realized who I was. I was in the upper echelon of Tremayne's inner circle. I wasn't a frigging donor like she was.

"Ladies?"

All five turned to him.

A shiver went through me with anticipation.

The women formed a circle around Tremayne. Waiting. Tremayne's eyes went soft. He made a complete turn within their circle. Then he dipped to one—a blond with red highlights—and took her chin in his hand.

As though some silent command went through the other four, they all silently stepped to the divan and arranged themselves on it; long, willowy legs crossed, their eyes expectantly on Tremayne and the girl he'd chosen.

Unable to help myself, I watched, too. My stomach did a flip as he stepped behind the girl who faced us all. Her head lolled back into his hands, his large fingers slipping through that bountiful golden mane.

Tremayne's eyes slid shut, lips curled back and then he opened his mouth wide, and I saw the fangs grow from his mouth. Large. Pointed. Deadly. I sat enthralled. I couldn't move if I'd wanted to, and funny, but I couldn't tell if I were merely mesmerized by Tremayne, or by what he was about to do to the girl. It was sort of like knowing two cars were going to collide, but you still had to watch it in all its glorified horror.

He made a low purr in the back of his throat, holding her head against his chest. Head dipping, I watched his tongue slide from her shoulder up the column of her neck, insanely slow. The woman's eyes fluttered open as she released a shuttering gasp, waiting, as if her toes were on the edge of a diving board, waiting for someone to say "fall".

Tremayne's head pulled back, eyes closed, as though he were enjoying prolonging this ordeal for some reason.

Then it happened. His neck arched. Eyes filled with a haunting, golden-red cast. Fangs fully exposed, he speared down on her exposed, delicate white neck.

The room filled with the girl's sudden shriek, and Tremayne's growl.

He withdrew his fangs almost the moment he'd impaled her. Twin crimson rivulets ran from the girl's neck, until he lapped at them from behind with a large, cat-like tongue—he never sucked at the wound, but actually allowed it to flow and he lapped it up. The girl stiffened against him, gasping delicately, still unable to do anything, except to quiver and groan in his arms while he lapped at her blood.

Finally, after a few minutes, the wounds winked closed. I experienced shock waves shuttering through me while I watched the girl wither in his arms like a dainty flower. Tremayne let her gently down onto an empty spot on the divan to the other side of the room.

An overwhelming panic had me in its grip. He put out a hand toward the other four, in a welcoming way. I couldn't speak. I couldn't move. But I sure wanted to. I wanted to yell at the top of my lungs *STOP.*

"Jasmine," he said.

Without hesitation, the pretty and petite Oriental girl slinked toward him. The same thing happened; he bent and licked along her slim neck. She moaned a little more excitely than the last one, as though he had actually pierced her skin, when he hadn't—yet. When it happened, she let out a scream, and then her whole body went into wild convulsions as he licked the blood that trickled down her porcelain neck. One of his hands slid up her dress, his hand to her crotch, making her buck a little more. I had to close my eyes at this perversion. It was like watching two people in the privacy of their own bedroom.

When he was finished with her, he settled her onto the couch near the first girl. They both wore that odd expression on their faces, like they'd had the best sex in their life, but it was more than that, and I simply didn't get it.

He chose the third one in the same way.

I wanted to leave—vanish into thin air. I couldn't move, though. It was like I'd been tied to the chair—or still was. I was locked into watching this repulsive act, viewing it like someone who's made to watch some porno flick again, and again, and again. I knew then that Tremayne was commanding me as much as he was commanding the other girls there in the room. I sure had to admire his ability to multi task.

When he was finished with the third one, and set her down on the divan, I expected him to take the fourth girl and do the same thing. He didn't. Instead, he grabbed his open shirt and ripped it open all the way, letting it fall off his shoulders to flutter to the floor. Head back, mouth open, he let go a primal roar. It scared me half to death, and I figured it had to have the rest of the people in the restaurant running for cover.

And then the most extraordinary thing happened. Invisible veins beneath that opalescent skin suddenly darkened, as though filling in with the blood of the donors. Each vein snaked and course down this arms, his chest and neck—everywhere. Then his skin turned back to white, and began to glow, like he'd swallowed the moon. Light poured from him, like a low-watt bulb, and then it intensified briefly, so brilliant I had to look away. After a few seconds, when the light faded, I looked again. He appeared normal once more. Vampire-white with a rosy hue. He also looked more robust, if that were possible.

Almost… god-like.

Emotions swelled inside me. Tears welled up in my eyes as though I'd witnessed some sort of miracle. Like watching a glorious, rare and beautiful sunset, or a beautiful double rainbow, and then have it *touch* me in a meaningful, emotionally-charged way.

As much as I wanted to believe he had merely glamored me, my brain told me this was the real deal. I had witnessed something that had taken place from the beginning. Something prehistoric, in fact. Vampires had been with man down through time, and he wanted me to see this so I would know and understand who and what he was—that's why he'd made me come to this room.

While I was going through this emotional thrall, the two girls who had not been chosen, jumped up, surged forward, and then fell to their knees before him.

I sat in absolute awe questioning what they were doing.

Face relaxed, Tremayne's eyes slid to me. Hands hung limp at his sides, now in desperate grasps by the two frenzied girls at his feet. Kissing his hands, they chimed, "You live, you live, you live... take us, take us now!" continuously, like a chant.

"Sabrina," Tremayne said low, but I could hear it above the women's little chanting. "You have witnessed the blessing. The blood of my disciples now courses through my veins." He drew the two girls to their feet, and wrapped large arms about them. They all turned as one, and strolled toward the opening.

"Have a good evening," he said over his shoulder to me.

Chapter 14

Numbed to the core, I sat staring as a tray of orange juice in glass goblets was ushered in and dispensed to the three remaining girls still lounging with the afterglow.

I didn't know how long I'd been sitting there when the curtains were drawn back once again.

I looked up. Nicolas stood there evaluating the situation. Our eyes met.

Leif sidled up beside him, looking momentarily flabbergasted at the sight. "Tremayne's blood dolls," he choked out, then looked to Nicolas for a clue. "She didn't become one, did she?" he asked, leaning toward Nicolas as he spoke low.

"No, I don't—" A troubled expression crossed Nicolas' face. His gaze flitted from the three girls and then to me. "You witnessed?" he asked, astonished. He obviously knew what had overcome them, because his bite probably did the same thing to his donors. He could plainly see the bite marks and some little blood trails left on their necks that Tremayne hadn't lapped up. Oh, yes, and the looks of ecstasy on their faces. Whereas I had none of these tell-tale hallmarks.

"I guess," I rasped. Standing unsteadily, I eased past two girls still lounging back on the couch. I certainly didn't want to brush against them, lest I get some sort of visual, or an emotion off them.

"Then you must have impressed the hell out of him," Leif said, stepping aside.

I blinked at him as I pulled up. "What?"

"Tremayne wouldn't have allowed you to see that, not unless he was impressed with you, and felt you were trustworthy enough," he explained.

"You mean you don't all glow like that when you bite someone?" I asked, pushing through the curtains angrily.

Nicolas and Leif drew up beside me on either side. "No," they answered in unison.

"We aren't masters and old as hell, like he is," Leif explained with a smirk.

I glanced back into the room. The emotions I'd felt while in there now lifted. I was relieved to be away from there.

I followed Leif and Nicolas through the restaurant, into the atrium, where Darla joined us. I saw a back bag in Darla's hand.

"Is that the bag you found down in the garage?" I asked her.

Leif took the bag from her and turned to regard me. "Oh, yeah. Tremayne told us to go and find it. It was near where Heath was shot. Why? What's it all about?"

Nicolas shifted from his spot next to me, staring at the bag.

"It's the one that Solange got her clothes and the crossbow from," I said, sliding my gaze from one to the other.

"Really?" He held it out to me. "You want to have a go, then? See who put it there for her?"

I glanced at him and then at the bag, but didn't move toward it. I regarded Nicolas. He seemed strangely silent.

"If I find out who it is, what will happen to him—or her?"

"It depends upon whether he is a vampire or a human," Nicolas said after a few seconds.

"If it's a vampire?" I asked, my eyes shifting to take in Leif's expression. The old saying that if looks could kill, I knew what the answer was right away.

"We will deal with him within our own laws," Nicolas said clinically. "Causing the death or attempting to kill another vampire is a very serious crime."

"Eye for an eye," Darla sneered, and then licked her lips as though the idea was mouthwatering. I didn't care about vampires so much. They had their own laws.

"Then, if it's a human, we all agree that you'll question them, clean their memories, like you did Solange, and let them go?"

I got silent stares. Finally Nicolas said, "Yes, as long as it is a human, who has been under a vampire thrall."

"Okay." I stepped forward, pulling the glove off my hand, moving to touch the black nylon bag. I pulled in a breath, closed my eyes and grasped the handle. I let my breath slide through parted lips. I waited maybe a couple of heartbeats and the vision came; it wasn't powerful, or overly dramatic. I had to backward the scene from when Leif and Darla had found it, to Solange who'd touched it, right before that.

Then, I saw what I wanted.

A man took the bag out of his trunk. His car was an older red Honda Accord, parked in the underground garage. He stepped quickly to a dark area to a spot near a pylon where no one parks, and set it down. When he rose, I saw his face, and I knew his name.

I didn't recognize him. But the name was there. I opened my eyes seeing expectant gazes from the vampires.

"His name is Al Brisco. Human. I think he works in the hotel, on the human side," I said, and shook my head of the vision when it didn't clear right away. I glanced around to find Nicolas' hard gaze on me. Lips pressed into a harsh line, his eyes took us all in.

"A human? You're sure?" Leif said somewhat disappointed.

"Yes." I said, flicking my gaze back to Nicolas as I continued. "I saw his name tag. I—"

A sudden sound like someone ramming a fist through a wall made me jump. I glanced back, to find Leif extracting his fist from the hole in the wall, bits of wall crumbling and falling to the

193

floor sounding like small stones, as he did. The startling thing was, it wasn't drywall. It was mortar and brick.

"I'll kill him!" Leif growled, his body shifting toward the exit.

"No!" Nicolas was a blur, getting right in front of Leif before he could get far. They faced each other.

"Get out of my way!" Leif growled, trying to break his hold, but Nicolas held him with his greater power.

"No, Leif! I understand what you're feeling. Believe me."

"Let go!" Leif struggled against Nicolas. Their face-off made me back into the wall, where I felt relatively safe as long as no one took a punch at it.

"Leif! Get hold of yourself. Your brother lives!" Nicolas reminded him. In a milder tone, he said, "I assure you the bolt wasn't meant for your brother. It was meant for Sabrina."

Well, thanks for reminding us someone wants to kill me.

Leif's stiff posture eased, and he blew off a few calming breaths. "Fine." He jerked his hands away from Nicolas. "Fine. He's human. He must have a reason for doing this." Leif backed off a few paces, relenting to Nicolas, straightening his shirt and jacket.

"Ms. Strong?" Someone's voice nearby made me jump. With a hand to my chest, I turned to see a man in black standing three or four feet away.

"Oh, crap!" I blustered. "You scared me!"

"I'm sorry," Dante said, bemused smile on his face. "Are you ready?"

"For what?" I asked somewhat irritated.

"I'm to take you home."

I gaped with my mouth open, unable to comprehend.

"Then I will say goodnight to you." Nicolas stepped in front of me, clearly putting himself between myself and Dante, nudging the shifter away. I was completely surprised and confused by his sudden interest in me, whereas before, he looked more ticked than affectionate toward me.

"Grasping my hands, he said, "I will call you. Later." He paused to glance back at Leif. "After I have taken care of our little problem." He then kissed the backs of my hands in a romantic way, sending shivers down my spine.

"Okay," I muttered. He leaned in and kissed me on the lips. Shocked by his attentions, a vision popped into my head. It was brief, but curious, and I couldn't piece it together while he was commanding my attention. The kiss ended, and he stepped away like a charming boyfriend.

I hoped that my sudden look of shock translated to the fact that he'd kissed me in front of everyone. What had actually shocked me was I'd gotten a brief vision of Nicolas with a beautiful woman. I stored it away.

"Yes. Later," I breathed, more out of relief.

"We need to leave, now, Ms. Strong," Dante's clear, deep voice reminded.

Chapter 15

Dante and I arrived at the garage in silence. We stepped along the exact place where my whole weird night had begun with Heath, Solange and Nicolas.

Stopping, I turned to see which way he was headed.

"This way." He moved off to another section. We stepped through a wide archway, while I pulled in faint exhaust fumes, oil, and other car smells.

Distractedly, I thought about my last vision—the one of the mysterious, beautiful blonde woman in Nicolas' head. I knew she was a vampire. I tried to pick out more details, but it had been so brief. I only knew that the two were having a conversation. Both their faces had seemed intense. Whatever they'd been discussing was important to them both. It had all the earmarks of some sort of deal. They shook hands at the end of it.

Other thoughts distracted me, as we walked. Assuming the faceless someone in my vision of Jeanie's abduction was Vasyl, why had he abducted her? Was he trying to piss me off? Because that worked.

Something about all this didn't fit. It was like putting together a puzzle that had all the wrong pieces—or missing pieces.

With these thoughts floating around in my head, as well as the dark thought as to what was happening to Al Brisco, and Solange this very moment, I nearly walked right into Dante, but stopped short. He glanced back at me. *God, he must think I'm a flake.*

We stood in front of a long row of cars. My boots scraped against the cement. Dante's were silent, wrapped in those moccasin-boots.

Two mustangs were parked side-by-side. Exactly same models, but one was white, the other was black. I had a definite vision of being inside the black one.

He hit the remote on his key chain.

The black car on the left started up with a roar, lights blinked on it everywhere, making it look as though a spacecraft had landed. My heart jumped, until I realized what had happened. I smiled. *Damn, I'm good.*

He stepped to the passenger side and opened the door for me.

"Cool car," I said, easing myself inside, slipping my butt across black leather.

"Thanks."

After closing my door, he jogged around and folded his frame behind the wheel. My eyes roamed the all-black interior, gazed at a dash and controls that looked as though it *could* take us up into space. I slid my gloved hands across the buttery leather seat. This was like all the other nice cars the vampires had.

Dante turned on the GPS and a map blipped up on a small screen. He was pressing some buttons on the control panel. "Where are we heading?"

"Oh," I said coming back down to Earth, and took in the fact I was in a muscle car, and this gorgeous guy was going to drive me home.

"My house? Yeah, get yourself on 290, to I-88, head west. I'll tell you when to get off."

"No. Give me an address. I'll punch it in," he said.

"Oh!" I rattled off my address.

He punched it out on the keypad. The GPS kicked in and a pleasant female voice told him exactly how to get to my house, complete with a map.

As soon as we were out into the open street, all my tensions eased from me. Dante slipped out a disk from somewhere inside his coat, inserted it into the CD player and on came this country swing music with a beat and a guy who had a country-twang voice. It was more than toe-tapping music. It made me want to kick up my heels.

We drove—well, he drove and I rode—without talking for quite a while. Dante was either not big on talk, or he was shy. But I knew he had to have questions for me, because I had some for him.

"So, your place," he said out of the blue, "is it big?"

"It's a big house. Yeah," I said somewhat startled.

"You have room then?" His question sounded somewhat hedging. I wondered why he was asking me about how big my house was.

"Yeah. Why?"

He glanced my way, then back to the road. "I'm wondering if you have a room for me? I mean to stay."

"Oh!" If I sounded startled, I was. "I—uh—I didn't realize that you'd be staying. But, yeah. I've got a room. My brother's old room."

"Yeah. That'd be perfect. When I need it, that is."

"Sure." I nodded, looking straight ahead. My palms began to sweat. I knew my face was red, because it felt hot. Good thing it was dark.

"You knew, didn't you?"

"Uh, yeah—I mean, well, I recall that someone said I'd be getting a body guard. I didn't put it together that you'd be staying at my place."

"That's sort of part of the job. I stick with you. Guard you. *Stay* with you." His sarcastic tone was sort of refreshing, after all the serious vampires I'd been with tonight.

"Right. Got it." I chuckled nervously. "They don't want me getting killed on the job, or when I'm at home."

"Yeah. I was told you had a visitor, last night?"

"Yeah. Nicolas couldn't find him." My mind suddenly went to the vision of the woman with Nicolas. This was going to bug me all night. I just knew it.

We became quiet again. We listened to the CD, until it ended. He didn't play anything else, and it became quiet as the miles swished by. I'm normally a quiet person, so if the other person I'm with isn't talkative, it gets pretty quiet. But I was curious about him. I decided I'd start with the obvious.

"So, you're Native American, right?" I know it probably sounded lame, and maybe a little silly of me to ask, but I didn't want to assume.

"Three-quarters," he said. "My dad was full-blood Lakota. My mother was part Italian."

"That's interesting." I nodded, pulling on the fingers of my gloves. "That's why the name?"

"Yep. She liked poetry. Don't know if she'd ever read anything of Dante's, though."

"You know it's a cool name. I mean, you don't run into someone with that name, and you sure don't expect him to be part Indian. Can I say that word without insulting you?"

"Why not?" he said. "We've been called everything from animals to devils. I hardly think the word *Indian* can hurt us any more than those did." He had stressed the word *Indian* a little bit, almost as though it were a vulgar word. I'd decided I wouldn't say it again in front of him. Native American, or Lakota, was all I'd refer to him as, other than Dante.

"I hear you," I said, treading carefully. I had done a paper in high school on Native Americans. My paper had centered on their treatment when white men first came to America, up to the present. The stories were not nice. In fact, some were horrifying.

"I understand you were bitten by a Were?" His question startled me a little bit, but it shouldn't have. I guess they were all talking about me at one point.

"Yeah," I said, looking down at my left arm that was covered by my coat sleeve and glove. "I don't know what will happen when the next full moon comes."

"If you go through any changes, some might be evident sooner than next full moon."

"Sounds like you know about such things."

"Yep, since I'm a shiftchanger." He glanced at me in the glow of his dash and the wash of lights at a junction.

"Forgive me; this is all new to me. Is it anything like being a Were?"

"Shiftchangers aren't Weres," he said patiently. "A were-anything needs the full moon to change, or to become extremely angry; a shiftchanger doesn't. We can shift whenever we want into whatever we want."

"Sweet."

"Yes, it is, but changing takes a lot out of us."

"I can imagine."

"Changing more than once in a twenty-four hour period taxes the system, depletes nutrients. It could make us sick, in fact. So, when I change, I change for a reason. Not to show off to my friends."

"Got it." I nodded.

"When were you bitten?" He glanced at me. Although it was dark, I saw his smoky eyes, and he looked right through to my soul—that was uncomfortable as hell. I averted my gaze, pretending the red taillights ahead of us were more interesting, which they weren't by a long shot. I found myself in the company of someone who could actually change his appearance into any animal he wanted. I was in awe of him.

"Two nights ago, on the second night of the full moon," I answered.

He shrugged. That little movement softened his stoic posture a little bit. "Maybe Nicolas got all the venom out, and you won't have to worry."

"But if not, then what? Will I change fully? Or just partially?"

His gaze flicked over me. "You're not full-blooded. So no, you'll definitely not be changing into a wolf. Something more half-and-half." One hand on the wheel lifted in a gesture and he brought it back down. I noticed he talked with his hands. Definitely an Italian thing. "In the very least your hearing could improve, possibly your sense of smell would improve. All positives."

"And what would be the negatives?" I asked, and wondered if I really wanted to know.

"Any Were or shifter within a mile will know you're in his range and come sniffing. Especially at the full of the moon."

I took two seconds to think about that and then threw caution to the wind. "So, what do you change into? Or do you have a favorite animal?"

"I prefer a jaguar."

"Like with spots?" I was getting chills all over. I simply couldn't imagine being able to change into any animal you wanted, when you wanted.

"No. Black. I'm all black."

"Oh." I was quietly pondering that for a few seconds when he went another direction.

"Are you and Nicolas seeing each other? I mean, it's not any of my business, but..." he trailed off.

I didn't know how to answer that. "You mean like are we dating or something?"

"Yeah. He kissed you. I'm just—it's none of my business, really. I just wondered."

Slightly embarrassed, I became quiet. According to Tremayne, Nicolas had no business kissing me, or anything else for that matter.

"Don't take it wrong. I've got my orders not to touch you straight from Tremayne. It's the smell of vamp on a woman is a big turn off for me." He chuckled, head making a little shake of disbelief. "He didn't have to bother."

"You're saying that he pretty much marked me as his territory?"

"Yeah, you could say that. In his own silly vampire way." He sounded indignant.

"So, vampires and shiftchangers don't get along as a rule?" I surmised.

"Oh, we get along, alright. You won't see us all hanging out together—me with a beer in my hand, and a Real Red in theirs at the bar." We both chuckled as he maneuvered through traffic.

"Doesn't matter, though. It won't interfere," he said abruptly.

"Interfere with what?" I asked.

"You and I are to work together... metaphysically, that is."

"We are? I didn't know that." I was pulling the finger ends of my gloves off and twisting them again.

"No one told you?"

"No." I looked at his face cast against the glare of streetlights and headlights. Dante turned the full measure of his eyes on me while driving one-handed.

"That figures." He sounded slightly irritated by the lack of communications. "I'm a telepath, by the way. And you have second sight, but I'm sensing that you also have a bit of telepathy in your make up, as well. Together we will be like a super sensitive duo."

"Oh, really?" I wondered what he meant. "How? I mean what do we need to do?"

"We need to be together for a while, you know, get comfortable with one another. That's why—or one of the reasons why—*I'm* taking you home, not somebody else."

Something about the quality of his voice and the way he'd said he was taking me home made my stomach clench.

"You said you'd stay overnight. But in your own room?" I wanted to make sure.

"Yes." He gazed at me and I saw a quaver of a smile on his lips. Something about this amused him. "Don't worry," he said with a chuckle, seeing my obvious discomfort. "We don't have to get to know one another *that* well."

"Oh," I breathed. I made to snap my fingers, but I couldn't because of the gloves. "Darn."

He laughed at my antics. Good, I liked that he could understand my lame jokes.

"Anyway, that's why Nicolas kissed you?"

"Yeah, probably."

"You and I are to be working partners, since we're the only humans in Tremayne's circle. It's actually more like we complement one another. Like yin and yang—you being the yin, and I being yang."

"Oh, heck," I griped playfully. "I wanted to be yang this time." He chuckled with me.

"Anyway, our combined powers will only be enhanced while we're together, but we have to feel one another out. Hopefully our powers are compatible. The last one"—he shook his head dismally—"we didn't get along, not metaphysically, not spiritually, not intellectually, and not personality-wise. Plus, she was a smoker. I don't smoke. Not even a pipe as my forefathers did. I'm sort of a new age Indian."

"Wow. That sounds difficult," I said finally.

"What's difficult?"

"All of it. What if we don't match—those things you mentioned?"

He smiled a little broader this time. I saw a flash of white teeth. "Oh, we'll match alright."

"Oh? So you're also a psychic?" We both chuckled. "I've been known to have second sight on occasion."

"Cool. Me too."

After our chuckles died, Dante drove on quietly for a time. It wasn't until we were passed the Aurora Toll Plaza that he spoke again.

"I've been briefed on your various attributes and background," he said, breaking the silence. "I've been told that Vasyl turned your mother, and bit you when you were ten."

"Yeah. My mother was his victim."

"His victim?" Disbelief laced his voice. "She may have been the one who'd invited him."

I gaped at him. "What? I don't believe my mother would invite a vampire to bite, or turn her!" My voice came harsh, and louder than I expected.

"I'm sorry about your mother. Her name was Julie, wasn't it?" I nodded. "But Vasyl hasn't turned anyone in a long while, not in at least a century, before your mother. It's on record," he countered gently.

"What record?"

"Our vampire who's who site. Thousands of vampires are listed, their human names, as well as any names they go by as a vampire, plus their approximate, or actual date of ascension, that sort of thing."

"There's a site that has all this?"

"Yes."

Still overwhelmed, I shook my head. "What are you saying? How does anyone know that any vampire has turned anyone?"

"It's supposed to be recorded. The World Wide Vampire Association requires it. If it isn't, then the vampire is considered a rogue."

"But I thought Vasyl *was* a rogue," I argued. "That's what everyone I've talked to has said about him."

"It's not an exact science, but someone has been entering Vasyl's information, including every one of his turns. Your mother was the last one, according to the information on that site. It's been updated recently."

"Do you think Vasyl himself would have done this?"

"I highly doubt it. It might have been one of his minions, or a scion."

"Why do you think that?"

"Because, Vasyl shuns modern technology. In fact he shuns pretty much all technology, including automobiles, electricity, et cetera."

I frowned into the night-scape as he drove on. "You seem to know a lot about a vampire who's considered to be a rogue, as well as crazy."

I caught the gleam of his smile in a passing car's lights. "You might say I have an interest in rogues. Especially the unconventional ones."

"I see."

"It's a side interest of mine, actually," he added. "Working for the Tremaynes has logged me thousands of hours on the computer learning as much as I can about their most revered, or feared foes. It's part of my job. I may spend days, maybe weeks, on the computer compiling information on anyone they deem a threat."

"So, what is Vasyl? Revered or feared?"

"Both, actually. He's more powerful than any vampire I've ever come across—uh, virtually speaking, that is."

My stomach dropped at his words. "And he bit me, and turned my mother."

"And I understand he's making your bite hurt?"

"Yeah, once in a while my bite site itches or burns."

"That would be him making a visit, in a vampiric way. He's sending you a message that he's ready to come to you, whether you're ready for him, or not."

"And if I refuse him?"

Dante merely looked over at me in silence, and looked away.

"Oh, right. Vampire. How silly of me." I flipped a length of my dark hair behind my shoulder, and adjusted my seatbelt. "I had a vision today, about what happened to my friend Jeanie. The strangest thing about it is that his face was missing."

"I beg your pardon?" He sounded half-amused, and half-alarmed.

Smothering a chuckle, I looked over at him. Driving with one hand on top of the wheel, he met my gaze.

"Yeah. I saw everything perfectly fine, but not his face. Why would that happen?"

"I don't know. That's unheard of. Are you sure about it?"

"Yes! Very sure."

Dante turned his eyes back on the road, and made a grunt while pondering on this. "It's almost like someone didn't want you to see their face in order to identify them."

"I figured that. But how could that happen?"

"If a vampire has had your blood, he could control your mind, even from afar."

A shudder went through me. Both Nicolas and Vasyl had had my blood. I didn't like the idea that either one of them could command me from afar. Bad enough Tremayne's powers were such that he could give me an orgasm without ever having touched me.

"Tell me what Vasyl looks like," I prompted. I had to know what this vampire looked like so I knew him when I went to kick his vampire ass.

"Well, he has long, black, wavy hair."

"Yes. I know."

"He's French, and lived during the first century, during the time of Charlemagne, and the beginnings of Christianity in Europe."

"What's he *look* like?" I prompted again.

Dante struggled with that one. "Like, well, I don't know. Closest I can tell you, I once came across the picture of Charles the First of France. It was spooky, to tell you the truth, it looked so much like Vasyl. So, I looked a little more into the kings of France and found out he looks more like his son, Charles the Second."

"Could he be? I mean could he be Charles the Second?"

"No. From everything I found out about Vasyl, his human life span came way before that. He lived during the early Middle Ages, about the eighth century. King Charles the First and Second lived during the Renaissance. It's said that Vasyl was the illegitimate son of Charlemagne. He became a priest during his life time."

"Oh, darn! He isn't the king of France?" I snapped my fingers and the sound was dull. "I was hoping to marry him, get all his money and I'd be set for life."

"Another one of your little jokes?" Dante asked, amusement playing across his face.

I let go a loud sigh. "Yes. It's the only way I know how to relieve my stress." *Well, one of the ways.*

Chapter 16

Once home, I pulled off my coat—not bothering to hang it but throwing it over a chair—and raced into my father's office and switched on a desk lamp. My father's encyclopedias were old, but they had a lot of information in them. It might have been quicker to use the computer (and geekier), but it wasn't on. So, pulling out an encyclopedia, and looking up Charles II wasn't all that time consuming, really. I merely had to find the correct book—BURNAP to CHARM.

The book smelled musty, the pages were slightly yellowed, and heavy, as I hefted it to my father's old roll top, and paged through it, all the way to the back. Almost as though my fingers knew exactly where they were going, they flipped open to the page in the back. There were a lot of entries for CHARLES, but when my eyes landed on the picture; my heart thudded inside my chest.

There it was. That face. The one that had been featured in my dreams repeatedly over the last eleven years: Heavy-lidded eyes, saucy lips, prominent chin, long dark wavy hair; a roguishly handsome man. Minus the chin beard and mustache, that was my dream vampire. How was it possible that Vasyl looked almost exactly like King Charles I of France was beyond me. Had I seen the portrait in this book once when I was small and somehow had transposed it into my subconscious and began dreaming of him?

I doubted it.

This was the vampire who'd bitten me when I was ten, and turned my mother?

I hadn't put it together, but why else would I have been dreaming of this man's face, knowing instinctively he was a vampire? And yet I didn't realize he was the one who *had* bitten me.

There were pages written on the psychological perspectives on vampires and why humans were fascinated by the myths. Freud posed that Bram Stoker's dark novel, *Dracula,* was an obvious reflection of the Oedipus complex, and incorporated incest, necrophilia and sadism, and interpreted as the age-old father-daughter relationship acting out repressed incestuous strivings. I remember reading about it in a book on vampires once. Vasyl wasn't much older than myself, and didn't look anything like my father, so screw Freud who didn't know that vampires actually existed.

I'd been bitten by a master vampire who wanted to—what? To claim me, everyone was saying. Claim me for what? His lover or his donor? Maybe he thought I was this sibyl. I hated to disappoint him.

Why did he bite me when I was ten, and then basically forgot about me, until now?

Like I said, leaving me alone with my thoughts was not a good thing.

Tremayne had given me his little demonstration with his "disciples" in order to throw some fear into me. This would forever give me a new perspective on how vampires viewed us humans. We were something to screw and feed from.

I wondered what Freud would say about that.

My mind raced as I climbed upstairs to get ready for bed. Dante, who may have read my mind and decided that his staying inside my house the first night would make me feel uncomfortable, opted to stay outside and go snooping around in jaguar pelt. Honestly, I drew a big sigh of relief when he'd told me. It would be difficult enough to shut my eyes and not think about everything. My strange vision of Vasyl from earlier today was gnawing at me. How was I going to find him, and save Jeanie without giving in to him? I understood he was turning this into a game. Yes, I was so vulnerable. But, I would use my powers to find him *and* Jeanie.

Slipping into my nightgown, I looked forward to becoming unconscious, hopefully. As I slid between the sheets I heard a sound. It was my new cell phone. As always, I'd brought my purse up with me, mainly because it had everything in it I might need. I stretched across the bed and looped my hand through the handle of my purse and hauled it into my lap where I sat in bed. Digging down I found the little twittering thing and answered it.

"Hello?"

"Sabrina?"

"Hi." My heart executed a somersault. Nicolas.

"You are alright?"

"Yeah, I'm fine."

"I felt you thinking too much," he said. "I had to call and make sure." This was the vampire's ability to *know* what I was feeling because he'd had my blood. That felt too weird, almost like he was spying on me. "Where is Dante? Is he there with you?" *Spy. Spy. Spy.*

"Ah, no," I said, shivering—and not from the cold. Adrenaline rush from talking to Nicolas, I was sure. I used to get it with my first and only boyfriend, Jack, whenever I spoke on the phone with him. "He's outside at the moment," I said. "In fact, he said he was going to spend the night outside." When there was silence at the other end I added, "He shifted."

"I see. Then he is outside and you are inside?" It was like he was trying to make sure we weren't together smooching, or something. Could he be the jealous type? "Are you going to bed?"

"I *am* in bed," I gushed, trying not to giggle like a tenth grader.

"Hmm, wish I were there," he teased.

"I bet you do," I rallied. My mind replayed that damned kiss he laid on me the night before, here in my bed, before he stopped abruptly. And the one tonight wasn't exactly innocent, either.

"Why were you so upset before I called?"

"I'm working on this thing with Vasyl taking Jeanie. I need to find her before it's too late."

"You will, Sabrina. Give it time."

"I may not have much time!"

"Calm down, Sabrina," Nicolas' voice was soothing. "Get some sleep. Your mind at rest may solve your dilemma."

"When I do, will you help me get her away from him?"

Again he paused. "It will be very difficult to catch him off guard—that is if we *do* find him."

"But you will help me?" I asked hopefully.

He sighed into the phone.

"What? You afraid of him, or something?"

"Sabrina, I cannot warn you any more stringently. Vasyl is very dangerous. A rogue vampire is dangerous enough. But Vasyl is—"

"Utterly mad?"

"Yes."

"You all keep saying he's mad, but he's outsmarted you," I pointed out.

"That is true," he observed. "We must be on guard even more. We will have to make stringent mind checks into those who work for us to guard against another attack from within."

"Did you find the guy?" I asked hesitantly.

"Who?"

"Al-something-or-other. Remember? We discovered he was the one who'd left that bag for Solange."

"Ah, yes, yes. We did," he said briskly.

"And?"

"We have yet to interview him," he said. "It's his night off."

I didn't know what more to say. We chatted a little longer about non-life-threatening, non-vampire things. I began to yawn, and he said he had to let me get some sleep. As if that were possible.

As we said goodnight, I noticed it was now ten minutes after two in the morning. *Where had the time gone?* My eyes felt grainy, and closing them felt about as good as rubbing salt into them. But I snuggled into my pillows and pulled up the covers around my neck. I did feel safe. Well, not every woman has a jaguar guarding over her in her backyard.

As I lay back down, and closed my eyes ready to sleep, I thought I heard a flapping sound outside my window. It had been on the porch roof, and it was large. I thought about getting up to look, but I was too tired to care. As I lay back thinking about it, I thought it sounded like the night before, when I'd seen the shape of a man at my window.

Was it Vasyl come to visit? Funny. My vampire mark didn't so much as tickle.

On that curious note, I simply drifted off to sleep.

When I woke the next day, feeling rested, and with sunny bars in on my rug, I knew I'd slept the whole night, into late morning. From the angle of the light I guessed that it had to be around noon. My clock read 11:43 A.M.

I dressed in sweats, because I knew Dante would want to come in and maybe have some coffee. I kicked on the furnace, before I ventured into the kitchen. While I made coffee, I heard a car door slam. I looked out the kitchen window. Dante strolled away from the black Mustang, toward the porch in his languid gate, carrying what looked like a soft over-night bag.

He'd obviously returned to human form, and was now dressed, waiting to be let in—like my pet shiftchanger.

I hit the brew button, and padded swiftly to the door, and opened it to the black-clad Native American shiftchanger.

"Morning," I said, smiling, crossing my arms to hold the warmth in.

"More like afternoon," he observed.

"Yeah, but it's morning to me. Want some coffee?"

"I'd kill for some. It's my only weakness."

"Mine too," I said, holding the screen door for him. I stepped back as he entered and looked around. Everyone looks around at the dining room, the ten foot ceilings, a homespun-look to the wall paper that was beginning to peel at the top, oak wood trim, and the open arch doorway to the living room. Beyond the living room was the double French doors, and my father's office was closed off with a massive oak paneled envelope door.

"Nice place," he said, nodding, still looking around. "I feel good vibrations here."

"Thanks. Good to know I've got a house with good vibrations." I shut the door to keep the chill of the fall day out, and expensive heat in. The chill reminded me I would have to call the gas people soon to come and fill my propane tank before winter. The cost would be up there. That's when I remembered the two thousand dollar checks in my purse. I'd have to get them into the bank before I forgot about them.

I led Dante into the little kitchen, and pulled two cups off the mug tree.

"Cream? Sugar?" I said pointing to the creamer and sugar bowl I'd sat out on the counter.

"Sugar," he grunted, reaching for a spoon. "My only other weakness."

"Indulge."

After we got our coffees all adjusted for taste, I said, "I'm sort of low on food. I don't have any eggs, nothing but cereal for breakfast, and barely any milk."

"No problem. We'll go get something to eat in town some-where."

"Sounds good. I have to stop at the bank anyway."

We both sipped our coffee, getting the full effect of caffeine into our systems. I rose and went to the cupboard, in search of cookies. I had a near-empty cupboard. I really needed to go shopping. I took out the package of cookies and set the nearly empty package on the table. "Cookie?" I offered.

"Sure." He snagged a cookie and inhaled it in one bite.

"Have another," I said through my mouthful of sandwich cookie, and he took another one and we ate the cookies until they were gone. It would hold us for the time being.

"Care if I use your shower?" he asked, rinsing and then plac-ing his empty cup on the counter.

"No. Not at all." I set my cup down and thought about him prowling around outside all night in a jaguar pelt. I wondered, distractedly, how that must feel. "You find anything interesting, last night?" I stepped out of the kitchen and he followed me to the bathroom off the dining room. I pulled out a clean towel and washcloth from the linen closet. I used the upstairs bath, so this one was clean—thank goodness. I handed him the towel and washcloth folded on top, feeling like quite the hostess.

"I don't know," he said. "Let me think in human form on that."

I nodded, placed the towel on the closed toilet seat and headed back into the kitchen. I wanted to tell him I thought that Va-syl had made an appearance last night, but somehow the whole event seemed more like a dream, so I remained silent.

"Have a good shower," I said, watching him haul his overnight bag with him into the bath.

"Thank you," he said before closing the door.

"No problem," I said. And it wasn't a problem, really. This was a guest bathroom. The bathroom upstairs was mine, and it needed to be picked up. Suddenly I'd become busy with a job, and not used to having to plan a day to do laundry, get groceries, or do housework—because I could always do those things, before. And now I had a guest. I wasn't sure exactly how long Dante was going to be my guest. It definitely felt weird to have a man in the house again. Especially one that was practically a stranger to me.

"Sabrina?" his voice filtered in from the bathroom.

"Yeah?" I ducked my head back through the doorway and saw him lean out from the bathroom. His long hair spilled down over one bare shoulder. The sight shocked me a little bit. I wasn't prepared to see bare male chest. I had to yank my eyes back up to his face—only because I didn't want to stare. Well, I did, but I had to be polite, as he was my guest and supposedly I was to work with him.

"Don't answer the door, if someone comes."

"Why?"

"Just don't. I'll be out in a little bit."

"'Kay," I said, and drifted back to the kitchen table, claimed my coffee cup, poured more coffee, doctored it up and waited. I looked out the window for a while. I watched rabbits eat dandelion leaves, and the squirrels race after each other in the boughs of the trees, trying to protect their nut cache. I thought about how Nicolas had floated off my roof, and he hadn't used wings in order to do that. I wondered if I'd been hallucinating the wing sounds. Why would Vasyl need wings? I thought about asking Dante if he knew anything about that, but thought it sounded stupid.

After fifteen minutes of such contemplations, Dante emerged wearing a clean pair of blue jeans that fit him better than the gloves fit my hands. His straight, jet black hair falling down over his bare shoulders was still damp. The no-shirt thing had me blushing—again. I wasn't used to his male body being exposed to me—and was alluring, to tell the truth. Of course when Jack and I were living together, that was a different story. I knew

Jack. I didn't know Dante. Was he flaunting his body, or had he no shame? *Damn, did he work out or what?*

I had to avert my eyes, as he padded barefoot back into the kitchen to get another cup of coffee. He smelled of shampoo and soap. A yummy smell for a guy, and making me a bit crazy. Hot guy parading around for me and I was too shy to take advantage of it. I was suddenly wondering if he was going with anyone. I hadn't *felt* a someone in his life, but then again, I wasn't the mind reader.

Trying to distract myself from my new male guest—and his freshly washed scent—I turned to look out the window. A red GMC pickup truck pulled into view.

"Oh, shit!" I said, nearly spilling my coffee.

"What?" He was suddenly by my side, looking out the same window.

"My ex is here. What the hell does he want?" Was this a co-incidence, or what?

"I'll handle this," he said, moving away from me, drying lengths of ebony hair flying.

Excited by the prospect of seeing Dante answer the door in wet hair and jeans to confront the man I'd left would satisfy a dark need in me. It would be good to see Jack on the receiving end of what he'd given me.

I paused at the kitchen threshold and watched Dante stop, dip, and dig something out from his bag. Turning, he stuffed the something into the waist band of his jeans at the small of his back.

There came the expected knock. Dante crossed the room and opened the door. I saw the butt of a gun sticking out of the tight fitting band of his jeans, barrel pointing down. I sure hoped the safety was on.

There came the exchange of 'hi' from both men.

"Can I help you?" Dante asked in a pleasant, yet curious tone as if he had no idea who he was.

Standing against the wall behind the door, I edged a little closer to hear the exchange.

"Is Sabrina here? Tell her Jack wants to talk to her," he said in that plaintive voice I'd come to know oh so well. "It's about her friend, Jeanie Woodbine?"

At the name, my stomach did a nervous flip. I strode away from the wall where I'd been hiding.

"Jack?" My voice made Dante half-turn to look back at me. When he did, he revealed Jack standing in the doorway, looking in at me.

Jack's blue eyes darted from Dante to me. "You sure don't waste any time, do you?" he said, accusingly.

I knew what this looked like. Dante's wet hair, and going shirtless looked like he lived here. A small part of me felt a pang of guilt. The rest of me felt justified if it made him feel a teeny bit like I had felt when I'd learned he had been seeing someone else on the sly.

Dante stepped back, but like a guardian—or jealous boyfriend—he folded his arms over bare chest and watched. Dante was a contrast to Jack who was a blue-eyed blond from Swedish stock, and they were both about the same height. Jack was the type of man women would have to turn around and goggle if he walked by, if only to confirm they hadn't seen something god-like. Yes. He was that pretty. His bowed lips and large blue eyes were intoxicating. That was one of the things I'd hated about being with him. He didn't try and hide the fact that he didn't mind this type of attention. But he had assured me that looking wasn't the same as touching. Thing was, I had believed him. I thought I was special, and the only woman in his life. How wrong I'd been.

This was all in the past. But I really didn't like seeing him on my doorstep. Not now, not ever. I was still in the hating stage. Eventually, I was almost certain, I might get to the point of not giving a crap about who he screwed. But he'd mentioned Jeanie's name, and I wanted to know what this was about.

"Right. If I'd been more like you, I would have had a guy on my arm well before I'd broken up with you," I countered. "What do you want, anyway? You said something about Jeanie?"

"Yeah, um—" his glance darted to Dante and then back at me. Dante was wearing an appropriate scowl. I could tell his mere presence made Jack uncomfortable. "I—um—look, I heard that you sort of had a vision about Jeanie?"

"From who?" I asked briskly, arching my brow and cocking my hip.

"From Mark, Jeanie's brother. He said his mom was there—saw it herself?"

"Yeah," I said. That seemed like a week ago. It was only yesterday morning. "So?"

"Ah, nothing. It was sort of freaky, you know?"

I twisted my mouth in thought. "Freaky?" One of the reasons we were able to date was the fact that Jack had thought my clairvoyant abilities were pretty awesome—not 'freaky'. I had given him a few demonstrations so he would know exactly what I could do, so he wouldn't be paranoid about it. Afterward, he understood why I wore the gloves.

"Well, you know Jeanie's mother. Her up-bringing and all? She thinks you're a witch."

"I know she does, but she sure wasn't thinking it was wrong when she saw me in action."

"Yeah, I know." He searched my face hopefully. "You figure out where she is?"

"Not yet." I let out a small gasp of disappointment. "But I'm still working on it."

He nodded, his blond hair was lifted in a slight breeze and he had to give his head a shake to get the golden strands out of his eyes. That was a move that might have made my heart throb a few months ago. But no more. I was relieved to find I was immune to his gorgeous looks. "Well, anyway, I wanted to tell you that there's going to be a candlelight vigil tonight at seven."

"Where?"

"At St. Paul's." That was the Woodbine's church.

"Okay," I said. "I'll try and make it."

Jack frowned. "Try to? What would you be doing that's so important you can't come?"

"I have to get out of work," I said. "I'll have to call and—"

"Work?" he repeated in disbelief. "Where are you working?"

I narrowed my eyes at him. I knew he thought—like everyone else thought—I couldn't get and hold down a job. Fist jammed into my slim waist as I said, "I work at Tremayne Towers in Chicago. I started this week."

"Oh, I didn't know," he said, sounding slightly impressed. "Really?"

"Yes, really."

"What do you do there?"

"I'm—uh—a consultant," I said, hoping I sounded convincing enough. I didn't dare look back at Dante. Dante was doing an upstanding job of pretending to be my boyfriend. "Any way, I'll try and be there. Now, if there's nothing else, I need to get ready to go to breakfast."

Jack didn't hang around, and was gone in a half a minute.

Closing the door, I turned to face Dante.

"Sorry. That was Jack Rasmussen, my ex."

"And now he thinks we're a couple?"

"Yeah," I said, stepping toward the stairs. "I'm sorry. But you didn't need to answer the door"—I looked him up and down—"without a shirt, and with a gun stuffed into your pants. Hair all wet. What would *you* have thought if you had been him?"

He smiled. "We'll let him go on thinking it."

I smiled back. I liked that idea.

"So, you're going to that vigil?" he asked, as I began up the stairs. I turned to regard him.

"I should. There isn't any problem, is there? I mean with you going into a church?"

"I'm not a vampire. And no, I've no problem with it."

"Good."

Twenty minutes later, the bank teller pushed out the dispense box, and I got back a small wad of cash from the two one thousand dollar checks I'd deposited. I asked for two fifties back, because I'd never carried that much cash around before—and almost never had a fifty dollar bill on me, unless my dad had given me one for spending on myself. I stuffed the two fifties into my billfold and smiled to myself.

I then directed Dante to the downtown, and he parallel parked as though he'd invented it.

O'Reily's was the only place in Moonlight that served a decent breakfast all day long. Dante and I got stares as we walked in. It wasn't me as much as him. Again, another guy that drew stares. It was like they'd never seen a Native American before. Maybe it was the long, unfettered hair. I found it flattering in a way, since I was with him. For the first part of my dating years, I never could catch the attention from male admirers. Now it seemed I had one too many. Although Dante was acting as unboyfriend-like as he could, being with him boosted my morale.

Dante had a big appetite, and ate everything he'd ordered. I could barely finish my pancakes and he offered to clean them up too. He explained it was his due to his turning into an animal and back again that had given him such a huge appetite.

Since neither one of us were due at work until later tonight, I talked Dante into having dinner at my place, something we could put together ourselves-something easy, and not pizza. I was surprised Dante was up to it.

Ten minutes later, while at Moonlight's Market, we agreed on tacos. When it came to what to drink we each had our own tastes on that. Dante told me he didn't drink alcohol, so he bought root beer in bottles, and I picked out a bottle of wine for myself.

Earlier, we had decided that he would pay for our breakfast, and I would pay for the dinner—since I needed groceries anyway. We both agreed to these terms, working to find a comfort zone, since we were work-mates trying to find a "melding" point.

"So, tell me about Jack," Dante said, as we strolled out of the store, plastic bags in hand.

"What about him?"

"Why is he your ex?"

"You might say I caught him messing around."

"You might say?" he asked, hitting the keyless remote. The car's lights flashed on, but not the engine. Apparently there was a separate button for starting up the spaceship.

"Yeah," I said, stopping at the car, plastic grocery bags hung heavily from my fingers. He placed the root beer and wine in the back on the floor. "I didn't exactly catch him in the act, but I knew he'd been with another woman. He didn't believe me. So, I told him what her name was, what she was wearing, and what they did—all of it, and in great detail. And then I left."

He looked at me pointedly. "Remind me not to piss you off."

"Note taken," I said, and paused to look around as he took my bags and settled them inside the backseat.

This was approximately where I'd found Jeanie's car. My vision going hazy, I was half aware that Dante realized something was happening to me. He took the bags from my hands.

"Sabrina? You alright?"

Hand up, I stood still, staring at nothing. "Yeah… yeah." Barely cognizant of where I was, I cocked my head, eyes still closed.

Forest green house with mustard-yellow trim, open porch with railing and decorative newels and carved posts. Old, maybe circa 1886-87.

"What are you seeing?" Dante's voice pulled me back to the now.

"I think I know what the house looks like," I said in a harsh whisper, skin pricking with both the excitement and fear.

"What house?"

"Where Jeanie is." The vision was still with me, and it switched to a different point of view and I saw something in the background, behind the house. *A church's steeple, limestone, with red accents, and a huge rose window.* "Oh my God!" I gasped.

"What is it?" I heard Dante's voice, but I couldn't see anything but my vision.

"The house."

"What about it?"

The vision vanished, and I sobbed into my hands.

Dante grasped me by the shoulders. "What is it? What's wrong? Tell me." I looked up into his concerned face.

"The house where Jeanie is, it's near the church where the vigil is being held."

Twelve minutes later, we pulled into my driveway and carried in the groceries. I was feeling wiped after that revealing vision, and had to lie down. Plus nervous and confused as to how I would go about saving Jeanie. I knew I was the only one who could do it, since I'd seen the vision where she was being held. But I needed help, and although I knew Dante would be at my back, I wasn't so sure about Tremayne and his vampire camarilla.

It was going on five in the afternoon when I pulled the frying pan out and set it on the stove.

"Hey, I'll do dinner," Dante said in a soothing voice.

"What? Really?" I tried to hide my utter surprise, which was impossible.

"Yeah. I'm known as the Taco Kid." He smirked.

I chuckled lightly. "I knew there was something special about you the minute I met you."

"Your eyes don't lie. Why don't you call Nicolas and tell him that you've had a vision of where Jeanie is?"

"I should, I guess." Who was I to argue with a guy who wanted to do the cooking?

Scrounging for my cell phone in my purse, I left the room to make the call. I figured he was up by now, since he had been able to call me in the late afternoon before, and the sun was going down.

He answered on the second ring.

"Hello, my dear." His voice sounded like warm chocolate to me, and I melted into it like a marshmallow.

"Hi. How are you?" I asked automatically. I was eager to tell him about Jeanie's whereabouts, but I suddenly knew something wasn't right on his end, and didn't plunge into my news.

He gasped lightly.

"What's wrong?"

"It's Toby."

"What about him?"

"He went on a trip with his culinary class for a few days, so I wasn't worried."

"So, you miss him?" I was clueless.

"Not exactly." He sounded off to me. Not himself.

"What's wrong, then?"

"Because I am his master I have him always on my radar, but right now I can't seem to *feel* him, any more. I do not know where he is. He is my scion, and I have a strong mental contact with him. I always know where Toby is. But now, I cannot feel him, and he has not answered his cell phone. He always calls me when he is gone for any length of time—to check in with me."

I was surprised that any vampire would let their scion roam away from them if they weren't on some mission for their master. Nicolas had given Toby his blood. I figured out slowly that this sort of exchange between a human and a vampire created a stronger bond. I was glad I'd made the choice of not having Nicolas' blood that first day. I would probably have become very bonded to Nicolas too. I wasn't quite sure, but I suspected that the more blood a human took of a vampire, the stronger the bond. Toby had told me he basically had had Nicolas' blood replace his own in order to get rid of the drugs in his body.

"What do you think happened?" I asked.

"I fear he is gone."

"Gone?"

"No longer alive," he clarified.

I was a little startled and fearful. Who would have killed Toby and why? My thoughts jumped to the fact someone had abducted Jeanie. Could the same person have gotten them both before we discovered who was behind it? But I couldn't figure out the motive. Jeanie and Toby didn't know one another. It simply didn't add up.

"What will you do?" I asked.

"I have called the hospitals… as well as the police," he added darkly.

"I'm really sorry, Nicolas," I said at last, and there was a long pause.

"Was there a reason you called, *dulceață*?" he asked, sounding morose.

"Oh. Yeah. I had a vision where Jeanie is being held."

"You did?" he sounded surprised. "Where?"

"Well, first of all, I have to tell you that there is a candlelight vigil being held for her in a church. I saw the house *and* this same church in my vision. The house is very close to the church."

"I will send the twins to join you. Tell me directions to the church." Happy he was going to help, I gave him directions, and the name of the street it was on.

"You must promise me that you won't do anything until I, myself, or Tremayne gets there," he warned.

"Alright," I said, trying to mollify him. I knew in my heart that I wouldn't be able to wait for Nicolas. In fact, I was getting more images flitting through my mind of me standing by myself in that house surrounded by vampires, and maybe a few Weres.

After saying goodbye, I closed up my cell phone and turned around to find Dante right there behind me. I let out a small screech. Those moccasin-padded feet of his were panther-silent.

"Sorry." He smiled sheepishly. He didn't look all that sorry, and I was sure he had enjoyed my reaction immensely. "What's up? I'm getting something about Toby?" That's right. He was a mind reader.

Hand over my heart as it thumped against my chest, I said, "Oh, yeah. Nicolas said Toby is missing."

"Missing? How can a scion go missing from his master?" he scoffed.

"Ah, as in dead?"

"Oh. Wow. How's he taking it?"

"I really don't know. He sounded bummed. Sad. For a vampire that's sort of rare, isn't it?"

"Toby was his scion. There's no reason to not think he felt something for him—a fondness. Scions aren't chosen arbitrarily." I realized he was telling me something significant. "Did you tell him about the vigil?"

"Yes. He's is going to send the twins to meet us at the church."

He made a grunt. "Almost sounds like we're going to a wedding, instead."

I frowned at him. "I'm going to get dressed."

"For the vigil? What's wrong with what you have on?"

I knew what I wanted to wear—and it wasn't jeans—because I'd seen myself in something else. "I'm going to my best friend's vigil where no one knows what happened to her, but me. I have to look… appropriately sad."

While Dante continued to work on dinner, I went upstairs to get dressed for tonight. I opened up my closet, wondering what would be appropriate to wear to a candlelight vigil. Then I revised my question: What did one wear to face off with a master vampire?

I decided black was the appropriate thing to wear for tonight's activities, and a pair of boots. Spying the only pair of black boots I owned, I snagged them and set them aside. High heeled, they went all the way up to the knee. Since my black pants were in the laundry, it made my decision easy. I would to wear a skirt and found a black skirt that laced halfway up the sides, which was purchased at the same time as the boots, and I knew how it would make me look if I chose a scooped necked top. Slutty. Was slutty a good look to throw into a master vampire's face when you wanted to flaunt it and not give in to him? Well, no. I guess not. But it was exactly the look I wanted to achieve to throw into Jack's face, who would be there at the vigil. Did I mention I was in a naughty mood? Naughty and somewhat reckless. Well, maybe a *lot* reckless.

After I slithered into my attire and checked myself in the mirror I realized why I'd bought the whole outfit—and never worn it. Jeanie had helped me pick out the boots, and helped me match it up with the skirt. It laced up on both sides and tied at the hem and could be tightened or loosened. This was not the look of someone about to go meet their vampire master and tell him to fuck off. But, a vision of me wearing this same exact outfit had played in my mind while we were in the store, earlier. I had to do it the way I saw it play out.

I needed one more thing to bring it all together—or at least have some sort of protection from a vampire. I opened my mother's old jewelry box (it had been her great-grandmother's, and I'd inherited it), and rummaged around in it and found the large silver cross. I took it out and gazed at it. Heavy and made of silver, it had tarnished some. I hadn't known if my mother was especially religious. We'd gone to church when I was young. After my mother's disappearance, dad and I simply quit going. (This had made his mom, Grandma Rose, really disgusted in him.)

I weighed the crucifix in my hand with my indecision. Finally, I looped the silver chain over my head. A sudden thought entered my head and I wondered if we would have time to run to the Walmart before the vigil. Somehow I didn't see that happening. But I knew that I had to be in that church tonight, it seemed crucial I was there. And not for the obvious reasons.

When I returned downstairs, I found Dante in the kitchen, a wonderful aroma issuing from the frying pan, while he chopped tomatoes, lettuce and olives up for tonight's meal. He moved around the kitchen like Rick Bayless on speed.

He looked up. The hand holding the knife over a tomato paused in mid-slice, as he stared at me. I smiled inwardly as I carried the bottle of Moscato to the counter, on the other side of the sink from where he stood. Feeling his eyes lingering on me, I suddenly became self-conscious, and nervous.

I maneuvered around him to rummage in the drawer for the cork screw, making the clutter in the drawer shift as I extracted it. I pulled off my gloves and used my fingernails to pull the bit of foil off—doing this with gloves was impossible.

"Here, let me do that," Dante said, coming up from behind me, his hand brushing against my arm. A sudden electric snap I hadn't anticipated hit me. I shrieked and jumped away, staring at him.

"What the hell?" I said on a gasp.

"Sorry." Stepping back, he smiled apologetically. "We need to find our melding point. This is gonna keep on happening until we do—what you just felt." He grabbed the cork screw, and in a moment the wine was uncorked.

"What the hell was that, anyway?" I was still trying to understand it. Similar to having a static shock, but there was something else to it. I'd felt *something* course through me. I was quickly reminded that Dante was as far from your normal human as one could get. I already knew this, but *that* was freaky as hell.

"Our auras are trying to adjust to one another."

"Okay, I guess that explains it." I scoffed, hands up as I backpedaled toward the freezer. Opening it, I dipped into the ice bin with my bare hand and dumped the ice into a stemmed wine glass on the counter. He poured the wine for me, and leaned against the counter with arms crossed, taking me in.

"What's the matter?" I asked self-consciously.

"Nothing, actually. But, that's really a hard-on inducing look. Are you serious with that get-up?"

Wine glass in hand, I looked down at myself. "What's wrong with the way I look?" I sipped on my wine and speared him with a tenacious look.

"Nothing, but I'm wondering what the plan is."

"No plan," I said. "I'm going to the vigil. After that I'm going to grab Jeanie and run."

He squinted at me. "I can see you hefting a full-grown woman over your shoulders and running with her down the street in high heels, with half a dozen vampires on your ass."

"It's been known to happen."

Chapter 17

St. Peter's was a honey limestone church with the classic pointed arched windows, and a huge rose window dominating the front. Dramatically angled roofs, and the tall steeple rose well above all surrounding houses and buildings painted crimson—as in blood. Tonight, the rose window looked more arresting all lit up from within.

People had converged on the front lawn of the church, holding candles with Dixie cups jammed over them to catch the hot wax. Faces glowed in the amber cast while they gathered beside the wide steps of the church. I easily picked out the faces I knew as we slowly drove by. And, yes, Jack was there. I also saw my brother, Randy, and his wife, Constance, and felt a tingle of relief knowing I wouldn't have all of Jeanie's relatives to deal with by myself.

I had stepped foot in this church on other occasions, once to attend Jeanie's middle brother's wedding two years ago. I remembered the reception after much better. I'd gotten to dance with Mark, but also, that was how I'd met Jack. The memory gave me an odd pang in my chest. Bittersweet. I'd been carrying a torch for Jeanie's brother, Mark, for several years—since sixth grade—then Jack came into my life to complicate things. Oh, yes. I wanted to flaunt what Jack could no longer have.

Now, of course, things were more complicated, as we arrived at the vigil. I knew what had happened to Jeanie, but I couldn't tell anyone. How would I be able to look Mrs. and Mr. Woodbine in the face and act like I didn't know what had happened to their daughter? I knew she'd been abducted by vampires, and now knew where they'd taken her. This wasn't something I could tell people without seriously sacrificing my credibility—what little I had.

We had to drive two blocks away to park, carefully observing the one-way streets, paved with old brick in this older section of town.

Dante took my hand, and we stepped out into the chilly night. Ozone and autumn was on the air as we walked through the fallen leaves on the sidewalk, now soggy from the rain that had fallen earlier. Butterflies began a tango in my stomach. I simply couldn't ignore Dante's sexual aura every time I got within two feet of him. He made me a tad nervous, and a bit anxious about being alone with him. It wasn't that I didn't trust him, because I knew he'd been told not to touch me. A master vampire has a way of making sure his underlings obey him. But I had more than a feeling we'd become much closer—eventually. And my Knowing is never wrong.

I thought back to last night, when he had put his arm around me when I'd turned away from the blood rite between Nicolas and Steve. I figured that as long as his intentions were to protect me, it was okay to put a hand on me. But all day, he'd made a concentrated effort to *not* make physical contact with me, until that moment in the kitchen. Later on, during dinner, I'd asked him what he'd meant about our auras mingling. He'd shrugged and said our spirits would eventually mingle, and we would be able to read one another's minds.

As we approached the church, my nerves were jumping for a different reason. About mid-block, I saw a parked car and someone standing, leaning against it. The orange glow from a cigarette caught my attention. I pulled up. Dante stepped in front of me, and we kept moving toward them. *Something* spilled from him. It was tangible, I didn't know if it had to do with our earlier brief physical contact where I'd felt that jolt from him, or what. I wondered if it could be his aura. He'd said we would begin to feel our auras mingle. Was this what he'd meant?

"Who is that?" I asked low, pulling out the crucifix from underneath my black shirt. I didn't want Dante to see it before we'd left—I didn't want to have to explain why I'd worn it. I'd had plenty to think about as the night drew toward the moment of our leaving, and now that we were here, my stomach was tied in a knot.

"Leif, and I think Darla," he said.

"You see that well in the dark?"

"Almost as well as a vampire."

"'Bout time you two got here. Been making between the sheets?"

"That's Leif," I said with disgust. Heath would never have made such a comment. And then I heard a wolf-whistle.

I rolled my eyes. Sure, I deserved it, but it was too late to go back home and change.

We stopped a few feet from him. I could smell the exotic smoke from whatever he was smoking. Darla was wrapped around him like a snake.

"Nicolas called, told us to meet you two here. You going after Vasyl, then, luv?" Leif asked.

"Yep."

Someone emerged from the darkness—I didn't see from where—and I knew from his form it was Heath. I was happy to see that he was back to normal after last night. I held back my joy; I wanted to hug him in the worst way, after seeing his horrible pain last night.

"Vasyl's demented, he is," Heath said.

"Fucking demented, luv," Leif repeated his brother's words—in his own way. "Are you sure you want to do this?"

"I have to. He has my friend."

"You've thought about how to go about this?" Leif asked. "I mean you can't simply go in and announce you're there to crush his balls, because he won't like that. And in that outfit, you'd be lucky to get out with all your blood."

"I think I'm drooling me self," Heath more or less groaned.

Leif turned to regard him. "A little bit, and your fangs are out, mate."

"Shit!" He pulled the cap off a black bottle and took a long swig.

Ignoring the vampires, I turned toward the church. The air was redolent with moisture. It had been sprinkling a little as we arrived.

"Church has holy water, right?" I said. "It burns... vampires... doesn't it?"

"Oh, it burns, luv."

"Depends upon the vampire, though, don't it?" Heath made a point. "I mean someone who wasn't a Christian in life wouldn't be affected."

"True," Leif agreed.

"Well, Vasyl was a Christian when he was alive, right?"

"Hard to say what Vasyl was, luv. But you could try it, see what happens."

"I bet the get was a Protestant," Heath sneered. Leif and Darla both chuckled.

"No, he was most definitely Roman Catholic when he as alive. In fact he was a priest for the Holy Roman Church," Dante argued. I trusted his word on that, since he seemed to know quite a lot about Vasyl, more than anyone else.

"Well, now," Leif said after a pause, "what will you do when you get the holy water? How do you carry it?"

"I'm working on the how part," I answered vaguely. I had thought of filling up balloons, but abandoned it. I mean, how would I hide water balloons?

"And what will you do once you've burned him?"

"I really don't know."

"I love your haywire plan, luv. It might just work." With Darla in tow, he strolled toward us and stopped at the edge of the sidewalk. He pulled in a deep breath. "Oi! Smell that, do you?"

Darla took a deep drag on the rain-fresh air and I wondered if they meant the rain. It had made the autumn smell of leaves a somewhat more fragrant.

"Wet human?" Heath guessed.

"Yes!" Leif said.

"Yum!" Darla said.

"You can smell that?" I asked, looking up at Dante.

"Of course," he said. "The rain intensifies your scent."

"Is mine intensified?" I asked low as we walked along.

"Yours is always intense."

"Wow," I said, mystified and a little nervous. "These are all my friends, I hope you realize."

"Not to worry, luv. We had a bite before we left the city," Leif assured. I didn't know how literal I should take that.

We stopped at the corner across from the church, letting a couple cars go by before crossing to the church.

"Jack will be here, right?" Dante asked.

"Jack *is* here," I said.

Dante grabbed my hand. "Won't look right if I don't act like a boyfriend."

"Got ya," I said, and found his hand warm over mine, yet not possessive. I looked around for the others. "Where did they go? Heath, Leif, and Darla?"

"You've a lot to learn about vampires. They're seen only if they want to be seen."

"They can't go onto the churchyard, though, can they?"

233

"No."

We crossed the street and stepped up onto the grassy lawn, joining the throng that had gathered there. Two girls, in their mid-teens, handed us lit candles. The warmth of the flame on my face and at my hand where I held it was welcomed as we walked across to where others had gathered.

Mark spotted me first. His longish, blond hair glinted in the candle glow and outdoor lights on the lawn. Candlelight revealed lines around his eyes and mouth I'd never noticed before. He looked older, somehow. Stress did that to a person. I knew he loved his sister. A tug at my heart, thinking how things would be if I didn't get her back, caught me by surprise. I wouldn't be able to forgive myself.

"Hey," he said, blue eyes darting from me to Dante, and back to me.

"Hey, yourself. How you holding up?" I asked.

"Okay, I guess. You?"

I shrugged. And then he put his arms around me and we hugged briefly. It shocked me at first, but the Woodbines were a hugging people. Other than a dance with him, I'd never gotten this close to Mark. When we parted, Mark turned to Dante.

"Oh, this is Dante—" I suddenly couldn't remember his last name.

"Dante Badheart," Dante supplied, and they shook hands.

"This is Mark, Jeanie's brother," I introduced, shifting my purse to my other hand.

"Glad you could come," Mark said. "There's refreshments, over in the tub. But I brought something a little stronger." He held up a silver can—obviously a beer. "Got some in the back of my pickup. You're welcome to it."

Dante waved him off. "No thanks, I'm driving."

"Thanks, Mark," I said as we drifted away. Jack's face peered out of a nearby knot of people, and we skirted by them. I could still feel his eyes on me, burning holes in my back.

Slipping around several people standing somberly next to the church, I found I was getting stares from a lot of the men, married or otherwise. Yeah, their slut-o-meters were going off, thanks to the way I'd dressed. I was glad that Dante had a possessive arm around me. Constance's voice arrowed toward me and I turned to see her in another group of people made up mostly of women and children. The candle in her hand cast unflattering shadows on her face, but I recognized her quickly and walked over. We gave one another a hug. Her two girls were running around the throng of adults with the other children, screaming, giggling, and laughing as though this were a birthday party. When we came out of the hug, her eyes focused on Dante. I introduced them quickly. Then I introduced him to my brother, and they shook hands.

"I didn't know you were dating," Constance said to me, looking a little surprised, but happy about it. At least she didn't add "again" to that. She brushed a swath of honey-blond hair out of her eyes and asked, "Where did you two meet?"

"We met at work," I said, giving Dante an anxious look while we held hands. I didn't like lying like this. But what else could I do? If he was to stick to me like glue, I had no choice, unless I wanted to try and explain that I had joined a den of vampires and Dante was my body guard, and oh, by the way, he's a shiftchanger. Yeah. That would get everyone off my back.

"At Tremayne Towers," Dante explained.

"Yeah, we went to lunch the first night, found out how much we had in common, and we've been hanging out ever since." I shrugged. "It's like he can read my mind." We all laughed at that, and Dante and I gave each other knowing smiles.

Within a minute of meeting, Dante and my brother began talking about the Bears and comparing notes about the last game. I was happy that they had something to talk about.

David and Brian Woodbine were both standing next to a planter where several unclaimed candles glowed in the soil.

Brian was Jeanie's youngest brother, and I could hear his husky voice from where I stood. David was five or six years older. David's wife, Jen, was yelling at her youngest child. Children's voices rose in whatever game they were playing while running around the adults, or up and down the steps of the church. Girl's screams punctuated the air. Distant sounds of traffic were muted, and then a train whistle blew a couple of times about a block away, and that pretty much ended the shouting competition until it went by.

Aside from seeing the church in my vision earlier, I had also seen a Buick dealership across the street from the house where Jeanie was being held. I knew the house was only two streets away from here.

"The house is that way," I whispered into Dante's ear, and pointed.

He followed my pointing finger. Pulling out his cell phone, he spoke quietly when the number connected.

"Okay, Josh! Damon! Stop running!" Jen yelled at her two young boys who were chasing each other with water pistols.

Suddenly a searing pain bit my vampire scar and I gasped, holding it. It felt wet, too. *The water in the guns?*

Two small boys charged around our circle, pointing plastic pistols at each other. I received a spritz in the face, and my arm became soaked while Josh and Damon ran around their father again.

The pain of my vampire bite quit burning. *Weird.* I gasped in surprise. I pulled my sleeve up, and looked at it in the diminished light.

"Josh!" David yelled. "That's enough!"

Finished with his phone call, Dante swiftly moved to snag one of the boys who angled right for us, and had him up off his feet, almost above his head. "Whoa there, partner." He delivered the boy into his father's hands.

"That's enough, I said!" David said sternly to the boy's face, shook him a little, and set him back down and gave him one good whack on the butt. Little Josh's face wrung up in anguish.

"I told you I'd paddle, didn't I?" David said, and turned back to his conversation. Josh rushed to his mother and clung to her legs crying.

"I'm sorry, Brie," Jen said, seeing me wipe my face off with a tissue. "They're wound up tighter than tops tonight. I don't know what's gotten into them," she said in her slight southern Illinois drawl.

"Oh, don't worry about it. Give a boy a squirt gun, you're just asking for trouble," I said, sliding my gaze over to my brother standing in the midst of another group next to us. I remember him ambushing me more than once on a few summer days with his Super Soaker.

I eyed the two squirt guns in Jen's hands. An idea blossomed in my head. *Would it work?*

"Jen, how much did those squirt guns cost you?" I asked.

"What? Oh, heck, I don't know. I think we got them at the dollar store. Why?"

Smiling, I pulled out my wallet and handed her a five. "I need to buy them off you."

"What?" She looked shocked at the money in my hand. "What do you need squirt guns for? And I don't need your money, honey."

"Okay, how about I give it to the boys so that they don't feel like I've taken something away from them?"

"You want to *buy* the squirt guns?" she said, her voice drenched in disbelief.

"It's really complicated, but I need to pull a joke on someone, later on tonight?" I said, trying to sound like it was no big deal. "I've also got a little job the boys can do for me. I'll give them each five dollars, if that's okay?"

"Five dollars for what?" Damon cried, staring up at me wide-eyed.

"Auntie Brie is going to give you each five dollars if you give her your guns," she repeated, handing me the water guns. Although I wasn't really their aunt, I was around the Woodbines so much that I was considered part of the family. I'd gone to picnics, weddings, and one funeral—and didn't want to go to another one any time soon, if I could help it.

The boys looked at their guns in my hands, and then at me.

"Sure! For five dollars!" Damon, the oldest, was first to agree.

His younger brother mimicked him, "Sure! For five dollars!"

"Wait, this is a secret pact," I said low, and lead them over to the side, away from the adults. I bent down to them, doing my best to keep my balance on the high boot heals and had to put one knee to the ground. I asked them where they had filled their guns. They told me pretty much where I had guessed.

"You think you can do it again without being caught?" I handed them their guns back.

They both giggled and nodded.

"Okay, then you need to do exactly what I say." The two were eager to please me and I figured if they were able to do it once, they could do it a second time.

Josh and Damon zoomed off with my instructions. Their small legs took them up the steps and inside the church.

Dante came up behind me, his hands grasped me by the shoulders. Voice low, he said, "What are you up to? As if I didn't know."

"The water they used in their guns came from the baptismal. Some of it hit my bite and it quit hurting."

"A Super Soaker would work a hell of a lot better on a nest of vampires, but you'd never be able to hide it."

"My thoughts exactly." I squinted at him. "I'll bet you read that right out of my brain."

He tapped his temple. "I'm telepathic. Didn't I tell you?"

"Slipped my mind."

He took a sip from a soda can.

"You're really going to do this?"

"Yes." A sudden burst of anxiety hit me. Leaning against a tree, I took some deep breaths. I had to hand it to Dante for not trying to talk me out of this. I thought he would.

By the time my breathing was normal, my little agents shot back out of the church, and roared up to me, panting perhaps a little more than necessary in order to sell the fact that they had worked hard to earn their five dollars. I asked if they did exactly as I'd asked. Excitedly, they assured me they had, and gave a full report of what risks they'd taken, and that Reverend Paul had nearly caught them, but they'd hid behind the altar. I patted them both on the head, and they were each five dollars richer.

"I'm ready to go," I said to Dante.

"*Wasté*, Ms. Vampire Hunter. Our back-ups are in position. More are on the way."

"Good." I shoved the guns into my coat pockets, made my apologies, and Dante and I swiftly left.

Moments later, we slid into the Mustang and Dante started it up. "Where do you think you're going to put those?" He nodded toward the two water pistols. One was a 6-inch yellow see-through, the other was a 5-inch see-through blue, both filled with holy water—not exactly deadly to a vampire, but hurting them was big on my list of things to do.

"I don't know." I held them in front of myself. They were wet, and bigger than I'd thought. I replaced them both back into the pockets of my jacket.

"You can't go in there with guns blazing like John Wayne." Dante said, as he maneuvered us away from the curb. He gazed over at me as he came to a stop sign, and turned to me. "You understand for this to work you'll have to walk in alone and ask for Vasyl."

"I know," I said, feeling anxious. I thought I would throw up. The realization of it all suddenly hit me. I was not a heroine. Really I was a big chicken. I'd rather run the other way, but this was Jeanie.

"They'll probably pat you down. Make sure you aren't carrying."

I bit my lower lip. "Didn't think of that."

I twisted the fingers of a glove, wet from the pistols.

"And what was the purpose of the crucifix, anyway?" he wondered. "Trying to piss him off?"

I looked down to see the crucifix dangling against the black shirt.

"A crucifix to a vampire is like flipping off the guy in the car next to you in the worst of neighborhoods in Chicago. You're just inviting trouble." His voice was in a low warning tone. "Some vampires are immune to the cross. Not all were religious when they were alive."

"I know." I frowned. He drove down the block and stopped for a stop sign. "But you said Vasyl had been religious. I'm betting it'll be effective."

Dante merely blew a sigh and shook his head. "I don't like this. I'm supposed to protect you, not send you into a den of dangerous vampires."

I looped a finger through the large silver chain. "Exactly why I'm wearing it," I said defiantly.

"I suggest you at least hide it for now. And decide where you're going to pack those two *very* deadly guns." I saw him roll his eyes. His sarcastic tone was not lost on me.

My mind worked on that as I shoved the crucifix down inside my invented cleavage—I was *not* going to go into a nest of vampires without some protection.

Something came to me then.

"Don't look," I said, as we sat at the stop sign.

"What?"

"Don't look at me, keep your eyes straight."

With a heavy sigh, he slouched his head on a fist, elbow on the window, as he drove slowly down the street one-handed. I checked to make sure he wasn't cheating and then took one of the guns, and shoved it into my bra. I shoved the other one on the other side. I had to experiment a little to get them in a spot that was comfortable. The handles stuck out, but they would stay put, since my bra was stretch cotton. Well, the six inch one was really a bit top-heavy, but I tucked it in so it wouldn't slip out.

"Okay, hot shot. How are you going to hide them?"

I looked down at the bulges in my shirt. "Didn't think of that."

"You need a larger jacket," he suggested. "A heavy coat to conceal them underneath."

I released an exasperated sigh and tried to reposition them a little. One was really rubbing me in the wrong place. "Ow, ow, ow!" I said while I re-adjusted the gun. I looked down at myself. "Now my bra is wet."

He gave a bark of laughter. I had to laugh too, and when I did the guns jiggled and one popped out. I caught it, and we both went into a fit of laughter.

"Am I insane to do this?" I asked, repositioning the water pistols as our chuckles died.

"Yes."

"Don't answer that—"

"Sorry, too late."

"What do you suggest?"

"I'll give you my coat. They may not pat you down, but if they do, they'll pat down your sides, hips, and legs."

"Wow. You know the drill."

"I do." Dante pulled over to the curb and turned to me, one arm on the steering wheel. "When you get inside, keep calm, be conscious about your surroundings, who's there, and so forth. I'll read your mind."

"Okay."

"When you get inside, as soon as you can I want you to yell, 'Tremayne and your minions come in'."

"Got it." I nodded. "The house is back over that way," I directed him.

Dante drove around the block, slowly. My mouth went dry as we neared the Buick dealership, and the house that sat across the street.

"There it is," I said, wonder in my voice as I saw it exactly as in my vision.

Dante drove by, turned and drove through a small lot next to the dealership, and parked the Mustang.

"Wait here," he said, and hopped out.

As I adjusted my weapons, which, by the way, were really uncomfortable against the mammaries, I heard him talking on the cell phone. Another car pulled up right beside us. I looked out the driver's window. The twins and Darla were here. Dante was still on the phone, I presume to Tremayne. If I was wrong to do this, I didn't care. Jeanie's life depended upon me.

Finished with his phone conversation, Dante stepped up to my side of the car, and opened the door. He helped me step out. Then gallantly gave up his beautiful heavy black leather coat.

"What if I ruin it?" I said as he helped me into it.

"I'll buy a new one." He shrugged. No big deal. He'd buy a new expensive coat.

It fit loose, of course, and the sleeves were too long. It was obviously not my jacket. He helped adjust it in such a way that it hid what I was trying to hide. It smelled of him—an incredible scent that pulled me in. More alluring than Nicolas'. I had to mentally slap myself.

"Nicolas and Tremayne are nearly here," he reported.

"How's this look?" I held out my arms and made a turn.

"Nice," he said, nodding. "You are candy for the eyes, babe."

"Wonderful. Bad enough I'm going to walk into a house full of vampires—and who knows what else."

"Are you sure you want to do this?" He kept asking me this.

"I don't have a choice!"

"I got that part." He moved to drape his arm around my shoulders in such a liquid motion, I thought he'd vamped out on me. My brain was frazzled. "You go knock on the door. When they answer, you tell them you're looking for Vasyl. If they look like they don't know what the hell you're talking about, get out. Right?"

"Right. But what if he *is* there? And more importantly, what if Jeanie is there?"

He paused and let out a breath. "You stay calm. Don't do anything to make them angry. Find your friend, and remember, I'll be reading your mind. You get into any trouble, I'll know it."

I tried to swallow. My throat was parched as though I'd inhaled a corner of Death Valley. Heart hammering inside my chest, I turned and saw Darla, Heath and Leif give me the thumbs up.

"We'll be here, when you need us, luv," Leif said.

I turned down the alley and headed toward the house, trying to fortify myself with the knowledge I was doing this for Jeanie. She had to still be alive. If not, I would kill Vasyl myself. Quickly, I reminded myself that I wasn't a character from some TV show that could kick vampire butt. However, I was determined to do this, and they might not expect my little surprise, and the big one to follow, if Tremayne got there in time.

"Remember, babe, talk to me through your head. What you see, or experience. Got it?" Dante reminded.

"Yeah. Got it," I said over my shoulder.

Wish I had a crossbow.

Chapter 18

It didn't help that a dozen feeble visions flitted through my mind as I crossed the street and neared the house. None of them pleasant. In fact, each one more horrible than the last. I was seeing things that had gone on in the immediate past, too. What I saw—in my mind—made my stomach clench horribly as reality closed in on me.

I was armed with only water guns and if I acted too quickly, or missed, I knew I would be on the receiving end of a whole lot of hurt—from about a dozen or more angles.

My clacking steps sounded magnified to my ears along the cracked cement walk. The old Victorian-style porch was painted mustard-yellow. I was surprised to find it in good repair. Voices within became more pronounced as I took the steps one at a time. Power hummed all around me, it was like walking into a high voltage area, and it seethed with vampire pheromones. For me to know everything about a house before I walked into it, was now a blessing, and for once I was extremely glad of my second sight, but it was doing a number on my nerves, and threatened to give me sensory over-load, but I did my best to block it.

I found the courage to knock on the door, and waited. I was astonished when the door opened almost right away, and I was looking at a man with black hair styled into a sort of pompadour—retro look. Perhaps he was an Elvis impersonator on his days off, but the eyebrow and nose piercing really put a new spin on it. His eyes roved my form.

"Who are you and what do you want?" his voice was more curious than intimidating.

"My name is Sabrina, and I'm here to see Vasyl. Is he here?" I asked boldly.

"Vasyl? Yeah, but he's preoccupied." He gave me another up and down look and said, "But, you can talk to Jason." He smiled wide, stepped back and held the door open for me. I was relieved when he didn't pat me down.

I was guided into a hallway. An open stairway led up to the second floor, and the hallway had a few wide doorways opening on either side. Mr. Elvis Impersonator led me toward a beaded doorway, and thrust his hand toward the room.

"C'mon in. Jason loves new blood," he said, and made a high tittering laugh that put me on edge.

I inwardly grimaced. Whoever Jason was, if he came at me with fangs he was going to get a face full of holy water, for starters.

I took in the tastefully decorated room before its bizarre array of occupants pulled my attention away. There was a fireplace in the center of one wall, between Victorian-styled windows, and the effect would have been stunning save for the aluminum foil that lined each one of them. Wall sconces were on the dimmest possible setting. All around the room were vintage couches or wingback chairs, and mismatched chairs were positioned around a large table where a human skull was used as a candle holder. Sort of like visiting my grandmother's house in Rochelle—except for the skull, and the vamps in the room.

Over the hum of conversation, there was a constant voice that stood out, too alien to belong to this den of evil. This beautiful male voice spoke in some other language, and it sounded like prayer to me. I'd attended church with Jeanie from time to time—Christmas being one of those times—and had heard the clergy, or priest, pray in Latin. This was pretty much like what I'd heard. Bizarre, unreal, and yet soothing to my troubled mind. I clung to it, listened closely, and let it all wash over me. It became a calming balm to my soul.

A hush fell over the room as I entered through the beaded entryway, the plastic beads made a clicking sound as they fell back into place. Now, all I could hear was that one clear, beautiful male voice. It *was* prayer. I was sure of it.

Disturbing this small island of beauty, hope, and prayer, obnoxious odors assailed me; a blend of sex, pot and something else I wasn't used to smelling, but from having been privy to Tremayne's blood orgy, the coppery stench told me it could only be blood.

The praying man was approximately ten feet at my two o'clock. I quickly counted fifteen vampires, but there were more, unseen. One woman with short bubble gum-pink hair and white-framed sunglasses was standing quite close to me. Head tilted, she gazed at me like I was an unusual exhibit. Most likely she wanted a taste of me.

"Ooo, pretty," she cooed. Or maybe she'd said "pity", I wasn't sure as she had a lisp because of the fangs. She wore white boots and a vinyl micro mini to match, and black netting for a top, no bra. She was not one bit ashamed either, and I could hardly blame her. Either she'd had a boob job while alive, or after being turned, but it was all I could do to pull my eyes off the blanched woman's huge breasts. Her nipples were red and hard as rubies and pierced, and a long chain looped from one nipple to the other. *Interesting.* Everyone else's eyes in the room were glued on me. Go figure.

The male vampire who stood before me hit me with his thrall, and I nearly caved, before I quickly averted my gaze, shifting it down to his tight, torn jeans. I realized I'd forgotten to pull out my crucifix to divert his thrall. He was a young vampire who needed eye contact with me before his thrall could take affect—thank God.

Realizing what I had done, he snorted, "Oh. So, you play hard to get? I love it!" Large, pale blue eyes took me in like I was frosting on a cake and he was the birthday boy. Cocking his head, his gaze fell to my chest of what I thought was curious appreciation. At least I hoped so. I didn't dare look down at myself. Of course, the water guns made the jacket stick out, and gave the impression I was nearly the size of Miss Nipples.

"Well, who do we have here, Dan?" The head vampire's gaze went behind me to the guy who'd led me in.

"Said her name's Sabrina. Said she wanted to meet Vasyl," Dan answered while leaning against the door frame, arms crossed. I noticed his arms were covered in tattoos. Definitely a Were.

"Really?" the head vampire said on a chuckle. "Well, he's a bit occupied." His gaze shifted briefly to the praying individual, across the room and to my right.

I looked over and thought I'd been transported to someplace else, momentarily. There were lit candles all around, several on the floor, and on two end tables. It looked like a shrine. He knelt before a couch where a woman was reclined—I couldn't see the face. He wore a drab brown robe, like a monk. His long, black hair fell down his back in waves. His feet were bare, and he was praying in flawless Latin—at least from my lay point of view. He made the sign of the cross, like a priest would, over the person he was blessing.

"Besides, I'm the best thing here. Come on babe, let's give you a ride," the vampire in ripped jeans said.

I threw him a nasty glare. "You need to get over yourself." Chuckles burst all around.

Outside, in the distance—and completely devoid from what was happening in here—a loud muffler sound moving closer. I was pretty sure that it belonged to a Harley.

"Come on, baby," the young vampire with the ego said, cutting off my thoughts on who would be on that Harley. "I'd like to get to know you real good, if you know what I mean?"

"If that's your only opening line, you need to change it," I countered heatedly. More chuckles. All went silent as a shift of emotions filtered through them all. A sort of expectant feeling. They looked away from me and to the other end of the room.

The eloquent prayer had stopped. I turned to see the praying vampire's head lift slowly. The long black hair fell in abundant waves down his back and around his shoulders. My heartbeat went into a deeper rhythm.

"I have marked her," the praying vampire said in that wonderful voice doused in a heavy French accent. His pale hand made the sign of the cross one last time, and he lifted himself off the floor in such a liquid grace it was hard to not think of a dancer.

I held my breath as he turned around.

Finally I was going to meet Vasyl. My mouth when dry, my knees nearly caved. *Oh, shit, I'm dead.*

The air around me shifted again as his glowing face came into view. His was more handsome, his features more robust, and roguish than the pictures of either one of the two kings I'd looked up. This was the face that had haunted my dreams.

Oh, yes. My dream vampire had stepped into my reality. I was so stunned I hardly knew what to do with myself. I slid my tongue over my lips while his dark eyes took me in. His head drawing back, as if to look down his nose at me, and then lowered it as if in a silent acknowledgment. His eyes were so hypnotic, I now knew this was what a deer felt like in car beams at night.

"Sabrina Nicole Strong," he whispered harshly.

"You know who I am?" I asked, startled.

"But of course." His movements, and everything about him was majestic, and I was utterly captivated. I couldn't move. "Why are you here, *ma petite fille?*"

"Because—" I lost my voice momentarily. I tried again. "Because my friend was taken against her will and brought to this house. I came to rescue her."

Sharp laughter was stalled by Vasyl's up-raised hand.

"Why are *you* here?" I asked, pissed.

"I was told of the one who is losing her life. I came to pray for her soul. This is your friend?" he asked, turning to gaze back at the woman on the couch.

As I glanced over, realization hit me like a bucket of ice. Jeanie was the woman sprawled on the red Victorian couch. She was partially nude, bitten in several spots. One arm hung off the side of the couch. Her skin looked white as bread. Her lips were turning blue. Dried blood, the color of tincture of iodine trailed down the arm from a breast, and from her neck.

"Oh, my God! Jeanie!" I moved toward her, but Vasyl stepped in front of me. I stopped. I absolutely couldn't move any further. Vasyl hit me with a thrall so powerful it nearly knocked me over.

"What have you assholes done to her?" I didn't lose my power of speech, however.

"Hold on, sweetheart. Someone brought her here. Said she was for Vasyl," the first vampire, explained quickly, but without compassion.

"I don't believe you!" I was shaking, I was so mad. "I don't—"

Vasyl's hand came up, and in an elegant sort of way, waved it before my face, and I suddenly couldn't speak.

"Jason, tell Sabrina what you have told me," Vasyl commanded.

"What? About the vampire who brought her here?" He pointed to Jeanie.

"Yes. What did he tell you?" Vasyl prompted.

"Well, he said that she was for you." Jason nodded to Vasyl. "A gift, he'd said." He made a snorting laugh.

"And, of course, you left her for me?" Vasyl's tone was sarcastic.

"Well, I sort of tasted her," Jason hedged, trying to look guileless.

"That would be your marks on her wrists, neck and breasts, of course?" Vasyl said. Then he lapsed into French. It sounded like an insult. "This is why you do not earn my protection." Vasyl's gaze came back on me, he winced apologetically. "Our need... it consumes us." Vasyl's voice rippled through me, taking a step or two closer in that vampiric liquid motion. I was suddenly on fire; the bite on my arm tingled, and the tingling went up my arm, down my spine and settled in my groin—not in any way it had ever felt before this. My spine rippled, and then arched with a need for his touch. I think I gasped or groaned with the exquisite torture of wanting him to touch me, but wouldn't. His mere touch would probably make me explode.

Unable to move my feet, I watched as Vasyl came around to stand right behind me—the position that a vampire usually feeds from his victim, if they are still standing, that is. His breath was absolutely intoxicating on my skin. I shuddered as my eyes slipped shut. Breath exploded from my lungs ending in a deep groan. His pheromones were filling me to excess, and I had no way to siphon them off. He spoke French to me, calling me *cherie*. I had no idea what he was saying, but as long as he kept it up, I was floating like a feather on a pleasant breeze.

"You wish to ask something of Jason, *'tite belle*?"

I nodded once, feeling as though my mind had split; one part was humming along with his glamor, the other part was trying to be analytical, and think clearly. *This is totally weird.*

"Ask," he whispered quietly into my ear. It tickled the shell of it wickedly.

"What was the vampire's name who brought her here?" I formed the words, although I didn't know if I had actually spoken.

"Didn't say," Jason responded.

"What did he look like?" I asked.

"Black hair, not very tall. He was a newbie. Had an eager look to him." I suddenly saw a flash of a vision. I saw the dark haired vampire who'd brought Jeanie to the house. These were quick flashes, but they were clear. Realization shocked me. *Him?*

"Will she live?" I asked, trembling.

"She is near death," Vasyl said solemnly. "I have said her last rites, and prayed for her soul."

"Why?" I whispered, and then sucked in a breath because his luscious lips landed on my neck. *Oh, God, what is he doing to me?*

"It is what I do," he spoke, his intoxicating breath against my skin, then his fingers traced lightly along my neck, finding the silver chain of the crucifix. I could hear something sizzle, smelled burnt flesh and opened my eyes, but I couldn't look. I knew his fingers were burning from the touch of the silver chain, and yet he seemed to be oblivious to it. He pulled the heavy chain, and what dangled from it, out from under my shirt. He held the crucifix out with the back of his hand, his flesh smoldering. The reek of his burnt flesh cloyed my air, I could barely stand it. He was tall enough he could bend toward the relic over my shoulder, as he brought it up, and touched it with his lips. The sound was like a drop of water on a hot griddle.

I heard the room as a whole groan.

"Shit!" Jason swore, eyes bulging. It was one thing, I guess, to see a vampire kneeling and praying; it was another thing to see him touch a crucifix to his lips reverently.

Into my ear Vasyl said, "Our time is not yet to be, *mon amour.*" My crucifix now hung outside my shirt, gleaming for all the vampires to see. Vasyl had possibly blessed it, I didn't know, but there was fear in the eyes of all the vampires who were watching. The Weres looked a tad uncomfortable, too.

"Understand, all of you. Sabrina Strong, is mine. You will not harm her, should you survive tonight. Or I will hunt you down and destroy you."

The vampires all exchanged looks of apprehension.

"*Ma petite*," Vasyl said into my ear again, and a throbbing need for him to take me right there and then went through me. "Call those who are outside. Invite them in. I have no qualms with Tremayne, and must leave you, for now." His hands lifted from me.

My eyes roved the crowd around me. I'd be attacked. "But—"

"Use the holy water," he whispered. "*Au revoir.*" In the next second the air around me crackled, and sizzled to the point of slight discomfort, and my ears popped. Vasyl's possession of me lifted as though it never were there. I turned in time to see him vanish in a cloud of vapor.

"Hell, I wish I could do that," Jason said, sounding awed, and slightly annoyed. His attention turned fully on me. His thrall zeroed in on me, but it was so insignificant, compared to Vasyl's, it was like having a puppy nip at my heels. "Fuck this shit. You're mine, bitch!" He lunged toward me. Several of the other vampires egged him on.

Before he got within six feet of me, I brought my hands up. Having to cross them to grasp both water pistols' handles, I yanked them out from their prison in my bra—*ouch! Shit!*—and began to squeeze the triggers, aiming almost haphazardly—as vampires had surrounded me—I hit five right away in both streams. They screamed and covered their smoking faces in agony. I aimed a stream of water on Jason, hitting him straight in the face. He shot straight up, screamed, and streaked from the room.

Within seconds the whole room had become like a hive of angry hornets. In the next few seconds I pumped several arcs of holy water across the room, hitting as many of them as I could. I knew once the burning sensation eased I was dead meat. The stench of burnt flesh cloyed the room and became more than I could bear. It smelled like a barbecue gone way wrong.

The two Weres, or shifters, standing guard at the doorway, growled baring teeth—albeit human teeth—I turned on them, aiming my pistols at them, but didn't shoot, since I knew it would be useless. They suddenly stopped in their tracks and gaped at me, and then at my weapons. Once they realized I had plastic toy guns, they lunged.

Quickly I ducked and moved out of their range, avoiding their diving bodies. The two large men collided like linemen at the fifty yard line, and fell in a heap to the floor. The house shook like an earthquake had erupted.

The place became a miasma of noise, and the vampire's movements were so fast, I couldn't keep up with any of it. The five inch water gun was out and I dropped it to go clattering to the floor, and held the other one in both hands like it was a real gun.

One of the Weres was up on his hands and knees, shaking his head, trying to focus. The other one was on his haunches and he was changing into his beast; I heard the ishy bone-cracking, and sticky sounds that characterized his transformation. I had to do something to make things more even, and pretty damned fast. The rumbling outside became louder, reminding me I had a backup of vampires right outside, ready to burst in.

"Bjorn Tremayne, and all your minions, come in!" I cried.

There was an explosion to my right, making me, and everyone else, dive for cover. The large picture window shattered; glass sprayed all over as something huge, sounding like a Lear Jet, soared into the room. My eyes took in huge chrome pipes, fenders, and two still-spinning wheels. A golden haired, broad-shouldered man, with the face of a god, and the determined air of a warrior rode astride it wielding something long, shiny, and deadly. He twirled it around with one hand like a propeller, cutting through the crowd like a scythe cuts wheat, before the Harley came down smack dab in the center of the room. Thundering along, he crashed into objects, upended the oak table; lamps and other things crashed, and parted the crowd that had all been intent on killing me. In the next millisecond decapitated heads fell, bounced heavily and rolled at my feet as the Harley stopped at the end of the room—and now the room looked small in comparison. I was too shocked, or busy worrying about getting the hell out of there to be grossed out. A small bud of hope blossomed in my chest—I was saved!

A huge sword like a—well—a Viking would probably have used, gleamed in Tremayne's hand. He sheathed it on the side of the Harley behind his leg, then maneuvered the motorcycle, turning it around at the end of the room, and aimed it toward me, throttling between all the rolling heads and headless bodies.

"Hop on!" he shouted above the piston-popping noise, and wiggled his fingers for me to move toward him.

Working to not eye the carnage, I surged forward, tripping on something heavy. I glanced down and saw the head of that pink-haired woman vampire with the boobs. She looked up at me in a death grimace, sunglasses gone. She wouldn't need them anymore. Her head rolled and stopped next to her naked torso, resembling a Picasso painting. I took ruthless satisfaction upon seeing she, and other vampires, were among the slaughtered. I had to hope that Jeanie could be saved—that she wasn't dead; that they hadn't drained her completely—despite what Vasyl had said.

In the seconds after Tremayne crashed through the window, Nicolas, Heath, Darla, and Leif all poured in through the broken window like specters, striking vampires who were still standing, performing impossible gymnastic tumbles, flying through the air, or became blurs as they fought their foes back.

"Get on!" Tremayne shouted again, and with one swift movement decapitated a changed werewolf who leaped at him from a dark corner.

"But Jeanie's—"

Another motion yanked my gaze off Tremayne. A huge werewolf stood directly in my path. Yellow eyes blazing, he snarled at me with a full complement of sharp teeth, reminding me of the one that had bit me the other night. There wasn't anything scarier to me, and I froze.

The werewolf lunged. At that exact same second, a large black cat—as big as the wolf—leaped through the window and tackled the Were in mid-lunge, knocking it down. I screamed, and maneuvered around the sudden loud fight between the two beasts. I saw the jaguar's large teeth chomp down on the Were's throat, tearing it open in a sudden neck-breaking motion. Blood sprayed, and I avoided it, taking one last leap over a headless body, hiked my skirt up, and tried to straddle the Harley. I couldn't manage it. *Stupid skirt!*

Tremayne's hands were on my waist. Suddenly I was hoisted into the air and came down on the seat behind, and slightly above him. Before my mind could catch up, we were speeding down the hall toward the door. I wrapped my arms around his large body, and ducked; the crash of wood filled my ears, the smell of smoke, oil, and gas made me gasp for air; we smashed through the door, then bumped down a set of steps and down a sidewalk.

When I looked up, we were in the street, the heat of the house gone; the chill of the night shocking me back to the now.

The last thing I saw as I looked back was Heath (or Leif), with Jeanie over one shoulder scrambling through the hole in the window, disappearing into the night.

I turned back around, buttoned up and snugged into the leather jacket I still wore, aware that my shirt was wet, my nipples hard, and grasped Tremayne's broad, muscular shoulders for support. Tremayne's hands were busy guiding the Harley, as he took turns like a demon.

Behind us, I heard an explosion—very loud—and I could almost feel the heat from it. The house (I knew from a sudden vision), had exploded.

Tremayne didn't slow down, as he took a corner. I heard wolf-whistles. A few moments later, I heard sirens screaming down streets somewhere behind us.

I knew almost right away Tremayne wasn't taking me to Chicago, or to my home—I was getting a read through my wet gloves. He seemed eager to get there.

He now had me all to himself.

Chapter 19

After possibly thirty minutes of riding a somewhat curvy and bumpy road, a cluster of lights on the horizon zoomed in on us.

Tremayne slowed the Harley's speed in half, then in half again; the gears shifting, making me rock slightly to and fro as he went through them. I peered out from my hunched-over position and saw that we approached a much larger metropolis, and in a matter of moments we were suddenly on a one-way, three-lane street.

Traffic snarled. It felt like we were crawling at a turtle's pace. I was real hopeful that we would get to wherever we were heading soon because my skirt was hiked up, and I found it uncomfortable as hell riding in the cold October night like this.

He took several corners, bumped over railroad tracks, as we entered an old industrial area. Finally we pulled up to a large sprawling, old factory encircled by cyclone fence. The windows were mostly broken out, and boarded up. Some had corrugated steel sheets over them.

We sputtered by docks that were long ago boarded up. Slowing, Tremayne maneuvered up a short, cracked cement ramp and stopped at a twelve foot tall gate. It looked sturdy and fairly new with razor wire at the top—a good deterrent against trespassers.

Tremayne hopped off the bike, left it running with the stand down, while I waited still perched on the bike. He unlocked the gate, came back and jumped on the hog, moved us through the gate, and stopped at a corrugated door. It looked like an average garage door—only impervious to WMDs. He used something like a garage door opener, and the galvanized steel door went into noisy motion. He drove through, and we both hopped off. After shutting off the Harley—cutting the ear piercing noise— he ran back out, closed and locked the gate and returned. He shut door and it sounded like a draw bridge coming down with a resounding, final clang.

I was now trapped with the most powerful vampire I'd ever known. My mind was in turmoil. Had I traded off one danger for another in those quick moments back there?

He pushed his Harley inside a small enclosure with bars around it. I moved to join him. We now stood in near darkness. Only his headlights threw a cone of light against a brick wall. Then he shut those off, and I was suddenly floating in darkness. I heard a switch thrown, and I was doused in industrial overhead lights. We stood on a steel platform.

"What is this place?" I asked, finally able to speak at a normal level instead of a shout, and my ears weren't ringing quite so much.

"This is home away from home," he said, and I realized we stood on an industrial type of elevator open all around, with metal pipe for railing.

"Home? This is your place?" I asked, incredulous.

He took up a different device with a large electrical power source hooked to the railing, and pressed a button. We rose slowly on this noisy contraption and arrived at a cement cliff overhang. Opening a keypad on the wall next to the steel door, he then tapped out a code. I looked down and noticed we were at least two floors up.

This door rose noisily, like the one before. Dubious, I stared into the darkness of the next area. I was telling myself for the hundredth time that if Tremayne had wanted to drain me of blood, or rape me, he could have done so well before this.

"Come on. It's not as bad inside as it looks on the outside." Tremayne stepped onto a wedge of space—that's really all I could call it—and like a dumb sheep, I followed. It took me a moment before I realized we were walking on a sort of catwalk and I clung to the steel rail, because I couldn't find my balance for a moment. Our footfalls clanged softly beneath us as I followed him inside his domain.

Tremayne stopped at a large panel of light switches. With several loud clicks, lights flooded several areas. The catwalk, I found, continued to a series of steps that wound down into a living space. It appeared to be a large studio apartment, or loft.

"This place all yours?" I asked, astounded. There was a bar and kitchenette along one end, and a long wooden table took a spot in the middle of the open room. Black leather chairs, couch, end tables with large black and gold ceramic lamps were arranged before a cozy fireplace.

"Yes. And only a few people know about it besides me."

"Really?"

"Nicolas, Dante, and now you," he said, sauntering forward, his steps echoed oddly, then became lost.

"Come on," Tremayne called to me from his loft below, moving in that Uber-vampire way that blurred if I made an attempt to watch him.

"Warm yourself," he invited as he slowed down, and strode into the middle of the studio. Grabbing a remote, he aimed it at the fireplace. Up rose toasty blue and orange flames on fake logs. My heels clacked noisily as I made my way down to him. He aimed another remote at a large plasma screen on the wall. The screen came to life. I thought a movie would blink on—so trained was I in this thought that TV's were for entertainment only.

I was quite wrong.

Instead, there stood Nicolas looking out at us, larger than life, face grim. Darkness shrouded him while a portion of his face and body glowed red. I thought that perhaps it was some sort of satellite feed from a cell phone, as it looked grainy.

"How is she?" Tremayne asked.

"The transfusions are not helping." Nicolas' voice solemn.

In the next few seconds my brain finally clicked on what was being discussed: Jeanie. I stood on wobbly legs gaping at Nicolas. His eyes moved as if to take me in, but he returned his attention back on Tremayne.

"Where is she?" I asked, because I knew they couldn't be back at the Towers yet. We'd only just arrived here, ourselves.

"The back of a private ambulance. The Sanguine Team has been working on her since we delivered her into their capable hands," Nicolas told me gently. "Alas, we have but two choices. Either we will allow her to go to a natural death, or—" I cut Nicolas' words off.

"What? No!" I lunged toward the screen as my eyes teared up suddenly. Tremayne's strong hands caught me by the shoulders before I could jump into the screen.

"You didn't let me finish, Sabrina," Nicolas admonished me gently. "I was going to say we could still save her."

"You need to decide what it will be, Sabrina," Tremayne's voice was calm, but urgent, as he spoke into my ear from behind. "We need your permission."

"What do you mean?" I asked anxiously, looking back at him.

"She will die, unless you want one of us to turn her."

The meaning of his words slammed into me. Jeanie would die because of what had happened to her. The only alternative was they could turn her into a vampire.

"That's like asking me to pull the plug on someone."

"We cannot act on our own. It is against vampire law," Tremayne explained.

"We don't have much time," Nicolas reminded. He held a cell phone to his ear.

"Wait!" I said, twisting the fingers of my gloves. I turned toward Tremayne. "If she dies naturally, then can she be brought somewhere so that she can be buried?"

"No. I'm afraid that isn't possible. It would raise too many questions about how she died. The bite marks are too obvious."

I shivered uncontrollably as tears pooled in my eyes.

"Okay," I said, shallowly. "Okay. Bring her over."

"Who?" Tremayne asked me. "Your choice. Who will do this?"

I looked up at him and then at Nicolas.

"Does it matter?" I asked.

"Whoever it is will be her master. A newly ascended vampire will need help from their creator, as they will go through a difficult phase. She will become his shadow. So, who will do it? Leif or Heath? They are with her now."

I definitely didn't want Leif to be her master. Besides, she would compete with Darla, as she was his shadow (how many shadows a vampire could have, I didn't know).

"Heath," I said on a heavy sigh.

"Heath, then," Nicolas said quickly into the phone. He was nodding. "Yes, yes." He turned his dark gaze back on us. "I will contact you later when the process is underway."

"Contact me in the morning—unless there are complications," Tremayne said sternly. Well, that made me *real* comfortable.

Nicolas nodded, and the screen faded to black.

I stood with my arms wrapped around myself, shivering. The adrenaline drop made me feel suddenly week; my legs felt cold and rubbery from the ride on the Harley.

"Come, sit." Hands still on my shoulders, Tremayne directed me to the couch. It was all I could do to make myself walk without falling over. "Wait," he said, and we stopped near the couch.

I looked back up at him.

"You smell of shifter." He was scowling at the coat. "This is Dante's. No wonder I had that scent in my nose the whole way. Take it off."

When I hesitated his scowl lifted to engage my gaze.

"Take it off," he repeated on a snarl.

I took off the offending coat, but didn't know what to do with it.

"Here," he said, and with a large pinky finger extended, he lifted it away as though it were infected with the plague, walked it across to a stainless steel wall peg and hung it.

"Sit. I'll get you something to calm your nerves—and mine."

I sunk into a leather cloud. Meanwhile, he angled through the apartment looking real comfortable. More so than in any of the other places I'd seen him in.

His kitchenette was basic. Cupboards were open and had nothing much in them. Naturally, because what would a vampire do with food, cups, saucers, and plates? There was a sink, next to an electric stove. Next to that was a side-by-side stainless steel refrigerator and a microwave.

While Tremayne played host, I noticed small wood carvings of things like bears, life-size eagles with outstretched wings, and fish caught in their talons. Smaller pieces of animals decorated shelves, or tables. I turned to study a two-foot statue of a Viking on the table next to me looking as though a strong wind was blowing his long beard and hair. These were magnificent works of art.

"Who's the sculptor?" I asked.

He looked back from the stainless steel refrigerator. "Me."

"You?" I said, and tried to halt the astonished end of it but failed.

"Yes. Why's that so surprising to you?" he asked, busily pouring what looked to me like red wine into a tall-stemmed wine glass.

"Well, I don't know," I said, looking around. I noticed that he had a second floor loft, I presumed designated for sleeping—or other activities.

"What?"

"Nothing. I guess I didn't expect you to be, uh, artistic."

"That's so difficult to imagine?" he asked, his voice saturated with sarcasm as he extracted a tall green-tinted bottle from the fridge. He poured the thick red liquid into another wine glass. Turning back into the room, he kicked the door of his fridge closed. "Is it because of my being a vampire, or something else?" He placed this glass into the microwave and punched a button, and it whirred for a few seconds.

"I'm sorry. It's surprising to me, is all. Will you forgive me if I say you're an excellent artist?" I more or less squeaked. The turn of our conversation was welcomed. I didn't want to dwell on Jeanie, and what was to happen to her.

"Yes, and thank you." The annoying beeping on the microwave was canceled when he opened it. Exhuming his now warmed drink, he stepped toward me with the bowls of the glasses nestled in the palms of his huge hands.

"So, this is your secret hiding place?" I said. He handed me my glass of wine.

"Yes." He sank into the cushions next to me, then took a quick sip of his liquid refreshment. "I come here to get away from everything. You must admit, it is a great hideaway. No one has a clue that anyone lives here."

I took a sip of wine, hoping it would help me dissolve some of the images from tonight's rout that were still doing loops in my head. I could still see scenes from our battle in my mind. It was like some sort of horror movie, and I was the stupid, hapless woman in the middle of it all. *God, I'm so pathetic.*

"How long have you had this place?" The wine skipped my stomach and took a direct path to my head. Perhaps becoming inebriated would free me from my living nightmares—past and present. But I highly doubted it.

"Twenty years. This was my very first place, in this area," he said, gazing around at his abode. "I'm absolutely safe here, lest someone drops a bomb, or something." He chuckled. "I come here at times to get away." He tipped his drink to his lips and drained half of it in one swallow.

Crap. I hoped he had more of that in the fridge. A lot more.

"Really?" I said, going along with his train of thought, doing my best to sound calm, although my heart was throbbing like a deep bongo. "But what about that nice cushy penthouse of yours?"

"I hate it. I don't spend much time there."

"Really?" I said, astounded. "But it looks like you do. I mean, you've a little butler, and all the decor—the mounted animal heads."

"Letitia had someone decorate it. I had to mollify Letitia, but truthfully, I loathe it." He threw back his head, looked about himself, and expelled a huge sigh. "No. This is my real home, when I need to get away, do my thing, or just relax." His eyes slid in my direction. "Relax with someone I really want to get to know."

Double crap. The sinking feeling that had been hanging over me earlier swooped down and nearly floored me. Damn. Right when I was beginning to feel more comfortable around him—to a certain extent.

I coughed. Setting my drink down on the coffee table, that last swallow was having difficulty going down. I coughed some more.

"That wasn't meant to make you react like that," he said, watching me closely. "I meant it as a complement."

"A complement?" I coughed out.

"Yes. You need some water?"

"No. No, I'm fine." I cleared my throat.

He set his drink down, and laced his large fingers together, one arm draped over the back of the couch and leaned in toward me. "I brought you here to show you I'm not the big bad guy you seemed to think I am."

"Oh, but I don't—"

"I admit I may have said a few stupid things—I admit it—and I really want to amend them. I'm an asshole. Okay?"

I said nothing. When a guy admitted to being an asshole, one should never argue with him. Tucking a length of hair behind one ear, I crossed my legs. Well, *crap*. His vampire pheromones were *making* me relax.

"I can't be the only other woman you ever brought here," I said disbelief rang in my voice. I reminded myself it took three women to satisfy his thirst, and two to satisfy his other lust, last night. I was only one woman.

"Letitia was the only other woman who ever knew about this place. We lived here for a time, together. By the way, your shirt is still wet," he observed, nodding toward my chest.

I looked down. My shirt *was* wet. I also saw that my crucifix gleamed in the limited light.

"Nice bauble," he said, reaching toward me. Reading the shock on my face, and the way I'd flinched away from his reaching hand, he stopped his motions. "Don't worry, I'm not going to grab a boob or anything. I only want to see the hardware."

I was incredulous when he lifted the crucifix in large fingers. *His* flesh didn't burn at all. "Nicely made. Heavy too. You wore this to ward off Vasyl? Or vampires in general?"

My mouth had been open and I closed it.

He chuckled. "Not all of us revere the cross, sweetie. I was a pagan in my lifetime. I was the church's *enemy*." He snorted lightly and let the crucifix fall heavily back onto my chest.

"Vasyl kissed it," I said, and wished I could take it back from the look I received.

"I won't be kissing any crucifixes tonight," he said. "I'd rather be kissing something else, instead."

My heart lurched when he knelt in one fluid motion in front of me. "You're still tense," his voice went into that hazy, lighter tone. "You need to relax more. Let's get the shoes off."

I had no choice but to uncross my legs and let him unzip and pull off my boots. Once they were off, his hands began to massage my feet. I almost complained, but it felt *too* good. I gasped with the exquisite feel of the massage. Then I couldn't help but let myself relax back against the sofa and moan a little. I pulled in more of those wonderful pheromones, which made me relax more.

"Good. That's better. Now, I must tell you, you made me extremely angry tonight," he said.

"I'm sorry," I sighed. His hands were marvelous. Strong, and yet, at the same time gentle. He actually massaged the tension from me. It drew another moan from me.

"It was a very reckless, stupid thing." His hands slid up my legs, giving me electric tingles as they went.

"Yes. I know. But she was my friend." I stifled a shiver best I could.

"I understand human loyalties. They are not quite as strong as a vampire's, but when I see them, it still amazes me. Why risk your life? You are so weak, vulnerable. To kill you would be so easy for a vampire. Why, with one hand"—he held his huge hand up—"I could crush you without a thought. What I'm doing to you now takes concentration to *not* hurt you. Why would you—how *could* you dare to attempt such a thing?" His hands had stopped moving along my thighs. I was glad they had, there wasn't much more room for his hands to go, except beyond the hem of my skirt, which was now hiked up some. I admonished myself for making it easy for him to touch me by wearing this skirt, but *he* hadn't been in my plans for tonight.

He planted a kiss on my knee, just below where my nylons ended in a lacy edge. I gasped, startled by his touch. His eyes flicked up to engage mine, a grin splitting his face.

"Very sexy stockings," he admired.

I did an eye roll. "We were talking about Jeanie."

He rose off the floor and settled next to me on the sofa, now slightly closer. *Smooth move.* I grabbed my skirt and yanked it down, as far as it would go.

"Explain your relationship with Jeanine," he coaxed, relaxing again with both hands clasped as before, but he was close enough to touch me with his elbow now.

"She's my *friend*," I said forcefully.

"I know. Tell me why she is your friend. I find it interesting."

I frowned, sipped my drink and thought about why Jeanie was my friend. "I tell her things that I know and she believes me."

"Like?"

"She believes that my mom's a vampire."

"Okay, but why would you risk your pretty little neck for her?"

I made a frustrated sound in my throat. "Why do you want to know?"

He leaned his cheek on a fist, looking maddeningly superior. "Tell me and I'll tell you something about myself."

I rolled my eyes. But truthfully I hadn't thought about why I had done this. I loved her, of course. But if I told him this, he'd still ask why. Finally I came up with a story that would put it all in perspective for him.

"I was in junior high," I began, and saw his blank look. "You don't understand junior high, but it's hell. Hormones in a teenager are at their peak."

"We married back in my day at twelve or thirteen. But go on. This sounds like a good story." He smiled and turned, and leaned toward me in that relaxed pose, one elbow still on the back of the couch, hands clasped once again, one kneed bent, thigh on the couch, touching me at the hip.

"Three boys began to tease me about my gloves." I held up my gloved hands.

"Right. Go on."

"The boys surrounded me—they were a couple of years older than me and a lot bigger—and no one did anything to stop them. One boy somehow got one of my gloves off my hand and held it above his head, teasing me.

"No one would stop them. A teacher went by without saying a thing. Then, suddenly, Jeanie came out of nowhere and slugged the kid in the gut. He dropped the glove. She threatened them with her two brothers if they teased me, or came near me again." Tears pooled in my eyes as I remembered this. I swiped them away with a shaking hand. "She didn't have to do this. She could have gotten the principal. But she knew that if I touched anything with my uncovered hand, I would go into a deep trance, one that would make me out of it for days. She saved me that day. Although those three boys were a lot larger than her or me, she did what she had to do." I was sniffling as I finished my tale.

He handed me a cloth napkin and I daubed my eyes on it.

Breathing out as I cleaned my eyes, I said, "Okay. Your turn."

"Okay, I'll tell you about how Tremayne Towers came to be. My brother had this plan that we'd buy up as many small hotels as we could, make money, sell them, and buy more expensive ones. On and on, we went through twenty decades, until we made money, kept most of it in a Swiss account—of course—and at the end of those years we split the money and each built a hotel. His is in L.A. We became the wealthiest vampires in the states. We each share the dominion of this country, by power of the Council."

"Council?"

"Our own governing powers. They're made up of the oldest vampires and demons, we call them Watchers and Elders. They're older than myself by thousands of years."

"So, that's it?"

"That's it. And," he said low, leaning in, "I'm still furious with you. Vasyl could have taken you easily."

"But he didn't." A little shiver went through me.

"No. And now you're with me."

I nervously sipped my wine trying to forestall this conversation.

"You realize I must bite you. My bite will cancel Vasyl's bite. That way this won't happen again—he won't be able to call to you anymore."

I looked away, my breath going out of me. I'd be his paramour.

"What is it?" he asked, brows furrowed.

"I don't get a choice in this?"

"Did *he* give you a choice when he came to you the first time?"

"Well, no, but—"

"I don't mind telling you that I'm turned on by you. The fragrance coming from you… your hair, your skin—" He breathed in, and let it out in a heavy sigh. His voice was velvet and seductive, changing suddenly. "It actually drives me to distraction. I can't stop thinking about you. Even when I'm not around you I think about you. I need to make you mine. I want to possess you. In every way, not just with the bite. I want *all* of you, Sabrina."

I bit down on my lower lip. I wanted to run. But I was a prisoner here.

"What if I refuse?"

"You can't refuse me, Sabrina. I mean to do this. Before the night is done, you will be mine. Totally. Unequivocally, unquestionably mine."

I swallowed. He would bend my will and take me, if it came down to it. Well, he'd have to then. I couldn't just give myself to him.

"You can't be anything but a vampire's paramour now. You'll never be able to lead a normal life, because every fucking vampire in a hundred mile radius will come hunting for you. You need the protection of a master. You need *me*."

I sat there, stunned over my predicament. I swiped at the tears that had begun again.

"It's your blood, you know? It's intoxicating. I'm the only vampire here that can put the fear into any of them. They wouldn't dare touch you, once my scent is on you, and my bite clearly on your pretty little neck." His head ducked a little and his closest hand gentled the hair off my neck. A sudden sensation of desire sizzled through me, exactly like before—but much more intoxicating—when he'd put the whammy on me in his office. I made an attempt to fight it, but I couldn't. He was as strong as Vasyl.

He moved slightly forward, and the leather creaked a little. "I'll be very gentle. I promise," he said softly.

He leaned forward, our faces on the same level. He took my face in his hands and our lips met. His kiss, tender at first, mounted to something wild, with the promise of something wilder. His fingers slid into my hair and became all tangled up. I had my hands on his expansive chest. The rise of passion began, making me abandon my thoughts of right and wrong. This was simply *too* good to refuse now.

In a moment of heated desire, I was pulled into his lap. His lips clamped over mine again. His fangs scraped my lips, sending chills through me.

He cursed in some other language, hauled himself up with me in his arms, and carried me hastily up the stairs to his lofty bedroom. He slowed once he entered the bedroom. Motion-sensitive lights blipped on, and the unusual large bed filled my view. It was unlike anything I'd ever seen before. The whole thing was suspended from steel beams by industrial-sized chains. As he settled me down on top of satin covers, he knelt beside the bed. The whole thing swayed, like a giant swing.

"Sorry. I made it this way because it makes me think of the ship."

"Ship?" I said hoarsely.

"Yes. We made our beds this way—to sway with the rocking motion of the ship. If you didn't, you'd fall out of your bed." His explanation was accompanied by the clinking sound of chains. I looked down to see him attach a chain from the floor to anchor the bed with a sound totally unrelated to anything I might do in a bed.

Kneeling beside the bed, he bent to kiss me. Hands roamed my body; it felt incredible. I gave in to the feeling. I didn't know if what I experienced now was created by his glamor, or if these feelings were true. At the moment, I really didn't care. His shirt open, I slid my hand underneath the heavy cotton. With a quick movement, he ripped the shirt from himself. He was one incredible specimen of a man—vampire or not. I suddenly had an eyeful of Viking chest—dark hairs covered the upper chest, and trailed down to end at a large gold buckle. I saw various scars—battle scars from when he was human, I guessed.

He rid me of my shirt in one smooth movement. Now I was nearly as bare as he. Bending to me, he kissed all along my neck, my throat, between my breasts, and down my abdomen. I would not remove my gloves—I couldn't dare. Knowing his past would give me a huge synaptic overload, and send me into a semiautomatic state for a week afterwards—unless he could bring me out, like before.

Leaning halfway across the bed, his hands rounded my back, one found the bra fastenings and suddenly freed that article of clothing from me. Now we were skin to skin. He felt chilly against my warmth. I heard him groan deeply with pleasure, filling the room, as he aligned himself beside me on the bed. The chains held, thank God.

He began kissing his way down, covering me with tingles as he went, stopping to engulf each breast in turn with his large mouth. What he did with his tongue was incredible. While I was preoccupied with what he was doing to me there, one hand went up my skirt to cup me. Then, in one smooth movement, off came my panties. He gazed appreciatively at me, my skirt was hiked up around my waist, my nylons were still on—amazingly the rubber bands had held up to this foreplay.

"Aren't you going to take my skirt off?" I asked.

"No, I like it like that. The nylons too," he said and made a little growl and threw himself back to where he'd left off.

My whole body tingled from head to toe. Eyes watching me, mouth open, fangs fully extended—and they were huge—he hovered over me, hand going back to lightly stroke my thighs, from the hip to the knee, and then he slid it between them giving me a slight shock of concern. It took me a moment to get used to his cold touch, but he absorbed my warmth. And while I waited to see what next he would do, he nuzzled me, kissed and licked me. When his finger entered me I pulled in a gasp of surprise. He paused for me to get used to that rather large invasion, and didn't move for a moment. When his finger began a rhythm I wriggled and bucked. The need in me strong as I sought an elusive climax. Then, an explosion of incredible sensations rippled through me. In a matter of moments I groaned, melting back into the pillow.

He stopped his motions inside me, and took his finger away. He rested that hand on my other side. Rising to one elbow, he gazed down at me. His eyes were focused on my face, then darted to my neck hungrily.

"You are mine, Sabrina." He opened his mouth exposing huge fangs. I didn't scream, but I did brace myself, thinking this was *really* going to hurt. He growled, like a large cat. Lunging, his fangs slashed toward my neck. A sting at my throat made me jerk. Not unlike when you nick yourself shaving, and it stings initially.

Suddenly, he gave a strangled cry of anguish; his head flew up, arms straightened as he stared down at me for one brief second. A look of—I wasn't sure if it could be horror, but maybe surprise was closer to whatever he experienced. Then, in the next two or three seconds, he became mist; the mist zoomed straight up, and then whooshed out of sight in one fluid motion. One, long horrible cry trailed after him.

Then all was silent.

Chapter 20

I woke up from a sound sleep to someone calling my name.

"Sabrina?"

Adrenaline surging, I rolled over and cracked open one eye, startled when I realized there was someone in here with me.

"Sabrina, it's me! Dante!" he called from somewhere deeper inside Tremayne's lair.

Worried he might come searching for me, I yelled, "I'm up here! Wait down there!" I sat up, and pulled the covers over my bareness, trying to assess my situation. My movement brought the lights on in the room.

I thought last night had been a dream—or a nightmare—but seeing that I was in a strange bedroom, half dressed, confirmed what I'd been up to last night.

"Fine. I'll wait down here," he called back.

I flopped the covers off myself. The bed was surprisingly comfortable. I wondered how it might have been if it had rocked me to sleep. It took me ten seconds to recall what had happened—at the end—and I still wasn't quite sure about it.

I located my clothes. In five minutes I was somewhat wrinkled but presentable, and stepped out of the room. There was no door, and I looked down into the living area from the top of the steps. Dante stood in the center of the room, hands on hips looking back up at me.

"You okay?"

"Yeah. What time is it?"

"Half past ten in the morning."

Frowning, I padded down the stairs. I was in no mood to take questions from a shiftchanger. I found my boots and slid them back on, remembering how Tremayne's hands had felt on my feet—and elsewhere.

"You sure you're okay?" he asked again as I stood trying to smooth out the wrinkles in my skirt (and mind). I'd put it back on to keep warm because there were no blankets, only sheets. Vampires.

"I'm fine!" I snapped.

"You don't sound fine." He eyed my neck, and then squinted at my face.

"What?" I said, hands on waist, hip cocked to challenge.

"Nothing. Just wanted to make sure you were all right."

"I'm great! Never felt better in my life! You?"

"I'm fine too. Jeez. Just trying to be cordial."

"Can we just get out of here?"

"Sure."

I climbed the steps and stopped at the steel door, waiting for him to open it.

"Here."

"What?"

He was holding the black leather jacket that I'd been wearing last night—the one that had made me smell like shiftchanger. Pulling in his scent, I slipped it on, trying to be inconspicuous about breathing in his musky scent. I don't know, shifter smelled as good a vampire to me.

In a moment, the steel door slid open, and we were out of Tremayne's industrialized Taj Mahal.

"Forgive me," Dante began in an apologetic tone. "I'm sorry, but I was my animal. I didn't find out officially. How is your friend, Jeanie?"

We stepped onto the industrial elevator. He hit the button and we rode down the noisy contraption.

"I honestly don't know. The last thing I do know is I gave them permission to change her," I yelled above the noise.

"Change her?" he had to yell too.

"Bring her over. You know, become a vampire."

"Oh, you mean *turn* her," he said, looking grim. "I'm sorry."

Right. I didn't have the exact wording down, but same difference.

The lift came to a resounding stop at the bottom, and we stepped off. In another moment we were outside. The sky was blanketed in dark clouds. I didn't speak again until we were in his warm car.

"It was either that, or she'd become nothing. No burial, because she was bitten too much. I guess she'd lost so much blood they couldn't revive her." I couldn't believe how clinical I sounded. My night had been total hell; not only did I *not* save Jeanie, but Tremayne had seduced me—and then left before he'd bitten me. Or anything else. In hind sight, I was relieved I hadn't become his party girl, or whatever they called them.

"Yeah. They can't have the authorities looking too deeply into strange deaths."

"Whatever. So, I chose Heath to do it."

"Heath?" he said, starting up the car, foot on the clutch. "Heath will be good for her, I'm sure. He's nothing like his brother."

I hunched over in my seat, burying my face in my hands. "God, what have I done?" Tears burned my eyes and back of my throat. I'd lost my best friend and my father within the same year. I could barely contain my feelings.

Dante took the car out of gear, and held the break with his foot. His hand reached for mine, and he squeezed it. "You did what you felt was the right thing to do."

"I don't know," I bawled.

"I know you did," he assured.

"I hope she won't hate me for it." I looked up at him, tears still pooling in my eyes.

"She won't. She'll have her youth forever." He kissed the back of my hand, then let go.

"I don't think that was important to her. Jeanie was pretty special and down to earth. She'd be pretty, like her mom, well into her fifties, or sixties." I rambled as I wiped my tears with a gloved hand. Dante produced a tissue and held it out to me. "Thanks." I blew my nose some.

He eased the Mustang away from the curb.

Depressed, I leaned my elbow against the window, head in hand sniffled a few times, and blew my nose again. He drove out of town—I learned we had been in Aurora—both of us lost in our own thoughts. Miles must have swished by before either of us said anything. The subject was weather. It was going to rain, and we agreed it might storm. Blue-black clouds were already forming in the west. Then we were silent again. Oddly enough, I was comfortable with him, not having to find something to talk about. I guess that's what was meant by companionable silence. He was the first man I'd felt that way with. Jeanie had no problem filling in all silence with constant chatter. But she was my friend, and she'd bring me out of a bad mood, or depression. I was going to miss that. I was going to miss the old Jeanie, and I had to wonder what Vampire Jeanie would be like. Would she remember me? Us? I worried about that. I needed to ask someone.

I was suddenly reminded what I'd learned last night, about *who* had taken Jeanie in the first place.

I had to talk to Nicolas about it. My stomach tipped with realization. It had to have been obvious to him that Tremayne was going to take me as his paramour, since he'd taken me to his hideaway. I wondered how he felt about that.

I also wondered what had happened to Toby. Was he really gone? Too many things at once. I simply couldn't concentrate on any one of them, now.

"Are you sure you're okay? You want to talk about it?" Dante asked. "I was told to come and get you. I have no idea what happened, but I've gotten some things—uh—thoughts from you."

Right. He was telepathic. I'd forgotten.

I let go a heavy sigh. I decided if I didn't talk about it I'd explode. I had no one else to turn to with this.

"Tremayne was going to make me his paramour and negate Vasyl's bite," I began, while staring out the windshield. "He had me in bed." I stopped right there, fidgeting with my gloves, my face going warm with embarrassment. Could I tell a man all this without being embarrassed? Eventually I found my resolve to continue. "He was about to bite me. And then, I-I thought he had, but suddenly, he became mist, and took off like a bat out of hell. I mean literally, he became mist and whooshed out of there!"

Dante bent his head slightly to peer at me. "You don't know if he did bite you?"

"No." I had my ungloved hand to my throat, searching. I flipped open the mirror on the sun shield and arched my neck to see if something was there. I saw two small scratches. Enough to bleed a little. I saw a bit of dried blood too.

"Oh, shit. He *did* bite me."

"Where?"

I turned toward him, pointing to my scratches. "See?"

"Yeah, I see. But why would he stop? Why would he—"

"I don' t know."

Dante scraped fingertips over his beardless jaw. He seemed pensive, like he might know something.

"What is it?"

"I don't know..." He looked at me, and then back at the road. "What did he say to you?"

"When? I mean, we said a lot of things last night."

"Anything about your individual scent?"

"Yes. He said it was mouthwatering."

Lips went into a purse as he deliberated on this. "I think you should call him."

"Huh? He left me, last night. Why would *I* call *him*?"

Dante turned to spear me with a significant look. "You're very lucky he did."

"What? Why?"

"You'd be as dead as Jeanie, right now. Deader, in fact. He wouldn't have left a drop of blood in you."

My jaw dropped.

"I think you should call him."

"I don't understand."

"It's the blood thing with vampires. They can control their thirst with a human. It takes a lot of practice, but after their first year they can control themselves really well, when to take blood and who to take it from, and how much is safe—for both of them. They have the will-power to take only a little at a time from any donor."

"What are you trying to tell me?"

"I remember something. That maybe once in a vampire's existence he might come across someone whose blood is so incredibly alluring that if they begin drinking it, they won't be able to stop. Sort of like a drug to a drug addict. They can't stop taking it."

I made a sound somewhere between a gasp and a screech.

"You don't realize what Tremayne did, how he must have gone through agony to leave you like he did."

"That explains the screaming I heard as he left."

"Yes. It would be a good idea that you not be in close contact with him again."

"My thoughts exactly." After a moment's pause I asked, "Is my purse still in here?"

"In the back. Why?"

"My cell phone's in it."

"It's all still there."

I looked to the back seat and saw my jacket folded neatly on the seat, purse on top. I couldn't reach it. We were nearly home, anyway. I chose to wait.

"You want something to eat, before we get to your place?" he asked as we turned off the tollway.

"Starved. Let's go into town."

I gave Dante directions, and in twenty minutes we swung into Moonlight's only fast food drive-up and swung back out with the car reeking of fries and burgers. We took it all home. I didn't want to get anything on the black leather seats or the carpet (he'd said it was a loaner from Tremayne's private garage, but I still didn't want to mess it up).

We ate in my kitchen while discussing what I was going to do today. Besides call Tremayne, I was going to clean the house and do laundry. I offered to wash anything of his from his stay. He thanked me, telling me he'd already taken his laundry back to his place.

"I need to tell you something. Something I found out." I had to tell him before I forgot it, or burst with anxiety.

"Okay," he said, wiping ketchup off his mouth, then snagged a couple fries and dipped them in a pool of ketchup and devoured them in two chomps. I found everything about Dante fascinating, especially when he ate. He looked ravenous, as though he hadn't eaten in days. But it was the way he ate, something about his mouth, and large white teeth that pulled my attention. I'd never known anyone who could look so attractive eating, but he did. I watched silently as he sucked ketchup off his fingers.

He stared back at me. "I'm listening."

"Oh, um, yeah." Embarrassed, I tried to hide my infatuation by blinking and looking down at my food. "I know who brought Jeanie to that house."

"You do?" He stopped his motions and stared at me, looking slightly stunned. I had the feeling I could never completely stun Dante, since he could read my mind. But I guessed that he wasn't always reading my mind, in order to allow me some privacy. I figured it had to have been both a salvation as well as a curse to be able to read minds. I knew what he went through, on a daily bases, because of my own curse.

"I got a vision of Steve, right there in that house, with Jeanie in his arms."

"Really?"

"Yes."

"Who else have you told this to?"

"You mean about Steve taking Jeanie to that house?" He nodded. "No one."

"Keep it to yourself." He gave me a significant look. "For now."

"Why?" I paused, thinking. Too many things were swirling around in my head. I tried to wrestle them down, but a lot of them fluttered out of my reach. I only know my night was sheer hell, and learning about Tremayne's lust for me, and that he might kill me because of it, didn't help either.

"You told me that it took two vampires to abduct her?"

I nodded. "I told you that the face was blurred, but the hair was like Vasyl's?"

"Your mind was blanked by a vampire."

His words stunned me. "Can all vampires do that?"

"Many of them can."

"Although the vampire in my vision had the same hair as Vasyl, I'm thinking that it could have been a wig."

"A wig?"

I shrugged.

"Okay, for argument sake we'll go with that. We don't know why these two vampires took Jeanie?"

"No. I'm not yet sure."

"How was it Vasyl happened to be there in the house last night?"

"Steve actually told them that she was for Vasyl, so Jason's scion went and got Vasyl. Vasyl was there to pray over her because by the time he got there she was already dying."

"And you believe him?"

"Yes! He was kneeling next to her—he prayed over her, like a priest." The memory rocked me, but I went on. "He—" I had to stop and take a breath before I could go on. "He could have taken me, Dante, right there and then. He could have done anything to me, but all he did was thrall me." Heavily.

"Who bit her? Was it Steve? Or—"

"No. The head, or leader of the nest. His name is Jason," I said, my voice going hazy with emotions. I swallowed and continued, "Vasyl asked Jason if he had bitten her, and he admitted it." We sat for a few seconds and I added, "Vasyl isn't the villain in this. He didn't take her. Steve did, but I don't know why, or who put him up to it." I knew this because they said they had sent for Vasyl. "Steve had told them Jeanie was for him. But I remember Vasyl admonishing Jason for biting her, before he got there. It was like he'd over-stepped his bounds and then Vasyl said that was why he didn't earn his protection, or something like that."

"An offering." Dante had quit eating and clasped his hands and settled his chin on the thumbs. "For Jason to over-step his bounds like that, Vasyl had every right to kill him himself."

"Offering?" I scoffed at the sound of it.

"Yes. Often to appease a master vampire to get his protection and blessings, lower vampires will snag a human—I'm sorry—" he made an apologetic wince "—and send for the local master vampire and offer the human up to him. He can either take the offering or leave it. But it's not something that is done often, now. But once in a while, and not so brutish, today. The vampire who is offering won't touch the offering before he gets there. However, since Vasyl is considered a rogue, and the vampires who were trying to appease him, were rogues, they would capture humans this way and for this reason."

I made a disgusted sound and looked away, tears brimming in my eyes. "But Steve wasn't part of their group," I protested.

"As far as we know, no, and that's what bothers me. Keep this to yourself. I'm sure nothing good will come of this. I've a feeling we don't know the whole truth yet."

"Now you're really shaking me up," I said.

He stood and his large brown hand came down on my shoulder and squeezed a little bit. "Don't go anywhere," he informed, pulling on his black swede coat—the one I'd been wearing.

"I have no place to go," I said getting up to walk him to the door. "I have housework. Remember?" He chuckled.

"I'll get back before sundown." He strode toward the door, stopped and gazed at me, his eyes roving down and then up. "I hope that outfit makes a second appearance, by the way."

I looked down at myself, remembered suddenly what he'd told me about it. I chuckled. "Maybe," I chided. "If I get an invitation for dinner?" I leaned against the threshold of the kitchen. I wasn't good at flirting, but it suddenly came easy. Was it him, or was it me?

His eyes fluttered up briefly, lips pursed as he hummed at the idea. "I hope to take you up on that."

My heart did a little dance.

"Pack an overnight bag. You're to stay at The Towers." Hand on the doorknob, he opened it.

"Alright." I didn't want to be all alone, especially after last night. But Dante had his life too.

"Don't open the door to anyone while I'm gone."

I rolled my eyes. "Why?"

"Because." He gave me a stern look. "There is still someone out there killing vampires. They know about you and your clairvoyant powers, and probably know where you live."

"Yes, and they'll come out here to murder me because I know too much. Right."

"Behave," he warned, keys in hand.

Once Dante was gone, I began to throw the whites into the filling washing machine. Something had sparked my memory; that missing puzzle piece that would answer who was killing vampires and was now out to get me before I could nail them was right there, on the edge of my brain, but I couldn't shake it loose. This would bother me the rest of the day, or until I remembered it.

I'd gotten in one load of laundry when my cell phone rang. My heart knocked on the walls of my chest as I looked at the readout.

Quickly I opened it up and answered. "Hi."

"Good day, Sabrina," Tremayne's deep, rumbling voice sounded a little tired. "How are you?"

"I-I'm fine," I stuttered, my face turn red with the memories slamming into me. "How are you?"

He released a heavy sigh. "I'm fine. Better than I should be. Anyway, I wanted to apologize to you, Sabrina, for—hell—everything."

A smile tipped my lips. "Okay. Apology accepted. Now will you explain what happened—I mean, why you left like you did?"

"That's actually the other reason I called." He paused. "This isn't easy for me."

"Because you find my blood so *mouthwatering*?"

"Oh, you have no idea," he almost groaned. "Who tipped you off? Dante?"

"Dante said that you could have killed me last night, and that I was lucky you had the will power to leave like you did." I stepped over piles of clothes in the laundry room, shut the door to the noise of the machine, and paced around the kitchen with the phone to my ear.

He made a groan of relief. "It surprised the hell out of me. Me, of all people! I never thought—after over a thousand years of never running across this—I would ever actually find a human woman who was my soul mate."

"Your... huh?"

"Soul mate. You know—"

"What? How could I be—"

"Let me explain, Sabrina, my love."

His endearment silenced me. I plunked down into a kitchen chair because the room began to spin.

"Vampires live so long that it's quite likely they will come across their soul mate at some point in their existence. When they do, the blood is sweet, the need so great to possess that soul, that we can only take it. Since our soul has already been harvested, we can do nothing else. We want to mate with you, but, the hunger is too great, and we take your blood—your soul—instead."

"I... see." *Not!* It was difficult for me to form anything but monosyllables at that point.

"That's why when I discovered your blood tasted sweet to me—too sweet, really—I knew I had to get the hell out of there fast. I would have fucking killed you."

I swallowed again. The events of last night with him kissing me, and doing things to me made me dizzier than before, and gave my libido a rude awakening, right there in my kitchen. How did he do this over the phone, no less?

"Sabrina? Are you still there?"

"Yeah." Barely. "I'm trying to take this all in. You're saying we're soul mates?"

"That's right. If I were a living man, we would fall madly in love with one another and probably fuck each other until we couldn't walk."

"Oh!" I gushed, that familiar tingling at my groin made me squirm. Once I could speak again, I said, "So, we can't be together like that, again. Right?"

"Not until I become desensitized. It will take some time," he went on, and my brain jolted to attention once more on what he was saying.

"Desensitize?"

"Yes. It will require your cooperation, of course. You'll have to donate blood, and I will drink it. Once I find I'm used to its allure, we can be together."

Silence.

"Sabrina?"

"Yes. I'm here. I don't know that I want to do this."

"Why not?"

"Do you need a reason?"

"Sabrina, if I'm not desensitized to your blood, in time I'll come hunting for you."

I leaned my forehead into my hand, elbow on the table. How many vampires did that make? If I included Leif, Nicolas, and Vasyl, it made four vampires wanted to turn me into their paramour—and take my blood.

"Sabrina?"

"Okay. When do I have to do this?"

"Tonight. I'll make an appointment. You'll be all set up to give blood in the usual human way. They'll get the blood to me post haste. I'll feed and feel a hell of a lot better and I won't want to hunt you."

"Okay," I said. "Tonight."

"Thank you, Sabrina. Thank you. I feel better all ready." He did sound relieved.

I wasn't.

Chapter 21

Rain beaded on the black, glassy surface of the Mustang as Dante pulled into the Tremayne Towers' garage.

"I'll get your bag later," Dante said, parking in his slot.

I unfolded myself from the car, turned and saw Heath standing there in the glare of overheads. I stared at him, then back to Dante.

"What's going on?" I asked suspiciously.

"I'm here to take you to the donor pool, where you're to give your blood," Heath said, eyes pinched apologetically.

Dante sidled up alongside me. "I'm really not a hundred percent for this."

"I'm not so warm and fuzzy about it either," I said, and we all moved toward the elevator.

"Do I get a vote on it?" Heath asked.

"Sure," I said. I wanted to hear how he felt.

"I'm bummed about it meself."

"That's overwhelming majority," Dante put in.

We took the elevator down in silence. Dante stepped off at Level A, explaining that he needed to go to his office. Heath and I continued down to Level C, then led me to Data and Personnel where Sally gave me a little worried look when Heath explained I had to have my status upped to "Donor-Exclusive", meaning that my blood goes to only one vampire—namely Tremayne.

It took a while before they got to me, as they had a number of other people in the half-prone position behind green curtains. The woman who took my blood was about my age, a pleasant young lady, with large brown eyes, no elf ears—but I knew she was one all the same. She was all smiles about my giving a donation, saying they'd been expecting me. When I was done, she put a band aid on my arm and gave me a glass of orange juice, and I drank it quickly. The dizziness went away after a few minutes and I was directed back out into the waiting area.

Heath got to his feet in one of those liquid vampire motions, and it had me thinking I was still dizzy until I reminded myself where I was.

"How'd it go?" he wondered, smiling.

"Fine," I said glumly.

"Great, great," he said, seeming to not know what more to say. "Uh, we're done, aren't we?"

"I was wondering—er—I mean as long as we've a few minutes, would you like to see Jeanie?"

I gaped at him. His question hit me like he'd slapped me with a cold wet towel.

"You can, if you want, you know."

"But isn't she—I mean—she's not awake, or anything?"

"No. She's still undergoing the transformation process. The ascension takes three nights for it to be complete."

I was still hesitating. "She's not in a—I mean there's no coffin, is there?" I knew I sounded like a complete idiot asking him this.

"Oh, no," Heath said with a light chuckle. "Come on, then. She's in isolation. I'll have to take you there meself. They don't allow humans in the ascension area, except in some rare cases, and you've been cleared by Tremayne."

In a few moments, we stepped out of the elevator on Level D. It looked like any hospital wing I'd ever been in. Nurses in their silent soled shoes, either mint green or dusky-blue smocks with matching pants. They looked like any other nurses, except for their pointed ears.

We stepped up to a counter, and behind it stood a blond woman of the fae. Heath announced he was there to see Jeanie, and that he was her sire. I had to show her my ID card, and sign in. Then Heath led me down the hall.

"These are elves that run this hospital?"

"Yes. Their blood is very toxic to us vampires. We avoid it at all cost," he explained patiently.

"Oh." No wonder the elves were in charge of the blood.

In a few turns, he announced, "It's right here. You can view her through the glass." Heath pressed a button, off to the side. Curtains on the inside slid open, revealing a small room. It was large enough to hold a hospital bed, and nearly every available space around the bed was filled with monitoring equipment. Several different screens either blipped, or were quite blank. I saw nothing on the heart monitoring screen—of course. That's what I didn't understand. Why would they have her hooked up to a heart monitor? Weren't vampires actually un-dead?

Upon seeing Jeanie there, stripped to the waist, her pale chest dotted with electrodes, an IV pumping something red into her arm, I stiffened. Her skin was wedding-gown white. She looked frail as a daffodil, yet more beautiful than I could ever remember seeing her. Tears flooded my eyes, and I broke down. Ashamed, I had to turn away. Heath pulled me into his arms and I wept against his shoulder.

"Don't be sad," Heath's voice soothed. I found myself able to stop crying. Of course, his pheromones were working on me, but I didn't care. I gazed up at him. Heath didn't look exactly like his brother. His jaw was a bit heavier, and maybe his nose was longer, and he had a mole high on his left cheek, usually hidden when his hair was down, but tonight he had it tied back and I could see it.

"Sabrina? Sabrina," he said, taking me by the shoulders and more or less pushing me away. "My brother is right. You have—something about you—that's hard to resist."

I frowned, confused. "I do?"

"Here." He handed me a handkerchief from his breast pocket. It matched his electric blue shirt. It was definitely silk. I hated to ruin it with my tears and mascara.

"Thanks." I took the handkerchief and dabbed my eyes. "I'm sorry."

"What? About crying, or being so alluring to vampires?" He was smiling. It lit up his eyes, I noticed.

Closing my mouth, I revised what I was about to say to him. "I'm really that alluring?"

"Yes. Your scent, for one thing. But mostly I'd have to say it's your *aura*, rather than just your aroma." He sounded real positive on this.

"Wow. You mean you can see my aura?"

"Yes, I can, actually."

"Can all vampires see the aura?"

"No. That's something I ascended with. It's my special talent. I'm surprised you haven't been attacked or approached, by at least a dozen other vampires."

I shrugged. "Only Vasyl, when I was ten. But, I live in a small community."

"A good thing, that."

"I don't understand though, all—this." I turned back toward the room. "I had no idea this is how it's done."

"This is how we do it, now. This is much more reliable. The technology is here, why not use it to our advantage?"

"But a heart monitor? Excuse me, but I didn't know you had any heartbeat at all."

"It's real slow, goes almost undetected by usual standards."

"Does she have a heartbeat now?"

"Oh, yes. She does. But you'll have to wait around a while to catch the blip." He was smiling. "Right now, she's in a comatose state. There is hardly any EKG, as well. But once the process begins to come to a close, everything will begin to accelerate. All those monitors will begin blipping and showing readouts. It'll be exciting." He was staring into the room smiling, hands in his pockets, going up on the balls of his feet, looking like a new father. Weird.

"I thought you'd have to bite her. Like they do in the movies and books."

"No. The bite isn't what turns a human into a vampire. It's the blood. Enough vampire blood would have to be consumed on three consecutive nights in order to make a human turn. A human doesn't need to die before they turn—or ascend, as we like to call it, now. In fact, the body can't die."

His words struck me. "Wait. Can someone change into a vampire simply by drinking vampire blood?" I was remembering something someone had said to me, only a few days ago. I was having a hard time remembering who had said it, what with all that had happened to me.

"Yes."

"This killer—they've been drinking the blood of their victims," I said, my eyes going out of focus for a few seconds. He turned away from the window, giving me a slightly startled look.

"What's that?" he asked, sounding alarmed.

"The killer. They've been drinking the blood of all their victims."

We stared at one another. This was significant.

"There's been, what? Two victims?" I couldn't remember.

"Yes, two as far as we know," he said. We stepped away from Jeanie's room.

"Would two be enough?" I quizzed as we walked swiftly up the hall.

"I really don't know. It's the nights too."

We jumped on the elevator. Heath pushed the button for Level B.

"How long until I can see her?" I ventured the question, because I didn't know.

"Jeanie?"

"Yes."

"It will be a while before she can be around humans. A month, at the least."

"Why so long?"

"A new vampire has very little control over their appetite, and will need time to get used to the regulated feedings. The program takes three to four weeks, usually, before the new vampire is able to drink from a donor without draining them of too much blood."

"Right." I recalled Dante telling me this.

"And, I must also caution you, Jeanie will not be the same. She will not respond to you as she once did. She'll remember you, of course. But she is no longer a human with human emotions."

"Well, I knew there would be all sorts of draw backs to this. I don't know why I didn't let her go on to her reward."

"You loved her," he said simply. "Human love is a jealous love. It's hard to let go."

"Wow, that's putting it into perspective." The elevator's doors slid open and we stepped out. Lines of people were heading down the hall and we paused to let them go by.

"You didn't have enough time to think it through. But look at it this way, I now have someone. My brother has had Darla for a year. I've sort of felt a little jealous. You've given me someone to be close to, intimate with. She'll be my shadow. Believe me, Sabrina I'll take real good care of her. You'll see."

"I know you will," I said feeling a blush coming on. "I hope that it works out for you."

He beamed. "I think it will. We aren't able to take someone for our own, you see? The Vampire Counsel forbids it. We can only take those who are near death, or are already turned for our shadow, or life-time mate. I just haven't found the right one to be me life-time mate, yet. I hope that Jeanie will be the one."

I nodded. Thinking about these things overwhelmed me, it wasn't what I wanted to think about right now. We strode forward, following the crowd.

"I'll tell her all about you—as much as I know. In time, when she's able to be with you, you can tell her more about her human life, and what she meant to you."

"Thank you," I said wanting to end this conversation. "What's going on? Where is everyone going?"

"Must be break time. Hungry? I sometimes forget that you humans must eat at regular intervals. We only need to feed once, unless we've exerted ourselves." Heath escorted me down the hallway, and then through a set of open doors. Inside was a large cafeteria with hot food bins, a salad bar, and servers there to spoon out whatever you wanted. Cashiers in the rear.

"Go ahead and get what you want," Heath said, moving in a direction away from the main food aisle. Wonderful aromas pulled me in. It wasn't culinary delights, but good enough to eat. I grabbed myself a tray, a plate, napkin, and cutlery, and began to drool. I got roast beef, mashed potatoes, gravy and green beans, a large roll, fruit salad, and desert—a large piece of chocolate cake, (I figured I was entitled).

I met up with Heath at the pay line, he was ahead of me with a black bottle of Organic Red, and a plastic cup. He paid for his and offered to pay for mine, but I showed him the ten in my hand, and he backed off. I knew he was only trying to be gentlemanly.

"Are you sure this is all you want?" he asked, eyeing my pile of food on my plate as we walked out to the tables.

"Okay. Funny. Ha, ha," I said, catching the glimmer of his smile. I turned to follow him out into the dining room. We sat by the window that looked down into the billiards room, on the lower level. The huge screen TV which hung over the tables showed some scene from a movie. No one was playing billiards, but I thought I could hear bowling balls crashing into pins, out of sight, somewhere below us.

We sat at a table nearest the window. I plowed through my meal, and Heath sipped his bottle of Organic Red—thankfully not pouring it into the cup. Leif suddenly appeared in a chair next to us. It startled me, but I managed not to spill anything. He must have been using his vampire speed, and I simply missed it with my slow, human eyes.

"Hello, luv," Leif said, casually.

"Brother? What's wrong?"

"Haven't seen Darla, have you?" He was gazing around, looking a bit anxious.

"No. I've been busy," Heath said, eyes slipping over to me, and then back to him.

"I see," Leif said on a suspicious note.

"Why? Isn't she coming to your summons?"

"I haven't summoned her, yet. But I may have to." He had his cell phone out and looked at the read out on it. "She's having some issues, and I'm a little worried she might rip out some poor bloke's throat. Excuse me." He put the phone to his ear.

I gaped, astonished at what he'd said. I glanced at Heath.

"Darla has only been a vampire for a year—maybe less, I can't recall—"

"A year on November tenth," Leif interrupted, still holding the phone to his ear.

"Yes, that's right." Heath touched the bottle to his lips, seeming to test it for heat or something. He took a sip and made a sour face. "I don't know. I think this batch is horse blood, or something." He grimaced at the bottle.

"Organic Red?" Leif said, eyeing the bottle. He sputtered. "You got yourself Organic II! That's mostly horse blood, you nitwit."

"Oh, well, no wonder!" Heath looked at the label on the bottle. Sure enough, it had the Roman numeral II on it after the words Organic Red.

Leif was still on his phone, but not speaking into it. He stretched over to look down into the lower level, then sat back. "Darla. Answer your fucking phone," he hissed, and then gave an exasperated gasp, throwing his head back dramatically.

"I notice you have a billiards room," I said to Heath, needing to fill in the silence at our table while I inhaled the gravy and potatoes. Every other table was brimming with people talking and laughing, enjoying their respective meals.

"Yes. There's a bowling alley down there too," Heath said.

"Are you part of a league? Like The Vampire League?" I joked, shoving another mouthful in.

Both Leif and Heath chuckled.

"What would be the point?" Leif said, seeing my expression.

"Yes, especially since we can pick up a bowling ball and throw it like a baseball and put it through a wall."

"Tremayne once crushed one in his hands."

"I recall that," Heath said, a reminiscent look on his face. "Oi! The bowling alley remained deserted for several nights after." He went into a fit of laughter and had to put his drink down.

Leif was up on his feet suddenly. "I see her. Damn it!" He was gone in a flash.

Heath and I simply returned to our respective meals in silence, as though someone moving around at the speed of light was a regular thing. I was beginning to get the hang of this.

The chirp of a cell phone sounded. I ignored it.

"I think that's you," Heath said.

"Oh! Damn. I keep on forgetting that I have one," I said, and rummaged around for it in the depths of my purse. I finally extracted it. I didn't read the number, but opened it and answered.

"Yes?"

"Sabrina," the deep voice vibrated through me like a bow on a violin string, and I had to grasp the table to keep my equilibrium. The sudden throbbing in my clitoris I had no control over. *Damn him!*

"Oh, uh, hi," I said, resisting the urge to put my hand between my legs. *This is embarrassing!* I cleared my voice. "Uh, how are you?" I plugged my free ear in order to hear him over the chinking noises and conversations around me.

"Much better," he said on a gasp. "Thank you, Sabrina. You've no idea—I've been an absolute beast all day waiting for—for your donation."

"I'm sorry. Maybe I should have come in sooner." I crossed my legs, in an attempt to ease the throbbing—it only made it richer and I had to close my eyes and simply enjoy it. *God, I hope no one knows I can get off on Tremayne's voice but me!*

"No. That's alright. I'll have to get used to the wait, anyway. You can't donate again for a week, and I'll have to wait until I can have it then."

I was silent. The throbbing subsided. I released the grip in my thighs. It was almost like holding the need to pee.

"I'm fine. Really, I am," he assured.

"So am I," I whispered, smiling to myself.

"I'll be able to maintain for a while. I can now safely say that I can look at you without wanting to devour you whole." His voice was filled with sarcasm.

"Oh, really? You sound so positive." I had my doubts.

"Turn around and look up," he said.

"What?"

"Look up, into the level above you," he directed.

I turned around, and looked up at the windows of the next level—Level A—it stair-stepped slightly over the dining area, as this level did over the bowling/billiards room below. The glass gallery curved above and there was Tremayne standing at the railing. It was the way to his office. I remembered having stood there myself and looked down. He waved at me.

Relief flooding me, I waved back. It wasn't his voice over the phone that had thralled me, it was his standing in sight of me, sending out his—whatever it was to give me an erotic ride. *Thank goodness!*

"There, you see? I'm able to look at you without wanting to come after you. This is marvelous." He was smiling, looking pleased.

Behind him stood Nicolas like a shorter shadow, dressed in a dark business suit, a suitcase in hand. He was leaving? I wondered where he was going. Our eyes met. Before I could ask, my vampire bite burned slightly. It hadn't done that since the night before.

"I have a suite ready for you. You'll spend the night," Tremayne's words yanked me back to the conversation.

"You mean the human side, right?" I wanted to make sure.

"Yes."

"My own suite?"

"Of course."

"Well... thanks," I said.

Ten minutes later Dante met us when we got off the elevator on Main. I said good night to Heath and thanked him again for letting me see Jeanie. It was like the men were changing guard, or something so Renaissance, and I was a maiden being taken to her end of the castle.

Dante led me through the mall, and to the entrance to the North Tower hotel. We could have gone through the outside entrance to get to the South Tower, but we'd have to go all the way around the building, and he said entering that way was more involved.

"It's something like what you'd go through to board an airplane," he explained.

"You mean they x-ray you?"

"No. They make you touch silver. I can't do that. So…"

"Oh, right."

From the end of the mall we entered a hotel lobby atrium. It rose five stories high, and my knowing told me this was the vampire hotel, not the human one. There was a glassed-encased elevator that went up to the fifth floor. The atrium was lavish, and I hadn't noticed it the other night when I went to dinner with Tremayne. The huge black piece of marble with the surrounding pool and waterfall stood a few feet inside its entrance. You had to walk around it to get to the hotel desk. This was the first time I'd seen what lie beyond that wall of black marble.

Dante took me beyond the hotel desk, and toward a blank wall with what looked like elevator doors. But they weren't the elevators. Above the door were the words SOUTH TOWER: HUMANS ONLY. Below this was something written in vampire script. I couldn't read it, of course, but I imagined that it may have been warning vampires they weren't allowed on the other side, or else it may have been merely decorative.

As Dante swiped his card he explained, "No vampire can gain access to this side of the towers, unless he has an unrestricted pass. You will need to use yours in order to gain access either in or out of here. Humans on the other side can't come through to the vampire side."

I had to wonder if a vampire couldn't get through if he really wanted to.

"Who has an unrestricted pass?" I asked. The doors whooshed open and we breezed through to the other side.

"Tremayne, naturally."

"Anyone else?"

"To my knowledge, only Tremayne."

The human side of the towers was no less lavish than the vampire half, but not as much red. Here the tones were mahogany, tan, and hunter-green with cream, and peach accents, and lots of mirrors. I had to smile, knowing what I knew now about vampires and mirrors. I couldn't help but think it was a private joke.

We strode through a hotel lobby. Brown leather chairs and sofas were huddled around a hooded fireplace. Huge crystal chandeliers hung from the expansive ceiling. A lavish sweeping staircase wound up to the second floor.

Arriving at the elevator, Dante asked me for my swipe card, to make sure it worked. It did. The doors opened to us, and we hopped on.

"After I take you up to your suite, I'm going down to get your things from my car." He then wagged a finger in my face. "Under no circumstances open the door to even the maid. Understood?"

"Yes."

He squinted at me.

"I'm not opening the door except to you."

"Good. Not even to Tremayne."

"Especially to him," I said and shivered.

The elevator stopped, and we strolled out onto a gold and navy carpet. It still smelled new. The walls had a fresh-paint smell to them. A lovely floral print, half way up, papered the walls.

We stopped at a door. Brass numbers announced we had arrived at room 1806.

"This is your suit," Dante said, pulling out a black card from his pocket. "Mine is across the hall." He pointed to 1805, then swiped the card through the swipe pad. The door buzzed, and he opened it to let me in.

"This is your key to get in." He handed it to me. I noticed it had my suite number on it. He back-peddled. "I'll be back in a bit."

"Okay." I watched as he strode back to the elevator.

I breathed out a sigh of relief as I shut and locked my door. Turning, I placed my key card in my purse, then threw my purse on a chair and took in my new place.

The couch, love seat, and chair were overstuffed, and done in brown suede, or a faux suede—I couldn't tell. The lush carpet was a deep forest green with a strip of peach running about one foot parallel with the walls. A glass-topped coffee table, and a side table with a jade green-based lamp and shade stood between the love seat and chair and gave the room a look that I couldn't achieve if I'd bought it all off the floor at a furniture store and brought it all home. The gas fireplace looked cozy, and it was lit, as though I'd been expected. Paintings on the walls were of Italian villas and florals.

The kitchenette was complete with cupboards, a full-sized stove and refrigerator, a microwave, and a breakfast bar separated the kitchen from the living area.

I detected a flower-sweet scent. Stepping past a large, flat screen TV stationed above a sideboard, I peered down a short hallway. The perfume was stronger here. The door of the bathroom was to my right, the door to the bedroom was straight ahead. It was dark back there. I flipped a wall switch. A ceiling light illuminated a recessed space devoted to a short credenza with three drawers. A bouquet of red roses, in a sea of white daisies, and a spray of pink freesias spilled out of a crystal vase.

There was a tiny envelope with my name scrawled on it. With trembling fingers I picked it up—had a hard time opening it up with my gloves on, but I managed—and read the card inside.

To Sabrina, my love~

Bjorn

Oh, crap. I was somewhat startled by the words on the card.

I stuffed the card back into the envelope and left it on the credenza. I was at a loss as to how to handle Tremayne's lust for my blood, and my body—and my lust for him, as well. When I was with him, I wanted him, too. Away from him I was absolutely frightened of the big, powerful vampire. Especially now that he'd nearly killed me.

Turning to the bathroom, I shuffled in, hit a wall switch, and found myself in luxury. The jacuzzi resided on a raised platform, a shower/tub was situated on the other side. Black ceramic, with gold faucets met my eyes. The floor was done tastefully in black and white marble in a diamond design. I'd never in my life seen gold faucets, until now. After pushing my eyes back into their sockets, I ran the water until it became warm and washed my face with a very thick, black washcloth that was somewhere in between velvet and velour. I patted my face dry on a matching towel that had satin running along the edges. Replacing my gloves on my hands, I turned out the light and returned to the small hallway leading into the bedroom.

I paused, thinking I may be the very first person to actually occupy this suite. I pulled off one glove and reached for the light switch to the bedroom. Almost nothing. No hard flash of any memory, thought, or emotion.

I let go a sigh of great relief. Only in my own home could I take off my gloves and relax. Now, I had a home away from home. This was somewhat exciting for me.

The bed was king size, a white and gold satin comforter with matching pillow shams. Like I needed a king sized bed. And then my mind worried what that might mean. Dante had said that Tremayne was the only vampire who had access to this side of the towers. The words on the card pretty much said it all. Now, as I looked at the bed, I knew what this all meant. At some point, Tremayne would make a visit—when he was used to my blood.

A knock to the door, interrupted my thoughts on all this. My heart jumped a little, but I knew it could only be Dante. To make sure, I looked out the peep hole.

"Sabrina, it's me. Dante."

Relieved, I undid the locks and let him in. He breezed by me with my small suitcase in hand. A black duffel sat out in the hall, near his door.

He paused. "Where do you want this? Bedroom?"

"Sure," I said. He marched through the suite. I knew he would see the flowers. He glanced at them in passing. In a moment he returned to the living room.

"Who sent the flowers?"

"Tremayne," I said, feeling some emotion roll off of him I couldn't quite identify.

"Thought so," he said. "Look, it's none of my business, of course, but be careful, Sabrina."

"That's me. Careful is my middle name," I said, smiling as brightly as I could.

"You know what I mean."

I let my gaze fall. "Yeah."

He lifted my chin to make me look up at him. "You're important to me, babe."

"Why?" I asked. I really didn't know what he felt toward me, other than some sexual attraction.

"What a question," he said, smile stretched across his face. He bent and kissed me, smack dab on the lips. It was quick.

Startled, I watched him move in a swish of raven-black hair into the hall, shutting the door before I could counter him with a look of dismay.

"Good night, Sabrina," he said through the door. "Lock up."

I stared at the door, trying to figure out what had happened. What *had* just happened?

"Lock up, I said. I'm waiting until you do," Dante said more firmly.

"Alright, alright." I turned the lock and threw the safety latch. Not that this would hold if a vampire really wanted in. But then I remembered a vampire needed an invitation before entering anyone's home, or apartment.

After a hot shower, I toweled off and slipped into my nighty. The suite was quiet as a tomb. My own place in the country wasn't this quiet. I wished I had more than one window to look out. The city skyscrapers became boring to look at after a couple of moments. After my long day—and I really didn't want to think about it at all—I was exhausted. I climbed into that huge bed, pulled the covers over myself, turned off the lights, and tried to find a comfort zone in a huge, strange bed. The pillows seemed a little overstuffed, but I managed to punch one into submission for my head and draped one leg over another. Satin sheets felt cool against my skin. No light came in through the only window in the bedroom—obviously, this was designed with a human in mind, not a vampire. Eventually sleep found me and I closed out the world.

* * *

When I heard a rap I was disoriented as I cracked open my eyes. It took a while before the cobwebs parted, and I came more fully awake. I finally figured out where I was. Not exactly where I wanted to be, but I felt safe, and I hoped that whoever was rapping on my door would not change that.

Another knock on the door came while I sped through an up-date in my mind on the day's events and why I was here. My last memories of Dante's warning about allowing anyone in resurfaced. I padded through the dark apartment, flipped on a switch and the lamp in the living room drenched the place in ambient light. I did not have a robe (it wouldn't fit in my small bag). I went to the door in my flimsy cotton night gown that came midway on my thighs.

Feeling trepidation crawl up my spine, I looked through the peep hole.

Staggering against a dizzy spell, I found myself standing at my opened door, looking out into an empty hallway. I had no idea why I was standing there with my door open. When had I opened it? Somehow I'd lost time, somewhere between looking through the peek hole and now.

The door across the hall flew open, startling me. Dante stood there, his male body eclipsing the minimal light from his own apartment.

I opened my mouth to speak, but Dante's raised hand silenced me. He launched out of his suite, closed his door and on silent bare feet entered mine. I backed away as he entered wearing nothing but black pajama pants with small white designs I slowly recognized as leaping cats. The ends of his loose hair fluttered as he turned. He closed my door, locked it and peeked out the peep hole. His silence and my inability to remember what had happened sent a chill up my spine that gave me sudden shivers. I wasn't wearing much for male company, and my male company wasn't wearing much either.

Finally he turned to me. "Are you alright?" His eyes took me in. I was as undressed as I could be with a man standing three feet away.

"Yeah. Weird, huh?" I worked my expression into something I thought was cool and aloof.

"Why did you open your door?" he asked, stepping closer to me, tripping off my libido by his nearness and bare male skin. I had to cast my eyes away from his bare chest. Something about that nice, hairless chest had me wanting to put my hands on him and explore the smooth, dark contours.

"I was compelled to," I said, shrugging. I edged back from him, putting a little more space between us. My nightgown wasn't see-through, but my goose bumps were giving him a lot of information. Fortunately he didn't pursue me. I wouldn't have control over my actions if he closed the gap. I couldn't understand my sudden desires, but whatever the reason, I found something about Dante triggered some primal need in me that I could barely control. I wanted to jump him, throw him down and ravage him. At what point had I become a nymphomaniac?

"Go on to bed. I'll stay here until dawn."

"Why? What was out there?"

"A vampire," he said, moving to look out the peep hole again. His edgy voice and actions made me nervous. That, and what he'd said.

"Who?"

"Nicolas." He looked over his shoulder at me. "Go to your room, and lock the door, Sabrina."

"Wow. You're scaring me," I said, backing away.

"It's for your safety... from me. I can't be here, near you, without wanting to act on my desires. Now, get into your bedroom and lock the door."

With his words, I practically ran to my room and locked my door. I stopped to listen. I thought I heard those odd crackling sounds that I *knew* to be a shifter going through his change. Whatever the reason Dante shifted—whether it was to guard me better, or to keep his male urges in check—I didn't really know, and at the moment it wasn't really important. What was important was I was safe from both vampire and shifter. I was too chicken to act on my own lusts. *Chicken, chicken, chicken.*

I eventually fell asleep and dreamed that Nicolas was standing next to Jeanie in a parking lot. Steve was behind her. Steve bit Jeanie on the neck from behind, and Nicolas smiled as he dipped two fingers into the blood oozing from her neck, then touched it onto the back of a silver car, and drew a V.

I woke up drenched in sweat, screaming.

I thought I heard a noise at my only window. I sat up. It was still dark out. I heard the sound of wings slapping the air. Then it faded away.

My vampire scar throbbed for a moment, and then it quit. The clock on the bedside table read 2:39 in blue numbers.

Chapter 22

My phone rang, waking me. I found myself in the middle of a huge bed. I rolled, and then swam my way across to the edge. The clock read 8:28. I located the phone and answered groggily. At the voice in my ear I became wide awake.

"Good morning, Miss Strong," Tremayne said in his richest baritone. It sounded halfway between a growl and a purr.

"Morning," I said in a courteous tone, and waited for his thrall to hit me over the phone. Thankfully it did not. I was a little startled he was up at this hour of the morning. The sun was out, sky was blue.

"I trust you had a restful night?"

"I... did." I paused, thinking. I remembered the knock at my door and the strange thing that happened after I went to see who it was.

"What's wrong?" he caught me in my hesitation. I didn't know why Nicolas had come to my door last night—or why he'd made me forget he was here—I wanted to give myself time to figure it out before I blew the whistle on him.

"Nothing's the matter. Um, was Nicolas leaving or something?" I asked, remembering that he'd had a suit case in his hand when I saw him with Tremayne, last night.

"Yes. Why do you ask?"

"Just curious. You'd think he'd want to find out why Toby is missing."

"I had something I needed him to do. Anyway, scions come, scions go."

"And did he?" I asked, trying to ignore his lack of concern.

"Did he what? What's wrong? What aren't you telling me?"

"Nothing's wrong." Yet. "I wondered when he left."

"His flight left at midnight. And speaking of flights, my brother is flying in tonight. That's why I've called you—other than wanting to hear your voice."

I smiled at that. "Nice to hear yours too."

"Anyway, we're going to a concert, and dinner tonight. I'll have a dress and everything you need brought to your room. I need your sizes."

"Me?" Startled out of my half-sleep I shifted some pillows to arrange them better behind my back and relaxed against them.

"Yes. What's your dress size?"

"I'm a ten."

"Shoes?"

"Seven. So, I'm coming with you?"

"Yes, you, and Dante, of course."

"And you won't attack me?"

"I'm, uh, making arrangements in that direction," he said, sounding distracted. "I hope your accommodations are alright?"

"Very. And thanks for the flowers," I added. I rarely got flowers. I thought it was a nice gesture.

"You are most welcome. Until tonight, Sabrina, my love."

Gulp.

Twenty minutes later, the tapping at the door threw my heart into a deeper rhythm when I emerged from my shower, dressed and ready for my day—whatever it would entail besides going out with two of the most powerful vampires in America later on. Dante was not there when I'd cautiously emerged from my bedroom, earlier. I'd wondered if I'd find a man or a jaguar in my living room. My Knowing kicked in. Dante was at my door.

I looked out the peep hole. Yep. Dante in man-form. Exhaling a sigh of relief, I opened up.

"Good morning," I said, smiling, recalling our strange moment in my suite, last night, and how he'd sent me to my room like I was some sort of temptation.

I stopped all motions and thoughts. The most wonderful aromas hit me. Behind him was a cart filled with silver domed-topped platters. "What's this?"

"Breakfast. Hungry?"

"Starved!"

After setting finding plates (they were white and square), and silverware, I set the breakfast bar with the plates, and we divvied up the food, and tucked in.

"So," I began, moving a forkful of scrambled eggs to my mouth, "why do you think Nicolas was at my door last night?"

"I don't know," he said, and inhaled a sausage whole. "A better question would be why did you answer your door to him?" he said after swallowing.

"I told you, I don't remember opening the door." It was a startling thought, now in the light of day. "You're sure it was Nicolas?"

"I know Nicolas' scent." He was right. I'd detected it too.

"Tremayne told me he was leaving last night on a flight. How would he be able to come to my room in the middle of the night, when he's supposed to be on a plane, and also, how would he have gotten over on the human side if he doesn't have a pass?"

"All good questions." He wiped his mouth. "First of all, if Nicolas really wanted inside, it wouldn't take much for a vampire of his strength to gain entry."

"Strength?"

"I misspoke," he amended. "His powers would allow him to move about as mist. Out of all the vampires under Tremayne,

Nicolas is the most powerful. I'd have to say he's as near a master as any other vampire under Tremayne, except for one other, but he lives in New York. At any rate, shape shifting is one thing only masters can achieve. The only thing he hasn't been able to master is to vanish completely, and a few other essentials."

"So, you're saying he came over on the human side, got up here—however he did it—to come to see me, and then made me open my door to him, and then for some reason made me forget he was at my door?"

"Yes." He was frowning at me. "In order for him to do that he would have had to have bitten you."

"But he didn't," I said, incredulous.

"Let me see your arm, the one with the bites."

I pulled up my sleeve and edged down my glove (since Dante had entered my living area, I'd put on my gloves limiting any reads from him, and in order to eat). He merely glanced at the vampire bite at my inner elbow, but his eyes went to my Were bite. Gently he took my wrist into warm fingers and brought it up closer for his inspection. The touch of his fingers was warm, and pulled memories of my lustful thoughts of him last night when I was banished to my room, so that *he* wouldn't be tempted.

Lifting his eyes to engage mine, he let a long breath ease from sexy lips, and said, "You've been bitten by a vampire." He released my arm. I pulled the sleeve back down and covered my wrist again.

"Yeah. Duh." I rolled my eyes. "Vasyl bit me."

"No. This bite is over your Were-bite."

"Huh?" My mouth fell open. "Nicolas?"

"Yes." He nodded. "That night when Nicolas took the venom from you, he also took blood—which he couldn't help, of course. This alone would not give him the ability to make you do anything against your will if he never bit you. I'm positive he has bitten you."

"You mean he put me under his thrall and made me open my door against my will last night?"

"Yes."

"So, you're saying—"

"When he took your blood that first night, he bit you. He probably couldn't help himself. The moment the blood scent is inhaled, the vampire's natural instincts come into play." I was nodding, remembering Steve's reaction over my blood. If it hadn't been for Nicolas' commands he would have bitten me. "Drinking blood stimulates the vampire's lust that revolves around their need to feed. To feed, they must bite and that's probably what happened. Nicolas may not have realized he'd bitten you, at the time."

"But he knows now," I finished. "I think he's always known. Oh crap."

Dante took a sip of coffee and held the cup before his lips. I caught a slip of his white teeth and had to dart my eyes away. I saw a vision of us together that took my breath away. Was it a vision of some future event? Or was it me thinking about becoming intimate with him? I couldn't decide.

"A vampire's bite injects a chemical into your blood system, connecting the two of you on a metaphysical level. Anytime the vampire is nearby, he can command you to do just about anything. Some can do so from afar."

"Oh-h, crap." I sat there thinking about the night he had come into my bedroom. "What can I do to stop him? He's already been inside my house."

"Wear the crucifix," he pointed to the one I still wore.

My hand went to it automatically. "I had it on last night."

"That may have been what saved you from his gaining entry."

Sighing my relief, I squinted in thought. "That's like what someone did with Solange?"

"Exactly. Someone bit Solange, gave her an edict and she could do nothing but act upon it."

There was something I needed to ask him.

"You seem to know a lot about vampires, and such," I said, shoveling my fork through the eggs. "What do you know about the sibyl?"

"The sibyl?" he said, looking thoughtful as he sawed into the waffles that he'd smothered in syrup. I eyed the waffles jealously. They were golden brown, I knew they'd be wonderfully crispy on the outside and delicious on the inside and I watched the oozing blueberry syrup running down the sides. I licked my lips. He made me take the eggs and ham, telling me I needed the protein because I'd given blood.

"Yeah. I'm curious because it's come up in conversation."

He shoved the mouthful of syrup-drenched waffles into his mouth and put down his fork, smiling as he chewed. A dribble of syrup leaked down one side of his lips. He wiped it off. I frowned. I wanted to lick the syrup off his lips.

"The sibyl is basically an ancient prophetess," he said after swallowing. He skewered a sausage and bit into it with the whitest teeth I think I'd seen on any human, and shrugged.

"Anything else?" I cut into the ham—it was off the bone, tender and not overly salty.

"Well," he said, around a mouthful. "The original sibyl in Greek mythology was the offspring of a shepherd and a nymph."

"That's what Nicolas told me. What's so special about her?"

"The sibyl multiplied and became thirty or forty—so the legend says. They were female oracles who usually predicted disasters like floods, wars, famines, things like that."

I stared at a spot on the table, thinking. "I've heard say there's a ring?"

"Yes. It makes her immune to vampire thrall. It's to be given at the time of the prophecy being told to her at a young age."

"Okay, since I don't have a ring, and vampires *can* make me do all most anything, I guess I'm not the sibyl."

"I didn't say you weren't. You could be. Possibly the prophecy hasn't been revealed to you for a real good reason."

I blinked at him. "What would be the reason?"

"We're talking about a very ancient prophecy. Plus, the ring is something that comes from *their* world, not ours." He sipped his coffee, gazing off in a corner of the room for a few seconds, looking thoughtful again. "The ring is also called Solomon's Ring. It's engraved with a mystic pentalpha that subdues demons and vampires alike."

"Can you look into it? I'm curious."

"Sure. Who mentioned it to you, by the way?"

"Actually, no one. I overheard Leif and Nicolas discussing it. Leif asked Nicolas if he thought I was the sibyl, saying that I was a very good clairvoyant." I shrugged.

"There is a prophecy in ancient vampire text that mentions a seer of great prowess."

"Do I have great prowess?"

"I think you do." His brow arched devilishly at me, and I giggled.

A half hour later, we were in Dante's car. He had tunes going but turned it off after we left the city behind. I'd told him that I hadn't brought that many things—I only had one pair of jeans, and had only one change of anything else. If I were going to stay for a few more nights, I would need more clothes. He was happy to drive me back to my house.

The whole business with Nicolas and the revelation that he had bitten me pulled a new memory from me and I suddenly felt a need to tell him.

"I had a vision of Nicolas with a pretty, blonde woman vampire. They were in a secluded spot, talking. But the conversation seemed—oh, I don' t know if intense is the word I want—but it was serious. Neither of them smiled the whole time—until the end of it."

"What did she look like?"

I described the woman to him.

"That sounds like Ilona Tremayne. Erik's wife."

"Erik?"

"Yes. Tremayne's brother."

"I was wondering," I began on a new tangent, "can you read any vampire's mind?"

"No. Only Tremayne's."

"You can't read any other vampire minds?"

"None. Except for Erik's."

"Erik's? Why?"

"Because, I was Erik's scion first. Now I'm Bjorn's."

"I didn't know you were a scion. You mean you're bound to do as you're told?"

"Pretty much," he said on an expulsion of a sigh.

"How did you meet Erik? I mean, I don't get how you came to be with them." I wanted to know more about him and hoped he was at a place where he could reveal something about himself to me.

"I was twenty-one when Erik came to me," he began with a heavy sigh.

I turned a little in my seat to listen.

"I was on top of this bridge, going to end it all, you know? When an angel—or what I thought was an angel—came to me." He glanced at me, gave me a slight smile and went on. "Actually, I thought it was a hallucination. This angel asked me if I wanted to live, or die? I told him I wanted to die. I was going to throw myself into the river below."

I made a small noise of concern, but didn't interrupt him.

"He knew I was telepathic. Of course, I knew that too. Then, he told me that I had another, hidden talent. He told me I was a shiftchanger."

"You never knew?"

"No. I didn't."

"Oh, wow."

"When this angel told me that he would take care of me, make me feel better than any drugs or the alcohol that I'd been abusing, I scoffed, but I had no will of my own. He bit me. There was pain initially, maybe slightly more than that of a needle going in, but then warmth spilled through me, a warm pleasure that surprised me. I think I fainted—no—I know I fainted. When I came to, we weren't on top of that bridge any more. We were in a nearby park. I felt like I was coming off a good high. He was standing before me, glowing like a light bulb. Well, by this time I knew he wasn't an angel, but not exactly human. I mean his wings weren't like an angel's, they were like a bat's."

I nodded. The memory of the man at my window—Vasyl?—had had wings too.

"Then he commanded me to drink from his arm. I watched as he bit his own wrist. The blood gushed red and thick down his arm. It tasted sweeter than I thought blood should taste, and slightly thicker as well. But when I drank his blood it was like I had been blind all this time, and someone had given me the gift of sight back. I felt free, and at the same time the knowledge of who and what I was, was simply *there*. It hit me all at once: My abusive father, and the way he'd beat us all, including my mother. All of my past slammed back into me, and then left me, as if a huge weight had been pulled off of me.

"Instead of feeling like shit, I felt wonderful. Strong—stronger than I'd ever felt all my life. My mind was crystal clear. No more drugs or alcohol lingered. I was freed from it and wanted it no more. I knew then what I really was. My father had repressed us all—he himself didn't admit to the fact that we could alter ourselves. I knew now that the beast lived within me, and all it took was the will to pull it out. It took me some bit of practice, finding the right way to call it out, but soon I was able to shiftchange without much problem. I think about becoming the animal, and it happens."

Dante turned to regard me now, as he pulled to a stop after we got off the tollway. He paused there, waiting for the light to change at the intersection. "Erik bit me, and showed me who I really was, and revealed all my potential. I owed him more than my life. At the time, I didn't know how I would properly thank him, but he had that all figured out." He chuckled humorlessly.

Dante's story surprised me. I would never have guessed he'd started out that way. But that was exactly how Nicolas had cured Toby of his drug addiction, and made him his scion. But I was getting that Dante had a stronger will than Toby had—he probably didn't have the needy thing that someone weaker who became a scion would. I figured it had more to do with the fact that Dante was a shiftchanger, than anything else.

The light changed. Dante made the turn and drove the quarter mile to the next stop sign and related the rest of the story to me.

"I stayed with Erik. I did anything he needed me to do. He would often have me read people's minds—those who were against him, those who might have cheated him. If he wanted me to kill—as the beast—I did that. I figured that it was all part of the deal. I would have been dead, if it weren't for Erik. I can't walk away from this, or them. I don't want to. I do what I'm told." He fed me a long, level stare. "And, yes, the money and perks are worth it."

I pondered the fact he had no problem killing for the vampires. Well, I'd seen him in action the other night. He had killed a werewolf, who was a man. There was no way I could ignore this fact. I just had to hope that whoever he killed had been very bad and had done terrible things to justify it in my own mind.

"So, how did you come to be with Bjorn?" I asked once I got over the initial shock of his admission of killing people.

"Bartering. The brothers often exchange humans."

"Doesn't that bother you?"

He shrugged. "No. Not really."

That surprised me a little bit. But I wasn't him. I wondered if that would be my lot.

"Where's your family?"

He didn't glance my way. "My father is dead and my mother lives in Phoenix, now. I found my mother a nice place to live and I'm paying on it for her. It's the least I could do, after her rough life."

"So, your father died of something?"

His lips curled into a soft, humorless smile. "That's something I don't talk about to anyone, usually." He looked my way. "Maybe when I feel you need to know, I'll tell you."

I nodded. I'd pushed him too much, and had to back off. I *knew* it was a terrible story, and his father hadn't died a natural death. He was good at blocking me. When he was ready, he would tell me.

Dante reached into his pocket and pulled out his cell phone. He must have had it on vibrate, because I didn't hear it ring. "Hello? ... Yes, we're almost there." He listened for a moment, gave me a sidelong glance, then said, "I can do that." I could hear the voice on the other line, but not what was said, I knew the voice belonged to Tremayne. "No problem," Dante said, and hung up. I was curious, but didn't ask what that was all about. I knew I would eventually find out.

Once we pulled into my drive, we extracted ourselves from his car and in a few moments we were inside my house.

"Where's your room? I'll help you pack," Dante offered.

"Upstairs." I shrugged off my coat. He had his off and we hung them on a coat rack. I lead him up the stairs, down the hall and straight to Randy's old room.

"I need the luggage out of this room," I told him, pointing at the closet.

"I'll get the suit cases," he said, moving toward the closet. "You get started with gathering your things."

"In a hurry?" I asked with a smirk.

He turned to me, smiled again. "Never, my lady." He made a slight bow, and I giggled, as he turned to dig out the luggage in the closet.

I walked back down the hall, and entered my own room. I really needed to check my phone messages on the house phone, but I could do that after I was finished up here.

I opened the top two drawers of my dresser and decided I could take everything with me in my underwear, sock, and glove drawers. One never knew what one might need at any given moment. I really didn't know how long I'd be staying in the Towers. *Forever?*

Dante lugged the suitcases into the room and set them down inside the door. I was grateful for his company, if only to interrupt my dismal thoughts.

"How much clothes do you think you'll need?" he asked, indicating the suitcases.

I darted a look over my shoulder. The suit cases had been my father's. Large matching Samsonite's, black with soft sides. They were old but had plenty of room in them.

"I don't know," I said eyeing my closet. "I'll need some things from my closet too."

"This is going to take a while, isn't it?" he asked, moving across the room, looking around. He spotted my teddy bear collection and paperbacks lined up in a bookshelf stationed beside my bed. I could tell his curiosity about me brimmed over.

"Not too long. Could you bring one of those over, please? Open it for me on the bed?" I said, and turned with an armful of clothing. He was standing one foot away, my load of socks and under things between us. Okay, this was awkward. Brown hands came up to cup my face and he kissed me lightly on the lips, his tongue darted out and teased. I dropped everything then. Stunned, I looked up at him when the kiss ended.

"Dante? What are you doing?" My laugh cut off, thinking he was joking around, but I could tell he was serious.

"At the moment, kissing you," he said, and he did it again. Feather light, with another flick of the tongue that rippled a thrill through me.

"Dante, I don't think—" He tapped my lip with a finger to silence me.

"I have to tell you something."

"What?"

"I want to make love to you. I've wanted to for a while. Since we met, in fact."

"O-kay." It was one thing to think about it in my head, but having the nerve to act it out was another thing, I quickly found out.

"But if you don't want to, that's alright. I can live with that. But I definitely have to scent you."

"What? Scent me? Why?" This was confusing.

"Orders," he said. "From Tremayne. If you don't want Erik, or Bjorn to become overly attracted to your blood, then we need to do this."

"That has to be the lamest excuse, or the worst line I've ever heard for a guy to want to screw," I sputtered. He had been making passes at me ever since that second night in my house. And truthfully, I couldn't resist his charisma and aura. No matter the reason, I was hot for him too. I made up my mind that I wouldn't try and play hard to get with him. I really liked him.

He caught my chin with his fingertips. "Tremayne doesn't want to lose you to his brother. *I* don't want to lose you."

"There isn't any other way? I mean…" I trailed off, eying the bed. Couldn't he simply rub on me? Well, sex was rubbing, wasn't it?

"The best way is skin-to-skin."

"I see," I breathed out slightly rattled. Dante would be only the second guy I went to bed with. I couldn't count Tremayne since we didn't exactly go all the way.

"Don't worry," he said quietly. "I'll make this easy. I'll do all the work. You lay back and enjoy." He grasped the front of his shirt and with a jerk popped all the snaps and exposed his hair-less chest to me—*nice*! His denim shirt was on the floor along with my undies and socks.

"Oh, boy," I blew out, and I sort of dipped with my weakened state. *God, he must work out.*

"Sabrina, Sabrina." He grasped me under the arms and held me up like a rag doll. "Don't be afraid. I don't take blood, okay? I'm not going to bite you. It's just me, human as human can get. I'm not deformed anywhere, I'm a regular guy. Actually, I'm told I'm better than average, but nothing over the top. Okay? I don't do kinky, we'll do it mission style, and that's it."

It was like he was explaining it all to a numb-skull idiot. "I'm, uh, not on the pill," was all I could choke out.

"Not a problem." He reached back and suddenly held up what I knew to be a condom.

"Shit," I said, looking away, snorting a laugh. I didn't do this. I didn't hop into bed with every guy who asked. Not that there'd been that many—none except for Jack, that is. This was *so* to-tally not me it was ridiculous. But I wanted this, didn't I? I'd fantasized about doing it with him last night.

"Okay," I said. "Have your way with me, then."

He snickered, sounding like a dry wheeze. "No need to get so melodramatic."

Like he said, he was not in any hurry. He kissed me, like be-fore. Tenderly, with the tongue thing. I parted my lips and his tongue slipped in. Then he flicked his tongue in and out of my mouth, settled into a rhythm that I knew was to be repeated with our bodies joined on the bed. Wild desire swept over me. I let myself go with it.

His hands slid under my shirt in the back, he undid my bra, and nearly as quickly as he had disposed of his shirt, mine fell to join his. We were now chest to chest. He felt warm—hot actually—and his musky scent anointed me. Winding my arms around him, with my gloves on, I explored his broad back, and muscles, while we kissed. His hands were all over me, as much as mine were all over him.

"You're beautiful," he whispered huskily.

Kissing down, he captured one nipple in his mouth. The sensation melted me, and I was suddenly in his arms. He carried me a short few steps and settled me on the bed.

He stood next to the bed, undid his pants and as I expected, he was going commando, and stepped out of them. As promised, he was an average guy—not that I'd known that many, but he didn't have any surprises, and he was raring to go. I was surprised to find he had nearly no body hair anywhere except a little on his belly, heading south.

He slipped my boots off, dropping them to the floor, and then peeled off my jeans. He lay beside me, head propped on one hand, looking down at me appreciatively, his other hand glided over my ribs, coming to rest on the full mounds of my breast, stroking me. His hand was like a warm glove.

"I like your voice. Your laugh," he said. "I love your eyes."

"Hey," I said. "You don't have to say such things to me."

"I *want* to. I'm not making these things up. I want you to know you turn me on. I think you're a sexy young lady."

"And you're... an older guy," I said stupidly, instead of what I really wanted to say. I thought he was terribly sexy, and I really liked him too.

"I would have rather we got to know each other in a normal way."

"Right. Like going out?"

"Yes," he purred in my ear as he nuzzled my neck. I shivered again.

His hand ran down my hip along the length of my thigh. It was like he'd placed his hand inside an oven for a half-hour, his body temperature was that much higher. He leaned over and kissed me, did the same sexy tongue thing again. His hand slid between my thighs. His fingers found me warm and wet. I jerked from his touch, and he pulled his hand away and looked at me.

"Hey, hey," he breathed.

"What?" I realized I was trembling.

"You okay?"

"Yeah," I breathed raggedly. "I'm just—you know—nervous."

"Don't be nervous. I know you've done this before. I mean you're not a virgin?"

"Oh, yeah. I mean no! I'm not a virgin!" *Jeeze!* "It's been a while."

"Don't worry. Relax." *Yeah, right.*

Dante leaned further over me, lips coming over mine and he slid a knee between my thighs. He was on his knees, hovering over me. I heard something rip, and I knew he was sliding on the condom. I trembled as he got into position and I tensed with the anticipated invasion. To my surprise, he didn't hurry. He paused at my opening. I squirmed slightly, then let out a little sound in the back of my throat as he kissed me. I arched my back to him, unable to stand the anticipation.

His hips thrust forward, and he filled me in a sudden, eye-opening motion. I pulled in a shocked breath, and he held still.

"I'm sorry," he said. "You seemed to want that."

"I did, but," I caught my breath before going on, "it was a little shocking. But not a bad one."

"Should I continue?"

"Oh, please," I begged.

Arms caging me, his long hair draped around us like black curtains, he began to move inside me, slowly at first and then he went into a deeper, hungrier rhythm and I arched to meet him at each stroke to bring him deeper. Together we worked toward that delicious, bright moment. It seemed out of reach until, yes, a little more, please, please...

"Oh, yes! Yes, yes, yes!" I clawed at his sides—not easy with gloves on. The glorious feeling was more surprising to me than I'd remembered it, and so *very* welcomed!

Afterward, we lay panting, soaked in sweat, side by side, wrapped in each other's arms.

"You want to shower with me?"

"More rubbing?"

"If you want."

"I want."

Chapter 23

Driving through the underground garage of Tremayne Towers felt eerie as always. Since that attack on Heath, I would never feel comfortable entering this dank area. I would forever be expecting a catastrophe to happen whenever I entered this section of the building. Not a good feeling to have.

Dante parked the Mustang into its own private parking slot, and cut the engine. I sat quietly, as I had the whole way back into Chicago, trying to make sense of the way my life had suddenly made this crazy turn; the danger, the vampires, shiftchangers—having sex with them—and finally meeting my dream vampire, Vasyl. I was surprised at myself for my recent behavior, but truthfully, I had to admit I'd enjoyed it—all of it. My boring life was suddenly turned around. Men wanted me, whereas before I was lucky to have a date.

After our lovemaking, Dante and I had showered. I thought his dark body was magnificent and his straight black hair actually came down to his butt. He was excited again, as the hot water ran over us. We did it in the shower. He pulled out right before his release, and held me against himself as he came and I had to wonder how or where he'd learned to do this. Jack certainly wouldn't have thought to do that. But Dante was older, more experienced than Jack. And then I *knew* how he'd gotten his experience. While we were naked in the shower, I'd had brief visions of Dante with other women. I knew then that he had, at one time, prostituted himself for money (he was younger looking in these visions). I knew what he did with that money, too. His life before Erik Tremayne was terrible. Horrible.

I knew my life had been changed, maybe not quite as dramatically as Dante's, but things had certainly changed for me in as far as dating regular guys. I knew I couldn't go back to dating boring, human men again. Dante had been such a superior lover, I could only compare him to Jack, and there was no comparison. Jack had been a selfish lover. Dante was not.

The door on my side opened and my private thoughts, and all my analyzing it came to an abrupt end. Dante looked in at me, then held out his hand to me when I paused.

"My lady, are you coming?"

"Do I have to?" I asked.

"I don't think you want to stay down here. Do you?"

"No." Resigned, I took his hand, and extracted myself from the relatively dark, warm interior of the car. I stood in the cooler, damp atmosphere of the parking garage as he closed the door. He suddenly grabbed me, hauled me up against himself and kissed me in a demanding way. He was hard again. I didn't need to use my clairvoyant abilities to know what he wanted to do—again.

When the kiss was over I looked into his intoxicating, smoky eyes.

"I want you again," he purred.

"Wow. How many times can you do it in a day, anyway?" My question was really rhetorical, but he answered me.

"As much as I please."

I blew out an amazed sigh.

"I get into this mating thing around the full moon, and I can't ignore it. I want you in my bed. I want you to belong to me, Sabrina." He gave me a sad look then and I understood. My stomach was in knots, knowing why Dante had made love to me—an edict from his master vampire—he had wanted to do this since he'd met me.

"Well, you'd better take a number, because I think the boss would have a thing or two to say about that." I hated when I was right.

"I know. That's what makes me hesitate."

"You don't seem hesitant to me." We both chuckled.

Hands braced against the car on either side of me, he let his head dip down to rest his forehead against my shoulder. He blew out a sigh, then lifted his head and went wordlessly to the trunk of the car to extract the suitcases. The suitcases were old, but they had wheels and I wheeled one along, while Dante grabbed the items I'd brought on plastic hangers from my closet. We hopped on the elevator and rode silently up to Main, then breezed through to the human side (using our passes), and went through the lobby to hop on that elevator. It was four in the afternoon, and plenty of people (humans, of course), were milling around, some were checking in, and some were either coming back from their tour through the city, or leaving to do the same.

We stepped into the elevator silently. I was comfortable with him, as though I'd known him my whole life—more so now than before. His silence spoke volumes, and anyway, he was probably reading my mind again. He said he could now read my mind (since we'd done it), so clearly, I wouldn't have to try and mentally tell him something—it would come to him.

He made another deep purr, a smile on his lips and our eyes met. I was thinking about having sex with him. I was terrible, I thought. What kind of woman walks around thinking about sex all the time?

"You're not alone, my lady," Dante said, a smile tipped his lips. Although we both had sex on the mind, he didn't approach me. He stayed a respectful distance away. He looked up at a point on the elevator. I looked to see the camera. Yes. They would be spying on us.

What about down in the garage? I wondered, knowing he would hear my thoughts.

"Not as many. More spaced out," he said.

I smiled, feeling excited that he could read my mind so easily, and now we were doing this covert thing. No one but us would know what we were talking about.

We arrived on our floor. Silently, we walked down the hall, and I swiped my key card, and we entered my suite. He didn't have to ask where to take my clothes, and I followed him into the bedroom. I knew what he wanted to do, and he knew what I wanted to do. We dropped everything and fell on the bed together. He shoved his hips between my legs and began dry humping me.

"I'm sore," I moaned. I was *very* sore. Three months of no sex and suddenly I had done it with a shiftchanger twice within the space of thirty minutes. "I'm sorry."

"Get un-sore, fast," he groaned.

I laughed and he resumed rubbing against me. I got into it and we were working ourselves into a real frenzy, then suddenly he groaned and jerked, and I knew what had happened. We lay there together, catching our breath.

"I guess you scented me real good today," I said.

He laughed as he lifted himself off me. "I'm going to go take another shower."

"I'm not joining you this time."

"Smart move," he said. "I'd only ravage you again."

I rolled my eyes, pulled in a hissing breath and let it out in a frustrated groan thinking about that.

He sauntered toward the door, turned his head, and threw me a look that utterly melted me. Without a word, he padded silently through the apartment, and only when I heard him say, "Lock up!" did I rush out of the bedroom and saw him close the door behind himself. I locked the door and leaned up against it thinking about all the unpacking I had to do.

But I had to change my pants first.

I had changed and put my clothes away when a knock on my door interrupted me. I went to answer it, wondering if it was Dante. It wasn't. It was a young pimply-faced guy holding something that looked an awful lot like a garment bag.

I opened the door the fraction with the security on. "Yes?"

"Ms. Strong?"

"Yes."

"I was told to deliver this to you soon as possible." He held up the long garment bag, and the way he held it in two arms made it seem heavy.

"Oh, okay," I said, and took the security off, and opened the door.

"Here you go," he said, pushing it toward me.

"Are you sure this is for me?" I asked, pushing my hair over one shoulder.

"Uh, yeah. Room eighteen-o-six, you're Ms. Strong, right?"

"Yes."

"Well, I guess this belongs to you. Mr. Tremayne sent it up."

"Oh." My memory kicked in. *Duh.* My mind had been a million miles away. *The dress.* I made a little sound in the back of my throat. "Thanks." I held out my hands and he settled the dress on my arms and it almost put me to the floor. "Whoa! Heavy."

"Yep. And here's the shoes." He settled a smaller bag that held a shoe box inside on top. "Have a nice evening, Ms. Strong." The young guy turned and lurched down the hall.

After he left, I placed everything on the love seat, unzipped the black garment bag and saw sequins and seed beads covering an ankle-length, sky-blue dress. I unzipped it all the way and pulled it out. Sleeveless, it dipped down low in the back and low enough in the front to make me feel self-conscious. What was I going to show off in that? As a matter of fact, since I'd never gone to my prom—or any prom—I didn't know what sort of bra I could wear with it.

Curious I checked the tag. *Dior.* It was a frigging Dior? Matching elbow-length gloves, shoes, and a clutch purse included. And inside the bag was a white mink stole. No wonder it was heavy.

I paced around the room in quick steps patting my warm face to make sure I wasn't dreaming. Heart racing, I stopped and extracted the matching blue, three-inch heels, and tried them on. They fit, what do you know? I was making little incoherent noises while stepping around in the shoes. I felt like Cinderella.

The knock made me stop what I was doing.

I peeked through the little peep-hole. Tremayne stood at my door. A wave of nerves hit me.

I opened it, not bothering to use the security this time—since it was still off. I asked him in, trusting he wouldn't be here if he was a danger to me.

"Did you get the dress?" he asked as soon as he swaggered in.

"Yes. See?" I moved to thrust one foot forward. "Shoes. Dress." I pointed to the dress.

"Try it on. I want to make sure it fits you."

I didn't hesitate, but grabbed the dress and darted into the bedroom to try it on. I closed the door to have privacy. I found that it had a built-in bra (well, duh), and once I zipped it up, I found that it fit like a glove. A heavy glove. It might have been ten or fifteen pounds of sequins and seed beads that covered the whole thing that reached my ankles. The gloves came over my elbows and I realized you wore them sort of slouched down a little bit. They had a spiral of sequins decorating each one. I slipped on the shoes again, and stepped out and found I had an all-male audience. Dante and Tremayne both were standing in my living room. They stopped talking, turned and stared at me for a long quiet moment.

"Nice." Tremayne said.

Dante nodded his agreement. His look said it all.

"I have a woman coming up to do your hair and nails," Tremayne said, looking at his watch, "in about twenty minutes."

I went into hyper drive. "What? I haven't showered!"

"Yes, you did," Dante said, squinting at me. "At your house. Remember? Before we left?"

"Oh." I stared at him pulling the memory up. My face warmed. "Yeah, that's right. How could I forget that? Silly me." I giggled nervously, and twisted the sequined fingers of the gloves—they felt strange and heavy. This was a sweat inducing moment. It was a good thing that Tremayne wasn't the mind reader—he could read my emotions, but not my mind, since he'd had my blood.

"Since this is such a big evening, and since my brother is joining us—" Tremayne's voice trailed off. Moving my direction, he pulled something out of his pocket and out came a glittering necklace. Once again my heart stopped. He held a diamond necklace—a journey-style pendant with the largest rock at the bottom, ending with the smallest one at the top. He came up behind me and fitted it around my neck, his fingers giving me little chills as he did.

I turned. He gazed appreciatively at it, as he stepped back. Pointing, he said, "Take care of it. It put me back a little."

I gulped. "Y-you'll want it back, of course."

"No, Sabrina. It's yours." He held up his hands. "A gift from me."

"Gift?" I said. This couldn't be happening to me.

"We'll be leaving in an hour." Tremayne turned to Dante. "Your tux come?"

"Just arrived, that's why I was in the hall," Dante said, and slid me a look.

"Good. Now, unfortunately, I have to go and get into mine," Tremayne groaned slightly. "Will you do me a favor and meet us half way, in the north lobby? Escort Ms. Strong?" He was directing this to Dante.

Dante made a bow. "Of course. My pleasure."

Both men exited, but Tremayne paused before closing the door. "You're going to knock them dead tonight, my love."

"I hope not!"

He laughed. "Just an expression." He turned away, and then a thought stopped him. He turned back and said, "By the way, my brother is *my* sire."

I nodded. "Nice to know both of you are older than dirt."

He chuckled.

"An hour, then," he said.

"An hour," I repeated.

As soon as he left, I went and slipped out of the dress, shoes and gloves, and got back into my street clothes. Nervous, I sampled the sparkling water in the fridge, noting that there was one bottle of wine and a couple of bottles of Real Red chilling. It was good to know that I could entertain a vampire after a long evening.

The hairdresser, and the manicurist both arrived within moments of Tremayne's exit. The hairdresser had wild white-on-black hair, and black, plastic rimmed glasses with sequins. Her name was Tosha. She chewed gum the whole time and talked around it. The manicurist was older, with long blond hair. Her name was Dev. They had a shop in the North Towers called *Manes & Thangs*. I knew they weren't vampires, but they weren't wholly human. I tagged them as Weres of some sort— the vampires would be too attracted to these two to leave them alone, I knew they had to be unsavory to vampires, whatever they were.

Dev said she'd do my nails in a "French manicure," with the tips blue to match the dress, although I'd told her not to bother since I wore gloves.

"Oh, honey, they'll look great, after. Y'know?" she argued lightly.

Okay, whatever. I braced myself to block out her emotions as she touched my hands. And nothing happened. Weird, I got nothing from her, not so much as a blip. I didn't understand this. Same from Tosha. Nada. Zip.

A hundred bobby pins and about one and a half cans of hair spray later, they helped me slither into the dress, and zipped me up. I stood in the full length mirror noting I'd never looked this way before. I thought, *if only my dad could see me now.* Then tears burst into my eyes suddenly. Both women were caught up in my emotions and hugged me. Well, hell, they were elves. When they hugged me, I saw their pointed ears. Possibly my clairvoyant powers couldn't read an elf. Good to know.

Dante stepped through the door as the beauticians pranced out. It was like I had a starring role in a movie or something. My mantra went, *This couldn't be real.*

"You—um, ah—"

I looked up at him as he stood there in a tux looking as though he'd been hit by a stun-gun. I thought he looked handsome, but different. His hair was braided on both sides. I decided it was probably because I was used to seeing him in jeans with his hair down.

"Who are you?" I asked.

"I might ask the same thing of you. Wow," he said, taking me all in. "That's Indian for wow, by the way."

"Back at you. Hey, I speak your language!" We both chuckled.

I sashayed toward the door and tripped half way across the room, only to fall into Dante's arms. I looked up into his eyes and knew what he was thinking.

I hauled myself to my own two feet—the weight of the dress really threw my balance off. "You'll have to keep those thoughts on hold," I said, re-adjusting myself inside the gown.

"I'll do my best, but it's going to be real hard." I caught the double entendre there, and couldn't help choke back the chuckle that erupted. Swishing away, I waited for him in the hall. Once in the elevator, he pressed for Lobby.

"I need to brief you on Erik," Dante said. "You're about to meet the most powerful vampire in North America. He has the authority to make the decisions that Tremayne can't."

"In what way?"

"The American Vampire Association?" he said, voice going solemn. "Think of it as their version of the mob."

"Oh. Got it."

"He's got a shrewd business sense, and he's not afraid of going up against anyone, anywhere, and in any way he pleases. Usually, baring teeth. But normally, on an everyday level, he sends one of us."

"Us?"

Dante shot me a quick glance as we arrived at the lobby and stepped off. "Someone like me, or another shapeshifter, or vampire under him." We strode briskly across the lobby.

"I see," I muttered. We dodged people coming and going, making our way across the lobby until we stood at the doors that only we could pass through. I caught the curious stares out of the corner of my eye. "So, you're saying he's deadly."

"Deadly, yes. And ruthless. Whatever you do, don't piss him off. Don't say anything that might be misconstrued, either." He paused and turned to me. "Erik will be curious about you, and want to take you from Bjorn." I tried to interrupt, but he pressed on. "He and Bjorn will argue possibly all night, about it. You'll have to ignore it all."

"Damned vampires. Think they own us."

He brought his hands up and grasped me by the shoulders, turning me to face him. "The one thing to remember, under no circumstances touch him. He'll sniff you. That's considered acceptable and polite vampire etiquette."

"So, smelling the other person's dates—he's got Martha Stewart's backing on this?"

"Not funny."

"Sorry. I get nervous and I joke. Bad habit." I play-slapped myself on the cheek.

"He'll know I've been with you. He'll accuse his brother of setting this up. Whatever you do don't let him know that you've donated blood."

"Got it."

"Everything you're wearing tonight, it's yours. Bjorn will have told him you've been with us for about a month, that way he won't wonder too much about how you gained money to buy these things, or how well you're ingrained into our society."

"What about the diamond necklace?" I pressed my hand on it.

"Bjorn will have an explanation for that. Play along, whatever he says."

"Okay."

"Ready?"

"No. Wait." I turned to look at him. "Are we supposed to be lovers?"

"Yes. Bjorn will back that up. There's no other way to explain that you smell of me." He swiped his card and the doors slid opened to admit us through to the vampire side of the Towers.

This side was swamped with vampire tourists. They were checking in, naturally because it was now dark out, they had arrived from O'Hare Airport. I remembered that Tremayne Air was their special jet made without windows—or the windows were fake—for vampire passengers, from that video that Nicolas had shown me that night we'd gone to Earthly Pleasures. It wasn't until now I made the connection.

Dante took my arm, led me through the lobby and it really wasn't hard to spot the two head vampires, as they were the tallest ones in any crowd.

Entering from the human side to the vampire side took a little getting used to. It was almost like entering a totally dark room where some sort of party was going on; I saw vampire women with vampire men, looking as though they were normal people checking in—except they had really pale, to opaque skin. Those of African American descent, or other dark races had a washed-out look. When Dante and I stepped through, heads turned to stare at us—because we were the only ones with warm blood in us. The worst case of heebie-jeebies hit me. Dante's arm slid around me and he gave me a reassuring peck on the side of the face.

"Don't worry, I'm here, my lady," he whispered in my ear, and it tickled.

Eric Tremayne was first to spot me from our party—and boy was I glad I had a party to belong to. Then his brother turned around. There was a great resemblance, and plenty of difference between the two men. Erik was slightly taller, not as robust, and in the looks category, much more handsome, and in the vampire world you really had to split hairs because they all looked uncommonly beautiful—men as well as women. Erik's hair was longer, absolutely straight and platinum blond. His nose was slightly hooked, his lips fuller, and his eyes were startling. Not blue, but I-swear-to-God silver with a darker shade circling the iris. The instant he sighted me it was as though a laser from an otherworldly battleship had found me and tugged me in.

Standing next to Erik was a pretty, light-skinned African American woman with straight blond hair, wearing a red dress that was cut lower than mine, had a slit up the side, to her hip, with her G-string showing, and she wore four-inch ruby red heels. She clung to Erik like he were a life saver and she was in a riptide. I had news for her.

As we moved closer, and entered their circle, I noticed that Tremayne also had a woman clinging to him. Blond, she'd chosen a black chiffon number that gave the red one a run for its money. Although I knew my evening gown cost more than what the other two wore all together, I was over-dressed—material-wise. My hem came to the ankle, and although I did have a slit, it only cut right above the knee. I didn't have cleavage anywhere near what these two had. Once more, I merely felt like I were a stand-in for the real stage actor. Tremayne had set this up perfectly: He had a date, Erik had a date, and Dante had a date. That made six of us.

I wet my lips thinking this might work out. I realized the woman with Tremayne was one of the women he'd chosen the other night. The other one might be from the donor pool—considering that vampires don't share their donors.

"Sabrina, Dante, good of you to join us," Tremayne said in a smooth-as-silk voice. "Erik, I'd like to present to you, Sabrina Strong, my clairvoyant," Tremayne introduced.

"How do you do?" Erik said with a British accent, as he moved with the grace and slowness only a vampire can achieve when he really wants to. He floated toward me, closing the gap easily. I was disoriented by the force of his silvery eyes—as well as his overwhelming thrall.

Dante held my hand firmly while I held still. This was something like meeting your friend's new dog. *Hold still and let him sniff you. He won't bite. Really, he's quite gentle.*

Erik was so tall that he had to bend down to breathe in my scent, and he did so as though he were sampling just-corked wine. His eyelids fluttered shut, and he groaned lightly, as though I were quite scrumptious. He straightened and looked at Tremayne.

"Tender, sweet morsel, Bjorn! Where did you find such a spry young thing?" His surprised voice seemed on the other side of too syrupy. I wondered if his English accent was put on, rather than acquired, too.

"Dante actually found her," Tremayne said. He was playing his trump card right away.

"I see," Erik sneered. "His scent is all over her. Is that the way of things, then?"

"I felt Dante deserved a little cunt now and then. What's wrong with that?"

My face must have turned beet red. I opened my mouth to make protest, in a lady-like way, of course. Dante's tightened grip and slight jerk stopped me. This at once earned him a disgruntled look from me.

Erik gave a rich laugh and stepped back—or rather he melted back—and the woman who had been on his arm didn't realize he'd stepped away from her. She sort of shifted back into position on Erik's arm and giggled like an eighth grader.

My thoughts ran the gambit of everything I would have liked to do to both big vampires at that point. Where was a crossbow when a girl needed one? Since I couldn't run, and I sure as hell wasn't going to slap anyone, I merely stood there like a live volcano and waited until the trembling stopped.

"Did you at least taste her before you let the shifter take her to his bed?"

I saw a tight smile on Tremayne's lips as he slid a look toward me. "Of course. She was a good lay, but nothing extraordinary, and the same could be said of the blood."

Arms crossed, I pulled in a breath and let it out slowly—glaring at him with everything I had.

"Why not give her to me?" Erik suggested. I froze again, listening to the two vampires talk about me as if I were a baseball trading card. Well, Dante had warned me, hadn't he? Still.

"I've given you two witches, a warlock, *and* my last clairvoyant. What do you want with this one?" Tremayne sounded disbelieving as he said this.

Erik shrugged. "Perhaps, then, for a night of debauchery. I won't hurt her any more than you could have."

Dante and I exchanged glances. This really wasn't going so well.

"I'm hungry," the blonde woman at Tremayne's side whined. "I thought we were going to dinner."

"Our reservations aren't until eight. We're going to the concert first," Tremayne said patiently.

"We'd better be going, or we won't make the concert," Erik suggested, glancing at his watch.

And the debate, for now, was over.

Chapter 24

Eric and Tremayne turned and we all trouped through the front doors—I didn't know where the front doors were, until now. We stepped past a metal detector for the entrance. Everyone who entered had to pass through it. Two security guards stood on either side of the doors, directing people, making them take off watches, as well as their shoes (I thought was a bit much). One woman complained bitterly about this process. The man with her chuckled and said he wasn't sure why they were going through this, since vampires couldn't be killed by a bullet.

"Ah, but a bit of silver touched to the skin can hurt like a bitch," another man behind him sounded off.

I realized that no one could get inside if they had any weapons, unless they knew the garage way in, of course. I hoped they weren't wrong in not having the metal detector down there as well.

Something about that thought lead me to a sudden vision of Toby. He was in a dark place. *Where was he?*

We stepped out into the cold night. I was glad to have the stole, though I knew several poor animals had been slaughtered to give their pelts for it. I'd wished he'd found me something less luxurious, and something that hadn't belonged to Letitia. Earlier, I'd gotten a flash of her wearing exactly what I was wearing recently.

I wasn't surprised to find we were all ducking into a stretch limousine. It was white, the chrome shiny as though it came off the showroom, and the driver in his spiffy light gray hat and suit stood at the opened back door, waiting dutifully. The vampires and their dates went in first, Dante and I ducked in last. We sat backward, facing Erik and Tremayne and their dates.

I settled next to Dante, his arm casually across the back of the seat behind me, crossing his legs. I crossed mine, showing some leg, but not nearly as much as the vampires' companions.

Both women giggled eying one another and cried, "Champagne!" as if they'd gone through this before. I figured they probably had.

I watched as Tremayne pulled the bottle out of the ice bucket, then expertly uncorked it with only the slightest pop. He poured four glasses. We humans were handed a glass each. Meanwhile, Erik poured the red stuff into the same type of glasses and handed his brother one. Everyone had a drink. I was about to take a good belt when Dante nudged me. I caught his significant look.

Probably not a good idea for me to get drunk. I took a sip. It hit my tongue setting it to tingle—unfortunately it was good, and I really, really wished I could belt it back, if only for this one night.

The movement of the car as it took off caught me off guard. It felt weird moving backward in a car, but I got used to it. Other than the initial take off, I was barely aware that I was in a vehicle; the ride was smooth.

The woman with Erik shrieked. I looked up to see that he was nuzzling her neck. His touch and thrall had probably given her a hell of a precursor to bedroom sex with him.

I pressed a little into Dante, felt his arm go around me, his fingers ran negligently up and down my arm. I knew instantly what he was thinking about doing to me later, simply because it was there in my mind too.

Eyes were boring into me. A glance across the car, I found Tremayne's eyes trained on us. A warning look flamed there. *Oh, shit.*

We leaned away from each other slightly, and Dante quit touching me.

There was a sudden burst of sound like glass breaking. Both women screamed. I saw Tremayne's closed fist hovering above the ice bucket, now wet and empty where a second before there had been the champagne bottle. Champagne had sprayed everywhere, along with bits of glass. Tremayne's anger at seeing Dante so into me had pressed him too far. Erik noted this, a smug expression washing over his features.

While this one electric moment charged the air in the limo, I suddenly had a flash of vision, and made an incoherent sound.

"What is it?" Tremayne asked, handing a towel to the blonde who looked a bit on the soggy side.

"I'm not sure." I shook my head. I knew I was about to be pulled into a strong vision. "Something's going to happen," my voice filled with panic. I gasped as I took in the blond with Tremayne. I saw her body suddenly transposed into some future moment; unconscious, draped in Tremayne's lap, blood sliding down her neck and arm, dripping from her fingers.

I clutched onto a hand in desperation. I heard someone say my name—either in my head or out loud. The vision took precedence, and I could do nothing to block it as it came full-bore.

And then I blacked out.

* * *

Cool fingers were at my temple. Slowly my eyes flitted open to find myself looking up into Tremayne's face. He gazed down at me. Supine, I was in his lap. The blonde couldn't be unhappier about this new situation, and I couldn't be more uncomfortable to be so close to him. Of course, he used his mind-touch on me to bring me back.

"Tell me what more you saw," he said in one of his lowest octaves, it rumbled in his chest.

"It was flashes of scenes," I said. "I can't make any sense of it."

"Tell me!" His command startled me.

My eyes darted to the blonde, then back to Tremayne's face. "I saw someone's hand with blood dripping down from her arm. I saw something like a stainless steel wall, maybe with drawers or doors on it. Blood, I—I saw a bolt? No. Many bolts." I glanced to Erik. "You are hit by a bolt."

"Bolt?" At first he looked stunned, then a smile split Erik's face and he chuckled. "Your clairvoyant is entertaining, I'll give you that."

"I saw you go down." I stared at Erik.

"Maybe we should postpone this evening," Tremayne suggested.

"Don't be silly," Erik smirked.

My hands flew to my temples, my eyes squeezed shut. "Toby. Somewhere dark." I said in a warning tone. *Where the hell was Toby?* "Oh... I see it now. He killed them. Letitia and the others," I said calmly. Maybe my sensitivities had been dulled somehow. Opening my eyes I looked up at Tremayne.

Squinting, Tremayne's dark-teal eyes flitted around the confines of our luxurious ride. Suddenly, he made a low growl in his throat. Eyes slipping shut, he held absolutely still for a few long seconds. My heart pounding with dread as I watched his face go through some sort of terrifying transformation. His mouth fell open in a horrible low growl, and I saw the huge fangs run out. His eyes flashed open, they were no longer the color of the sea, but blood red. I was looking right into the fires of hell. Those horrifying fangs darted toward me. I couldn't move. I could do nothing but accept my fate at the hands of this master vampire.

Then, as if I were a piece of paper tossed on a gust of wind, I took flight. One second I was in Tremayne's lap, about to be a blood meal for all time, and in the next I was in Dante's lap. I'd been shifted from one lap to the other. I quickly righted myself on the seat next to Dante. I had no time to scream when I saw what was happening across from us.

A woman's squeal from across the limo drew my attention to find Tremayne holding his date like a rag doll. Fangs buried deeply into her neck, she went from surprised squeals to a deeper sound in the back of her throat; her body arching and jerking helplessly under his possession. Then she went suddenly limp on a long sigh. Tremayne threw back his head and roared like a lion, teeth stained red, blood dripping in strings from his mouth. Then, all exposed areas of his flesh glowed like a light bulb for a few seconds and went out. Something went through me as realization hit.

"Oh dear. We should have brought a couple of extra whores with us. Seems as though the blood lust has taken you by the dick, brother."

Tremayne released the girl, who now lay lifeless in his lap. I knew she was dead—not merely because she didn't move at all, but I'd already witnessed the scene I was faced with now.

Tremayne wiped his bloody lips with the back of his hand, and looked absolutely mortified by what he'd done. Blood stained the white of his collar, and elsewhere.

"Dante, call—" Tremayne didn't get the words out fast enough.

"Already on it." Dante had the cell phone in his hand and spoke carefully, but quickly into it. To my ears it sounded somewhat like a 911 call.

"They're on their way," he informed, folding the cell phone up, then replaced it in his pocket.

"Fuck!" Tremayne swore.

"What's come over you?" Erik asked, perplexed. "I haven't seen you this out of control since Mussolini declared totalitarianism in Italy. You went out of control then, drinking to excess. Tell me, are you on a rampage again?"

"No!" Tremayne gasped, still watching the woman in his arms. "No. I didn't mean to do this." There were tears in his eyes. His tears were tinted pink. I had no idea that vampires cried. Tremayne especially.

Erik lifted the woman's wrist. Dark trickles of blood slid down the arm as he did. He turned to look at me. "This was in your vision," he said to me, then two fingers to her bloodied wrist he waited for a pulse. He made an unconcerned sound and shrugged. "She's expired, I'm afraid." Dropping her arm, he licked the woman's blood from his fingers casually as though it were merely spaghetti sauce. He made a smacking sound. "Not bad. AB positive."

As though coming out of shock, the woman next to him began to scream really loud. So loud it nearly broke my eardrums and I had to cover them.

Erik rolled his eyes exasperatedly. "Oh, will you STOP!"

The woman stopped and slumped back into the seat, eyes closed as if she were merely asleep. He'd put her under a heavy thrall.

"I really hate it when they go all to pieces." He regarded me. "Your clairvoyant seems to not be very affected by all this."

"I've seen it before." *And almost had been there.* "There's nothing I can do, and screaming, and going all to pieces won't change things."

"Very bright young woman. Brother, you must trade me your clairvoyant! I'm in lust with her."

"Not a chance," Tremayne said in a savage whisper, and shoved the lifeless woman off his lap onto the empty space between himself and his brother. He slumped, white hanky to his eyes stained with red. Our eyes met. I knew that that would have been me had he not moved with that Uber-vampire quickness. He tried to convey this to me with a plaintive look as he opened his cell phone. He suddenly barked into his cell phone, "Get down to the garage and look for Toby! That's right! He's ascending. Let me know if you find him." I must have told him where to find Toby during my vision. I couldn't remember.

The limo pulled over and stopped. No one moved. The next moment, the door opened and a man in a dark suit slid in, and paused. Bent at the waist, he surveyed the interior. A pall of some heady mix of smoke, and something I couldn't identify, entered with him.

"Erik? Hell. I didn't know you were in town," the stranger said, as he moved to a small seat next to the door.

"Oddly enough, that's exactly what my second wife said to me, right before I turned her," Erik drawled, with a flick of the wrist.

Two more people hunched through the door, and it became really crowded in there. They wore Sanguine Team uniforms. The elves—a man and woman—knelt beside the dead woman. The woman elf put a stethoscope to her chest and the man tried to find her pulse at her wrist, like Erik had done.

The female elf turned to the other elf, and shook her head. "Gone."

They moved to check the African American woman.

"She's fine. She's just out," Erik said defensively. But they checked her out, anyway. They exchanged looks, and nodded to the man in the suit that the woman was as Erik had said.

"Give me a few minutes with them, please?" the man in the suit said. They left, and shut the door behind them.

"Who did this?" the man said, he had a pad and pen out.

"Me," Tremayne said exhaustively, flopping a hand up briefly to signal guiltily.

"This will cost you, you know," the man said.

I then realized it was the man from the night Nicolas had taken me out to the graveyard. I was trying to bring his name up when Erik said, "Fuck you, Crimmins."

Crimmins chuckled deeply. "You know the laws as well as your brother, Erik." Narrowed eyes slid to observe Tremayne. "You want to tell me what happened? Or do I have to drag your sorry ass down to H.Q.?"

"I've been under a lot of stress lately. My life-time mate was murdered, and I've just learned who the murderer is."

"And of course you called me right away to keep me informed," Crimmins said, the sarcasm falling easily from his lips.

"Again, fuck you, Crimmins," Erik said politely in his British accent.

Crimmins turned his large head Erik's way. I really didn't know what was going on, this bantering, for one thing was really strange. Crimmins acted like a cop, or detective. I knew he wasn't a regular human cop, but why were Erik and Tremayne acting like the guy had the upper hand, like he could lock one, or both of them up like a regular human? Two powerful vampires couldn't subdue this man?

"He's a Ba'al demon," Dante said low in my ear. "They can't be thralled; and their blood is absolutely deadly to vampires."

My eyes went wide at that. I slid a look toward Crimmins. He looked human enough. Possibly he was wearing a clever disguise, and underneath he was all green and ate large rodents whole.

"Who killed her?" Crimmins asked, bringing me out of my thoughts. "Or are you keeping that a secret from me as well?"

Tremayne let go an exasperated sigh. "Toby Hunt," he said wearily. I caught up with the conversation at hand.

"Nicolas' scion?" he scoffed.

"Yes."

"How?" Crimmins' mouth twisted into a snarl. "How was he able to approach and then kill Letitia? She would have seen him coming, wouldn't she?"

"He hit her with a bolt, somehow he'd gotten himself up on her balcony and waited for her to come out. I still don't know how—"

"Rope," I blurted. Everyone's eyes turned on me. "The ropes from the scaffolding. I saw it on Nicolas' balcony. Toby acknowledged he knew about it. I can't believe I didn't remember that! And I saw the vision of him in her apartment. You remember?" I looked straight at Tremayne.

"Yes. I do remember you saying something, but you never mentioned Toby at all."

"I-I'm sorry. I didn't think it was important at the time."

Tremayne held up a hand. "Don't worry about it."

Crimmins squinted at me. I saw his eyes register a glimmer of recognition. "You're Strong, right?"

"Weak as a kitten," I said. Okay, my little joke really didn't fly in this somber company. They all gave me dead-pan looks. Dante didn't smile, either. Slightly crest-fallen, I said, "Yes. I'm Sabrina Strong," I answered correctly.

"How do you know this?" Crimmins asked, his voice patient, sincere, and I detected a slight wheeze as he breathed, almost as though he had asthma.

"She's a clairvoyant," Tremayne answered briskly.

Crimmins nodded, and began scribbling something on his notepad. "Now, you say you saw that he used scaffolding rope?"

"Not exactly. I was at Nicolas' apartment one morning—uh—having breakfast. There was this coiled up rope there. Toby had said that workers were still working on some of the windows, or something. I hadn't thought about it since then. But I think he had to have used the rope to reach Letitia's balcony. In other words he had a way to get up there." My clairvoyant mind had the vision running in my head while we spoke about it.

"That's only five stories above Nicolas' apartment," Tremayne observed.

Crimmins turned to Tremayne. "But how would he have gotten this rope up there in order to use it to reach the penthouse?"

"He tied a smaller, or thinner rope to one end, and used a crossbow to shoot the other end up to Letitia's balcony—which is straight above theirs," I said, looking at Tremayne. "When he visited her that time, he used his visit as an excuse only to get up to her balcony in order to set things up. Pull that rope up and hang it so that he could get into place in order to shoot her."

"Ah, yes." He nodded. "I see how that would work." Crimmins turned away from me. "Who found Letitia?"

"I did." Tremayne plunged into the story from there, stemming off what I would have said—and probably screwed everything for him.

When he was finished, Crimmins asked, "Why was Mr. Hunt killing vampires?"

"He drank their blood," Tremayne said.

Crimmins made a sound of interest. "Nice. Where is the little asshole now?"

"He's ascending as we speak," Tremayne informed, and made a wheeze. "I've gotta find out where he is!"

Erik chuckled. "I don't think I've had so much fun on a trip to Chicago since Al Capone was shooting things up. Brother, you didn't tell me any of this, only that someone had killed Letitia." He tsked, and shook a finger at him. "Not nice to keep me in the dark. That pisses me off."

"You're pissed!" Tremayne gave a grunt as he fed him a withering look, then directed it toward the window.

"Toby can't ascend just from two nights of drinking vampire blood." Crimmins shifted in his seat next to the door.

"Three," Tremayne corrected. "We suspect he was collecting it as well."

"There was that third vampire you found in that cemetery," I said. "There was a bolt, similar to the one used to kill Letitia, I bet."

"Right," Tremayne said. "I'd totally forgotten about that. Didn't even think it was related."

"He meant it to seem that way," Dante said, glancing at me. I nodded.

"Then, he disappeared for a few days?" Crimmins asked.

"Yes," Tremayne said with a heavy sigh. "Nicolas had been under the impression he was at his school—something to do with it—but then he was unable to reach him by phone, or summon him. He later said he couldn't feel him anymore, that he'd lost the connection."

"Where is Nicolas now? This is his scion. Why isn't he here?" Crimmins said.

"I sent him on an assignment. He should be back by tomorrow evening," Tremayne said.

Crimmins leaned a little forward. "You still haven't explained why you exsanguinated this woman. What's her name? I'll need it for my report." He held his pen at the ready.

"Ashley Pierce," Tremayne said. At Crimmins' request Tremayne supplied her address, and he wrote it down.

"Now, tell me what happened here." Crimmins was going to grill Tremayne right here in front of all of us.

"I had a vision," I said abruptly, cutting off whatever Tremayne was about to say. "I tend to fall under heavy trances when I do. I won't come out of them unless a vampire pulls me out with a mind-touch. I had a vision about Toby; that he was ascending. I think it might have made him go over the edge." I nodded toward Tremayne, meeting his gaze.

He kept a poker face. I knew he would have admitted how attracted to my blood he was, and I wasn't sure what the outcome of that would be, since I really didn't know how much power over Tremayne—or any vampire—the demon, Crimmins, had.

"Then what happened?" Crimmins asked, penning everything we said. I was nearest him, and noticed he wasn't writing anything we said in English. In fact, the writing was mostly squiggly lines. I thought it looked an awful lot like some dead language. It didn't resemble anything I'd ever seen.

"I had to go with my donor, since Sabrina is not my donor." Tremayne's tone had become cold. I hoped Crimmins wouldn't go and check that out, because it was now in records that I was Tremayne's donor exclusive.

"Okay, what took you over the top to make you kill her like you did?"

"I don't know. Anger. I don't know," Tremayne said.

Crimmins sat back and pulled out a cell phone. "You older ones tend to fall back on the old ways every once in a while. I hate this part of my job. I really do." He seemed to wrestle with a decision while waiting for someone to pick up on the other end. "Douglas?"

He had it on speaker phone—I didn't know why, but we could all hear whatever was said.

"Whatcha got?" came the fuzzy response.

"Got a frigging DBE."

There was a long pause. "Who?"

"You won't believe it. Or, maybe you will."

"Don't leave me hanging, chief," the voice said, sounding only slightly piqued.

"Tremayne."

"No shit?" The voice on the other side sounded surprised. "Hauling him in? Or do we take care of it discreetly."

Crimmins looked up at Tremayne. "He hasn't been in trouble in over fifty years. I say we do this the easy way."

"The Watchers won't like it."

"I know. A fine, self-confinement, and a trial. That should keep them happy." He smiled up at Tremayne who held a look somewhere between disgust and loathing for the demon detective. "I think he'll like that much better than facing Valiente tonight and going into confinement there. We'll find a nice, cozy private place away from the rest of the scumbags there." Crimmins said this in a voice oozing with sarcasm.

"Okay, you're the boss," the person on the other end said.

Crimmins shut the cell phone and snugged it into a coat pocket. "Okay. I'm letting you off easy. Your record has been fairly clean, in the past fifty or sixty years. Fifty big ones is your fine. I'll give you twenty-four hours to get your affairs in order, and then you'll go into self-confinement until your hearing."

"Shit," Tremayne said. He slid his gaze to Dante.

"I'm on it," Dante said, and whipped out his phone once more. It sounded like Tremayne had to pay a fine for killing the girl. I gathered that this was like bond money, to keep him from going to their jail cell, wherever that was. And he was to go into self-confinement. Where, I sure didn't know, but it was possibly better than the jail cell for vampires.

While Dante called to arrange for the money—cash—to be delivered, Crimmins handed me his card, telling me to call him "for any reason", and exited the limo. The Sanguine Team re-entered, this time to take the body out. I don't know how discreetly they could do it without bringing the attention of the real police on them, but apparently Crimmins' car with that blue light bar was official looking enough. Maybe the vampires and demons *did* really run the world. I pondered on this, but really, I didn't want to know more about it.

The dead woman, Ashley, was covered in a blue sheet, and carried out on a stretcher into an awaiting ambulance—it looked like any other ambulance. I didn't know what would happen to her from here.

"Looks like the concert is canceled." Erik's voice was laced with sarcasm. "Too bad." He looked over at his date, who was still out, next to him. "I was so looking forward to afterwards." He let out a little sigh. "Well, I'm not going to let the evening be a total wash. We must dine, and I will tamper with the woman's memory, let her think she's been to a great concert—not that she would have gotten a charge out of Beethoven, I suppose." He made a little shrug, looking at the woman. "Then I'll take her up to my room, have my way with her and send her off."

Tremayne gave him a hard look, cell phone in hand.

"Hey, I'm only trying to save the evening." He turned to Dante and me. "You two look hungry. I'm sure dinner before you two jump in the sack would be the thing to top the evening."

Tremayne made a growl of protest.

Eyes narrowed, Erik aimed a look of suspicion at his brother. "You aren't coming clean with me, are you, brother?"

"You might as well know it all," Tremayne breathed.

Alarmed, I clutched Dante's hand and held my breath.

"I'm very attracted to Sabrina's blood," Tremayne said on a heavy sigh.

"Really?" Erik's silvery gaze flicked to me, then back to his brother. "No wonder you went off like someone had your balls in a vice!" He barked with laughter.

"I can't be near her."

"Or you'll do exactly what you did to that poor girl?"

He nodded.

Erik's gaze shifted over to me and then back to Tremayne. "I want to hear the whole thing. Turn the car around. Our dinner reservations are still intact."

"What is a Ba'al demon?" I interrupted.

"A type that you have to behead in order to kill them. Their blood is poisonous, and also burns. But it's their bite we fear. It is very poisonous to us, it's similar to silver poisoning. We slowly die from it; it eats us from the inside out." Erik's smile had become chilly. "That's why we hate the vile son of a bitch."

The car pulled away from the curb. My stomach did a flip as it made a U-turn, and with the momentum I had to lean into Dante.

I could now understand why they were so fearful of Crimmins—all snotty rebukes aside—they had no power over him, and Crimmins knew this. He had authority when the vampires stepped out of line—whatever that entailed. Obviously it included killing humans. There also seemed to be a hierarchy, since they mentioned the Watchers.

"They're placed in areas where the largest vampire population is, based mostly in cities where a vampire magnate resides—like myself, or like my brother here. They basically police us so that we keep in line with our laws."

"He said something about Watchers?" I pressed. This was the first chance I'd had to get some answers for questions I'd been harboring for the last few days—and new ones that had cropped up.

"The Watchers? They begot us," Erik said on a chuckle.

"So, they're vampires?" I guessed.

They all chuckled "No," Tremayne said, looking slightly uncomfortable, unable to meet my gaze.

"Let me try and explain," Erik said. "Watchers are fallen angels who took human women and... well, we're their off spring."

"You are?" I gave him a dubious look.

"That's not exactly correct," Dante spoke up. "Off by several millenniums, in fact, before the Great Flood. *There were giants in the earth in those days; and also after that, when the sons of God came in unto the daughters of men, and they bore children to them.*' Genesis 6.4. The Fallen Angels came to earth, and mated with human women who bore their children. You ever wonder what happened to their descendants?" He thrust out his hands toward the two vampires. "These two were born in the first century."

"You were born vampires?" I guessed, surprised.

"No. They both died a violent death, and became vampires after," Dante explained.

"And that's how vampires came to be?"

"It's how it all began. And you know now how new ones are made," Dante said. I nodded.

"Finished?" Erik snapped, and turned to me. "You must tell me what's been going on with Nicolas' scion, Toby. Killing vampires and drinking their blood? He's really buggered things up for himself. I'd like to grab him by the balls, rip them off, and feed them to him myself."

Chapter 25

The trip back to the underground parking at Tremayne Towers was probably only a few blocks, but it took forever what with the traffic. I had enough time to fill Erik in on everything—from the point of when I came into the picture up till tonight. Tremayne confirmed it all, once he got off the phone with Valiente.

The limousine let us off near the elevators. Erik was last to emerge with his date, who was now revived and told she had fallen asleep at the concert, but she hadn't missed much, and that Ashley had an unexpected emergency when she asked why she was missing. I wondered how close the two women had been, and when the truth would be told, if at all, to her. She looked terribly confused, but well rested—which was better than I was faring. After nearly being sucked dry by Tremayne, for the second time in two nights, I figured I needed a long, long vacation away from vampires, Weres and everything that went bump in the night. I also had to figure out if I really wanted to come back to this job. In fact I really didn't want to spend another night here. But here I was, arm-in-arm with a shapeshifter, surrounded by two of the most powerful vampires in America.

While we rode the elevator up, Erik had a brief conversation with his wife, Ilona, on his cell phone, telling her we were all going to dinner, and that he had a lot to tell her when he got home, and hung up. Because of my close proximity to him, I brushed up *accidentally*, and got a read, and knew that she was definitely the woman I'd had in my vision with Nicolas. This had me slightly on edge and I didn't know why. There was some connection, but I couldn't bridge it.

We were right on-time for our dinner reservations. Dante and I strode behind the others, following the same hostess, into Tremayne's private room.

Before any of us were seated, Tremayne suddenly surged away like someone had set fire to him, phone to his ear. "Stay with Sabrina," he blurted over his shoulder to Erik and Dante.

Something was wrong. Something was *very* wrong, and I was too spent to put it all together. *Had they found Toby?*

"I need the ladies room," I announced as I got up. I mostly needed to get the hell away from everyone there who was on their phone—Dante included. He was doing a lot of "yeah," and "okay" into his phone.

Erik and Dante lurched to their feet doing the gentleman thing when I rose.

Dante closed his phone. "Wait. I'll take you."

He directed me out of Tremayne's private room to the lavish restroom (again, gold faucets, black granite sinks). I took my time. I waited for some women to finish up, and washed my face. Toweling off, I looked into the mirror. I didn't belong in these clothes, with my hair like this. These had been Letitia's— everything I wore had been hers, right down to the shoes and necklace. I questioned why Tremayne had given the necklace to me. I'd decided to give it all back to him. Everything.

Something else was bothering me. It had to do with Ilona, but it also had to do with Toby. In my vision earlier, I'd seen Toby ascending—out of the trunk of someone's car down in the garage. This was something I'd forgotten. Possibly I'd blurted this during my vision, and that was why Tremayne had yelled into his phone for someone to go to the garage earlier. I hoped that's where Tremayne was headed when he'd left us.

Emerging from the lady's room, I was a little disoriented. I don't mean I couldn't find my way back to my party, but a sudden uncomfortable feeling washed over me. My brain was signaling a warning. I was hyper conscious of my body; my skin felt all tingly, the little hairs on my arms had spiked, my heart had gone into a deep pitter-patter, like it *knew* danger was near, and I wanted to run to somewhere safe.

I stopped in mid-stride and surveyed the restaurant.

Something—a sound, or a motion, or both—drew my gaze toward the entrance. A thin blond man wearing a long black duster took big strides toward me; his face a hard mask of harsh lines as he moved in that ethereal vampire way. At first I didn't recognize him, then my blood went ice cold with recognition.

Toby.

Arrowing toward me, he reached down at his side and pulled up something dark and deadly, and pointed it at me. When I heard that ratchet sound that only a shotgun could make, I instinctively dove to the floor, and rolled toward an unoccupied table for cover. A split second later, a cannon blast filled my ears. Screams filled the room. Tables turned. China, glass, and cutlery crashed to the floor as a stampede headed for the exit. Wait staff rushed by, surging back into the kitchen for cover. I tried to get to my feet, but the dress was cumbersome, and heavy, leaving me little room to maneuver. I wished suddenly to pull it off, but I had almost nothing on underneath. I managed to roll to another table that had been tipped over, and hoped he hadn't seen where I'd wound up—hoped that maybe in the mayhem, and darkness he'd lost me. But he hadn't.

The next blast hit the table I hid behind, taking a big chunk out of it, and actually made it jump at least a few inches off the ground. Bits and pieces of the table rained over me. Stifling a screech, I stayed put. I was sure Erik and Dante had to have heard the noise, in fact Dante would have read my mind and knew what was going on. The shotgun would not hurt Erik—much—but it would hurt Dante. Maybe they were maneuvering into positions to over-take him.

I was the only person left in the main dining area. Everyone else had run out of there screaming. The only ones left would be Erik, Dante and Erik's date (and if he were smart, he'd put a whammy on that screaming lunatic—I had to presume he had because I didn't hear a thing).

"Sabrina! Don't move!" I was surprised to hear Erik's voice call out.

Pulling in the sharp smell of gun powder, I peeked around the end of the table. The voice made Toby twirl and shoot. In the same moment, I saw something black fly through the air; tail, claws and teeth, like a black juggernaut, sailing right at him. A shot ripped the air, and ripped my heart in two when I saw the jaguar drop.

"Dante!" I screamed, and wanted to jump up and throttle Toby, but knew that I didn't have a chance. If he was human and not in possession of a fire arm, he was still larger and stronger than I was. Besides, the dress was like a hundred pound Python around my legs. I couldn't move. Spying a steak knife on the floor, I grabbed it, punched the point through, and began sawing at the material.

Toby's back was to me; I saw a crossbow slung there. Oh, hell, it was a multi-shooter.

"Toby," Erik admonished, and *tsk-tsked* him, somewhere from across the room.

"Show yourself!" Toby growled.

The tittering laugh gave Toby an excuse to shoot another round. Erik was drawing his attention off me and onto himself. There was no way I could telegraph that Toby was armed with a multi-shooting cross bow.

Cutting the dress off around knee length, I was freed, and moved to stand on my bare feet—my shoes had come off a long time ago, I didn't notice when I'd jumped out of them.

"Show yourself!"

"My boy, why are you in a hurry to kill us all? Who put you up to this? Tell me, and I swear I won't tear your head off."

"Fuck off, old man!"

Possibly twenty feet away, Dante, now in human form, lie nude and bleeding on the floor. My heart lurched at the sight, but my inner eye told me he would be okay. I had to stifle a sob right there and put my emotions back into a usable form. Like anger.

Erik blurred across an open area.

Toby whipped the crossbow off his shoulders, trading the gun for it. He shot several bolts, machine-gun style, across the room, trying to hit a very fast moving target.

Realizing I had an opening, I willed myself to move faster than I'd ever moved in my life, and pounded toward the kitchen.

Before gaining the entrance, I glanced behind myself. The last thing I saw was Erik take a bolt to the chest and fall backward.

Toby's arm came up, aimed, and another bolt shot from underneath the coat sleeve. Eric went down.

Adrenaline rushed through me as I lunged through the kitchen's swinging doors. Toby was after *me*, now. There wasn't another human or supernatural in the place to stop him. It was only me and him.

I tore through a deserted kitchen made up mostly of stainless steel. The smell of cooked food filled the air. I knew where the exit door was, and headed in that direction.

Heart thudding, I jogged around one serving station like a race horse as my bare feet pounded on the tiled floor until I hit something slick, and my foot slid out from under me. I went down hard, bumping an elbow that went suddenly funny-numb, and my hip took the brunt of the fall. The pain went through me like a knife.

Toby banged through the double doors.

Crawling further along the cold, filthy floor, tears flowed down my cheeks. My heartbeats pounded in my ears while I pulled myself along the muck. The mashed food helped me slide some. My gloved hands slapped the cold floor, becoming grimy. So much for the Dior and matching gloves.

"Hmmm," Toby simpered playfully. "I've been so busy killing, I forgot to eat today. Now I'm *really* hungry, and I smell warm human—and it's female." He paused for some effect. "Not exactly what I was looking for, but you'll do."

Oh crap.

I cast around for something, anything to use against him. I was surrounded by every kitchen utensil imaginable. I spied the range. A number of the burners were still lit, blue flames shot up like mini infernos. They'd do me no good, unless he fell on them.

"You want to play hard to get, that's fine," he said. "What's the chance you getting out alive? Hmmm? None."

"Before you kill me why don't you admit that you and Ilona made plans to take over the North American Vampire Association?"

He gave an indignant sound. "How the hell did you know that?" He sounded pissed.

"I'm a Touch Clairvoyant," I said. "Nicolas is involved somehow, too."

He laughed. "Whatever, bitch." He moved through the kitchen, arrowing toward me. I flopped back down on my belly. I managed to slither to the furthest end of the kitchen; the whole get-as-far-away-as-possible scenario was looking like the best and only idea for now. A bank of stainless steel doors covered the wall down here. All of this in my earlier vision.

"Did she come to you? Ask you to kill her husband and she'd give you your own area?" I taunted bravely.

He laughed. "Oh, if only you knew the extent of things. But I'm not stupid enough to tell you. I wouldn't want to *spoil* the surprise. If you haven't guessed anything from using your *gift*, then why make it simple for you?"

"And then you went to Letitia, using the excuse of needing to speak to her about turning you. But instead, you went out on the balcony and while she was busy with her male donors, you somehow brought that rope up from Nicolas' balcony so that you could use it to get into position to kill her later on."

He said nothing. I knew my guess was correct.

"Nicolas knows what you've been up to? He in on the plans?"

He gave a taunting bark of laughter.

"And how did Steve and Solange work into your plans? You put them up to trying to kill me?"

"I have no idea what you're talking about. I wouldn't want to take credit where credit isn't due." At least this answered how deep his involvement was. I had a feeling Ilona kept all the players unknown from each other. Toby was a means to one of the ends. I was a danger to her, and expendable.

I spied a wooden spoon on the floor, and grabbed it. It needed sharpening. I cast around for a knife. There wasn't any within my grasp. *Shit, now what?*

"I know exactly where you are," Toby boasted. Then he moved with that Uber-vampire quickness where in one fluid moment, he was across the long kitchen, and in the next he was right there above me. He hauled me up by the shoulders, and threw me against a cabinet. My breath gushed out of me, I couldn't scream properly.

Before I could pull in a breath he slammed me back into the stainless steel door. Dazed, I looked up into his face. Toby's face was twisted into an evil mask. His pupils pooled, leaving only a thin ring of blue.

Tears streamed down my face, as the vampire took me in. Toby's breath sent a chill over me while pinning my shoulders against the wall.

"How did you know it was me?" he asked, pulling one hand away from my shoulder to take a finger to tip my chin back. Eying my neck hungrily. "I was so careful."

"Yes. You didn't leave the coffee cup at my house," I said, trembling from the adrenaline rush, and him.

"No. I didn't." He smiled that crooked smile that I'd once thought was somewhat sexy. Now, it was a horrific smile with the fangs.

"I knew you were hiding something," I went on trying to put off the inevitable. "The rope on the balcony. Ilona visiting Nicolas. It all came together. But I was too late," I admitted, too afraid to wipe my tears and snot from my face. God, how could he do this? He was a monster, feeding off my fear, bringing himself to a higher pitch, waiting for the perfect moment to strike and get his high—now from *my* blood, not a vampire's.

"Yes. You are. And now, it's just you and me." Gripping my shoulders, he suddenly twirled me around and I found my cheek against the cold stainless steel door of one of the coolers. He pressed his whole body against me. Something warm and wet slithered across my shoulder and up my neck and it took about half a second to understand it was his tongue. "Oh-h-h. You're absolutely yummy. I'll have to tell Ilona what she missed." His hand went under my dress and clutched a buttock hard. A scream was wrenched from me.

"Mmmm, it'll be like old times. Only I'm the one having al-l-l-l the fun." He chuckled and his tongue slid up my neck as he pressed me harder against the door, hard enough my cheekbone hurt, and my arms were crushed between myself and the door, so I couldn't use them. Plus it was hard to breath. I couldn't get a scream out.

Then I heard the solitary sound of a zipper as he held me in place, and my world went into the toilet right about then—the end would not come quick enough for me.

"I'm going to fuck and drain you, bitch," he said into my ear. "You're my first. You won't be my last."

My scream came out in a sob.

"Oh, we can't have that. No," he whispered, cheek against my neck as he sent pheromones into me, and there came that tingle of desire when a vampire hit the right note. I wriggled and sobbed, my tears lubricating the stainless steel where my face was pressed against it. I saw how his possession of me would make me want him. His hand was under my dress again, yanking down my underpants. Somewhere in the back of my mind I was about to go mad. *This can't be happening! I have to find a way...* He was going to use me like a worthless *thing*, and then I would die.

A loud bang made us both jump. I knew it wasn't the gun; he'd left it somewhere. It was the door. Someone had burst in. It wasn't a guess on my part as to who. I simply *knew*. There was that familiar twang in the air that heralded only one vampire's nearness. My heart trembled with hope.

Toby's hands and body left me, and without him holding me up, my legs went out from under me and I crumpled to the floor. I managed to pull up my underwear, and then curled my legs underneath myself and sat back awkwardly, ignoring the pain. I swiped the hair out of my face and tried to gather my wits. My nerves jumpy, I was unable to think clearly. I should *do* something, but I could only watch the two vampires face each other.

A growl issued from Tremayne, and then some word was uttered.

"Oh, good, another one I can mark off my list of things to kill," Toby said, sounding trite.

"You!" Tremayne roared. His voice filled the room. "You cowardly son of a cur!"

Tremayne's face was stony, fangs out. The only emotion of any kind was in the eyes. They had become the same color of the cold-steel room, and the whites were bloodshot. I would not want to be on the receiving end of that look. I thought Toby, being a newly-turned vampire, was rather reckless. Either that or he had something up his sleeve—literally.

I was right. Toby brought up his right hand and pointed it at Tremayne, exactly like he had Erik.

"BOLT!" I shouted.

Something zinged toward Tremayne. In that split second Tremayne's hand snapped up to snatch the bolt out of the air—missing his chest by mere inches—and snapped it in two like a twig in his fingers.

Angered, Tremayne took two huge strides, and then blurred. Suddenly Toby was thrown across the room; he crashed through a salad-making center. Salad flew everywhere, and dishes crashed to smithereens on the stone floor. Before Toby could take stock of his predicament, he was thrown to the other side of the room. Utensils became musical cacophony as Toby sailed through an arrangement of pots and pans hung overhead, and another stack of dishes fell like bombs to the floor. I ducked and hunched against my only protection of the table, as the splintered pieces sprayed, hitting me like bee stingers.

Tremayne became an unstoppable whirlwind, picking Toby up and throwing him further along in the kitchen. Every time he did, he growled a string of things, and I could only make out Letitia's name once or twice.

Then Tremayne picked Toby up high, and threw him onto the burners. Flames engulfed Toby. His high scream went right through me and I had to shut my eyes tight, and close out those sounds with my hands over my ears.

After a moment, I heard no more screaming. I had to peek at the carnage. I was startled by what I saw. Toby was on his feet shedding his flaming coat, throwing it to the floor. The smell of burnt cloth, hair, and skin cloyed the room. Damn, but vampires were hard to kill, if a master vampire found the task somewhat difficult. But I had a feeling that Tremayne wanted to cause Toby as much physical hurt as he could for killing Letitia.

Grabbing Toby by the shirt, he landed several bone crunching punches to his face. Something flew at me. I ducked. That *something* clattered above my head, clattered and fell to rest right next to me. Looking down, I found it was Toby's other weapon. I understood how it fit on his arm with the Velcro straps. I picked it up and placed it on my glove-protected forearm, and fastened it with the straps. I found the wooden spoon that I'd picked up earlier. I needed to make it into a bolt, and fast. I shoved the bowl part between two heavy stainless steel units and broke it off. The end was needle-sharp. I fitted it into the slingshot.

I jumped when Toby's body hit the wall a mere four feet from where I crouched, and slid down next to me in a heap. I thought he was down for good. Then his eyes popped open. Filled with fire, they turned on me, and his lips slid back into a snarl, exposing his fangs. I took aim. I squeezed the trigger. The bolt thunked into him on the left side of the chest, the end sticking out a good inch where a blossom of bright red blood painted the blue of his shirt, making it dark purple.

I made a sound of wonder, realizing *this* was the blue shirt in my vision from a few nights ago.

I held my breath as the look of surprise on Toby's face turned to anger as his eyes turned back up at me. The thin, wheezy sound made it clear that I'd merely hit his lungs, not his heart. *Damn it to hell!*

My eyes refocused on Tremayne surging up behind Toby. Then Toby lunged at me. I screamed and threw my arms up over my face as a flash of steel arced through the air and sliced through Toby's neck. Toby's head rolled a bloody path across the floor. His headless torso slumped toward me. I thrust my hands out to pitch it away from myself. Eyes still open but unseeing, the head rolled a few feet and stopped against the leg of the work station. The long, bleached strands of hair twirled around it like spun gold.

Tremayne straightened, and gazed down at me. "I wasn't here. Got it?"

"Right."

And he vanished, making my ears pop with the displacement of air.

Chapter 26

Something cold touched my shoulder and shook me.

"Sabrina? Hey." The voice was soft, and plainly a man's.

I cracked open one eye. I was staring up into Leif's face. I think it was him. Or it might have been his brother. My brain was stuck in the heavy fog of exhausted sleep yet.

"What? What's wrong? What's going on?" I asked groggily, and saw the face double suddenly, and had to raise my head to focus with both eyes. The brown leather couch I lay upon made an obnoxious creaking sound. The fur stole, which had kept me warm, slid from me luxuriously and fell to the floor—and made a soft thud as it did. Leif—I was sure now—held my blue shoes in his hand, and picked up the thing that had fallen with the stole. He was looking curiously at the weapon.

"I'll take that, thank you," I said, and held my hand out to him.

"Here you go, my little Vampire Killer," Leif said, smiling—oddly I thought. Crouched beside me, he handed me the slingshot.

"Wait, what did you call me?"

"Vampire Killer," he repeated. Behind him Heath nodded vigorously.

"Our hero," Heath simpered.

"Who? Me?"

"Yes, silly," Leif said, helping me to sit up. He eyed my dress as he folded himself next to me. His smile vanished. Frown lines between the nicely arched brows formed. "Is that a new style? Or what?" He pointed at my dress—what was left of it.

"It's a new fad, they cut them now, I think." Heath sat down on the other side of me and fingered the jagged hem I'd cut with a steak knife in haste. It angled down across my thighs, ending in a length of torn, and now dirty—possibly bloody—material. "Grunge, I think they call it."

"No," I said. "I cut it so that I could run away from Toby."

"Ahhhh," I heard in stereo. They no longer looked confused.

"And this horrid looking thing you have here." He eyed the slingshot. "I'm certain it doesn't go with the ensemble."

"No." I rolled the slingshot up into the fur stole tightly. It had still been attached to my arm when I was brought down here by members of the Sanguine Team, along with all the other casualties of the night. Realization had spooked me, knowing that this had been the murder weapon that had killed Letitia, and the chef, Ivan Ivanho (who had been missing for a few days and only discovered tonight in the freezer in the restaurant, after they'd found me and what was left of Toby), and the rogue vampire in the cemetery. Oh, yes. I had been paying attention. Toby had been vague, but I could read between the lines. Ilona had put him up to this turning-himself-into-a-vampire killing-spree. I knew she was a powerful vampire without trying too hard to read it from Toby. After remembering something Tremayne had said—how scions come and go—I now knew Toby was no longer Nicolas' scion, that day I'd met him. It was all a ruse.

But he was not lying about one thing. He'd had nothing to do with the shiftchanger who had tried to shoot me down in the garage, shooting Heath by mistake. That had been someone else's doing. Probably Ilona. I feared that I would never learn for sure.

But, I couldn't part with my new weapon. Not yet. And some- how I highly doubted that Tremayne would want it as a sou- venir. But I didn't want anyone to know about it, and now I feared that I would have to trust the twins to keep it a secret.

"Do me a favor?" I said, giving them a pleading look.

"What is it, luv?" they asked, sounding cordial enough.

"No matter what happens don't tell anyone I have this." I held up the concealed weapon.

The twins exchanged glances.

"Please?" I added.

"Sure, luv. Anything," Leif said. "I love a bit of skullduggery."

"You're our hero, after all. What's a little secret between friends?" Heath said, smiling broadly.

"Thanks."

"Well, let's get you out of here, luv. This place is for the sick and injured."

"Wait, explain what you said about me being a vampire killer," I asked, refusing to move until I knew what he'd meant.

"You are, you know?"

"Tell her what Tremayne told us," Heath suggested.

"What? That if the V.I.U. knows that Tremayne was anywhere near her, his butt's in a sling?"

"That's paraphrasing it nicely, brother."

"I don't understand. I didn't kill Toby. Tremayne did," I said, making it clear I'd had nothing to do with it.

"Shhhhh!" The both of them said, fingers to their lips, looking frantically around for anyone who might overhear.

"Tremayne is not supposed to come anywhere near you, luv," Leif explained in a hushed tone. "He's supposed to be in iso- lation. C'mon. We need to get you out of here." Leif said in his newly acquired affectionate tone. They lifted me up off the couch as though I were as light as a pillow.

"Whoa, wait," I said, trying to straighten my legs. I found that every joint was stiff, and places I didn't know I'd hurt,

hurt: my right hip, both knees, my elbow, maybe a rib or two, hurt, and my big toe began to throb—plus I noticed I'd lost some fingernails—the fake ones, anyway. I moaned as I struggled to stand. I looked down at my big toe. It was bandaged.

They had ministered to me, here in the hospital wing on Level D. The nurses had been very nice to me. So was the doctor—whatever his name was—but an elf with a good ear-job, because I couldn't get a read from him.

Earlier, after the dust had settled in the restaurant's kitchen (and Tremayne had disappeared), I'd stepped on some glass as I exited Earthly Pleasures' kitchen. I found the Sanguine Team, Heath and Leif, and a bunch of people in suits, including Crimmins, swarming the restaurant. I hadn't realized I was bleeding until Heath, or Leif, had noticed the blood had made a nice path of regular red dots across the floor as I stepped along—barefooted. Blood was seeping from my foot, and hungry looks were in their eyes. I don't know, in all the confusion, who had rescued the blue shoes, but my purse was missing.

I now saw it in Heath's hand and reached toward it.

"Oh! My purse."

"Here. Everything is there," he assured, handing it to me.

"How's Dante? Is he out of surgery?" A panic went through me, thinking about his injuries. The gun's shot had given him various injuries; his face, both arms and chest had been peppered, but no vitals were hit, I had been told. He had been in surgery when I arrived to be tended to, myself. I'd fallen asleep waiting for word.

"Yes, Dante is going to be fine," Heath intimated, sarcastic tone etched in his voice. "He's a shifter. Weres and shifters heal faster than mortals."

"What about his face?" I worried. I had been told his face and chest had been hit the worst of all.

"He'll still be handsome, if that's what you're concerned about."

"I'm worried for him," I said. "How's Erik?"

"Truly, you want to know about Erik?" Leif asked, perplexed.

"I'd heard he took the bolt in the chest, and that's all I know," I said.

"Erik the Dread is dead."

I went silent for a moment, letting that sink in. I wanted to say something appropriate, but nothing came to me.

"Yeah, we feel the same, luv. Let's get you out of here."

The twins helped me out of the hospital wing of Level D. We stepped—well, I hobbled between them—onto the elevator.

"We were told you need to see Crimmins," Heath announced as the door snicked shut.

My head snapped up to regard him.

"Crimmins? Me?" My stomach lurched. "No!"

"He only wants to ask you some questions."

"I'm in too much pain. How about I call him, instead?" I remembered I had his card.

"That might work," Heath said.

"Can you guys get me to my room?"

"Sure. In fact, we're supposed to keep you under watch the whole night," Heath said as the two of them took me by the arms and helped me across the hallway. Making a small grunting sound, Leif pulled up. Both Heath and I looked at him.

"I think it would work better if one of us carries you," he suggested.

I rolled my eyes. "Okay, but this is going to look odd."

"No, not at all. Happens all the time, a man carrying a woman with a damaged Dior dress, and one bandaged toe."

Other than the clerk on the human side giving us worrisome looks, we went through without a problem. I had to punch in the number of my floor because the buttons had silver in them. The ride up was quick and we met no one—not on the way up, or in the hall. Leif stepped out ahead of us. Heath carried me as I told them my suite number, and dug out my room key card.

Leif unlocked the door and we all paused.

"Invite us in, luv, or we'll be standing out here forever."

I frowned. "I can take it from here."

"No. We're under orders," Heath refused.

I sighed, and rolled my eyes. "Okay, Heath and Leif, come in."

Heath strode forward with me in his arms, and Leif followed. I heard them both take deep breaths. "Smells like a bloody parade's been through here."

"I smell Tremayne, Dante, and... Nicolas?" Leif said, curling his lip in repugnance. "Dante's scent is strongest."

"He does live across the hall," I reminded drolly.

Leif surged ahead, toward the bedroom. "In here."

Heath stepped after him, me still in his arms.

"Hey, wait. When I said come in, I didn't mean *all* the way in," I protested, holding onto Heath's neck.

Leif threw himself onto the far side of my bed, head braced on a fist. He picked up a single rose from the bed—it was red, not the same ones Tremayne had sent me the other day—and now sniffed it.

"Ah, an admirer," Leif said, twirling the rose. "And a letter with your name on it, luv." He picked it up and sniffed at it. "Ahh. Bet you can't guess," he said, waving it. I gave him a nettled look until he tossed it toward me. "And a rather heavier, larger one." He held up the manila envelope and shook it. "Something in it."

Heath settled me down on the bed, three feet from his brother. I went to my knees grabbing at the envelopes.

I picked up the smaller envelope and opened it first. A check fell out. I saw all the zeros on it, and Tremayne's signature at the bottom. Heath whistled as he leaned over my shoulder.

"That's one nice bonus, luv."

My face warmed. It was the money that Tremayne had promised me—one hundred thousand dollars—for revealing the murderer.

The larger envelope was bulky and heavy. Something more than paper was inside. I opened the flap and up-ended it. Out came a set of keys and papers. Two keys with a remote which had the Pontiac symbol embossed on them. It obviously went to a car. I picked up the papers next. I saw a dealership name at the top and lots of legal mumbo-jumbo. My name was typed in at certain spots, and there were x's where I needed to sign.

"Ohmygod! I own a new car!" I shrieked excitedly. I saw the name of the vehicle: Solstice. I had no idea what that was, but I couldn't wait to see it.

"Notice she didn't shriek at the huge check, but at the vehicle," Heath said, smiling.

"Yes, your priorities are a bit jumbled, don't you think?" his brother added.

Someone's cell phone rang. It wasn't mine. It was Leif's. Sitting up, he whipped his cell phone out and answered it. "Yes?" In one Uber vampire move, he was up on his feet, striding away. "Of course. At once, sire." He dashed out of the room. "Bring her in here!"

"Wait!" I screeched as Heath scooped me up and scurried with me in his arms, back into the living room. Now I know what a pet gerbil felt like.

Leif had turned on my large screen TV. I couldn't figure out why he was turning on the TV.

When the image came into focus, I understood. Tremayne stood staring out at us, arms crossed over his broad chest. My heart did a tattoo then.

"I'm very glad to see you've returned safely," Tremayne said in a low rumble, and then scowled, eyes shifting to my vampire guardians. "Heath, why are you carrying Ms. Strong?"

"She hurt her foot," he answered almost sheepishly.

"My big toe, but my knees hurt when I walk, too," I clarified.

"I see," Tremayne said sounding almost mollified, arms still crossed. "Set her down. Make her comfortable. I wish to speak to Ms. Strong—alone."

"Yes, master." Heath turned, and settled me in one of the over-stuffed chairs.

Both vampires bowed to Tremayne, exited my apartment, and closed the door.

I waited and watched Tremayne's eyes follow the pair out. Once the door shut, his arms relaxed at his sides. He slouched in front of a desk, or table—I wasn't sure. The place didn't look familiar to me. There was some sort of colored window in the background—it looked like stained glass—and a large bookcase over his left shoulder.

"Good. Now we may talk," he said. "Did you speak to Crimmins yet?"

"Not yet. I'm going to call him, though."

"I'm sure that the twins told you why you are to tell Crimmins you never saw me?"

"Yes. And I hope you've wiped out any video from the restaurant cameras?"

"Already done."

Nodding, I quickly continued. "Thank you for the check, and do I really own a car?"

"Yes. The car has been delivered, I only need you to sign the papers from the dealership. It's the least I could do. I've put you through hell."

I bit my lower lip against the quick comeback I had in my head. "Where are you?"

"I can't tell you that."

"Okay." I guess I should have expected that. "What's going to happen to you?"

He made a sigh. He looked furious with himself. "I'm fucked," he said. "As of now I've been stripped of all my powers as a magnate. I'm to remain in isolation until my trial—whenever the hell that will be. Damned bureaucrats," he hissed. "In the meantime, Nicolas has been instated as interim magnate."

"Oh... oh, crap," I said, squeezing my eyes in dread.

"What's wrong?"

"Everything," I said, shaking my head. "I found out why Toby killed Letitia—or rather who was behind it."

"Who?"

"Erik's wife, Ilona. I don't fully understand how Toby began to follow Ilona's commands."

"Scion stealing and scion trades happen all the time," he said without hesitation.

"Really?"

"Sure. She was here only a few weeks ago. She was keeping company with Nicolas. I had her watched, but I had no idea what was going on behind closed doors."

"I think they either traded scions, or she might have stolen Toby out from under Nicolas."

"We'll never know," he said on a frustrated gasp. "And since I'm no longer in charge, I can't have anyone investigate it. Not officially, anyway."

"There was definitely a plan in place," I went on. "Toby came armed to the teeth. He wanted to kill not only me, but vampires. Plus, right before it all went down, Erik was speaking to Ilona, on his phone, telling her where we all where. Coincidence?"

Dipping his head, Tremayne ran a hand through his golden mane. I know he was swearing under his breath, because I could read his lips.

"Not only that," I went on, "remember what I told you about Nicolas being involved with Jeanie's disappearance? Steve abducted her before that blood ritual, but Steve was under Nicolas' command before that, but before the blood ritual, so he was free to do whatever he wanted. Or whatever someone else wanted," I clarified.

374

Tremayne blew out a heavy breath. His gaze came up to engage mine. "Nicolas can't have been behind any of this."

"What? Why not?"

"I trust Nicolas explicitly." Tremayne's frown deepened. "You haven't said anything to Nicolas about this, have you?"

"No. But did Dante tell you he came to my door last night? He erased my memory of it."

"No. I wasn't told of this. He didn't gain entry, did he?"

"No. Dante heard someone in the hall. I think he interrupted him. Dante spent the night in my living room to guard me."

"I want you to take some time off, Sabrina," Tremayne suggested. "You'll only come to the Towers to give your donation. Do it during the day."

"No problem." No vampires were up during the day—except for Tremayne.

"By the way, Nicolas is coming home tonight. In fact I'm expecting his call any minute because I have to up-date him on what happened. He has a surprise for you."

"A surprise?"

"Yes. Look, I promised not to say anything to you. This was his idea. I still don't see that his intentions were ever to harm you. He's tasted your blood. It's hard to not become territorial. Possibly he may have only wanted to see you before he left for England."

And do what?

"I hope you're right," I said, doubt filling my voice.

"Sabrina, I know him. I have to trust him—even if he was sneaking around behind my back to see you." And obliterating the whole thing from my memory in the process.

I resisted the urge to roll my eyes. Was I the only one who realized that Jeanie's abduction was to get me off the investigation? Problem was, I couldn't prove it. I had no witnesses, I had nothing. I'd never seen the other person's face—whoever it was trying to look like Vasyl. The only other person who knew anything about Vasyl having come to me when I was young was Nicolas, who'd had my blood. I stopped. Steve had had my blood too. Would he have been able to read my thoughts? Each vampire had their own special skills. I had to wonder what Steve's were.

"Anyway, I have to hand over the powers of the eastern half of the vampire state to Nicolas tonight."

"What about Erik's half of the vampire state?"

"Yeah," he said in a half-smirk, half-snarl. "Erik's wife, Ilona, will take over for him."

"So, this is how it's done? Power of authority is automatically switched over to the spouse?"

"In this case, it is. We don't usually marry, as in a ceremony, like humans do, or have a certificate of marriage. We simply choose a mate. If it lasts, it lasts, and if we want to part company, we do. Very simple."

"Works for me."

"But she wouldn't allow Erik to stay tied to his other wives, made them formally disavow any legal ties to his estate in the case of death. Ilona gets his estate, and his half of the vampire empire."

"She sounds like a shrewd, gold-digging, power hungry woman. You gotta admire that."

"That she is." He paused for a few seconds as if he was considering his next words. "Also a new faction is wanting to bring back hunting humans."

"No. Really?" I said, startled.

"Ilona is behind this whole flip-flopping the current legislation. She makes me ill."

I made a little gasp of insecurity, considering what this might mean for everyone who worked at the Towers. I really didn't know what would happen with the donors. I mean would they still be donors, or be hunted?

"Sabrina, promise me to steer clear of Ilona," Tremayne said, a dark look in his eyes, voice serious and deep.

"No problem. I will," I said, confident I could do this.

"I mean don't be in the same room with her at all."

"Why?" This was strange. "I'll make sure to wear a crucifix."

"No. That won't work with her. She doesn't need to look into your eyes. She only has to be in the same room with you."

I frowned, unable to understand.

"She's what's known as a psychic vampire."

"Psychic? You mean she can read my mind?"

"That, yes. But she can actually drain the energy from you. She's been known to actually steal a person's soul this way, killing them, eventually. She's extremely dangerous. I want you to understand this before I—" he broke off, gaze going away from me. He seemed to have to gather himself, looking a bit misty. "I don't know what's going to happen to me, or my estate. I can only hope that Nicolas will run it the way I've always ran it. But Ilona… if she actually did set things up, having Toby kill Letitia, and my brother, there's no telling what she'll do in order to take the whole North American Vampire Association for herself."

"She can do that?" I asked, bringing my hands over my arms; goose bumps rose and the hair on my arms went straight out. If I were a cat, my fur would be sticking out. My insides churned. "You can't mean you'll lose control that easily."

He shrugged. "I don't know what will happen." His gaze went around the room again. "I've incarcerated myself here. I can't leave. I won't even be given a donor. Just blood—somehow. I was told that no human or vampire can enter this place. Only a demon."

"So, you're saying you're going to be there until your trial, whenever that is?"

"Yes. Now," he sounded like he was going to begin with a new subject and I listened. "Both Heath and Leif are to stay and guard over you tonight."

"Okay." I nodded. Dante was in the hospital. Someone had to guard Tremayne's love interest, after all.

"In the morning go down to the garage. Go to wing A. My mechanic will be there to show you the car."

"Will I ever get to see you again—like this, or in person?"

"I really don't know," he said glumly. "Have a comfortable sleep, Sabrina."

"You too," I said quietly, and watched him fade to black. Finding the remote, I hit the power button. The TV winked off. I took a couple of deep breaths, easing them out steadily, because I wanted to cry, but didn't know why. I was confused over my feelings for Tremayne, and my deep attraction toward Dante, as well as my questionable quandary over Nicolas. My attraction for Nicolas had fizzled quickly because I simply didn't trust him.

Then there was Vasyl. Whatever he was all about was my other quandary, and I really wanted to get some answers, soon. Real soon. The *whys* were piling up.

I remembered that I had invited Nicolas into my home. What would keep him out, if he really wanted to come and visit me some night? The mere thought made my heart pound hard. That was one reason, maybe, that Tremayne had suggested Heath and Leif would become my guardians. Dante would be back, once he was out of the hospital.

The knock at my door shook me from my deep thoughts.

"What?"

Leif poked his head in from the hall. "Are you alright, luv?"

"Nothing ibuprofen, a bath, and a drink won't cure."

Both vampires entered, shut and locked the door, then sauntered through my apartment like they lived there.

"What can I get you? Wine? A pint of something? Manhattan?" Leif asked, as he angled for the kitchen. Funny how I'd never said come in, but here they were, the both of them, sticking their heads in my refrigerator.

"Wine."

Leif pulled out a bottle of wine and searched for a corker in the drawers.

"Oi, she knew we were coming! How cordial," Heath said, as he opened the two bottles of Real Red, and popped them into the microwave, and set it for a few seconds.

"Help yourselves, guys." I waved at them. Well, they'd more than earned it, I figured.

Leif finally found a corker in a drawer, and worked on the bottle of wine. The cork on the wine bottle popped softly. The microwave beeped, and they extracted their warmed blood, clinked bottles in a silent toast, and sipped tentatively at first, because the bottles were hot.

"Glasses are in the cupboard—go ahead and help yourselves," I said. They did, and poured the Real Red and my wine into glasses, looking as happy as vampires could look. I noticed that their fangs had popped out. Damn. Would I ever get used to that?

"I'll get the bath," Heath announced, and with his glass of blood in hand, he angled toward the bathroom, in regular human motion. Well, he sort of jogged.

I let go another sigh, remembering I needed to make a call to Crimmins. I dug into my purse, pulled out his card and dialed his number.

"Crimmins," a glum voice answered on the second ring.

"Oh, uh, hi, Mr. Crimmins. This is Sabrina Strong," I said, eyeing Leif as he angled toward me.

"Yes, Ms. Strong, I understand you've been hurt in tonight's scrimmage in the restaurant?" Crimmins said. "I hope you're alright?"

Leif came in front of me, handing me the glass of wine. I took the glass thankfully.

"Oh, yeah. And I hope you don't mind if we do this over the phone?"

"Not at all, Ms. Strong."

"Um, first of all, can I ask if you know if Toby was found with a cell phone?"

"I don't know. Why?"

"Because, I was wondering how Toby knew all of us had come into the restaurant. I think he might have been in contact with someone. You could look on his phone and see who called him, or who he called?"

"Very good suggestion. I'll have to see what we can find. So, what you're saying is that you think he had someone else working with him?"

"Oh, definitely," I said.

"Who?"

"If I tell you will this get out?"

"I promise you, Ms. Strong, the VIU works independently from the Vampire Association. We go on our own tips. Whatever you tell me will be most confidential."

"Good," I said looking up to see Heath pop out of the hall. He held two different containers.

"Bubbles, or bath salts?"

I covered my phone. "Bubbles." It then occurred to me that it wasn't every night a woman had one vampire make her a drink, the other a bath, and have a conversation with a demon over the phone.

Chapter 27

I knew something wasn't right when I woke and slowly stretched out in my own bed, back in my house on Sonata Road. Turning my head, I checked my clock. Red digits proclaimed it to be 1:39 in the afternoon. *Half the day's shot.* My father's favorite saying when I got up later than seven a.m.

First and foremost, I had no pain, when I knew there should be. The twinge in my hip, and the pain in my knees from my horrific night was nonexistent. I moved a little to test it, and it felt normal. Wow. That ibuprofen really works, I guess.

I had avoided a near death situation with only bruises, minor scratches, and a cut on my big toe. Which I should have been happy about, but I was actually furious that I hadn't had the vision until it was really too late.

Secondly, I'd had a dream of my mother stepping into the backyard when I was ten. Only in this dream, I was definitely the age I am now and I saw things I hadn't seen then more clearly. Or, perhaps I'd forgotten all about it. It's funny how as you grow older you understand the world differently. You also become slightly less gullible—hopefully—and a little more jaded, because you know how the world works.

There was something *very* important that I had forgotten from that time when I was ten. In my 'dream' I'd seen the vampire with long, wavy hair standing somewhere behind my mother with his face and part of his body in the shadows, watching the exchange. But at an unguarded moment I saw him—all of him. I understood it now. He had allowed her that moment to say goodbye to me. Then, later that night, he had come to bite me, in order to claim me at some point when I grew up.

Vasyl's regally handsome features, large, somewhat saintly eyes—and on a vampire was something of a contradiction—came to mind now. He had been the mystery vampire who'd starred in my dreams. I'd fallen in love with his face. I had known all my life I would someday meet him.

I *had* met him, but under real strange and harrowing circumstances. I needed some answers. It was imperative to get them because I knew my life was about to change drastically—more so than it had to this point—and he had the answers I needed for my continued survival. What was it I was supposed to be? The sibyl? Why were vampires so interested in the sibyl? I really needed to understand why Vasyl had marked me and took my mother from me. *Now,* not next week.

A sharp edge of anger drew over me as I fumbled in the fog of half-sleep to the bathroom. I tried to fight my way to wakefulness, and the feeling surged through me and somehow mutated. Stumbling, I entered the bathroom, and flicked on the bright lights around the mirror. I ran cold water, and splashed my face to wake up. *Why hadn't I asked to touch something of Steve's?* my brain screamed at me. I pounded a fist on the sink vanity with frustration.

That's what was bothering me. Had I asked for something that Steve had worn, a ring, a shoe—something—I might have found out who was behind Jeanie's abduction. *Too late now.* I was certain he had disappeared by now.

Oddly enough, my vampire bite actually itched this morning. I hadn't felt it since that night I'd met Vasyl. *Strange.* And I still felt that I was missing something, something important. Something I'd missed, but what? What was the question and what was the answer? It was one of those damned algebra formulas, like x + y=? I was lousy at math.

I examined my werewolf/vampire bites. Red, and they pinched a little, like the two bites were warring with each other to supersede. *Great.* I had two problems, instead of one.

Heath had made the comment later last night that my aura had changed slightly. He'd said it was slightly darker around the edges. At the time I thought nothing of it. But, now as I looked at myself in the mirror—my hair rumpled, my eyes bloodshot—I knew. I knew what was happening to me, I couldn't deny it any longer. The werewolf venom was still in me and things were happening inside, right now.

Grabbing a towel, I wiped my face dry, and grimaced as the thoughts tumbled into place, one by one. How had this escaped me?

My brain cells functioning at about seventy-five percent, I returned to my bedroom and slipped on my gray sweats. I realized only then my big toe didn't hurt either.

I lifted my foot. The angle was all wrong. I sat down on my bed and pulled up my foot so I could see the bottom of my toe. The band aide had rubbed all most all the way off. I pulled it the rest of the way off, expecting it to hurt and bleed. It didn't. There was no cut. It was a narrow, red line and welt, now.

What the hell? Did I dream of stepping on the glass and having the elf-nurses bandage me up?

I checked my knees. I *know* they had cuts on them. I remember surveying my various cuts in the tub, last night—in a drift of bubbles (Heath had used way too much bubble bath). I was a mess then.

Now, as I examined my legs, I found no cuts, or bruises. I'd healed overnight. Like a shifter.

Or a Were.

My aura *had* changed, not slightly, but a *lot.*

I needed coffee, and I needed it now. I was up on my feet and moving quicker than a few moments ago, heading down the stairs of my own house.

Last night I'd talked Heath and Leif into allowing me to pick up my car and let me drive home. Heath rode in my new car with me, while Leif followed in his own. They'd insisted that they were to watch over me through the night. I didn't argue, but my own home felt safer, no matter who was there with me.

While the coffee brewed, I went to my refrigerator and glanced out the window. There was a small zippy-looking car in my drive. It was red with a black rag top, a two-seater, and it would fit in the smallest parking spot available. My new car, the Solstice. I thought it looked really cute, and sexy at the same time.

Nicolas is coming out tonight, my memory dredged up.

My heart knocked hard a few times against my ribs remembering the phone call from Nicolas last night, before I had decided to come home. I had to remember what Tremayne and I had discussed while I spoke with him. I put everything I wanted to say to him on hold—because I wanted to say it to his face. I let him talk, and I merely answered in monosyllables.

"Sab*rrr*ina," Nicolas had said.

"Hi," I said, a chill going through me while holding my cell phone to my ear.

"I will be coming out to your place tomorrow night, to give you a present," Nicolas said. His voice rumbled smoothly, as though nothing was amiss, and reminding me of how he made me feel, once upon a time. Not anymore. I truly didn't trust him anymore. But I played dumb and agreed to see him.

"I'll be home," I said. We'd said our goodbyes and hung up.

And I would be ready.

After my quick meal of toast and coffee, I went up to my room and opened my over-night bag, and located that one important thing from last night. I picked it up with a gloved hand and stud-ied it. I'd need bolts that would fit. It was basically a slingshot.

The sun would be setting in about three or four hours. I was running out of time.

Chapter 28

My ammo was simple, and not hard to come by, in fact. My father had a wood shop in a small shed out back, and in his spare time he had made many wood projects. There was plenty of left over wood, and scraps, but my interest was in the dowels he'd had for some of his projects. I chose the narrow ones. I would only need one, but in case there was need, I sharpened four. I used an electric pencil sharpener, since these were exactly the same size as a pencil. In less than two minutes I had myself some home-made bolts—deadly if aimed at a vampire's heart.

Underlying all the familiar autumn scents, tonight there was a certain tang to the air. A moist loam filtered up to me. The soil was still damp from rain. Everything smelled about ten times richer than I remembered.

I could thank my brother for being the avid hunter and camper because he'd put the row of lights on top of the Jeep, and I pointed them toward the backyard where I stood. Once darkness set it, I hit the switch—something I thought I would never use—and a huge spotlight came on, revealing all of my backyard, well beyond the three catalpa trees that stood stately and tall about fifty feet away.

Breathing in a new scent, I lifted my head. I knew vampire scent when I smelled it. This individual scent was of leather and sweet hay—making me think of a horse barn. A quick flash of his image, what I remembered from childhood, and from the other night, hit me. Stunned me. My heart beat deeper, anticipating his arrival.

I wish I could say that I didn't know why my senses were heightened—but of course, I did. Nicolas hadn't gotten all the Were-venom. I had thought about this before tonight, in fact. I don't know how many minutes had passed from the moment when I had been bitten, to when Nicolas had sucked the Were-venom—and a lot of my blood—out of my arm. Five? Ten minutes? I don't know. Probably plenty of time for it to go deep into my bloodstream. It didn't matter anymore. The damage was done.

"Hello? Vasyl? I'm here," I said in a normal voice. I didn't need to shout. I knew what that flapping sound at my window had been, and it hadn't been a bird. Truthfully, I'd known all along what it was.

I heard it—a swooshing, sweeping noise, like enormous wings. My skin pricked from his familiar nearness—there was a definite bending of the atmosphere. A dark shadow passed overhead; the flapping became louder, more distinctive, and I ducked as it whooshed really low, and landed in the beam of the lights. The dark shape of a man, with huge wings, like that of a Pterodactyl, landed outside of the light's perimeter. The wings folded against his body, then vanished.

"*Ma 'tite fille*," the dulcet male voice sent shivers down my spine because it felt as though he were right beside me, and at the same time inside my head.

"The lights, *mon enfant*, they hurt my eyes. Turn them down, *s'il vous plait*."

"We need to talk," I said.

"Turn the lights down, I beg of you." He was touching me with his mind, I could feel it. I could do nothing but comply.

I reached into the Jeep, flicked the switch for the overheads, and left the ambers on—I had to see, after all, and the yard light would not reach this area of the backyard. I turned back to find him standing in the ambers—bare chested, wearing skin-tight, faded blue jeans and no shoes. Ebony hair striking against the marble white of his skin, I had trouble pulling my eyes in. He was a magnificent creature. He was perfectly sculpted, from his chest, down to his narrow waist. Throwing back his head to shake the wavy lengths of black hair out of his face, he brought his head down slowly, and stared out at me. His beautiful eyes wide. Saintly eyes—so deceptive. I got a sexual rush from that look; it intoxicated me.

After a moment, he found a different level with his thrall, like a lower wattage. He was making this difficult. He had quite a repertoire of vampire tricks.

"Why did you call to me, *mon enfant*?" he asked excitedly, his accent thick, I could hardly understand him.

"I need to ask you some questions I've wondered all my life," I said, determination in my voice.

"Ask." He thrust his hand out in invitation.

"Tell me how you came to know about Jeanie being in that house?"

"As I have told you, I learned about her through Jason's scion. He came to me of his own free will."

My lip trembled as the tears pooled. "I made a bad mistake and had them turn her."

"What has happened to her body is *peu important*—not important. What is important is that her soul is with God, now."

Closing my eyes, I pulled in a breath and let it out on a whisper, "I hope so."

"Believe me, *ma petite*."

Realigning myself, I cocked my hips, crossed my arms in a threatening pose, feeling the thickness of my weapon there on my arm. "Why did you turn my mother?"

"Your mother was dying. She asked me to turn her."

I took a deep breath, and let it out trying to calm myself. I had known that my mother had been sick, but no one had said what she'd had, or that she wasn't expected to live. "I don't believe you!"

"It is true. I gave her the one gift I have not given in over a century. She did not want to die, but to live on."

"Why would she leave and not explain it all to me before she left? Or, that night, when she came back?"

"Your mother will have to answer that question," he said.

"How can I ask my mother when she's not here?"

"But, I am," the silky voice that came out of the dark shadows of the catalpas shocked me. My heart skipped some beats.

"Mom?" Startled tears came to my eyes. "Mom?"

"Yes, Brie. It's me," she said. I watched a form glide out of the darkness across the long grass, and into the dim amber lights. Long hair glistening, she was dressed professionally, in a khaki pantsuit. I could only see her from the waist up.

"Mom?" I wanted to run to her and throw my arms around her. But I quickly reined in my emotions. She was a vampire. "Why are you here? What's going on?" I was staggered by this surprising outcome.

She smiled serenely at me. Turning to Vasyl, they greeted one another in French, and then she turned back to me. "I've just returned from Europe."

"I don't understand." I was struggling with this. "Did he—" she interrupted before I could finish.

"Nicolas Paduraru brought me back so that you could see me once more," she explained. "It was supposed to be a surprise," she added sheepishly.

"Nicolas?" The hairs on my neck spiked. She was my surprise?

"Yes."

That explained where he'd been all this time. I had to ask my questions quickly. I knew Nicolas would be here soon.

"Mom. Why did you have Vasyl turn you? What were you sick with you had to do this?"

"Oh, Sabrina," she sighed heavily. "I never wanted to hurt any of you. Your father especially. But, I'd been to the doctor a half a dozen times. Your father knew I was very ill. He was understanding, attentive. But he could do nothing. The day the doctor had given me the prognoses—actually my death sentence—that I had an incurable cancer, I was devastated. I didn't want to die. So, that night I prayed, but it was no good. I didn't know what else to do. I asked to be given another chance. I would give it all up—you and Randy, your father, the house, everything—if I could have life eternal. I really didn't know what I was asking for. Then, Vasyl came to me."

"How? I mean, you disappeared during the day—at least that's what they'd said."

She made a guilty sigh.

"Tell her, *cher.*" Vasyl said.

"For three nights he came to me," she began. "Oh, it was wild, so wonderfully wild!" My mother's voice had become excited. I could hardly believe she was revealing this to me. I had to steady myself with one hand against the Jeep. "He had warned me that I couldn't stay here. I would have to leave, go far away, that way I wouldn't be tempted to turn you and your father." She paused, eyes glittering, and went on. "Grandma was here, watching over you kids, that night." She turned her eyes downward.

"He turned you," I said. He'd given her his blood to drink each of those three nights. I knew how they did it, now.

"Yes," she said, looking back at Vasyl. "He took me some place where I could ascend. So, naturally, everyone thought I'd disappeared, or that I'd walked out of the house, that next day, when really I'd left that night."

"I also prayed for her soul, *petit,*" Vasyl put in.

Bowing her head, my mother's hand reached over to his. He took it and kissed the back of it, not like a lover, but more in a revered way. Their hands parted.

A noise caught me by surprise.

Suddenly, I saw Vasyl's eyes flash up, fangs out over full lips. Wings fully thrust out, he surged out of the beams of the ambers. There was a split second where I *knew* what was going to happen—because I had already seen it.

Everything went into Uber-vampire drive when a dark form swooped out of nowhere. I dropped into a crouch. Vasyl lifted up with a whoosh of his wings and dropped down in front of me, wings out, partially blocking my view—and my aim.

I pitched to the ground, onto my side, and took aim with Toby's slingshot under the scalloped edge of Vasyl's wing. I squeezed the trigger. The bolt sizzled through the air. Nicolas moved in a strange, undulating way, and the bolt missed him completely.

"Oh, hell!" I grappled to my feet.

I had to push Vasyl's leathery wings away as I stood to face Nicolas. Vasyl's wings vanished, like before, as he regarded me, concern etched on his face. "You are sure?"

"Yes," I said, still breathing hard.

Nicolas' eyes rose up to meet mine. I didn't see where my mom had gone.

"Sabrina, why?" Nicolas said, looking perplexed.

"You were in charge of both Steve *and* Toby," I said, shaking so much I thought I'd fall over. "Plus, you'd *bitten* me, that first night."

Nicolas gave a small shake of his head, looking repentant. I think he was relieved I'd figured out that he'd bitten me. "I am sorry, Sabrina. I had no intentions of biting you. I had come to your suite before I left to explain things, but Dante would have gotten in the way."

I nodded. Now I knew what he was doing at my suite.

"As for Toby, he became Ilona's scion. I agreed to it. But I didn't know that she put Toby up to murdering Letitia and the others." Hands out in a placating way.

"Well, she did. Erik is dead."

He nodded, looking properly put in his place. "I will head a full investigation into these things, as I am now acting magnate while Bjorn is in isolation."

"I know. What about Steve?"

"He is dead." That stunned me.

"Did you at least ask him who put him up to abducting Jeanie?"

"Someone had already killed him before I had a chance," Nicolas said. "I'm terribly sorry. As for the business with Solange and Brisco, they both escaped our watch. We have yet to discover who is trying to kill you."

"So much for my safety," I muttered despondently.

"I will have someone watching over you all the time," Nicolas announced in a formal tone.

"You are not welcome here. Not ever!" Vasyl growled, taking a menacing step forward.

"*Carpe noctem,* Vasyl," Nicolas said. "I have no quarrel with you. But she is my ward. She is *my* responsibility."

"She wears my mark, and soon will receive the ring signifying she is the sibyl."

"We shall see," Nicolas argued, his eyes glittering, brows arched like two dark slashes.

"I'm fine, now, Vasyl," I assured, glancing his way.

"I will not be far," Vasyl hissed. Wings becoming visible again, he spread them and lifted off, and was gone like a shot. Relief poured through me.

My mother glided out of the darkness, and pulled up right beside Nicolas.

She gazed at me, then back at Nicolas. "Thank you for bringing me here to the states, to see my daughter," my mother said.

"Not at all. My pleasure." He inclined his head toward her. "Shall we return? The hour becomes late, and I've many things to attend to."

"Of course." She turned to me. "Sabrina, I hope you understand things now."

"Yeah," I said feeling slightly lost. "Thanks. Both of you." I meant that too.

Turning to me, she said, "I love you, Sabrina. Don't ever forget that."

"I love you, too," I said, a trembling smile tried to curve across my face.

Both Nicolas and my mother shot out of sight as my eyes teared up. I figured that the party was over, and I doused the lights on the Jeep and trekked back toward the porch.

Unanswered questions were weighing on my mind. Am I really the sibyl? Will I ever see Vasyl again? Should I trust Nicholas? What will happen to Tremayne? Will Ilona try to kill me again? What will happen to Jeanie and will she ever forgive me?

Most of all, how is Dante?

My cell phone was in my pocket, vibrating. I opened it, not surprised to see the readout.

"Hi," I answered on a sigh.

"They've released me from the hospital."

"Really? That's great!"

"Had a few stitches out already."

"Cool. Which ones?" I asked.

"How 'bout I come over there and show you, my lady?"

I smiled. One question answered, more to unravel.

Dear reader,

We hope you enjoyed reading *Ascension*. Please take a moment to leave a review, even if it's a short one. Your opinion is important to us.

Discover more books by Lorelei Bell at
https://www.nextchapter.pub/authors/lorelei-bell.

Want to know when one of our books is free or discounted for Kindle? Join the newsletter at http://eepurl.com/bqqB3H.

Best regards,
Lorelei Bell and the Next Chapter Team

The story continues in:
Trill by Lorelei Bell

To read the first chapter for free, head to:
https://www.nextchapter.pub/books/trill-urban-fantasy

About the Author

Lorelei has always rooted for Dracula/vampires to be the romantic hero in books and movies well before it was "cool". Author of the *Sabrina Strong series* and The *Zofia Trickenbod Chronicles*, a "young-at-heart" Baby Boomer, avid bird watcher, naturalist, and member of Writers of Mass Distraction, and lives on a prairie reserve in the Midwest with husband of 26 years, and three feral cats.

Other vampire works include *Vampire's Trill,* the second book in the Sabrina Strong series. Soon the third book, *Vampire Nocturne,* will be available, and in 2014, the fourth book, *Vampire Caprice.* All available as eBooks @ Amazon.

Also, on a lighter, funnier fantasy note, her Zofia Trickenbod Chronicles: *Spell of the Black Unicorn,* is also available as an eBook on Amazon.

To find out more about Lorelei, and her books, you can follow her at her blogsite:

http://loreleismuse-lorelei.blogspot.com

Lightning Source UK Ltd.
Milton Keynes UK
UKHW021116021120
372650UK00005B/922